PENGUIN BOOKS

THE RAG & BONE SHOP

Jeff Rackham is Professor of English at the University of
North Carolina–Asheville, and has served as a Fulbright
Scholar in Portugal and Macedonia. In addition to pub-
lishing short fiction, he is the author of several scholarly
collections and a standard college textbook on writing.
The Rag & Bone Shop is his first novel.

The
Rag & Bone Shop

Jeff Rackham

PENGUIN BOOKS

PENGUIN BOOKS

Published by the Penguin Group

Penguin Putnam Inc., 375 Hudson Street, New York, New York 10014, U.S.A.

Penguin Books Ltd, 80 Strand, London WC2R 0RL, England

Penguin Books Australia Ltd, 250 Camberwell Road, Camberwell, Victoria 3124, Australia

Penguin Books Canada Ltd, 10 Alcorn Avenue, Toronto, Ontario, Canada M4V 3B2

Penguin Books India (P) Ltd, 11 Community Centre,
Panchsheel Park, New Delhi – 110 017, India

Penguin Books (N.Z.) Ltd, Cnr Rosedale and Airborne Roads,
Albany, Auckland, New Zealand

Penguin Books (South Africa) (Pty) Ltd, 24 Sturdee Avenue,
Rosebank, Johannesburg 2196, South Africa

Penguin Books Ltd, Registered Offices:
Harmondsworth, Middlesex, England

First published in the United States of America by Zoland Books, Inc. 2001
Published in Penguin Books 2002

1   3   5   7   9   10   8   6   4   2

PUBLISHER'S NOTE

This is a work of fiction. Names, characters, places, and incidents either are the product
of the author's imagination or are used fictitiously, and any resemblance to actual persons,
living or dead, business establishments, events, or locales is entirely coincidental.

THE LIBRARY OF CONGRESS HAS CATALOGED THE HARDCOVER EDITION AS FOLLOWS:
Rackham, Jeff.
The rag and bone shop / Jeff Rackham.
p.   cm.
ISBN 1-58195-105-1 (hc.)
ISBN 0 14 20.0225 9 (pbk.)
1. Dickens, Charles, 1812–1870—Fiction.   2. Ternan, Ellen Lawless,
1839–1914—Fiction.   3. London (England)—Fiction.   4. Mistresses—Fiction.
5. Novelists—Fiction.   6. Actresses—Fiction.   I. Title.
PS3618.A34 R34   2001
813'.54—dc21   2001026137

Printed in the United States of America
Designed by Boskydell Studio

. . . and yet when all is said
It was the dream itself enchanted me . . .

Now that my ladder's gone,
I must lie down where all the ladders start,
In the foul rag-and-bone shop of the heart.

—W. B. YEATS

The Rag & Bone Shop

Wilkie Collins

CHARLES DICKENS never tumbled a whore in his life, never let a woman know he felt lust. He truly believed all women were pure and virginal. When Miss Coutts approached him with a scheme for saving prostitutes, he saw it as the opportunity to fulfill a personal mission.

"I'm convinced they're better than people think," he told me over a pint of bitter one dreary London evening. "Fallen girls, of course. Some of them even criminals, I should think, but they deserve a second chance!" He pounded the table like an aggrieved member of Parliament. He was on a moral campaign.

"Wilkie, these are fallen girls with pure hearts."

"I'm sure they are, sir," I said. "I've known several myself over the years."

"If it weren't for you, Wilkie, there would be far fewer on the streets today."

"I take that as a compliment, sir. I do my best to help the working classes."

We were drinking in the Olde Pelican. As usual, a crowd gathered outside the window to watch Charles Dickens drink.

Eventually we requested a room on the first storey to avoid a constant pecking on the pane.

"Now, now, I'm serious here," Dickens said. "I'm talking about young girls, you see. Mere children who sincerely want to reform. They only need a place of shelter and love to find a better life for themselves. Miss Coutts and I have decided to raise funds for an asylum."

Dickens' relation to women had always been perturbing. He wrote stories about perfect young children, about angels and little girls, never about adult women with any hint of sensuality. One of his earliest stories was about an innocent child whose gin-sotted father sold her as a prostitute. In the story, I recall, Dickens wanted to save her because she was virtuous and pure, but she dies early and the reader is led to believe she goes straight to heaven.

Whore heaven, no doubt.

"In all due respect, sir," I said, "the larks I've known are more interested in a pint and a bed. Only two nights ago, in this very tavern, I met a gay young thing, told me she was an orphan in need of rent money. I immediately recognised the need for a little charity."

"Wilkie, you are a sensualist."

"Of course I'm a sensualist!"

I reminded him of my first sexual experience at age thirteen — with an older woman in Rome, a city I'd come to believe invented sensuality.

"I've never believed a word of it, Wilkie. It's impossible."

He sipped his bitter and looked about with studied unconcern.

He leaned across the board and whispered. "Now this woman in Rome. Was she what one might call a prostitute?"

"Absolutely not. She was a friend of my father's, one of his models actually, a fine matron of the arts. A married woman of spectacular person. You know what I mean. Luxurious attributes, as they say. A fullness of growth found only in Italian Baroque."

Dickens looked like a priest shaken by dark confession. "I don't want to hear about it. Not at thirteen. My God, Wilkie, Miss Coutts would faint." He leaned across the board and whispered coarsely, "What was it like?"

Poor soul. It wasn't until I took personal charge of his needs that Charles Dickens discovered true pleasures of the female sex. Perhaps it turned out badly, becoming, you might say, a lurid tale I couldn't have foreseen. But I want to make clear early, the story was never about Ellen Ternan. Ellen was a mere actress, playing a part of no great consequence, barely more than a slender child with oddly beautiful eyes and boyish hips. I wasn't at all attracted to her person. She had a charming, sly humour, always a little secretive, as if she knew more than she let on. She could hold the attention of a man attracted to innocence, to insouciance, to flirtation, a man like Charles Dickens.

Ellen Ternan appeared far too late to be a central figure. She floated about the periphery like a succubus dressed in silk. She was mysterious, beautiful, vital. None of us understood her. She was never truly at the heart of it, yet she was always there, her own double in everything. There was no way to penetrate her secret, and no need to because the story wasn't about her.

Let me begin again. As a mystery writer, I was better than Charles Dickens. Dickens knew how to create magnificent characters — better than anyone — I'll grant you that. But for me, it was brilliant plots and intricacies, plot remarkably superior to life. Full of intrigue and romance, shocking frights, and surprising resolutions. All quite intelligent. Life is more untidy. Set your goal, march off in one direction, and suddenly you find it's the wrong direction, or the wrong goal, or the wrong life. Charles Dickens knew how to create magnificent characters, but the plot of his life turned out all wrong.

All those stories about how he began as a poor young lad. Don't let them fool you. By the age of twenty-five he had pulled his literary sword from the stone. By thirty, he had slain all dragons, sat down to tea with the Queen, and found himself roundly cheered by the yeomen. By forty, he was famous beyond mortal understanding. You and I can't know what that kind of fame does to a man. The surge of inner power and vitality — lifting you like a windhover high above rippling clouds, soaring alone, I would think, in a lone and windless sky.

Everyone knew Charles Dickens, everyone tipped his hat, deferred to his decisions. They queued three deep to buy his novels. They pushed and shoved to see him act in a play or give a speech. They bowed and curtseyed to him on the street, as if he were Royal. He was more than a famous writer. The working class saw in Dickens an image of its own striving. The man who rises from poverty to wealth, who becomes a gentleman, yet retains great feeling for those he's left behind. He was a saint who remained in sympathy with clerks and kitchen maids, blacksmiths and coal miners. Without knowing quite how it happened, Charles Dickens found himself the standard for Christian virtue and manly character. He became rich and kept a carriage, two carriages, then three. He became a symbol. He became England.

Now. How can any mortal live up to that? In early years, he was exuberant. After a while, it was duty. Then, burden. Dickens discovered he had to grow into the man they wanted him to be, and after playing the part for so long, he became the part, the part the nation scripted for him. There wasn't any Charles anymore. Only the famous author, famous playwright, the Great Man, The Great Dickens. Even he got confused, you know. He wouldn't remember which one he really was. And then he couldn't find the other one. The dirty child, humiliated by poverty, driven to work day and night to overcome the shame. He couldn't find that one anymore. Like an actor who has played Shakespeare onstage too many times and been celebrated too often. Like Macready, who began to talk to his friends in blank verse, even in private. The voice changes. The truly celebrated ones begin to speak in sonorous tones. The posture arches. They talk to you with a three-quarter pose, their best profile toward you. They can't move their arms anymore except to make bold gestures.

I remember speaking to Dickens once and he seemed to be listening, when I realised he was only permitting me to talk. He was being generous. Tolerating little folk. And to my greater horror, I recognised that wasn't it at all. His eyes — grey with dark green, almost hazel, unforgettable and lost — his eyes were focused on the horizon, one ear cocked toward me, and I understood the truth. He couldn't hear me. Not that he wasn't listening. He couldn't hear my voice. It was too far away, too faint and distant for him. He wanted to listen, actually wanted to, but the voices mingled and overlapped now, like too many garbled whispers in a dream. The cheers and the hurrahs and the honours. Out there somewhere, my poor voice was lost with the others. He so desperately wanted to hear it. He smiled on, pretending, wishing, and feeling alone, so desperately alone.

*

I was in my twenties when I met Dickens. It was Augustus Egg introduced us. Egg was a mutual friend and a painter of some repute. My father had been a painter. So it all came about naturally, and we liked each other. Dickens asked me to perform in a play he was producing, a private showing before the Court. The opportunity to work with the Great Charles Dickens was the dream of every would-be writer in London. But I wasn't like the other toadies who slithered around him, wanting the afterglow of his fame to improve my own complexion. I had already published my first mystery novel. Dickens knew I was my own man. I answered him with blunt good humour, teased him, told him he was wrong when no one else dared contradict the Great Man. We became friends.

Even then Charles Dickens was rude, demanding, arrogant, and always right. Everyone could sense it. He had more energy than all the rest of us, working ceaselessly, serialising novels, organising theatrical productions, directing, acting, editing a journal, encouraging young writers. He entered a room like a volcanic wind. You braced yourself against a desk or a door and Dickens bellowed with laughter, shook a man's hand vigorously, shouted an order, demanded his barrister be sent for, stamped across the boards in heavy boots, and hugged his frightened scrivener. He was vigorous, there's no other word for it, and adored.

Yet he was unhappy. He never mentioned it directly, but there was increasing distance between Dickens and his wife. In the beginning, everyone said, Catherine was perfect. She was childlike, a frightened little bird with small black eyes. She was decent and maternal, easy to cry, confused. I've seen a photogravure of her. She had a small beautiful mouth, a sweetness about her, but something sad. She bore children like a rabbit — litters of them — and she grew pink and fat. She ate sweets and issued chocolate-smelling farts, little hissing ones that made her pause and listen to them, turning up her eyes and concentrating, as if measuring the sound or the smell by some secret standard known only to her.

By the time I knew her she was afraid of Dickens, peering out from behind puffy cheeks like a frightened child. She must have felt trapped inside that billowing maternal flesh. Decent and tender is how she struck me, easy to manipulate. I think she meant to please him in any way she could. She was the innocent child bride he wanted her to be. She had never been his mistress, not even his lover. And now all that was hidden deep under layers of overripeness. She had taken to wearing a flannel nightgown with a hole in it, centrally located. She refused to lift the hem, refused to move, or couldn't move. Afterward, Dickens would be up half the night, pacing, smoking his cigar. The next day he would shout at the scriveners, bark rudely to Forster, lock himself in his office, and write furiously for six hours. We would all tiptoe. The others thought it was temperament. I knew differently and teased him about it. I was the only one he allowed to tease him. Until later, when Ellen Ternan came along.

I seem to be rambling. Nothing like a tightly structured plot here. No clear good and evil, no villain, no comedy or tragedy. Just a famous old writer who had everything except what a man needed as a man. Not that he hadn't tried, mind you. In our early years, we travelled across Europe, searching out the best quality of women, the most charming and sumptuous. We drank heartedly with them, laughed and flirted with them. And that was all. In spite of rumours you may have heard, nothing happened. At the appropriate moment, Charles Dickens would disappear or grow suddenly ill or pass out. His conscience closed like a cold fist about his heart. Or perhaps he was overwhelmed by a terrifying fear his admirers might discover he was mortal. He couldn't explain it.

Still, it affected him. Dickens grew harder, master of home and hearth, morally principled, generous to the public, more and more sentimental in his stories, inwardly dead and empty. He wrote about angels and little girls. Something melancholy in him longed for passion. He began to drink an extra pint or two, he took up cigars, grew his beard like a wild thicket. In the smoke and haze of the Olde Pelican he told me Catherine was like a great sow with hanging teats. He was disgusted with her fertility.

"She's obese, Wilkie. Her body is like a pile of clammy pillows. She smells like wet face powder. Her buttocks are scarred with dimples."

He spoke under his breath, as if ashamed of his own feelings.

"Her stomach gurgles. Her chins wiggle. When I come to her at night, her little black eyes peek out with the hurt innocence of a fat, dumb puppy. She lies there in absolute silence, waiting for me to be done with it. Or she's afraid of me, I can't tell which."

Now what kind of reply can a friend make? What was I to tell him?

I told him about Caroline Graves, of course. A lovely woman, sensuous, mysterious in her own right, unbalanced, but totally irresistible.

I'd seen her first by moonlight in early summer, when the air floated with the last faint odour of lilacs. My brothers and I had been drinking and we were strolling home through the narrow lanes of North London, a few years before they put in the gas lamps. We were singing, pushing each other about when a woman's scream pierced the garden of a villa nearby. For a moment, every drop of blood in our bodies was brought to a stop. A great iron gate in the wall beside us rushed open and a woman dressed in white flew into the moonlight. She seemed to be floating over the cinders, and she passed without seeing us. My brothers gave each other a look but started on as before, arms about each other's shoulders. It wasn't our business, you see.

Yet inside my heart I felt something happening. It was all so foolish and melodramatic. My brothers only laughed, but I turned back and followed her, overcome by that old heritage of the English gentlemen.

"Wait," I called out.

She ran on, her footsteps crunching on the cinders. Finally, out of breath, and crying, she stopped, leaning heavily against a shadowed stone wall.

I heard her whisper, "You won't hurt me, will you?"

It sounded like something I would write in one of my novels.

"Of course not," I said, approaching her cautiously. "Are you in danger?"

She stared past me down the lane. Listening. We could neither of us hear a sound. It was almost midnight and the moon was full. The young woman was no more than twenty-two or -three, with wistful eyes.

"If you'll escort me," she said, placing a still trembling hand on my arm, "I'll be eternally grateful."

We crisscrossed the city that summer night, walking through moonlit lanes that shimmered like the mysterious canals of Venice. She told me her tale and I fell in love.

No, no, her story isn't important here. This is Charles Dickens' story, isn't it? But Caroline Graves is essential to what happened. I knew Dickens couldn't possibly find courage to rearrange his life, set up a second household, keep a woman not his wife for God's sake, without ever once toppling into the arms of a single courtesan. If I hadn't met Caroline, if she hadn't become my mistress, I would never have convinced Dickens he, too, should consider taking a younger woman under his wing. Dickens' story would be totally different. No disaster, no tragedy. Dickens would have maintained his purity, all the while letting a few selected friends believe he was whoremaster of the Continent, with a wink here, a droll story there. He would have lived a longer life, unhappy perhaps — definitely unhappy — but less dramatic and exciting. And Ellen Ternan would be a name forever lost to history. Don't you see, this is how a true plot develops, from a small incident that seems unrelated to the main character, while step by unforeseen step it leads to revelation and death.

Caroline Graves put it about that she was the daughter of a good family, but like most of her life, it was only part of an ever-changing tale. She told me her father was a gentleman and her husband a great squire in Northumberland. Later that night she stopped me as we circled back toward Regent's Park, placing both hands on my lapels, looking up at me with desperation.

"I haven't been telling the truth," she said. "I was afraid you might be part of the conspiracy."

"What conspiracy?"

"Promise you'll never force me to go back."

"On my honour."

She studied my face to be certain, and I studied those weeping eyes, so deeply frightened yet trusting, like those of a child awakened in the night.

"It's the Count, you see. Count Fosco. When he discovered my husband was only an army captain with no inheritance — a gambler who deserted me — the Count became outraged and began to chase me about the house with an iron poker. It was only my money he wanted. I'd led him to believe my child was my niece. It was horrid of me, I know, but I was desperate for protection."

"But what about your father, the Squire? Can't you seek his protection?"

"My father?" She looked puzzled. "Oh, he wasn't a Squire. He was the second son of famous clergyman. I can't reveal his name. He preached at St. Paul's."

"But you spoke about an estate in Northumberland."

"Yes, yes, originally. Before the Great Fire destroyed it, and we were forced to live with my aunt in Greenwich."

"The Great Fire?"

"Surely you've heard of it, an educated gentleman like yourself." She looked at me with sudden distrust, as if I might not be a gentleman at all if I'd never heard of the Great Fire.

"Do you mean the Great Fire of London? In sixteen sixty-six?" I asked.

Caroline placed her head on my breast in obvious relief. "Yes," she sighed.

"But Northumberland . . ."

"I know, I know. We were so very unlucky."

Her real name was Elizabeth. It took several months before I found out. Something had gone wrong as a child. She began to call herself Rebecca, then Isabella and later Caroline. Her father, I believe, was a stonemason, and in a desperate act to escape him, she married an accountant named Graves who died shortly after she gave birth to a daughter, a child she introduced for the rest of her life as her niece. The natural child of the Earl of Greenwich, she told people.

And still I fell in love. For a short while, I kept her a secret, but I had no need to. My father built a great reputation for himself and his family, painting portraits of the noble and the wealthy, painting landscapes to please the gentry, twelve and sometimes fifteen hours a day, painting to ensure that he left a small fortune for his family after his death. But to what end? I had to ask. To what end does a man do everything for others, for reputation, for wealth? Had he lived a full life?

No, in fact his life had been rich in art but empty of all other human experiences. When he took us to Rome, he didn't see Rome, he painted it. When he bought us a large house in London, he didn't sit before the fire and enjoy his sherry, he locked himself in his studio and sketched preening wives of the peerage. Did he laugh? Did he frolic? Never.

And so I took rooms in a small house on Howland Street, a foul lane of leaning shops where painters and writers lived overhead, wonderful rascals who taught me how to shed my foolish inhibitions, taught me to live life fully without concern for the bourgeoisie. And there I set up Caroline Graves or Elizabeth Compton (whatever she wanted to be called), and her daughter Harriet or her niece Alexis, and in those cold narrow rooms, we made love, we chased each other naked down hallways, we horrified the servants and drove them all away until we found one or two who merely tolerated our madness, and those we kept forever. Later, we found other lodgings, in Albany Street and then in New Cavendish Street, settling at last on Gloucester Place. But it was that first one set my life free, and it was that freedom the Great Charles Dickens never had, could not even imagine, which intrigued him and drew him to me like a hypnotised bird.

"Tell me about it, Wilkie," he said, with small beads of sweat on his brow. "Tell me what it's like."

"You must try it yourself," I urged. "Keep your family sacred, honour your wife, honour the proprieties, but for God's sake, man, find a mistress and experience the joys of sensual bliss once in your life."

I'd said it half in jest, raising my pint of ale in salute. Any other man would have raised his glass as well, and we would have toasted the pleasures of the opposite sex.

Dickens half-pushed his chair away from the table, as if someone had recommended he drown his children. "You know my history," he said, bitterly. "It will never happen."

"Come now. Man was made to whore. And woman — lovely woman — was made to spread wide her privileged flesh."

He tried to stop me. I was enjoying his discomfort.

"There's no wrong here, sir. Bury your face in a hot, voluptuous bosom, spend a night with your nose pressed between her sacred thighs, perfumed as they will be with oils from Morocco, and I promise you, sir, you'll return home renewed, refreshed, revived. Your loving Catherine will find you suddenly more interesting, and you'll find her unexpectedly attractive."

"Stop! I'll hear no more!" The man was truly Puritan. He had spent years seducing little girls in his stories and then letting them die of cholera to expunge his guilt.

I was having too much pleasure to stop. "Sir," I said loudly, "I'll find you a willing whore this very night. A dark-haired lovely who will suck you dry, and you'll be the better man for it."

Dickens rose abruptly, knocking his chair so hard it fell back to the floor. "Stop! I tell you." Even though we were in a private room, he looked about desperately to see if anyone had heard. I stood up as well, challenging him face-to-face, or mostly so, since I was shorter than Dickens and a little more tipsy, supporting myself with both hands on the board. "Two wenches, then! A night of passion with two sweating, laughing, brightly nippled women at the same time."

The Great Man flailed like a carp pulled from the Thames. "My reputation, Collins, my reputation." His gills gasped for air. "My admirers," Dickens said, glancing desperately at the door one more time. "The position I hold in society."

In those days his beard was still golden brown and well-trimmed. He looked at me with the most sorrowful eyes I've ever seen on a man. They were eyes of fear and loss and struggle and, most of all, confusion.

"No, Mr. Collins." He picked up his fallen chair, adjusted it to the table, and sat, wobbling once again, struggling to light his dead cigar.

He spoke in thoughtful sadness, almost to himself.

"You can have a mistress, Wilkie," he said in a resigned whisper. "Thackeray can toy with his children's governess on long afternoons. George Eliot can live openly with Mr. Lewes. But not Charles Dickens. No sir, I can't betray Queen and country, Wilkie. No sir, absolutely not. This is a moral position from which I'll never budge. I could not — will not — let down England."

I dropped into my chair. I felt astonished in a way I've never felt before or since. If he had said he couldn't tarnish the memory of his long-dead mother or his long-suffering wife or his tumbling children — or if he'd said he could not let down God — all that I could have respected. But England! *He could not let down England!*

"Sir," I whispered, "it's time for me to introduce you to the House of Madame Dubois."

He released a long curl of cigar smoke. "Never, Wilkie." He retreated deep within some hidden past. "I've come to know my own heart over the years, and this is a position from which I'll never budge."

Dickens, you understand, had been to France many times. He took his whole family, a wagonload of baggage, maids, cooks, friends, a carriage or two, and, of course, Georgina.

Georgina was his sister-in-law. She arrived years ago to help Catherine with the children, and then stayed, godmother to one child after another, consoler of an increasingly tearful wife, manager of the household, and perhaps most of all, confidante of the Great Man. She brought him cigars, she took dictation, she laid out his clothing, saw to his meals, ordered his bath, laughed and cried over his manuscripts. Georgina became his other wife. The little sister who adores us, defends us — the one we secretly wish our real wife was like. Or perhaps Georgina was the daughter who so admires her father she can see no flaws in him, who idolises his every thought and action against the wicked and unseeing stepmother. She was the perfect female he wrote about in so many stories, the one who silently and efficiently ordered the household, who never lost her temper and never made demands, who spoke with sweet humility. Sister, wife, daughter, companion. And pure, of course: *pure pure pure.* Not a hint of sexual feeling between them, as best as I could tell.

I despised her. Slithering about with the silence of an unctuous servant. Never there when he didn't need her, appearing like a biblical apparition the very moment Dickens was about to pull the bell cord.

"Ah, yes," he would say, beaming with the kind of pleasure we feel when a young greyhound admires us with uncritical eyes. "How do you do it, my little one?" And he took the warm tea she'd brought, or the sherry, or his tobacco, or the mail — whatever thing he had only moments before desired.

I despised her.

When he summered in France, I was often invited along, and there was no avoiding Georgina. Dickens rented the Villa du Camp de Droit in Boulogne, a marvellous old château on a high hill at the top of a road lined with plane trees. The harbour and red-tiled roofs of the village sparkled below. There were guests coming and going all summer, carts bouncing up the rutted road from the grocer, parties organised for the opera in Paris. In the shade of an awning, we drank Bordeaux and green Chablis from a dank cellar. Each morning, we walked in the rose garden. Every afternoon, we organised impromptu games of cricket in the meadow. We made up ragtag teams consisting of Dickens' sons, a neighbouring farmer, a carpenter who had come up from town to build a grape arbour, and various others who were in and out of the manor — even his daughter Katie at one point with her skirts tucked up — and Hubbard, Dickens' balding manservant who had to retire early after he couldn't get his breath. The wind blew every day from the ocean, snapping the Union Jack we'd erected on a nearby haystack with a great show of patriotism. We made kites for the children to fly until the wind tore them into shreds and they flailed and popped and dived into the hedges.

The first time I was invited, Prince Albert sailed into the harbour moments before sunset. The Royal yacht was flying all its colours, the deck aglow with lantern lights. That's what gave me the idea. I proposed we honour our Royals with some appropriate exchange of illumination. A token gesture, you understand.

Dickens, being Mr. England himself, assumed the role of Commanding General in charge of Naval Illumination. He sent servants flying for candles, every candle they could find. The children were organised into teams on each floor, one child per window. Katie was placed in charge of their overall command with a title of Honourary Lieutenant of the Infant Guard. Servants were called away from other duties, and Georgina was promoted to Majordomo. I was appointed Chargé d'Affaires (Dickens' little joke).

By the time we had everything organised, it was dark, a starless night with high clouds moving fast. We decided on four candles per window, every window in the villa, which a child or servant or neighbour stationed at the ready. General Dickens rang a bell, and each of us lighted a candle at the same time, a blaze of at least two hundred illuminations. The house burst into the flame of English glory, and all of us came clamouring out onto the lawn to admire our work. The Great Man led us in a rousing cheer for our own genius. Later, we heard the whole of Bordeaux rushed into the cobbled streets and stood openmouthed at the château on the hill. The Prince acknowledged our little display with a formal note without quite inviting us to join him on his yacht.

A real man, however, cannot live forever in the country. A château amidst wheat fields is all very good for family, but not for a man with needs. After a week or so, I visited Paris on my own. There were always new clubs to entertain one, old friends to dine with, and a bordello here or there. I always invited Dickens, mostly as a matter of course.

"Join me, sir. We'll have a light repast, some fine wine, and I'll introduce you to several charming friends."

He turned red-faced, or turned away entirely. Or he

laughed and urged me to go on with my frivolities. Another engagement held him, he said. Or perhaps little James was feeling ill and it was no time for him to abandon Catherine with a sick child. Or he turned prudish and snapped, "Go, Wilkie! Bother me no more about this."

"I can arrange everything confidentially, sir. Everything very discrete, and all government inspected, fully licensed you see. Not like Italy."

But my badgering was no longer lighthearted for him. I'd pressed too many times. It was still midsummer. Within a few days we would both return to London. Catherine and the family would linger on in Bordeaux for several more weeks. Dickens was needed elsewhere — his magazine called for him, financial affairs were pressing. He turned grumpy.

"We are never to discuss this again, Wilkie. If the subject arises again, our friendship will come to an end. That must be absolute. You understand, Wilkie, it is not a desirable termination for me. I wish our relationship to continue, but there will be no more talk of mistresses and whores in my presence. None whatsoever. No proposed trips for purposes of sin, no hidden assignations, no mysterious visits at night to whispered rooms. Understand this, my dear friend, I'll never again speak to you on this matter, nor will you broach it with me. Before you began to whisper of temptation and sensuality, I conducted my life as a model of purity, and I am determined to stay the course."

He relit his cigar and began to pace. He seemed fully resigned to the decision he had made, and he asked me to take his words seriously.

"Live as you wish, Wilkie, with your luxurious women, as many as you can afford, lay waste your powers between their open thighs, but don't broach the topic with me. I've resigned myself to stay the course. I'll hear no more bawdy talk of bosoms and buttocks, now. No more talk of dark scents that flare the nostrils and make one pant over turning flesh. Never again will immoral thoughts press such hot hands upon my brain and heart. I declare this to be my final word on the subject."

Two days later, Dickens and I set out by train for Paris.

We took a cab from the station. The moon was full and the sidewalks alive with cafés, lamplight, singing, laughter. Paris on a hot summer night is the most sensual city in the world. Except for Rome. Or Naples. Or Venice. Quite a different story, Venice, where the young women often turn out to be young boys.

I was wearing my old felt Wide-Awake, a great hat with a broad brim, like no one else wore except in Bohemia. And truthfully, I felt cheerful enough to light up a Turkish cigar. Our cab could barely press through the crowds. Dear Charles hid in the darkest corner, huddled in fear. I thought it might calm him if I explained the important gradations in French whoredom. "Let me go over it in French terms, sir," I said, leaning back and enjoying myself immensely.

"Now, because the French are connoisseurs of fine wine, they always grade their *Mignons* in the same way.

"They sip, taste, and sniff a whore according to very clear standards. At the bottom of the list, for everyday table use, so to speak, are spring wines called *Grisettes*. These are part-time girls — fifteen years old perhaps — girls who don't mind a pint and a tumble, but who truly satisfy only country boys or young clerks in back alleys. They're usually cheerful, even eager. But having been plucked from the vine too early and sold hastily at a cheap price, they'll age quickly and badly.

"Now, a wine with a slightly better label, one with fuller

body and perhaps a hint of cheerfulness — this would be your *Gigolette*. They're jolly and experienced, even if they do tend to announce themselves rather quickly, sometimes calling out to you on the street. They love drinking and gambling. They love the darker life, the jokes and teasing, a hand under the tablecloth, and an honest businesslike tussle in bed. Unfortunately, *Gigolettes* sometimes front for a lurking pimp, some dark tattooed gipsy who enjoys emptying your pockets and knocking you over the head like a bad hangover."

We moved into the darker sections of Paris. The crowds grew rowdy. Our cab jerked to a halt while a clutch of university men sang their way across our path. The Great Man huddled ever more darkly into the recesses of the leather curtain. I was afraid I might lose him soon, afraid he might take a sudden bolt for the door and run off wildly in the dark. I began to talk faster.

"Now if you lived in Paris most of the year, a gentleman would want something more secretive and dangerous. I would recommend a *Demi-monde*, one of those educated, upper-class ladies, married to a wealthy man of business or industry, but bored bored bored. Ah, the secret rendezvous, the stealthy exchange of notes at a party, the hurried delights. Love on hot afternoons, in boudoirs, closets, or stolen moments in the cool, dark cell of a chapel, and sometimes a stolen retreat to Marseille while she visits a sick aunt.

"These are fine wines from the best families, mature and satisfying. They deserve to be handled gently, tasted and sniffed, enjoyed with superb meals or late-night suppers. Their white limbs will envelop you in the finest bouquet. And best of all, *Demi-mondes* always return to their husbands. One never has to worry about the affair being mistaken for love.

"But let me clarify, sir. A *Demi-monde* should never be confused with a *Grande Coquette*. These are women of remarkable beauty and person who have demonstrated such a fine range of talents they're shared by only two or three gentlemen. Truly a select wine from the private reserves of Rothschild or Aquitaine. They usually speak several languages, and they're fully respectful of a gentleman's more refined sensibility. They can sing, play the pianoforte, cut and light a cigar properly, and pamper the most spoiled aristocrat with specialised tastes. Indeed, they're so valued they usually have their own apartments or a small villa with several servants."

The cab jolted over several rough cobblestones. We entered a more respectable alley of small galleries and cafés, where waiters in white aprons fluttered like moths about the candles on each table. We were almost at our destination if I could hold him another moment or two.

"Now, let me get to the point, Charles. We'll have no *Grisettes* or *Demi-mondes* tonight. No, no. Our *Poule de Luxe* shall be sampled from the vineyard of Mme. Dubois, whose young ladies, I assure you, could be classed among the finest champagnes in the world, delightful bubblies who will give you great cheer on any occasion, refresh your spirits, charm your palate, and improve your mood for days to come. These are the premier sparkling wines, spirited and full-bodied, they'll make you drunk with good fun, they'll take your breath away with sensuous pleasure, but never never will they come back to make your head ache the next morning, never will they demand more of you than the knowledge they've pleased you well."

I was quite charmed with my own description.

"Perhaps," I speculated aloud, "perhaps I should write a guidebook on the *Mignons* of Paris." Guidebooks were all the rage then. Dickens seemed unfailingly dull, however. He breathed heavily in his dark corner and gave no response until we stopped at number 37 rue de Charbanais.

"No," he whispered. "I can't be seen going into such an establishment. Someone might recognise me, Wilkie."

"Nonsense. This is an antique shop, one of the most exclusive in Paris, and I've made private arrangements for a showing of several Louis the Fourteenth paintings."

Dickens peeked through the curtains, saw the lighted shop windows, the armoires, the inlaid table with crystal vases, the painting of Versailles, and M. Bompard waiting for us in the doorway.

Dickens seemed confused and relieved. He patted my hand. "A fine idea, a wonderful idea." He almost leapt from the cab and strode head high into the shop. M. Bompard bowed low as Dickens nodded to him, moving across oiled floors to gaze about at fine examples of period furnishings amid the antique candlelight. I paid the cab, made arrangements for him to return sometime about three in the morning, and followed Dickens inside, tipping M. Bompard as I entered.

I guided Dickens away from a display of Oriental jewellery and led him, almost without his awareness, through a sliding door built into a bookcase. M. Bompard silently closed the door behind us. We found ourselves in a lavish salon, a circular room with a ceiling as high as a church and inlaid with gilt. A great chandelier with at least fifty candles hung in the center. Overlapping Oriental carpets covered the floor. Fringed shawls were tossed over sofas and fainting couches. But of course, one's eye captured all this indirectly. Dickens had come to an astonished halt with an intake of breath, not for the beauty of the room but for the human tableaux around the walls. A young Algerian boy, bare-chested, barely noticing us, plunked softly on the strings of a cithara.

Dickens started to speak, found he could not, and instead, let forth a puff of breath. There before him on a slightly raised stage against a painted backdrop of pastoral fields and mountains, in various postures of half-naked repose, lounged three young women in diaphanous costume, posing as vixen milkmaids. Dickens stared like a schoolboy. One of the models turned slowly. She looked meaningfully at him and stretched with a slow, sensuous gesture of her arm, like a mistress awakened from warm sleep to find her lover admiring her across the room. She held Dickens' eyes with hers and raised that arm slowly toward him until one breast was fully exposed, a pink nipple offered with bright charm. Dickens swallowed audibly. The milkmaid smiled and tilted her head to one side so that long silky hair tumbled and flowed down over the exposed portion of her person.

The Great Man stood transfixed. He had entered an underwater dream and found his limbs too heavy to move, his lungs suddenly empty and burning in his chest.

In the second tableau vivant, in front of a canvas painted to look like a mediaeval cathedral in evening mist, stood two innocent young women dressed as nuns. Dickens took them in, his lips parted. The young women nodded ever so slightly at us and then moved together, wrapping bare arms about each other in a slow embrace, and while we watched, they kissed deeply. One of them lifted a glistening bare leg from her black gown, wrapping it tightly about the other girl. Then, both looked back at the great author with dark eyes, soliciting his approval.

There were three other tableaux. In the first, fairies in diaphanous gowns seemed to sleep. In another, several African women lounged on bright robes, absolutely naked except for gold necklaces, earrings, and arm bracelets, all against a backdrop of painted lions standing guard over them. And finally, three bronze-skinned women — from Egypt or Syria, I suspect — were dressed as harem girls in gold embroidered gowns against a painted canvas of the minarets of Constantinople.

Dickens was still trying to find his breath. He seemed to weave slightly. Mme. Dubois appeared before us in a full-length Empire gown, a modest woman with a face as soft as polished leather. It was said she had made a small fortune by the age of thirty and now, at sixty, was one of the most wealthy women in France, one who had been known to provide services to the highest Ministers of State as well as the aristocracy. Let me assure you, that evening was costing me a small fortune as well, enough to feed and house a working family in London for a year, I suspect. But I felt certain anything less than the best would have frightened Charles Dickens away in an instant. To keep him there, it was necessary to overwhelm him. I had to go far beyond what his poor imagination might have envisioned. And as everyone knew, Mme. Dubois' salon was the premier bordello in Paris, and that meant it was the premier bordello in the world.

"So delighted to have you visit," she said, with only the faintest and most elegant French accent. She held out her hand for Dickens to take. She might as well have held out a slice of raw goat liver.

Dickens could not decide where to focus his eyes. He clearly wanted to turn away from the sensual tableaux all around him, but he could not find it in himself to confront Mme. Dubois' eyes.

"Charmed," I said, stepping forward and taking her hand. I bowed to kiss it. "I am Wilkie Collins from London. I hope you received my message."

"Certainement." Mme. Dubois looked me directly in the eye, in a way no lady would ever dream of. "You are ze mystery novelist, I believe."

"And this," I said, indicating Charles Dickens — whose knees had started to buckle at the thought he was about to be publicly introduced — "this is the world famous English author, William Wordsworth."

Mme. Dubois seemed deeply impressed. "You are truly welcome. I have read some of your poetry. How do you say it? Kubla Khan?" Dickens accepted her outstretched hand, glancing at me for my assurance that it was not going to harm him. Mme. Dubois seemed amused and, after leaving her hand in his slightly too long, seductively allowed her fingertips to brush Dickens' wrist as she drew back. It must have struck him like an electric shock.

A young woman appeared from behind a curtain, bringing a tray with three glasses and a bottle of champagne. She was clearly an American Negro, with spectacular long, black, kinky hair falling in flowing waves, split over her fine dark shoulders and barely covering her exposed bosom. Around her waist she wore a burlap skirt that brushed the floor as she walked, but the skirt was split up the front so that at each step polished black thighs were exposed for a brief flash of a moment.

I thought I might have to bring a chair for Dickens to sit down in, but he drew himself together and took one of the glasses, avoiding the dark nipple only inches from his hand. I took another glass, thanking the young Negro, who smiled at me with hot black eyes. She might have been fourteen.

Mme. Dubois accepted the third glass.

She raised it up to us. "We want to welcome you. May your pleasures be great and many. Everything you see around you, and much much more, is all available to you. We are your hosts and your servants, or" — she glanced meaningfully at the Negro girl who remained beside us and who was still looking me directly in the eye — "or your slaves, if you wish."

Mme. Dubois touched her glass to Dickens' and to mine, and we toasted our adventure, Dickens swallowing his whole, in a single dash, like a man about to be hanged.

"Mr. Wordsworth is stressed from the long journey, madame, and I suggest we proceed immediately to the *petit-souper*."

"Anything you wish, messieurs." She nodded imperceptibly to the models posed about us. As she led us out of the Grande Salon, I saw several of them lie back and look faintly bored. We immediately found ourselves in a rather small antechamber lit with gas lamps that flickered and hissed. All about us, on the walls and on tables, were displays of various toys, various mechanical devices, whips of the softest leather, oddly elongated tubes, marvellous dildos, feathers, fans, chains of various sizes and shapes, ropes, velvet cuffs, bottles of oil and perfume — a cornucopia of the Marquis de Sade's pleasure. But poor Charles saw nothing, I'm afraid. Although everything passed before his eyes, none of it made sense to him. To Dickens, it must have seemed like some mysterious museum of mediaeval torture.

Mme. Dubois had paused, clearly to let us make our choices should we wish — and if truth be known, there might have been several small items I would gladly have looked over for consideration — but I knew Dickens could not hold up much longer.

"No, no." I laughed. "The *souper*, if you please. Perhaps we'll consider all this later."

Mme. Dubois nodded with complete understanding and

guided us through a side door into a private salon. A single table had already been set and a small candelabra lit. The chairs were plush velvet, the silver glistened on a white cloth. About the room, on three walls from floor to ceiling, hung smoke-darkened paintings of nudes, their candle-warmed flesh stretched out luxuriously on sofas, in beds, in swings, alone or sporting in the woods with other glistening nymphs and coy cherubs. In the background were the inevitable dogs or jaguars or tigers lurking about. On the fourth wall hung a life-sized *Triumph of Venus* embroidered on blue tapestry. Mme. Dubois seated us across from each other and immediately poured us each a glass of claret from a bottle already on the table.

"Shall I choose two of my young pupils for you? Or would you prefer to share your wine for a while and then accompany me to the *Salle des Voyeurs,* where you can select your own companions with great discretion and pleasure?"

As for myself, of course, I would have preferred the opportunity to choose among the many, but for Dickens' sake I decided we should perhaps postpone that pleasure until another time.

"If you please, madame," I said, "Mr. Wordsworth and I trust your judgement implicitly. We'd be delighted for you to select the two finest young entertainers in the house. Your most talented, of course. And" — I leaned forward confidentially — "most of all, Mr. Wordsworth wishes discretion. I'm sure you understand. Discretion and talent, you see."

"No need to say more, monsieur. I assure you all my pupils are superior young women, born and bred as ladies, and all with exquisite beauty. You will not be disappointed."

"We'll wait here with great anticipation."

Mme. Dubois nodded gracefully and withdrew.

Dickens sat rigid in his chair and only gradually began to breathe. I do believe it was the first breath he had taken since we entered the establishment.

The wine was warm as silk, and I encouraged him to partake, which he did eagerly, as if he hadn't noticed it in front of him until that moment. He swallowed off an entire glass, and I refilled it for him. Only then did his eyes seem to take me in and recognise me.

"Are we here to dine?"

"Only the *petit-souper*," I said. "The French believe food and sex enhance each other. In the eighteenth century, Duc de Richelieu was said to dine with several lady friends in the nude, wearing only their wigs. A little too Parisian for English taste, don't you agree?"

Dickens was sweating uncomfortably. On the other hand, he'd begun to look around at the paintings and to settle back with his wine. For the first time I thought the evening might not be a total disaster.

No need for all the details of what we ate and what we said, of course. Mme. Dubois introduced Lutrice and Diedrie, two delightful young women, full of laughter and playful hands. Lutrice had hair slightly more orange than red. She was at least twenty, I'm sure, and with a rather luxurious fullness of person, even a little plump perhaps. I found her exquisite. Bright blue eyes and bare shoulders polished with oils. I immediately suspected her whole self might be equally oiled, and I silently marked her as my own. She spoke liltingly in English, with a French provincial accent, admitting with sighs and flutters of her eyelashes that she was the illegitimate daughter of a Cardinal, schooled by governesses and, if truth be told — which I never doubted for a moment — a virgin still, merely in hiding here from a reckless engagement with a scoundrel who had betrayed her. At any moment, it seemed, she expected the Cardinal would come to her rescue. Unless the Cardinal could not forgive her. And then, what-oh-what would she do?

She leaned toward me with moist eyes, placing her hand under the table on my thigh. "Monsieur, perhaps you will rescue me tonight, no? I do so long to be rescued by a gentleman of your reputation."

"Mademoiselle, I vouch that I will personally intervene in your private affairs this very evening. Your deepest wish is my deepest wish as well." I raised my glass to her and leaned equally toward her to whisper in her ear, her hand squeezing my thigh, you see, for support in her troubles. She smelled like sweet Turkish brandy.

"As a gentleman of highest rank," I whispered, my lips merely brushing the warm flesh of her lobe, "I promise to explore every possible opening into your salvation."

Dickens hardly noticed our plotting together. He was equally entranced by Diedrie. He had slowly regained his old self, his old confidence, and he'd begun to flirt, rather boyishly, it seemed. Diedrie was a worthy target. She was dark, with mischievous eyes. Thick hair lay coiled on her head like a black snake, held there with a magnificent diamond comb — a gift from a well-satisfied admirer, no doubt. She spoke English with an Island accent, probably from the West Indies. What I remember most about her was the flowing swell of that glistening bosom, barely contained in a low, square-cut gown. As she moved, her flesh moved, swung, rose, like gentle swells in a warm Caribbean sea, a rise and fall of sensual promise. She would reach for bread with one long shining bare arm and

Dickens hardly knew whether to devour her tender arm or turn to catch the front of her dress falling open or watch the teasing of her eyes.

"Oh, Monsieur Wordsworth," she said with delightful innocence, "you are so famous. I, too, have read your poems, have I not? Perhaps you will sing one for me, and I will swoon with your rhythm."

We dined luxuriously in candlelight. *Petit-souper. Petit-souper.* A delicious *petit-souper.* We became drunk on sauces and bread and cheese and seafood and wine, and on beauty, we became drunk on the pure pleasure of beauty itself, the luxury of all the senses in full play, the delight of anticipation prolonged, delayed, promised, and flowing ever forward like Diedrie's cinnamon breasts, almost but never quite tumbling out of her dress.

I remember we found ourselves guided up a flight of circular stairs, dimly lit, tumbling over each other and laughing, all arms and petticoats and blindly teasing fingers. I remember vaguely a long hall led to a door covered in dark baize. I remember Dickens laughing heartedly, boldly, happy. Until we entered the room and he realised for the first time in an hour, perhaps, just what he was about to do.

The room was enough to bring anyone to a dead stop. Three large candles on one side of the bed cast the only light. The ceiling was astonishing, a magnificent mahogany wood, hand-carved with angels and clouds.

"We've entered the Pope's private chamber." I realised I still had a glass of wine in my hand, and I drank it off.

A vanity of rare inlaid wood was adorned with statuettes, silver brushes, etched glass bottles containing liquids of various colours, small ebony boxes, and various articles of jewellery, gold and silver, tossed casually about. Above the dresser hung a picture of the Virgin and Child, painted in the style of Raphael.

The walls were covered with a deeply textured red paper. The floor was spread with overlapping Turkish carpets, like piles of velvet on my bare feet. (When had I become bare-footed?) And to one side, two curtains of rich blue silk over a primary layer of heavy navy blue velvet hid a recessed closet.

And the bed. A grand four-poster in the middle of the room, with white curtains, and more white curtains overhead pulled to a knot in the center and tied with golden rope.

Our young ladies tried their best, inebriated as they were, to drag Dickens into play, attempting to tug off his jacket, untie his cravat. They fawned over him with laughing hugs and squeezes, pressing their oh-so-ripe and flowing bosoms against him, embarrassing him, frightening him, until he called out to me, "Wilkie!" He attempted to laugh, but he was backing rapidly away, pushing at their gay hands. "Wilkie, Wilkie, this is impossible for me, don't you see?"

He cried out in delight when Diedrie nibbled on his ear and surprised him with a sudden grab of his crotch. To his credit he didn't run, but again his eyes caught mine and I re-alised he was about to panic.

"Come, girls! Allow the good man to catch his breath." I pounded the pillow on the bed. "Here." I pointed. "Here is your duty, the night is young. Mr. Wordsworth will no doubt join us momentarily."

To his relief, they abandoned him for me, undressing me while I undressed them, the girls squealing and laughing. We were all tipsy, sometimes stumbling against each other, some-thing that seemed oddly hysterical at the time.

Out of the corner of my eye, I saw Dickens watching us with greed, with lust, envy, fear, desire. He wished to join us, I'm certain, but something held him. He felt weak and needed to sit or lean against something. He edged backward, desperately, it seemed, thinking to find a wall or a dresser to support him, but touching instead the deeply hung velvet curtains of the small closet. I was, I admit, too busy rolling a slow stocking down Diedrie's thigh to pay close attention to Dickens. When I next glanced up, he had partly withdrawn behind the curtains. He had collapsed on a chair in the closet, half-sitting, half-hanging on to the curtains. Only his knees showed, but I could hear him panting heavily, like an obese man at the top of a staircase. He panted in fear or desire or both, and I could imagine him there, trying not to overhear the girls' giggles, trying not to hear the sound of their shoes kicked loose, holding his breath at the girls' squeals and the rustling cloth of their petticoats tossed, their stays loosened, each act more focused, with more whispering, love-biting, generous little moans of anticipation, teasing and giggling. I knew Dickens was holding his breath now, behind the curtains. He had become silent, his eyes tightly scrinched no doubt, heart pounding. One hand still trembled at the edge of the curtain between us, holding on desperately, as one might hold on to the past.

I had leapt into the feather bed, into the billowing piles of pillows, into the luxury of two warm and deliriously wet young women, all flowing breasts and welcoming arms, laughing as our hands searched for divinely yielding flesh, stroking and squeezing, a bend of legs, thighs all diffused, finding one's face and beard suddenly buried in the opening flesh, while other hands gripped the hot bone of our contention, all tongues and nipping teeth, until we became one undulating animal, aching, deliciously quivering, with breathful moans and sudden barks of laughter.

Lost as I was in the liquid sounds, in the heaving pounding of our breathing, in the taste and smells of delirious flesh pressing against me, I found myself aware of another sound in the room. It had been going on for some time, I knew, although it had been faint and now was louder. The delicious pantings of Lutrice and Diedrie were close in my ear. This was something else again. Distant, yet heavier, more painfully rhythmic than our triunal gasps and moans. Searching for it in the yellow glow of the candles, I saw out of the corner of my eye as I rolled gently from top to bottom and over and under, that the dark closet curtain had been pulled to ever so slightly. In the liquid candlelight, I could clearly see the single startled eye of the Great Man peering out at us. I could hear the pumping of his heaving breath.

Then, the scrape of chair legs rocking, beating out a rhythm on the floor, until at once the curtains flew apart, and Dickens and chair were pulled flying into the room by wild leaps, his trousers about his ankles. A divining rod of odd justice had led him to a certain destiny, the chair and his body rocked forth like a pony cart out of control, jerked into the uncontrollable mystery of those smoking candles, until the chair flew forward faster than Dickens, and he toppled backward with a shout and cry, holding himself with one last effort of will, seeming to hover in midair like a magician performing a breathtaking feat of illusion. Gripped by a fierce loyalty to all his past had ever stood for in his heart, and if not by the Catherine he knew now, at least by the one he married so long ago, and by his nine children, by a Proper Morality he felt sure he was expected to believe in, by all those factory workers and kitchen maids who idolised him, by the Queen herself sitting down to tea, and yes, yes, yes, by England, too, that grand bloody isle.

"Ahhhhhhhhhhhhhh!" Dickens shouted as he crashed to the floor at the foot of our bed.

Lutrice and Diedrie burst into applause and cheers.

"Bravo, bravo."

"Monsieur Wordsworth, oh, you are too much with us," Diedrie cried. "Late and soon!"

Ellen Ternan

H<small>E DASHED</small> across the stage, shouting at someone about lighting, then rushed back to correct Maria's gesture. I wasn't aware he had slipped around behind me until I felt his hand in the small of my back, fingers and thumb spread apart, guiding me like a dancer, two feet forward.

"Here, Princess," he said. "This is where you belong." His hand lingered for ever-a-second on my back before he dashed away to call for wigs.

Mr. Dickens was not a large man, but strongly built. When he looked at you there was a power in it that made you uncomfortable. That afternoon he was wearing a white jacket and a gold watch chain. About his throat he had tied a silk cravat, which seemed, to my mind, astonishingly rich. His famous beard looked like a wild broom attached to his chin. He didn't walk across the stage, he strode about with the ferocity of an old lion. The best part was the beard and his great wonderful moustache. He was a lion all right. The moustache hung down over his lips and made you want to lick it with your tongue. You can see how silly I was, but bold, waxed moustaches made all the girls silly then. I was just turned eighteen.

Mr. Dickens wrote the play himself, a profound tragedy. After the Queen asked for a private performance, everyone in London was talking about it. Katie and Mamie and Georgina — the whole family had taken a part. But you couldn't expect them to go onstage before the public. It would have been highly improper. So I took the role Georgina had played. She seemed to think it made us friends of a sort.

There was no part for Fanny, my oldest sister, but she came along anyway, telling everyone how relieved she was. "You can't imagine how tiresome it can be," she said, "all that sweating in some awful costume." She had taken to wearing green spectacles and reading *The Fool's Tragedy* by Thomas Lovell Beddoes. Everyone left her alone, which is what she pretended she wanted.

It was Maria who got all the attention. She was twenty-two and beautiful, with dark hair and eyes, like a sultry madonna. From the first rehearsal she flirted unconscionably with Mr. Dickens. She sought him out, made him laugh, brushed lint from his white jacket. Mr. Dickens loved it. He joked and flirted back. Maria thought with an extra show of her great talent, Mr. Dickens could not help noticing her. Maria thought he could help her career, and she was right. Afterward, he tried to promote her among the stage managers in London. He knew everyone with the right connections. I was quite left out and offended. Her behaviour seemed so obvious and insincere. Mr. Dickens was taken in like a schoolboy.

He hired us all at the last minute — Mamma, my sisters, and I — in London, where we'd been living for about a year. We met him for the first time at Euston Station, setting off for rehearsals in Manchester. The whole cast was there. Mr. Dick-

ens shook our hands in turn, beaming, joking, making us feel
as if we were going to be the only passengers besides himself.
It was August and sultry, too hot to be in London anyway. I
was wearing a brown satin frock with a travelling cloak. I had
worn it in Molière's *Highbrow Ladies*. It was still serviceable,
I told myself, until I saw all the finery the other women wore.
They were all laughing and flirting in their silks and crinolines. My sad brown skirt had no flair at all. It hung in dreary
folds, as if I'd just been pulled from a lake. Even Mr. Dickens'
youngest girl, all fluffed up like a little white duck, in white
lace collars and ribbons and polished leather shoes, put the lie
to me.

Mr. Dickens had rented several private railroad carriages so
we could ride together, wives, families. We all squeezed in
among them, sweating and fanning ourselves. He had arranged
for everything, as if it were a picnic. We ate cold beef and pies
and cheese. The men drank dark ale. I said I'd try half a cider,
but Mamma gave me a look so I knew I wasn't supposed to.
Mr. Dickens danced in the aisles. He was in constant motion,
moving from one carriage to the next, treating everyone as a
personal friend. We played games and sang songs. On the
train we were only one family among many. He offered us jel-
lies and convinced Mamma to sing a solo, but he did the same
for others. I watched in dark fascination, like an ignored child.
His eyes swept past me, hardly noticing. He was accustomed
to being stared at. He was oh-so-famous.

At the rehearsals, Mr. Dickens praised Maria rather loudly.
Praised her beauty, her feeling. "I've never seen an actress so
simple and unaffected," he announced to everyone onstage.

Maria flushed and looked down modestly. She was preparing for the biggest role in her life. I hung back with the scenery,
saying nothing, merely watching the Great Man as he went

about painting props, moving furniture, shouting for carpenters in that booming voice. He loved the theatre. He was a fine director, firm, domineering, never harsh. He must have thought I was such a twit. Every time he saw me I was watching him secretly.

He put his hand in the small of my back and said, "You stand here, Princess."

You have to understand, it didn't mean anything. I was eighteen and innocent. Everyone thinks an actress is a whore, but I was innocent, no matter what they say. Mamma chaperoned us. I had been onstage since I was three. I saw things, heard things. You will, of course, when you work in the theatre around adults. But our life was pure in every sense. Mamma wouldn't let us out of her sight.

A lot of men teased me, petted me. I was pretty, but Maria was beautiful. Everyone said so. There's a difference. Mr. Dickens flirted back with Maria, and she tossed her head and looked at him from the corner of her eye, as if she were so very shocked. Maria was older than me, and she was not innocent. I knew that for a fact. I'd seen her with Charles Heyworth in Nottingham after the final performance of *A Gentleman Never Knows*. It was an accident. I wandered away from a cast party on the stage and opened a wrong door. Mr. Heyworth was standing there without his trousers. His white legs poked out below his topcoat, all blotched with age marks like the diseased trunks of two birch trees. His wig had come off, and his hair was smashed down with grease. When I opened the door, he was buttoning the back of Maria's dress. Maria was trying to hold her long hair up out of the way of his hands.

"Ho ho!" Mr. Heyworth cried. "The second sister wants her turn."

"Damn your eyes," Maria whispered.

After that, Maria and I didn't get along well, where before we'd always been the best of friends. Mamma didn't understand why Maria was always snipping at me.

At the final dress rehearsal in Manchester, everything came to a stop while a settee was moved closer to the front. We were unusually silent and nervous, waiting. Mr. Dickens leaned toward Maria and made a big show of whispering, "If only I were twenty years younger." Everyone knew he was joking. Maria tilted her head and looked at Mr. Dickens with pouted lips. "Twenty minutes would be good enough for me," she sighed. Everyone laughed. We all felt the same way; we were all in love with him. The Great Charles Dickens, like an old rooster among his brown hens.

In the play, Maria was even better than she expected to be. The play was so deeply moving. At the end of the first performance, while Mr. Dickens died onstage in her arms, Maria bent over him and cried real tears that dropped into his beard. Then she collapsed and had to be carried off in the arms of a gentleman. All of us backstage were crying. The audience was on its feet stamping and cheering. Mamma had to revive Maria in a chair before she could take her curtain call.

To me, he said, "Here, Princess. This is where you belong." It would have sufficed.

We came from a family of actresses. Three generations of actresses. My grandmother was one of the last of the strolling players, almost a century ago. Moving on foot from town to town, like itinerant pedlars. Sometimes sleeping in fields or ditches. Acting parts from Wycherley and Webster in village squares during festivals. Collecting coins from a crown of openmouthed yeomen and their scraggy wives. My mamma could remember it all. How she walked the muddy roads as a child, playing a new part every day, singing and dancing from the back of a wagon in a mining village in Wales or a country fair in Sussex.

Both of them, my grandmother, and Mamma in her turn, raised children long after their men died or disappeared. They were independent, enterprising, determined. Most men admired their beauty, feared their independence. Sometimes they earned little more than enough to buy bread and lodgings for the night. They acted on stages with delightfully vulgar males, before audiences of men and whores who drank pints of ale and ate sausages while the play was going on, who shouted and cursed and leered at them, who smoked and talked, gambled and sometimes tried to climb onstage in a violent drunken stupor. That's still the way it was when I was born in 1839.

At night, by rush light, my mother taught us to memorise lines. She sewed our costumes, taught us to sing and recite. Sometimes we ate mouldy bread if the mice didn't get it first. When we had a bed, we all shared it, four of us, with the bedbugs and the lice. Some beds were worse than sleeping in fields. At least in a patch of hay there was no stink of wine and vomit and semen.

The women in my family raised us to be strong and talented. They weren't ashamed. They taught us how to control everything about our lives, except the public's attitude. To be independent and alone, to earn our way, to make decisions, to accept what was difficult and dangerous and sometimes exciting.

My grandmother acted with the best in her time. With Charles Kean. With the Kembles and Mrs. Siddons and Charles Matthews and Macready. We were related to some of them, I think. They married each other, raised each other's children — a solidarity among the great and the talented. The public called us whores. We sold our talent for the price of admission, you see. The attitude was different then. To be beautiful and sing or recite or dance in front of the lewd eyes of the world was impure.

When I was twelve, I began wearing tights onstage, and the men cheered and guffawed. One man became so excited he fired a gun in the air and shot another man in the foot in one of the boxes. Later, when I danced the part of a fairy in *The Winter's Tale,* two men crawled onstage and chased me until one fell off and broke his arm.

They disgusted me. They made me ashamed. I knew it was because I had beautiful legs and, as more than one man told me, a beautiful arse. Was I supposed to feel guilty for being pretty? I was always embarrassed by my own vanity, but I loved to dance and excite the idiots, especially the young men who stopped chewing on their sausages in midbite. I didn't develop as fast as my sisters. I was still wearing tights and playing boy's parts when we were recommended to Mr. Dickens. There was something about my face in the glass that seemed too innocent and young. And yet my eyes were mysterious, much wiser — or at least older — than I really was.

The newspapers proclaimed we created a breach in morality. They said we violated England's pure standards. We were women of lax principles. But I remember the same newspapers sent men to the plays to review them for the social set, and the reviewers praised our beauty, our "intoxicating charms," as they put it. I remember the name of one of the reviewers to this day. Mr. Blackwell. He signed his name at the end of the article. Intoxicating and lovely, he said about Mamma. And then in another article, a few weeks later, he signed his name again, calling on fathers to forbid their daughters the degrading life of the stage.

Fanny began on the stage at two. They say she was so talented. So clever and sweet, you see. For a time she was in such demand her income supported the whole family. Later, she wanted to become an opera singer, but we had no money for lessons. She grew disappointed and withdrawn, and by the time she was twenty-five, her beauty began to fade, like a young mother who has lost her only child.

Sometimes, we toured Ireland. That was when Papa was still with us. And our baby brother, who died. Mama insisted we carry his body back to England. We had to perform three nights in London to earn enough money for the burial. Papa died a few years later.

Of course, we knew more than other girls. We played the parts of lovers onstage when we were sixteen or earlier. I can't even remember. We knew what love was while most women in England didn't know their cunny from a stinking carp. I don't mean to be vulgar. It's all in Shakespeare, you know. The bawdy jokes. The innuendoes. Have you read *Romeo and Juliet?* The way Shakespeare wrote it? We knew what he meant, even if the audience didn't. Among the groundlings, we saw whores rubbing their bodies against the customers. In the boxes, we saw jewelled ladies stroke the inner thighs of gentlemen. Of course, we knew. Yet Mamma kept us pure.

We had to stitch our costumes and dress our hair and copy our parts by hand. We took lodgings where we could find them, above a millinery shop or in the cellar of a bakery. We ate sandwiches or cold meat on the bone. Mamma told us the story of Charlotte Dean. You may have heard of her. They say she was born into a wealthy family from somewhere, Surrey perhaps. She ran away to join a troupe of strolling players and spent seventy years tramping the roads of England, carrying her children in her arms. They said she eventually had ten of them by one actor, her husband, and seven more by a second husband after the first one died. She outlived them both. She was still acting from town to town when I was a little girl, and I saw her once in Cornwall. I remember the raw red face and her booming voice. She was playing the wife of an innkeeper in something by Sheridan.

Our life was not a good one, I suppose. By the time I was five or six, I was painfully conscious that being an actress set Mamma and my sisters apart from the lives of others. How strange, you see. I loved every minute on the stage. They told me I was pretty, and the audience cheered when I sang. I didn't think of myself as unfortunate. Yet I knew Mamma and my sisters were not like other women. They were the ones I felt sorry for. They seldom associated with their betters, they were almost never introduced to the proper sort. We lived apart. We lived in a world of men. We were strong.

Mr. Dickens' play came at an important time for us. Our acting careers were about to take off — or die. We couldn't decide. Mamma had moved us to London, and we were renting in Northampton Park. It was our first permanent home, and all of us were working. When I think about it now, the house wasn't much. Narrow and dark as a cellar. Water trickled down the wall behind heavy wool curtains in the parlour. I slept in the same bed with Maria. Fanny had chosen to sleep with Mamma. She was too old to sleep with her childish sisters. Fanny and Mamma sometimes shared a lump of coal for the fireplace in their room. Maria and I cuddled back to back under old comforters and thought ourselves lucky.

Then someone recommended us. We were to be paid, but Mr. Dickens pretended we were part of the family. Afterward, everyone said I planned it all, that I was cunning. That I used my acting charms to trap Mr. Dickens, to break up his marriage, to lure the Great Man away from his moral duty. But it was all a series of accidents. We were living one life, and then, without quite understanding it, we were living another. I couldn't have planned it. I don't even remember having a choice.

After the play was over, Mr. Dickens seemed far away. He was busy with other projects and had no more time for ours. Everyone wanted to be alone. The set was being struck. Costumes were folded into trunks. Wilkie Collins slithered about telling everyone how it was actually he who had written the play. You could never tell when Mr. Collins was on the side of truth.

I wandered up to the stage. A faint, greasy light seeped in from windows high above. Several carpenters were trying to pull down a back wall on the set. There's always something so lonely about a stage after the play is over. The heart aches, as if people once loved had moved away or died. You feel haltingly aware of your own mortality. During the play actors pursue their lives with blind intensity, then it's over, suddenly, finally. Like watching a hearse pull away from a church after missing the funeral. Everyone retreats into themselves, struggling inwardly with private echoes. Something living was there, and now it's not there.

I was standing in the wings watching the set come down when Mr. Dickens came up behind me, as if by accident, stopping close to my side, both of us pretending to be absorbed in the carpenters. I realised I was holding my breath. Or perhaps simply unable to breathe at all. The carpenters hammered and cursed. Mr. Dickens placed both hands behind his frock coat and began to rock on his toes. I could hear a faint squeak of his leather boots.

"Well, Miss Ternan."

It was the first time he'd used my name. In the wings across from us, I could see Wilkie Collins talking to Mr. Dickens' eldest son, Charlie. We couldn't hear what they were saying. Charlie was nodding and trying to edge away while Mr. Collins waved his arms.

Mr. Dickens rocked forward and back, never once looking at me directly.

"You must have other engagements lined up," he said. "A very talented family like yours. I suppose you'll be returning to London."

"Yes," I said, keeping my eyes on the carpenters. One of them wore a tight cap and had oogle eyes, like a fish.

"Yes, but then it's on to Doncaster in September. Mamma says we'll be playing a comedy."

"Ah." Mr. Dickens nodded. "A comedy." His boots squeaked back and forth. He seemed to be considering it. "Doncaster in September, then. The St. Leger Day Races are held there in September, aren't they? Perhaps we'll see each other."

Our play had no connection to the races. I felt quite confused. Across the stage Charlie had disappeared into the wings, and Wilkie Collins followed him. Somewhere in the auditorium behind us, several voices laughed in the dark.

"I'm sure Maria would be quite flattered to see you again," I finally said. "As we all would, of course. It would be a great honour."

Mr. Dickens held his tongue. In front of us, the set at length collapsed in a violent heap of dust.

Oogle-eyes cheered. "Halooo!"

The carpenters congratulated each other. With a man on each corner, they carried away the flat, like four men carrying a casket. We could hear them shuffling off through the darkness on the other side. A shroud of dust was left behind to float in the orphaned light.

Mr. Dickens stopped rocking and spoke very softly. "You see, it was you, Miss Ternan, who I hoped to call upon." His voice was hesitant. I wasn't sure he had even spoken. My chest felt as if the stays of my corset had been yanked so tight my lungs wouldn't work.

"Oh now," I finally said, trying to keep my voice normal. "Maria has so much talent and charm, she's become the star of the family. A delightful actress, everyone says it. Mamma says Maria will have the lead role in Doncaster. If you find it at all possible to attend the play, I'm sure you'll see nothing but Maria."

For a long, unbearable moment, Mr. Dickens didn't speak, and then he finally said, "Maria who?"

I laughed and pouted for him, batting my eyes like Maria, being braver than I'd ever been. I wasn't flirting. I was imitating Maria flirting, but I've never known whether he knew. Because he roared with pleasure and his eyes never left mine. And how is it we can say so much with the human eye? How can we share in an instant a meaning words never speak, or if they can, would only sound suspicious or banal or too clever by far? But there it was. And it hit me with complete surprise. I knew in an instant as God's truth what had just happened. Later, Mr. Dickens told me I looked at him with such puzzled perplexity that it was more sensual to him than anything else I could have done. It excited him because he knew his eyes had told me exactly what he wanted them to. And I understood.

His moustache had fine grey streaks in it and hung down over his lips.

Afterward, he said all along it had been my eyes. Quizzical eyes. Watching him on the train, watching him backstage. I discomfited him, he said. My eyes made him feel some inner something, like a deep mysterious flowing river, he said. Yet I only watched him, I swear, or if I looked at him with the eyes I sometimes practised in the looking glass, it had been playacting, for myself. How could I have known he saw me at all?

Don't let this child get away, he had thought. Or so he told me later.

"I'm sure," he said, "absolutely sure we'll see each other in Doncaster. Perhaps you and your mother would like to attend the races with me."

He bowed slightly and was gone.

Afterward, came the question. Did I love him? But he was so much older and I was so very young. Love and passion are very different from the thrill of being noticed. Especially when you're barely eighteen. I had golden curls and new breasts. I thought a lot about making love, yes, but not about love. I believed in taking risks. No, not even that. I didn't believe anything at that age. One does not *think* oneself into love or passion. For a girl of eighteen, love is nothing more than an emotion of possibility. For me, it was like the stage. The thrill of an audience, or performing, or winning the applause, or the whistles and calls. Of triumph. I began on the stage at three. How could I separate how I felt inside from acting how I thought I was supposed to feel? I was learning how to act a bigger part, one of excitement and passion and catastrophe.

Did I love him?

Of course. Probably.

It never occurred to me.

In September, we were all performing in Doncaster. The audience suddenly began clapping, a standing ovation before the curtain had risen. Someone had entered one of the private boxes. The rumour spread like a backstage fire. *Charles Dickens is here. Charles Dickens is here.* Many of the cast were peeking through the curtains, almost fainting from heat, from the sudden tension. After the performance a bouquet of flowers, along with a card, was delivered to Mamma.

> Would you and your daughters be so kind as to give Mr.
> Collins and me the pleasure of attending the races with
> us tomorrow?

Would we be so kind? Suddenly, others in the cast saw us newly. They were humble around us, fawning over us, unable to speak. They hadn't known we were friends of the Great Man. The greasy little manager ordered our dressing room cleaned. He ordered a hackney cab to take us back to our hotel. He helped us in, saying, "It's all my honour, I assure you, all mine."

We had never known the luxurious wonder of being celebrities, the thrill of others bowing, holding doors, looking at us with awe. We laughed all the way to the hotel.

Fanny said to Maria, with only a touch of jealousy, "Well, little charmer, you got what you wanted."

Mamma said, "Who would have thought Mr. Dickens would have been so taken with you?" She'd not yet made up her mind whether his fascination for Maria was such a good thing. Maria fanned herself, looking as pleased as a ferret who has trapped a mouse.

We slept until four in the morning. The room was still dark and chill. Mamma went down to the hotel kitchen and lit two candles from the embers. We'd always shared three trunks for the four of us, with dozens of costumes and petticoats and hats and gloves. For the next six hours we sorted through every dress to see which could be made over, fluttering and cooing about each other, like pigeons. Shades of a pink dawn eventually seeped through the hotel window. Fanny had dressed in a violent hurry, knowing she was not the object of this stir. By completing her wardrobe first, she was in a better position to supervise the rest of us, which, after placing green spectacles on her nose, she took every opportunity to do.

Maria paced up and down in her shift, throwing dresses about. "He can't see me in this! Only governesses wear grey. Absolutely not."

"Remember not to remove your gloves," Fanny was saying. "A lady does not remove her gloves. Not even to eat."

Maria laughed. "What do you know about ladies?"

"I've acted the part several times, which is all any woman can ever say."

"Hush," Mamma said. "Wear your gloves and be damned."

We all laughed. Fanny had a beautiful laugh with a rich, deep voice.

Maria thrust her boots at me. "Here, child. Make yourself useful and brush these, fast as you can."

"Brush your own boots, slug." I was trying to pull over my head the seventh petticoat I'd found, a flounced white one with only a few small tears. Fanny and Maria had already claimed the crinolines. I hadn't even chosen a frock, but I was not about to make the same mistake I'd made for the train to Manchester. If I couldn't have a crinoline, I would create fullness with layers of petticoats.

"Goodness, Ellen," Mamma said to me. "Hurry up. Stop thinking about yourself in front of the mirror for once in your life." She took the boots from Maria's hand and pushed them at me. "Here, this is Maria's day."

Maria had already turned back to Fanny. "Don't you think my stays could be tighter? I've hardly any waist at all."

"We could call in the Royal Fusiliers to tighten them further."

"Oh, my hair," Maria cried. She was close to tears. "It looks like a chicken's nest on top my head. I can't possibly be seen like this."

Mamma hugged her quickly. "Mr. Dickens will see only two things, darling, and both of them are on your chest."

We all laughed again, except Maria, who looked desperate. "Then I'll need a little help." She began tucking satin scarves into her bosom for padding.

The hotel keeper's daughter brought harsh black coffee and dry cake for breakfast. Her eyes surveyed the chaos of the room. Mamma gave instructions one more time.

"The moment Mr. Dickens arrives, you're to send up. Tell him we will be down shortly. Can you remember that?"

"Yes, ma'am. Of course, Your Ladyship."

"Tell him we will be down shortly, don't you see, and send up immediately."

"Yes, ma'am." She looked wide-eyed at the thought of Charles Dickens waiting in her lobby.

"Tell him Maria will be down shortly. Can you remember that?"

"Yes, ma'am. Of course, ma'am."

We sipped our coffee on the run. Fanny and Mamma helped Maria dress her hair. Maria had lovely black hair. They parted it severely down the middle in the new style, pulling it back tight from her face with a snood behind. It emphasised her large dark eyes and made her look stunning. Mamma prepared a flower- and lace-trimmed bonnet worn far back on the head, tied under Maria's chin with a wide white ribbon. Maria had chosen a frock of blue satin. Mamma spent two hours preparing a woven ribbon border. I brushed her boots until they had a rich gleam, and she wore them over dark blue stockings. Not that Mr. Dickens would ever see her stockings. I felt so envious of how beautiful she was. My chest ached from it, and in the mirror my face was splotched from regret. When Maria slipped on her white gloves, she was perfection, as if Ingres had painted her in light filtered through a cathedral window. In my heart, I knew Mr. Dickens would see no one else. Maria's waist was so small even my own hands could almost have encircled it. She had the charm and bravado to enthrall a ballroom full of dukes and counts.

I knew all along I had misunderstood Mr. Dickens' intentions. He had been probing to discover where Maria would be acting in September. And if he flirted with me, it was no more than he had with many others. Clearly, my own foolishness blinded me to think such a great man would be attracted to a mere girl. I felt stupid and nauseated for letting myself be deceived so easily, for being such an ass. Maria had a lively energy and deep powers of acting. Her nose was long and Grecian, with arched, almost half-moon-shaped eyebrows over almond eyes — the face of Desdemona, with a full bosom, now enhanced with no little degree of padding. Most of all, she had a flirtatious charm that appealed to a man of Mr. Dickens' energy. She had a lively voice and wit and confidence. If I had been a man at the height of my powers, I would have fallen in love with Maria. Or at least made her my mistress.

No man would ever make me a mistress. I was shy and awkward and uncertain, shadowed by more glamorous sisters. What had I been thinking? What childish girl playing with dolls could have romanticised anything more unlikely?

Fanny and Mamma continued in the now light-of-day to circle about Maria, adjusting a ruffle, pushing back a loose curl. The hotel room seemed so suddenly dreary. Skirts and bodices and stockings lay strewn about. In one corner, I continued my quiet preparation. My eyes burned from the shame of my own innocence. Ridiculous golden curls punched out from under my bonnet, sadly out of style, like a country schoolgirl's. In the rusted glass I looked like a child pretending to dress up in her mother's clothing. I had given up finding a frock that would compete with Maria's. The old brown one wasn't so bad after all, and with all the additional petticoats, it was nothing to be ashamed of. A little worn perhaps. Fine enough for someone in the background, a lady-in-waiting, someone to carry a tray or laugh on cue. The dress had a square neck with ruching on the day bodice. Over my shoulders I threw a mantle. Deep in a trunk I found a pair of lilac gloves (only slightly mended) that picked up on a hint of lilac in my bonnet. It would do.

It would do.

I steeled myself and waited for the knock on the door, almost hysterical when it came.

"He's here, ma'am! He's here! He's waiting downstairs at this moment!"

We stood about a suitable time, in silence. Mamma peered out the window to see what kind of carriage he had brought.

"A landau," she said. "Quite distinguished."

Mamma went down first, then Fanny, then Maria, then me. I was glad to be last, as if I were in no hurry, as if I weren't even interested. Our parade of frocks and petticoats swished down the dusty stairs like a hot seductive wind over the moors. In the dimly lit lobby, silhouetted against the light from the door, we could see the form of Mr. Charles Dickens, waiting, hat in hand, leaning on a gold-knobbed walking stick.

"So very delighted."

"So charmed."

"Such a pleasure to see you again."

"Such a real pleasure."

"And Mr. Collins?" asked Mamma. "Will we have the enjoyment of his company today?"

"We will, we will. He's waiting for us at the racetrack."

In the lobby of the hotel, a crowd began to gather, as it did whenever Mr. Dickens appeared.

Maria stepped to the front, her gloved hand lingering in Mr. Dickens' too long, throwing her head back and laughing slightly too loud.

"You can't imagine the things we've been saying about you," Maria whispered, cupping one gloved hand to her mouth as if she were about to provide him with the most humorous confidential gossip. "Truly awful things, I'm sure." She laughed.

Mr. Dickens nodded politely to her, smiled at Fanny, half-bowed to Mamma, who was still all aflutter, and turned back to Maria, who tossed her head and burst into the most deviously happy smile.

"Shall we go out?" he asked.

Maria lowered her eyelids demurely and held forth her hand to place it on top of his.

Then Charles Dickens moved ever so slightly, stepping graciously it would seem, between Mamma and Fanny, and pre-

sented his arm to me, there in the ever-brightening gloom of
the crushed velvet lobby, and I felt my heart go smash. It
would have been impossible even to smile. I focused on making my feet move vaguely in time with his feet. Toward the
light it was. Someone held open the door, and the sun was in
the sky waiting for us, holding its breath as several folk on the
sidewalk clapped and tipped their hats. I know there were
horses, a driver, a carriage. I know we all climbed in and the
carriage moved slowly out and away. Clusters of watchers
stood on the sidewalk as we clopped by. I know Maria sat
across from me and glared at me in trembling anger, yet I
remember only the feel of Charles Dickens' gloved hand
through my gloved hand, the pressure of his arm against my
arm, the silence of the stars somewhere up beyond the sun and
clouds and sky, as they whirled on their mysterious orbits
making small of such moments, while even then, so much
then, I felt myself finally breathe again — and smile, only the
slightest bit — and look at Mr. Dickens with disbelief and delight and puzzled perplexity.

"Good morning, Miss Ternan," he said to me, as if no one
else were with us in the carriage, his eyes talking to my eyes,
his moustache hanging down over his lips with touches of
grey in it, so close I could have licked it with my tongue. I
looked at Mamma across from me. She was seeing me for the
first time, stunned and afraid for me, but I was eighteen and
suddenly afraid of nothing. Mr. Dickens, sitting so close,
smelled faintly of brandy.

"Mrs. Ternan," he was saying, happy and full of good spirit.
"What a wonderful family of daughters you've raised. You
must be quite proud."

Mamma could not answer. She and Fanny and Maria could
only stare, as if I were a changeling before their eyes. When we

reached the racetrack and climbed down, Maria leaned over and whispered in my ear.

"You little bitch."

It turned out to be a beautiful September day, the kind only England can have. Sunshine and crowds at the racetrack, with the smell of horses, and all the women wearing new bonnets and gloves, and men smoking cigars. I cannot recall a more wonderful day. When the horses ran, they sounded like a hundred drums beating, and the crowd roared and pushed forward, and my heart held still. I tried to watch the race, but someone always seemed to be in front of me, and Mr. Dickens seemed but mildly interested. He flirted and joked as if we were the only two people there, as if the jostle of elbows and hoop skirts was a mere breeze around us. Mamma watched us out of the corner of her eye. I knew she was upset. She thought I was too young. In her worry about me she pulled and twisted one finger of her glove until the fabric stretched and dangled, as if she had some kind of limp deformity on her left hand. That day, for the first time, I realised she was growing old. Her face seemed tired. Standing next to Maria and Fanny, she suddenly seemed so small. I felt embarrassed by her, angry she cared so much. Maria looked peevish and sour, holding her chin high and refusing to enjoy herself. Fanny pretended to hide behind green glasses, and when the horses ran she lifted *The Fool's Tragedy* to her nose. I felt disgusted with them all for being so petty, so undistinguished. It was the finest day of my life, and they acted like miserable children. I was ashamed of them all and kept my back to them as much as possible, hoping Mr. Dickens would not associate me with stage trash.

Mr. Collins was there, too. I had met him at the play in Manchester, of course, but he seldom noticed me. He was a sometime friend of Charles Dickens, but not a good friend. A hanger-on of sorts, the kind of toady all famous people surround themselves with, the kind who like to make up intimate stories about their relationship. When we arrived at the racetrack, he met our carriage wearing checkered trousers and his odd Bohemian hat with a floppy brim. He pretended to smile, but he limped and hobbled about, seeming to have nothing but complaints. He had sprained an ankle on a hiking trip with Mr. Dickens through the fells of Cumberland. It rained every day, and Collins had slipped in the mud. He was of the opinion no one had ever hurt himself so badly, nor did so few ever show so little proper sympathy.

I could not see why Mr. Dickens kept him around. Mr. Dickens was generous and boisterous, a friend to all, while Wilkie Collins was small and mean with his money, a weasel with tuppence. He wore gold-rimmed spectacles on a pointed nose. The thick lenses gave his eyes a narrow, hungry look that would undress a woman in public. But he was not romantic, only sensuous, like a snake in a carnival act. He made me uncomfortable and uncertain of myself. He was a spoiled sensuous little boy, even years later, when he was an old man with a tortured beard.

"Ah, my God," he groaned. "I shan't make it farther, I'm sure. We may have to cut short our holiday, Charles."

He was leaning on the rail of the track between races, one foot held up like an injured thoroughbred.

"Poor Mr. Collins," I said. "Perhaps we could ask the horse doctor to shoot your ankle. I'm sure they could spare a bullet."

Collins looked at me in shock, as if I were an insolent child, the presence of whose mother alone prevented him from slapping me silly. Mr. Dickens threw back his head and roared with laughter. Collins opened his mouth to speak, saw Dickens' pleasure, and knew in an instant he could not thrash me, even verbally. He spun on his one good foot and hobbled off, mumbling, "Good day. Good day, I'm sure," to Mamma and Maria and Fanny, staggering a little to make certain we knew his pain.

I put my gloved hand over my mouth, shocked at myself, but when I peeked at Mr. Dickens my eyes were still laughing, and he was looking at me, trying not to laugh out loud. Both of us were trying to hold back our silliness, snorting together through our noses like naughty schoolchildren. Mamma glared at me with disapproval.

"Poor Mr. Collins," she said, quite sincerely, which caused Mr. Dickens and me to finally burst out laughing together, conspirators in crime.

It was a wonderful day. I refused to take it seriously, and that made it all the more fun. Mr. Dickens had flirted with Maria, now with me. Next, he would flirt with Fanny. I had to believe that. Even when he asked Mamma for permission to call on me the next day. Even when he asked if I would accompany him on a carriage ride the next day, I still didn't want to take it seriously.

"It would be my greatest pleasure," he assured Mamma. "We would be back long before dark."

Maria and Fanny opened and closed their mouths silently, like fish in a pond where the water is drying up. Mamma was polite, but shaken. She waited for him to suggest that perhaps Maria or Fanny could accompany us, but he smiled firmly at her and said nothing. Nothing at all, allowing no possibility for a chaperon. It would be wrong, of course, wrong to ride alone in an open carriage with a man, even worse to ride with a married man. It was shocking taste for him to ask.

Mamma was in such a dilemma. She twisted and twisted

the finger on her glove. How could she say no to Charles Dickens, the most celebrated man in all England? Our lives had always consisted of flaunting society, flaunting convention, yet Mamma had protected me, kept me pure. Mr. Dickens was in his forties. Could a mother, even a stage mother, merely offer her lamb to the lion?

She looked first to Fanny, who removed her green glasses from her nose and, with great show, cleaned them with her handkerchief. Then to Maria, who gnawed her lower lip in bitter disapproval. Then to me, searching my face for a sign.

And so I told her with my eyes. And in her eyes I saw myself and my history and our family's history. I saw in that moment a grandmother trudging the muddy roads of England with her children. I saw the strength of generations of women on the stage. Mamma's eyes gave all that to me, with courage and faith and no little sadness.

She took a deep audible breath and turned to Mr. Dickens. "Of course," she said to him. "Ellen would be delighted."

Something happened to her then. I saw it in her face, in the way she held herself, in the way she bowed her head in curtsey to Charles Dickens, and I knew deep in my heart that Mamma had changed in that moment, that some profound release had occurred inside her. The strength and pride and courage she'd always had was still there, but a portion of it had just been reassigned to me, and the youngest of her living children had become the one on whom her own future would now depend. She was afraid for me, afraid for herself, but she smiled and lowered her eyes as if saying, Yes, the future is yours and God bless you, child. Forgive me if this is the wrong thing to do, and forgive us all for being such heirs to the flesh, but you have my faint blessing if that is what's needed here, because it will be the only blessing the two of you will ever receive. I knew she would have hugged me, but she was being silly and old, and I was quite ashamed to be seen with her.

I took Mr. Dickens' arm in the afternoon light, and we walked back through the parting crowd and the still-strong smell of horse sweat and leather saddles, the Great Charles Dickens and me, holding my back arched and my chin high, my lilac-gloved hand (my gloves only slightly mended) over his gloved hand (pearl grey and very expensive with a tiny gold button). Behind us, Mamma and my sisters followed, now somewhat diminished, like small fishing boats following a four-masted sailing ship out of the harbour. Charles Dickens had chosen me, and it was not necessary to breathe, don't you see? Charles Dickens had chosen me, and there would be a full lifetime ahead to bother about breathing.

The next day, I wore a pale blue walking dress (the only one in our trunks). This time everyone rushed about helping me get ready, even Fanny, although she still disapproved. This time I got to wear the crinolines, which showed seductively below the hem of the walking skirt. And over my gold curls I chose a flat-crowned hat that made me look very young and girlish. It was daring, but I insisted. Some instinct told me it was not the full womanliness of Maria he wanted. It was vital to be a little girl. Mamma was trying hard to put the best face on it. "It's so flattering to our family," she explained to Fanny. "Think of the connections. We'll be able to play anywhere. Every theatre manager in Great Britain will call on us."

No one listened to her or believed her. She looked strained and very tired. At the last minute, with Mr. Dickens waiting alone outside the hotel by the carriage, hat in hand, Mamma suddenly squeezed my arm hard, smiling at Mr. Dickens as we came out the door, and whispered in my ear, "Absolute propriety. Do you understand? No matter how famous he is, you must never forget he's a man."

Maria and Fanny remained inside the lobby in the dark. For them, it must have been like watching a train depart the station, all steam and smoke and mixed feelings.

One never forgets the first time a man attends upon you as a woman. That day, Mr. Dickens had rented a gig, which even then must have been an antique, but a fine one, painted green and red with a dark leather seat. We drove through Doncaster openly, pulled by two spirited bays. The sun was out again, although clouds swept across the sky. Everyone recognised him, of course. They tipped their hats, curtseyed, gaped. And then we were out in the countryside, where the wind blew warm and luxurious.

We talked endlessly. There seemed so much to say we couldn't get it all in. Mr. Dickens talked and I talked. We stopped at the ruins of an old abbey and walked about through late summer flowers and ancient stones stained with lichen. I removed my hat, and we laughed at my daring. On the way home we ate in a country tavern, where Mr. Dickens had reserved a private room, a clean cloth, and a fire in the grate, even though it was perfectly warm. After we were seated and alone, after the waiters had hurried away with his order, I knew it was more than flirting. I was frightened and thrilled. I could hardly speak. He ordered French wine. (Who ever heard of such a thing?) And roast lamb, rare and pink and delicate.

The wine tasted like summer on the tongue. Mr. Dickens tipped his glass a little too far, so that it stained his lips and even the grey on his moustache. I laughed and tipped my wine too far and knew it marked my lips as well. It ran down my chin, and we laughed, but he was watching me ever so closely, and it was hard for us to breathe normally. By my plate lay a white linen napkin, and I wiped the wine from my chin, but not my lips. When I dropped the napkin back on the table, the white linen had a dark purple stain on it, and I felt flushed and hot.

"Waiter!" Mr. Dickens bellowed. "More wine here." We tried not to laugh when the waiter, a young boy with long fingernails, came running. He saw the stain and hesitated, not knowing whether to change the napkin.

"A wine from Italy, this time, full-bodied — very red, dark red — you understand. We've a lot more white linen to stain here."

I gasped and held back laughing only by clamping my hand over my mouth. The young man avoided our eyes. "Right away, sir." He spun about so quickly he knocked into a chair and stumbled over his own foot.

It was that afternoon I first sensed that Mr. Dickens had chosen me exactly because I could hardly breathe. He wanted me *because* I was shy and pure. It was an easy role to play because I'd always played that role. He wanted me to flirt with him, too. He wanted me to be suggestive and sexual and tempting. Like a little girl who is sexual to a man because she's innocent. And I didn't know how. I did know how. It surprised even me it came so naturally. Innocent and tempting at the same time.

It was not the kind of acting you do on the stage. It was the challenge of being a woman. How to please a man. An older man. I was shy, unsure, flattered. He was all-powerful, ordering waiters about, enjoying how impressed I was by his power. Pleased with my adulation, charmed by my youth, my pretty hair, my náiveté. And my daring. It gave me confidence to know that in his confidence he was nervous. I felt myself adjusting to the role, sliding into it as if it were natural to my very being. Not dishonest at all, simply the role a woman must always play with a man. The adjustment you need for whatever man you sit across from. But what was it he wanted from me?

He called me My Little Riddle, and I pretended not to understand. He called me Princess, and I understood everything.

We were back in the hotel before sunset. As the carriage stopped, Mr. Dickens said, "You know, I'm forty-five years old." He looked at me. "And you cannot be much more than twenty."

"Eighteen," I said, without thinking.

Mr. Dickens sighed. "Eighteen."

The truth was I simply held myself back from thinking anything at all. I knew the moment was fraught with all kinds of dangers. I simply wouldn't let my mind and heart consider any of them. Inside my gloves, my palms were sweating.

He turned to me. "I would like to see you again. I realise it's all very improper. I would do nothing to compromise your reputation."

I had to smile, didn't I?

"My reputation, sir? I'm an actress. An actress has no reputation to compromise."

"Not true. Not true. To be an actor is one of life's highest callings. And your family's reputation is impeccable. I've always admired the theatre. I'll let no one cast aspersions on it. No one at all. From the time I was a child, I wanted to act onstage. I still do. Writing novels is merely a substitute for what I always wanted. Being an actor or an actress is one of life's most distinguished professions. . . ."

He was losing his train of thought. I could see I would have to interrupt. "You were saying, I believe, that you wanted to compromise my reputation."

"What?" The great Charles Dickens flushed. "No, no, of course not."

We both laughed. He settled back, admiring me with his eyes.

"I will," he said quietly, "ask your mother if I might see you again."

"Sir, my mother would appreciate that. But I need to tell you. I speak for myself. You must ask me first."

Mr. Dickens blushed. He actually did. "I'm so much older than you."

The gig held perfectly still. The horses waited impatiently, shaking their harnesses. My insides wavered, as if we were riding a small boat at sea.

"Sir, I could wish you twenty years younger, but then you would not be a true man. Only a boy not much older than myself. I think I would hardly be interested in you at all."

He looked into my eyes. He relaxed and knew what we both knew.

"I'll call on you tomorrow, with your permission."

"Sir," I said, playing my greatest role, "I regret to say, I'm busy tomorrow." I stepped down from the carriage and swished my way into the hotel, where I know for certain I held my breath for two days at the point of tears, waiting. Until his card arrived with a small gift. A box of new gloves, lilac, made of softest silk. The card was addressed formally to "Miss Ellen Ternan." Inside was another card in his own hand that said, "For My Princess." That was me, but I had to keep reading it over and over again to be certain.

Georgina Hogarth

THE SCREAMING had gone on for an hour. At first the servants ran from room to room carrying tea and hot water and smelling salts, but nothing would stop the terror overhead.

"How is she?" Hubbard asked.

"You can hear for yourself," I said, hurrying upstairs with warm brandy from Cook. Katie and Mamie huddled in the front bedroom, peeking out as I went by.

"Nothing to report," I said.

In her room, Catherine had torn the drapery and broken one of Charles' most cherished mirrors. She spent the afternoon shredding dresses and throwing brushes out of the window — the window that looked out over Charles' favourite view toward Bluebell Hill. She'd flung open the sash and shamelessly screamed and cried. No doubt across Gravesend Road at the Falstaff all those drunken louts had been listening with smirks on their red faces. It was Charles' favourite tavern, and his drinking friends would be there hooting. The hedge prevented them from seeing the house, but they could hear the breaking and screaming.

Catherine began on the bed linen, tossing pillows and sheets and quilts into the yard below. She hurled Charles' silver cigar box so far it landed in a rosebush, and his best leather boots, which flew badly, rather like dying birds. At first, several of the servants scurried about trying to collect everything, but now they simply cowered in protection of the drawing room below and watched the litter accumulate. When I reached Cahterine's room with the brandy, her face looked bruised and tortured, like a smashed Christmas cake. I was the only one in the house who wasn't afraid of her at the moment. She was my older sister, of course, and that made a difference. She was in her forties then, and huge, like a lumpy old feather bed, humping about the room in a white nightgown, but she was still a child. You could see it in her eyes.

It was I who played the role of older sister, who consoled and advised and tolerated her tantrums with no little resignation. Even I had to admit this one was different.

She'd torn the room apart, but the gift box and the note that started it all still sat evilly on the centre of a small table near the fireplace. The silver bracelet lay smugly in cotton, the white card reading "For My Princess" in Charles' handwriting.

"Of course it *could* be for you, Catherine," I said as I came in, taking up the same conversation I'd been trying to have with her all afternoon.

Hubbard had told me the jeweller personally brought the gift to the door — a different jeweller — not one the family used in the past, bowing several times, Hubbard said. But Hubbard was suspicious from the beginning. He had served as Charles' manservant forever, first at Tavistock House and then at Gad's Hill, and he knew Charles never called his wife Princess or any other endearing name. Hubbard knew almost as much about their relationship as I did. He knew Charles didn't speak to Catherine if he could find anything else to do, and none of us could recall the last time he bought her a surprise gift, especially not jewellery. In the kitchen, Hubbard whispered that he'd tried to question the jeweller, but the man hurried away rather quickly. Someone down from London, Hubbard thought, someone who wanted to impress Mr. Dickens by being a little too eager. Delivering the order himself and then seeing something was all wrong. He had held out the package with a rather delicate manicured hand, the nails cut and polished as flakes of mica, Hubbard said. Bowing and scraping about.

"You see, the gentleman forgot to tell me where to deliver it," the jeweller complained, "so naturally I assumed I ought to bring it myself. Took the train to Rochester and walked all the way out here, I did, to his home, you see, that's what I said to Mr. Clark, my assistant, and we both agreed, someone of Mr. Charles Dickens' stature would just assume we'd deliver it ourselves, so if there's been some mistake . . ."

Hubbard claimed the jeweller was backing off the whole time, bowing and grinning with his gums, like a dog that's afraid he might be kicked. Hubbard didn't like the situation at all. At first, he left the small box on the hall table by the stairs, but each time he passed it the box had worked its way closer to the edge, about to leap off, Hubbard thought, about to spill evil all over the house. Hubbard had long since lost most of his hair, and when he was nervous he would slide his hands up over his bald head, smoothing back invisible hair he'd taken so much pride in twenty years ago. Today, he couldn't stop straightening and patting his scalp, trying to recover the tone of his nerves.

Mrs. Potsherd came by just then, carrying a tray of hot chocolate and cakes for Catherine's headache. I took the opportunity to slip the box onto the tray as she passed. It was not, after all, our business to get involved.

Hubbard raised his eyebrows at me. "As sly as a fox hiding a chicken feather," he whispered under his breath.

Of course, it's easy to fool Mrs. Potsherd. She's a silly old woman, blind and toothless in a white cap, who slithers about the house whispering to her dead mother about how badly we treat her. Catherine keeps her around to massage her swollen ankles. But there was the package on the tray, invisible no doubt to Mrs. Potsherd, placed directly on the bedside table next to Catherine, who sat propped up by pillows in her feather bed.

I slipped upstairs and stood behind the door.

"It's my bowels again," Catherine was saying to Mrs. Potsherd. "Gurgling and frothing about. Frankly, I believe it's nerves. I don't think I'll leave my bed at all today. So much to do as always, but no, I'm trapped here. Abandoned would be a better word. Abandoned with so much to do and my bowels acting up again. Sometimes, Mrs. Potsherd, I think you're the only one who cares. There are others I could mention too busy to care, simply too busy for a sick woman who has devoted the better part of her life to raising her children and is now abandoned."

Everyone in the house heard the scream. I stepped back in time to avoid a terrified Mrs. Potsherd fleeing past me down the stairs. Hubbard peeked around the door of Charles' study below. The children scrambled to their bedrooms.

I spent the afternoon trying to calm Catherine. It was one of those burdens I had to bear alone. "Of course, it *could* be for you, Catherine," I urged. "No doubt Charles intended it as a surprise to please you. I can just see him thinking he would like to please you. That's so like the Charles I admire."

By late afternoon, almost everything in the room that could be thrown through the window lay scattered on the lawn below. Catherine staggered about, desperate to find something else to throw. I'm sure she didn't know I had come in once again. She suddenly spied Charles' favourite chair and began dragging it to the window, where she studied the possibility of pushing the whole thing out. She began with the seat cushion, panting and heaving, her face growing increasingly purple and wet from the unusual exertion, and when the cushion became permanently stuck in the window, she slowly slipped to the floor and began to sob. It was silly, of course.

I looked on with my best face of disinterest, chin high, waiting for her to come to her senses. She seemed pathetic and fragile. "Aren't you ashamed," I said, to console her. "You've never been anything but a selfish child." I had no choice but to be firm. It was the only way.

"I'm certain Charles will spend another of his nights away from home now," I said, "just because of your selfish actions. All you had to do was say, 'Thank you, Charles, what a thoughtful thing to do.' And now look how hurt he'll be."

Catherine lifted the hem of her nightdress over her face and sobbed in her private darkness. Two fat dimpled thighs poked out like albino dolphins.

"I have no sympathy at all," I scolded. "Charles may simply decide to move out of the house, altogether. You didn't think of that, did you? And then, my charming sister, the whole burden of running this establishment will fall on my shoulders. You never think these things through. I really don't believe you've ever left off being a selfish little girl."

She wasn't listening, and after a while I called down to Mrs. Potsherd. Together, we got Catherine into bed. I closed the window and straightened what I could. At least it's over, I thought. But it wasn't. When poor Charles came home that evening, none of us had the courage to warn him, and he went straight to the bedroom. All of us held our breaths, and then we heard a wee small sound, like a piece of jewellery, a bracelet perhaps, hitting a pane of glass.

The screaming began all over again, with Charles' voice bellowing louder and louder, denying everything. They fought for several hours, until Charles finally tramped downstairs and out the front door, slamming it like stone. On the second floor we could hear sobs for a while, and then nothing. Catherine couldn't say I hadn't warned her. She's never understood Charles as I have. Never loved him as I have.

I'm not a novelist telling you plotted stories here, changing the plot every time a more fantastic idea comes along, all for the sake of rather shallow entertainment. I'm not an actress, either, pretending to be someone else. Pretending to be oh so innocent and alluring, inventing a life of make-believe to deceive men. What I'm telling you can be trusted. My memory is razor sharp, and I'm good at seeing through to the truth of things.

Of course, I'm little more than a governess, if you will, one whose children have gone off now, married, or to the military, to India, Australia even. Long forgotten all about me. The real mother to them all. Catherine never lifted a hand. She bore them and collapsed back in bed, leaving others to cuddle them, feed them, give them a moral upbringing.

I'm the sister-in-law who came once to stay for a fortnight and lingered on in the background, like a cold that wouldn't go away — for a month, a year, a dozen years. Somewhat an-

noying at first, I daresay. That's how they thought about me.
Helpful, you see. I was needed, especially with Catherine
pregnant so often, or unwell, taken to her bed, ballooning
larger and larger until Charles ordered his workman to build a
support brace underneath the bed out of bricks left over from
the carriage house.

I learned to be helpful. I was tolerated with forced smiles
and awkward politeness, a ghost who floated about the house,
silently from floor to floor. I learned to go up and down stairs
without making even a creak. When we moved to Gad's Hill, I
was rewarded with a front bedroom, quite large and comfortable, and a nice fireplace. I shared a wall with the bedroom of
Charles and Catherine, and somehow it seemed right. I could
sit on a small settee by the fire and hear Charles walking back
and forth. I could hear Catherine's muffled crying, coming as
always from the giant feather bed. I could hear Charles' frustration as he explained there were no other women in his life,
accustomed now to years of such charges, but bitter about it
nonetheless. I even mentioned once to Catherine how dangerous it was, how when a man is accused repeatedly, he'll start
thinking he might as well be guilty of it, might as well enjoy the
sin he's charged with. She would hear none of it. And so I sat
by my little coal fire and knitted or crocheted, and I listened to
Charles pace in his heavy boots, sometimes hearing it all as if
Charles were in the same room with me, sharing our frustra-
tions together as of course we should, Catherine being the
only thing that kept us apart, Catherine complaining and sigh-
ing and boo-hooing that life had served her badly.

Over the years, I made myself useful, indispensable really. I
helped my sister dress, as if I were little more than a lady's
maid. I gave instructions to Cook for dinner, as if I were a real
wife, because the real wife was too absorbed in nursing yet an-

other baby, or nursing another grievance, or more likely too absorbed in whatever illness or distress she'd thought of to occupy her time that day. I found myself more and more busy, guiding the children with their studies, resolving fights, laying out clothes. I took my tea alone. I could hardly sit with the servants, could I? And I did find it so depressing to take it upstairs with Catherine and her continual complaints.

There were lovely days when Charles was there and we had our tea together, sometimes with heavy cream and strawberries. In the dining room alone or in summer on a table in the backyard looking out over the new-mown fields of wheat, or later, after the conservatory was built, sitting amidst the tropical flowers and feeling the sun's warmth even in winter, with tea and cake. Charles and I both liked our tea with milk. We were similar in so many ways. He would talk and I would listen.

"This new scrivener will have to go," he would say. "Too many mistakes, just too many mistakes."

"I wouldn't tolerate him," I would say. "You're just too kind, allowing that sort to take advantage of you. You always think too well of people, Charles, giving them one more chance, and then they take advantage of you."

"You could be right, Georgina."

"You let folks take advantage of your better nature."

"Yes, quite possibly."

I spread clotted cream on his scones and then just the right amount of strawberry preserves, and he ate heartedly. He loved to be pampered.

I observed things, too, it was only natural. How he grew unhappy over the years, lonely even. I watched him, and I learned how to bring his cigar or a glass of sherry, at just that moment when it was most needed. Something a wife should do, of course, but Catherine had become someone who merely whined at him, begged, pleaded. I remember very well how Catherine had been such a sweet, innocent puppy in her youth. She adored Charles and he adored her, at first. I felt envious, but only because I was younger and it was all so romantic. He was incredibly handsome. She was pink and rather perfectly plump. Afterward she grew into a heavy-jowled spaniel with odd ringlets over her face, and — it must be said — someone who released long, slow, whistling emissions in company. My story can be trusted. Every word of it's true, isn't it? Because it *was* a secret, shared only with one other person, the other half of it. I'm sure you can guess who that was. I don't have to keep the secret any longer, not after all that has happened.

The stress of it began to tell on dear Charles. At night he couldn't sleep, and I could hear them arguing in there as usual. He had gone moody, quick to anger, bitter about Catherine's complaints and whining. Then there was the night it went on into the morning hours — until sometime about two o'clock. "Yet another actress," I could hear her sob, which made a morally principled man like Charles even more angry. Anyone could understand that. Charles must have dressed, because the bedroom door slammed, and again he stamped down the curved staircase in his boots, and out the front door. Only the next evening did we hear he'd walked thirty miles through the night across the fields, all the way from Gad's Hill to Tavistock House. Everybody was astonished, except me.

A few weeks later, Charles called me to the library — his study, really — closing the door behind me. It was a room I always loved, with a beautiful tiled fireplace and dark mantel, the glass-doored bookshelves catching a late autumn glow from the window, and that wonderful mahogany desk made just for him, facing the bow window so Charles could look out over the lawn, and out of the corner of his eye, see his rose garden. He'd been away so much during the autumn we'd hardly had a chance to talk. There'd been so many readings to give, in Edinburgh and Bury St. Edmunds and Liverpool, passing restless nights, because he couldn't face coming home to more accusations. In London, he worked late at the magazine — sleeping on the horsehair sofa. Catherine grew more and more frantic.

"After all," he told me confidentially, "I really haven't done anything wrong. I can tell you this with a clear heart. I've never in my life had congress with any woman but my wife." He blushed and looked away. "I know you'll forgive the blunt language," he said. "I want to make this clear. It isn't fair for her to accuse me of something I've never done."

"I understand perfectly," I told him. "Really, here at Gad's Hill we all understand. We know such a thing would never happen. You have our faith and confidence, just as you have the faith and confidence of the nation."

"Do you really think so?" Charles asked. It seemed to make him feel so much stronger. He gazed out the window of his study. Afternoon light had mellowed, like a glaze of amber frost on the bare trees. I could tell my support brought tears to his eyes. He needed that. He needed a woman to believe in him, trust him, stand beside him. Something Catherine had never done.

"There's something else." He turned back to me. "Something only you should know. I'm certain only you will understand the true meaning of what I'm about to say."

I bowed my head. "You can rely on me to the fullest."

"The gift, you see." He sat almost silent, studying his

hands. "I hadn't intended Catherine to see it. All my fault. I was nervous when I purchased it and forgot to tell the jeweller where to deliver it. Here's the point. Here's what is for your ears only."

I did not look up. Whatever he had to say would be sealed in my heart forever.

"The gift was intended for a young woman, one you've met, although you may not remember her. She played the part of Lucy Crayford in Manchester. It was your original role in the play."

"Ellen Ternan."

"Exactly. I'm glad you recall." He paused, as if remembering. "She did a decent job, of course, but not up to your performance."

"Thank you, sir."

"What I'm trying to say is, how much I admired the deeply felt way you played your part. In Manchester, the whole production suffered because you couldn't take the stage. I would never have asked you, of course."

"Of course."

"And really, Ellen Ternan could never substitute for how closely you and I work together. Do you feel the same?"

"Oh, I do, I do," I whispered.

I couldn't help myself. I found body and soul pulling me from the chair until I was kneeling on the carpet, holding back tears. I could not look up, but I clasped my hands in front of me.

"You don't have to say any more," I whispered. "I understand what you're trying to tell me."

"Yes, I thought you might. You anticipate my needs, my moods. I thought I might be able to rely on you."

"Oh, sir," I cried out. "I hereby engage my words and deeds to our union in silence about any of this. Let me assure you, I say this with the reverence of a sacred vow."

My eyes were closed. I tried not to sob. In the hall outside I could hear the old clock ticking. In the kitchen below, Cook beat faintly on a copper bowl. The sound of Katie's laughter drifted in from the yard. Charles and I were here, together in this reverential moment, immersed in an inviolate secret while the mundane world went on. How can I tell you what it felt like? How can I tell you how much I'd waited for this time to occur?

Charles moved in his chair, as if he were oddly uncomfortable with me kneeling on the floor at his feet, as if he were unsure what to say next. It was all that kept me from reaching out and taking his hand, and I'm sure he felt the same way.

"Yes, he said. "Well, yes. I wanted you to know about Ellen."

"I understand everything."

"About the relationship. It's pure, you see. Friends only."

"I understand everything."

"We meet secretly sometimes. Forster knows because I've told him. And Collins. But no one else. Still, there are rumours, as I'm sure you've heard."

"I understand everything."

"About the rumours. You've always been so much a faithful friend, and our relationship has grown over the years, don't you think? I've known you since you were a little girl. I rely on you. That's the point, I suppose. So much might happen I have no control over, but I didn't want it to violate our confidence in each other."

I could barely whisper. "I understand everything."

For a moment, Charles paused. He must have turned partly in his chair, looking down on my bowed head, my hands folded like a supplicant before a saint.

"Yes, well," he said. "I'm glad we had this talk."

Throughout the winter, Charles seemed violently distracted, spending fewer and fewer nights at Gad's Hill. We heard he'd begun telling everyone how difficult it was to live with Catherine, how fat she'd become, how slovenly, how terrible she was as a mother. All of which was truth, of course. It had to come out eventually. But Charles did not reveal our own intimacy: how I had become the mistress of the house so many years ago, taking charge from a wife who could no longer perform her wifely duties, or how it was me who raised the children, who loved them, cared for their cuts and bruises, schooled them. I understood he could not bring my name into it. It was part of his plan. But in some way, my name was mentioned. It was natural, unfortunately. The worse things became between Charles and Catherine, the more suspicious busybodies searched around for the cause, and his attraction to me was so very obvious. How could we disguise it?

In early spring, my parents wrote, complaining that rumours had reached even their ears. They felt certain I was not involved, but they sought my assurances. I was furious. That my own parents could doubt me. It was like Catherine's accusations against Charles. The purity of our relationship was inviolable. No one, not even Mamma and Papa, had a right to tarnish it. Naturally, I denied. I wrote back, rather intemperately I'm afraid, pointing out in the most carefully crafted sentences that certain types of love rise above the ordinary, soar above the physical, beyond mere friendship, romance, and even passion. Like Héloïse and Abelard, I wrote, there are relationships that endure because of higher truths. If they could not understand that, then they would have to choose which daughter to call their own.

Charles was busy fighting his own battle. Trying his best to divert attention from me by denying he was having an affair of any kind with Ellen Ternan. It was such a blatant ruse I felt sure everyone could see through it, but I knew it had to be done. His great public would never tolerate incest with his own sister-in-law. I kept mum and supported every word he said, especially to the staff, who had begun to whisper violently amongst themselves. Catherine had, of course, taken to her bed, stricken with gas. None of us paid her much mind, it was all so confused and shocking. The poor children huddled in their rooms with me alone to console them, to assure them everything would work out and they must only be brave and have faith in their father.

Then, Charles ordered carpenters in London to Tavistock House. None of us knew what work he had charged them with, until one morning when Hubbard caught me in the hallway.

"He's had the doorway sealed," he whispered. "I've just found out."

"What doorway?"

"*Their* doorway, don't you see? The doorway between their bedrooms. His and Catherine's."

"At Tavistock House?"

"That's it," Hubbard said. "Sealed up tight. And word is, he's preparing the house for Catherine to return. I've got it from Mrs. Champlain herself."

Mrs. Champlain was the housekeeper at Tavistock House, and because Charles often stayed the night in London, he kept the house open, with Mrs. Champlain there to serve his needs, and, of course, a cook and a liveryman, several others, I think. Mrs. Champlain was a domineering old fool who enjoyed ordering everyone about, although to Charles she pretended she was sweet as dogwood in May, and because Charles is himself such a decent honourable man who gives every human soul the benefit of the doubt, he trusted her implicitly. I had reasons to be suspicious, however. Mrs. Champlain was a little too sweet for my taste. A little too much the blooming dogwood — even a complexion the colour of dogwood — a sort of corpselike white skin with faint traces of purple around the nose, and deep open pores. I suspected her of being a secret drinker, but I could never prove it. A bottle of gin somewhere, I was sure, although she kept it well-hidden, like the deceitful biddy she was.

At Gad's Hill, the world began to fall apart. We were all in a state of confusion. The children avoided both their father and their mother, devastated and in tears. Catherine refused to talk to me, and frankly, I had no desire to speak to her. She was the cause of all this, you see. A good wife would have kept her husband happy, pleased her husband, made him feel as if he were the centre of her world. It was Catherine who drove Charles into fits, destroyed his happiness, made him doubt himself.

Katie seemed the only person who kept her wits. Little Katie, who was almost nineteen and pretty. And so very responsible. She stepped in to fill her mother's place, her own face as sober and full of pain as any I've seen. She was lovely beyond words, with eyes from the Hogarth side of the family, winsome eyes, like my own, with a touch of sadness that deepened as her mother and father had grown apart. She turned to me, as all the children did in their confusion, and I coddled them, gathered them to my bosom as my own, which in truth they were.

In March, I believe, or perhaps early April, after the door-way between Catherine's and Charles' bedrooms at Tavistock House had been permanently sealed, Charles summoned me to his study and told me he'd ordered Catherine to call upon Ellen Ternan.

For a moment, I felt staggered, waiting for him to continue.

"Sir?" I finally said, in half my voice. "You've asked Catherine to pay a social visit to Ellen Ternan?"

He gave no answer, standing near his desk, hands behind his back as he gazed out the window, rocking slightly on his toes.

"Do you think it quite proper?" I finally asked.

"She has insulted Ellen," he explained. "Gravely insulted her by numerous accusations."

He turned to me, and I could see his face gripped by a strain I'd never seen before. The eyes seemed tortured. The mouth twisted in such a small way. I had a sudden over-whelming desire to press his head to my bosom, to console him, he was suffering so much — trying to hide his love for me behind that silly actress. I had never understood the depth of his pain, and I felt gravely ashamed, rocked by the depth of his sensitivity.

'You of all my friends," he said. "You will understand when I tell you it offends against all decent morality to allow such accusations to be publicly circulated. The great offence and anguish it must cause the Ternan family is more than I can bear."

"Of course," I said. "The family should not be slandered."

"A great acting family," he reminded me.

"Very distinguished."

"Very distinguished," he emphasised. "I've ordered Catherine to apologise in person. It's the least I can do, Georgina."

He looked directly into my eyes and held out both hands

for me to take. It was the supreme moment of my life. I stepped forward, felt myself lifting my arms, holding out my hands to his, blinded by tears, and heard him suck in a deep breath to announce his final decision. "Afterward," he said softly, speaking to me alone, holding both my tiny hands in his great paws, his voice for my ears solely. "Afterward," he sighed, "it will be impossible for Catherine and me to continue living together."

I nodded, unable to speak.

"The children will stay with me, naturally. That will be my final decision on the matter."

"Of course."

"And you, my dear Georgina, you must make a decision that may well affect the rest of your life."

"Of course," I said faintly, knowing what it was, having known all along, having felt it in my bosom like a snake swallowing my heart, evil and terrifying and wrong, to be damned forever for love, like one of Dante's great tortured souls swirling about in the winds of eternal hell, unable to make any other choice, and making that choice with full and eager awareness of the consequences.

"Yes," I said. "Yes. I will stay with the children, of course. They'll need me. I would never be able to leave Gad's Hill, sir. Not as long as you're here."

"Thank you, Georgina. Once again I knew I could count on you."

For a moment more, he held my hands and then released them. They floated like heavy doves sinking in a setting sun, hovering in one last fading light until I reluctantly pulled them back to myself.

Ellen Ternan

I WAS STILL an actress, of course. I had a part at the Haymarket. A small part, but a good one. Reviewers said I had talent. Or at least reviewers said I was pretty. I kept busy in theatres around London. If I'd had more talent, I could have won better roles. Perhaps I could have gone on. It was such a heady time. Playing at the Haymarket and having a closed carriage waiting at the stage door afterward to whisk me away. Everyone was talking. Who could he be? What was his name? Couldn't I just give them a clue?

Mamma said it was too dangerous. Even if it led to an affair, what could I get out of it? A few jewels? A baby? The great Charles Dickens was not going to abandon his family, his wife of twenty years.

Mamma forbade me to see Mr. Dickens again. My reputation would be ruined if I went on with it. If the rumour spread, theatre managers would not hire me. No one would allow anything to harm the Great Man.

'It is *theatre*," Mamma said firmly, "*theatre,* don't you see? It must be theatre you hold central to your life."

Maria was even more insistent than Mamma. "Stop being a fool," she said. "This is too serious, too dangerous." She was seething with jealousy. She and Fanny joined together, the wicked stepsisters, whispering and plotting.

Fanny pulled me aside one evening, just as I was leaving for the Haymarket.

"Someday you'll need to support yourself," she whispered. "The burden will fall on you. The burden always falls on the woman. Trust me, baby sister, your Great Man will not be around at the time. He'll go back to his wife or he'll find another actress, younger and prettier. All you'll ever have that is yours, is the theatre. That's who we've been for a century and all we'll ever be."

Mr. Dickens had already sent a message he would meet me that night after the show. It was so incredibly clear they were all jealous, even Mamma. I shrugged off Fanny like a wet shawl and hurried out the door to my real life.

When you are with a man, you do not remember a mother's warning, and you deliberately defy a sister. You see his eyes looking into yours, somewhat nervous, and the grey-streaked moustache over the full lips. You realize that even though he's more than twenty-five years older, the most famous man in England, he's as nervous as you are. His eyes look into yours and you know, absolutely, without doubt, that he is yours alone.

Of course, he wasn't mine, was he. I was a romantic twit.

He belonged to his public. I didn't understand until later. He belonged to the sales of his books, to the weekly magazine, to his lawyers, to the letters that poured in, to his standing as the most popular artist of all England. Mr. Dickens was often gone. He gave readings around the country, in Alderbury and Bath and Broadstairs. And when he was in London, he had his great editorial duties, his business affairs. I would receive a package from him. Full of new hats. Or new frocks, shawls, shoes, jewellery. With lovely notes. "For My Princess." But I had to go on being an actress. Mamma was right. Maria and Fanny were right.

Then he sent dresses for Maria and Fanny. He bought a necklace for Mamma. He bought them scarves and bonnets. He began to visit us in the evenings. He would come by late and stir up the house. All the women fluttered, and Mamma would run next door to borrow a porcelain tea set. Mr. Dickens would stride across the parlour in leather boots, like a man who owns the world. We were so unused to anything masculine. He sat by the oil lamp and smoked his cigar. We did not have gas lights in the house; we were too poor. Mamma lit the lamp, and it smoked so Mr. Dickens offered to trim the wick. He liked being a man, and Mamma pretended it was something she could never do herself. She was so grateful to him. They chatted about the stage and actors they'd known. Fanny stood by the fire and sang an aria from *Figaro*, letting Mr. Dickens think she had played Susanna although really she'd only sung a small part in the chorus. Maria gave a reading from *The Duchess of Malfi*. Mamma pounded out a sonata by Liszt on an old secondhand spinet that came with the house. And later, over cards, Mamma and Mr. Dickens talked for hours. She flattered him and offered more tea or a nip of brandy (purchased just for him). She praised everything he'd ever written, especially *Pickwick Papers* (which she'd heard most about but never read). Of course she told Mr. Dickens how Fanny wanted to become an opera singer. Her heart was set on it, but it was impossible. There was no way to study opera except to go to Italy. You simply couldn't find the proper training in England. Out of the question.

Mr. Dickens had a sudden idea. He would pay for it. He

would send her to Florence, where she would study with the greatest opera teacher in the world. It would be his pleasure. Such a small thing for him to do.

Mamma would hear none of it. Fanny would be infinitely grateful, of course. So grateful, but it was impossible, you know. Fanny could not go off to Italy by herself. She would be turned down without friends to recommend her. Mr. Dickens was insistent, excited, carried away with his plan. He would write letters of introduction. He would pay for everything, the least he could do. And he would even send Mamma as chaperon. It was settled. What a wonderful opportunity for him to make some small contribution to our family.

There were tears and pleas and denials and gratitude. Charles Dickens gave orders, paid bills, bought rugs and brass candleholders and shoe buckles. Maria began to primp and use powder instead of rouge when she went out on the street. She wore silk frocks and complained she had no one to dress her hair.

Fanny practised her scales every morning, every noon, every evening. She turned down parts on the stage with gracious handwritten notes. She and Mamma bought hosiery and gloves and hats and writing paper. Passage to Italy was booked for late autumn.

We hired a maid.

The scandal began in the spring. The bracelet, the mistaken delivery. He told me Catherine had accused him of having yet another of his "little actresses." As years went by, Mr. Dickens seemed to think it was true: he came to believe he must have had many affairs with actresses. But he hadn't, you see. So with his wife he could play the part of being unjustly accused.

I can imagine how he roared and bellowed, how she mooed and cried. The whole house was rocked by it, they say.

Some way, he turned it all against her. I never understood. It became her fault and her foolish jealousy. She had slandered not only the great Charles Dickens but an impoverished family of struggling women. She must make public restitution. And suddenly, one afternoon, the personal maid of Catherine Dickens arrived in a black cab, a Mrs. Potsherd who seemed dazed and frightened. She'd been sent to enquire whether Mrs. Dickens might call upon us tomorrow afternoon. Mrs. Dickens. The fat sow with the pinched, humiliated face, in her ballooning white dress, would like the honour of paying us a call. A family of distinguished actresses.

Mamma was accustomed to surprises during a performance. A table collapsing, an actor falling down, a pistol going off. She faced Mrs. Potsherd on the doorstep as if one more caller could hardly make a difference. "It would be our pleasure," she said, with solemn dignity. "Entirely our pleasure, I'm sure."

Then we put on our caps and began to clean. We beat the rugs, we scoured the doorstep, we washed the curtains, we boiled the chamber pots, we polished the few pieces of silver we owned. We dusted and dusted. Mamma purchased cakes from the finest baker in the West End. We hired a second maid for the next afternoon.

When the hour finally arrived, we dressed and powdered and said nothing to each other. All of us waited in absolute silence. It was raining that dark and pouring April day. Water puddled deeply in front of our steps. A four-wheeled brougham arrived with horses snorting and stomping. A liveryman jumped from the box to hold a black umbrella over the great Mrs. Charles Dickens, who stepped forth, almost tilting over the carriage. She was a large woman. Her daughter Katie accompanied her, steadying her arm. Together they waded through the muddy water to our door, feet sloshing under the hems of their frocks and their white crinolines.

"So kind, so kind."

"So honoured."

In stiffness and near darkness we sat in the parlour while the clock ticked. The parlour too small for all of us by half. We should have laid a fire, but we had been too busy to remember. Mamma ordered candles lit. The maid brought cakes. Brought tea. The clock ticked. The rain beat in gales on the windows.

Katie was the same age as me. A little plump, like her mother, but pretty, with brown ringlets. She looked at us with bold curious eyes. First at Fanny, then at me, then at Maria. She was trying to decide which one of us it was. And her mother, the woman whose eyes were like small antique buttons hidden in the white pincushions of her cheeks, whose jowls rested upon her lace collar, the great Mrs. Dickens nibbled silently, sipped around the edges of her cup, and tried not to burst out in tears.

All of us, I think, wondered at how bizarre it was. Yet all of us were playing the roles Charles Dickens had assigned us. Mamma poured, acting her best part ever, the materfamilias, head of — according to British standards — a family of whores.

"So very honoured," Mamma said, "to be favored by such a fine lady and her daughter."

Fanny nodded graciously, turning to Katie. "I look forward to the opportunity of calling upon you sometime."

She knew full well Kate would rather bleed to death.

Maria said, "I recall meeting you at Euston Station, although there was such a large crowd. You probably don't remember me."

Katie forced a smile.

"We so enjoyed the train ride." Maria was too nervous to stop herself now. "Mr. Dickens was so humorous, don't you agree? And then, having the opportunity to act with Mr. Dickens in his famous play. Truly delightful. A challenge for me, you know. I was so overcome with emotion. By the end, it was not like acting anymore. I remember holding Mr. Dickens' head in my lap as he died. The tears simply poured forth and dropped directly upon his beard, his face was so close, you see, I could smell the pomade in his hair. I simply wanted to press him to my bosom in those dying moments.

She caught herself. "But, of course, not that close." She gave a broad smile to Mrs. Dickens. "It was only a play. With a lot of emotion. Mr. Dickens loves to play, don't he? Onstage that is. So flattering to have been selected by him for his attentions. As an actress, I mean. Quite flattering in a professional way, so to speak."

I remained silent, as did Mrs. Dickens, who never looked at me, who looked straight forward at the flowered wallpaper and finally said, in a voice so soft and broken we could hardly catch the words Mr. Dickens had instructed her to say, "I do hope any unpleasantness you might have heard can be forgiven."

Mamma and company protested.

"Why, what can you mean?" Mamma said. "I assure you we've heard nothing at all. What is there to have heard anything about?" She turned to her daughters for affirmation.

Fanny pushed up her green glasses and looked so very curious at the Dickens women, as if attempting to recall any affront she might have received. "I can't think any apologies could possibly be necessary."

"Really," Maria said, "we're so flattered — so honoured — by your calling."

Mamma leaned over the tea table. "Can I interest you in more cakes, Mrs. Dickens?"

The Great Man's wife rose like a white whale that suddenly realises it has left open sea and is disastrously squeezed into a narrow harbour. She rose, heaving waves of embarrassment about her, and nodded silently, with eyes that barely saw, leaving harbour under her own power, with great dignity, declining all help, acknowledging no one. Her footman assisted her into the brougham, steadying the carriage to keep it from tipping over as the great whale vanished forever to lock herself away in a dark bedroom, at Tavistock House we later heard.

Katie alone turned back from the carriage and walked up the steps to me, their liveryman scurrying to cover her with the umbrella. She offered her hand.

In the pouring rain, she said, "I'm sure we'll get to know each other better, someday."

I could not speak.

It shot through my heart: I was the exact same age as Katie. He could be my father. Everyone else had probably thought of it, but truthfully, it never occurred to me. Katie looked into my eyes and knew it was me. She had so much more wisdom and dignity than I did. The carriage drove off in the rain, splashing our narrow lane on both sides.

When I returned to the parlour, Mamma and Maria and Fanny were holding themselves with laughter. Fanny was pretending to be Catherine Dickens, pushing pillow after pillow into her bodice and up her skirt. She puffed out her cheeks, squeezed her eyes in terror, sipping the edge of her teacup as if it were poisoned. All of them laughed so hard they could not sit on their chairs. They stuffed their mouths with cake and called for more tea. I couldn't help myself, and I began laughing, too.

Mamma mimicked Maria: "Oh, how much I did so like Mr. Dickens' beard, it was such an emotional beard, wasn't it, as was his love for playing with actresses, at least those who cry real tears into his emotional beard, and don't we all love a beard pressed against our bosom, speaking professionally, of course."

We laughed until we were in pain.

Afterward, I went to my room and cried. I felt so degraded. For several days, none of us looked each other in the eye. We were all ashamed. We were afraid we would break out laughing again.

Mr. Dickens decided the house we were living in lacked dignity, or perhaps it was too small. Something made him want to lavish more money on us. He rented a new house, with more light, he said, on Gloucester Crescent, near Regent's Park. The location was surprisingly more exposed, but I felt I needed to trust his decision. Within the week, an army of workmen packed everything up and moved our few possessions, much to Mamma's fluttering dismay.

Fanny decided with a better address, Mamma should entertain more, although there were few we could invite except other actors. Sometimes, when Mr. Dickens wanted to be alone with me, we met at private dining rooms in inns or hotels, travelling in separate hacks. Or I would take the train to Southborough or Ashbury or Chester, wherever Mr. Dickens might be giving a reading. But we couldn't hide from everyone. Other times, he would cast caution aside, and we would attend the theatre together, sitting in the back of a box, of course. Somebody always saw us. Sometimes a member of the Royal Family would come out of a box beside us just as we exited ours. Mr. Dickens would bow low, and I would curtsey. There would be several moments of good-fellow conversation, and then we would all bow and curtsey again. For me, there would be a glance of acknowledgement. An acceptance so long as it remained unofficial and private. In a strange way, I took the same attitude. I spoke about Mr. Dickens to no one, not even my sisters, not even my mother, and never about "us." To say the word "us" frightened me. Eventually it became an odd eccentricity I could not overcome. I accepted who we were and what we were. But I kept it private in my heart. I nodded to it kindly, a tip of my hat, but I politely avoided any reference to myself.

That first year, everything seemed dangerous and exciting. Mr. Dickens moved out of Gad's Hill. There was a public announcement to cover up. It spoke about mutual agreements and great affection. But there were rumours. Some of his friends knew, and they must have whispered it about. Mr. Dickens was so upset his face hurt. He could not let down his public. Could not let down England. He was a frenetic man at times. Other famous men had mistresses, but he was a gentleman, he had obligations, duty, principles. I was not surprised when he told me about Mr. Collins living openly with a mysterious woman. But it was fretful to hear of Thackeray and Victor Hugo, not to mention Shelley and Lord Byron earlier in the century. I knew all about the morals of actors. Somehow, I imagined authors held themselves to a higher standard. In many ways I felt disappointed.

Mr. Dickens explained how the others kept their women openly because none of them were idols of the great middle class. As he was. It was the middle class made England ruler of the world, so said Mr. Dickens, who being older, often needed to explain things to me.

He kept explaining things to everyone, even though no one asked. Catherine had mental problems, he decided. Catherine could not take care of the children, she had always been a bad mother. Catherine was the one who wanted a separation for years. He broke off old friendships with those who could not understand his bitterness. He broke his contract with Bradbury and Evans, his publishers, and he refused to speak further with Miss Coutts, who wrote to him expressing her hopes that what she'd heard might not be true. He denounced Catherine's family, the Hogarths, as evil and wicked. Later, Mr. Dickens ran an editorial in his own weekly magazine, defending himself from something no one had ever accused him of. I told him he was foolish, but some days he was in such anguish he could hardly talk in complete sentences. His words slurred. His face blotched and twisted out of shape. He would hold me on his knee and pet me and ask for help. I would comb his hair and his beard, or press his face to my bosom, where he would breathe slow and deep.

We were never intimate.

After the theatre we went to his other lodgings in London, at Wellington Street, where he often stayed now. Georgina remained alone at Gad's Hill with the children. On Wellington Street, Mr. Dickens kept only his man, an older gentleman named Hubbard, who knew how to be discreet and whom I seldom saw.

We would arrive from Covent Garden, and Mr. Dickens himself would light the lamp and start a small fire in the grate. The smell of the fire would be warm, like someone's breath on your throat. He sat in an old stuffed chair from the Georgian period and held me on his knee. I could tell he was too exhausted to talk. I ran my fingers softly over his eyelids, stroked his face. I straighten his cravat. He seemed very distant or perhaps afraid of something only he could envision. Finally, I pressed his face to my bosom, where he breathed slowly and deeply. We cuddled in the flickering shadows, like father and daughter, you see. I cooed to him, sang to him, played with his thinning hair if that was what he wanted, and often it was. I felt hurt he didn't desire more, yet relieved and proud I knew how to give him the care he so clearly needed. We were never intimate then. He petted me, his fingers traced the lines of my eyes, my ear, my throat down to my high collar. He smelled like cigars and whisky, as always. His hands were so much older than mine, with heavy veins and the coming on of age spots. Yet I loved them dearly, loved the touch of his fingers on my bare arm.

When he was especially upset, I sang small songs in his ear, allowing my lips to brush his skin and my breath to warm him, sometimes brushing my cheek or my lips against his, as if accidentally. Passion is not always what we think it is. Passion is sometimes holding back, trying to control the rise and fall of your bosom as it presses against a man's arm or his chest, feeling the hot blind darkness of desire swelling in your throat, in your stomach, your thighs. I could feel Mr. Dickens tremble until I knew he was becoming afraid — of himself, I suppose — and I would suddenly remember something I needed to jump up for. Something in my bag I'd forgotten I needed. We laughed nervously, talking fast about other things, and before midnight, he sent Hubbard to find a hack. He escorted me back to the new house on Gloucester Crescent. The cab rumbled over cobblestones, with me leaning tightly against Mr. Dickens, saying little. While the driver waited, we said good night at the door like nervous lovers, illicit lovers, afraid we might be seen in the yellow light from the gas lamp. But of course it was too late to be seen by proper folk, who were all long since gone to bed. And we weren't really lovers at all, except in our passions, which we never revealed to each other.

He took on another reading tour in early autumn, and audiences cheered. The scandal didn't matter to his admirers, not a whit. Charles Dickens meant more to their hearts than any scandal could shake. Or maybe, in truth, no one really knew about us. Maybe there was no scandal at all. The public seemed aware only that he'd moved out of Gad's Hill, that he'd left Catherine. Or that she had moved out. It wasn't clear. The rest was rumour, or nothing. It may only have been the desperate fear and pain and guilt that haunted Mr. Dickens.

You understand, as an actress, I was accustomed to the public assuming I lived a life of scandal. I was accustomed to catcalls, the open assumption I was immoral. I could not fully grasp Mr. Dickens' deep pain. For a time, he seemed to lose his mind. His power and control changed to rage, anger, desperation. He was a bull bellowing at having been trapped in a pen. He was exhausted all the time. In some way, I knew I wasn't responsible, yet of course, I knew I was. I tried to mother him. It was what he needed. I held his head against by bosom, and I could feel the weight on my breast stirring deep sensations in my womb, a spreading heat through my body. Rocking him, a little boy now, a baby really. The great grey-haired Charles Dickens, only a baby against my own new breasts.

In the autumn, we heard rumours that Catherine had abandoned Tavistock House and returned to her parents. She settled into a windowless bedroom while the whole family sobbed and raged about Mr. Dickens. Georgina was in charge of the children now. Mr. Dickens arrived at Gad's Hill to inform them the arrangement would be permanent. Their mother, he announced, had suffered an attack of wickedness

and folly, brought on by monstrous misconceptions and mis-
representations of his moral character, all of which were
abominably false and entirely her fault. Nine children, it was
said, huddled in shocked and stricken silence. Only Charlie
disobeyed his father and slipped out of the house to follow his
mother. Mr. Dickens was doubly outraged, swearing he would
never again have anything to do with such a son, branding him
a cowardly traitor who acted from a most grossly false and
wicked deceit. The rumours reported Mr. Dickens had gone
mad.

Georgina sent me a note by the liveryman.

> My Dear Miss Ternan,
>   Our mutual friend is much distressed at recent turns
> of events and I fear for his safety and well-being. Al-
> though I'm sure you alone of all people understand the
> true relationship that exists between our friend and my-
> self, he has revealed the need for a secret meeting with
> you. I feel your presence might help me ease his pain. Al-
> though I hesitate to impose on your goodwill, would it be
> possible, at your convenience, to call upon us here at
> Gad's Hill?
>
>   Yours in Deepest Gratitude,
>   Georgina Hogarth

Mamma and Maria and Fanny were shocked, forbidding me
to go. But before I could even dress, another messenger arrived.
It was Mr. Hubbard in a long coat and wearing a bowler hat.

Mamma retreated, leaving us alone in the hallway. Hubbard
held his bowler in his hand. His bald head glimmered in the
dim light from the small rose window behind him in the door.
"It's like this, miss," he said, holding his dignity as straight
as his back. "A gentleman of our mutual acquaintance has
begged me to inform you he's moved out of Gad's Hill and

just this afternoon taken full residence for the time being at Wellington Street. He's given me express instructions to request — if you're not presently engaged — you should accompany me immediately. That's just how he said it, miss, and now I'm to say I'm at your service."

I expected to find Mr. Dickens pacing, but he sat slumped in his chair in front of a miserably weak fire, his head held by one hand that rested on the arm of the chair. His hair was tousled, as if he had been pulling at it. And for several moments after I arrived, he could not force his mouth to shape the sounds of words. I wanted to sit in his lap and hold him, but something told me he wasn't yet ready. Instead, I stood in front of the coals in the fireplace, the only light in the room. I felt shaken somewhat by the discovery of his weakness.

"Ah, Ellen."

He did not look up, pausing, unsure perhaps what else there was to say.

"It's all over," he whispered, his voice hoarse and trembling. "I've done it — or it has been done to me. Whatever could be done has been done."

The coals popped in the fireplace. Upstairs, I could hear Mr. Hubbard walking about.

"I apologise, my dear." Again, a long pause while he stared at the fire, and this time, under his breath, as if more to himself than to me. "I apologise."

"Why should you say that, sir? You've done nothing wrong, unless following your heart is wrong."

He nodded, but still looked away, speaking finally in a broken voice, almost inaudible. "I've torn asunder a family twenty years in the making. I've abandoned a woman I loved once, who I valued above all else in life, and who I vowed publicly and before God to care for. I've locked my children indoors and forbidden them exit. Miss Coutts no longer speaks to me. Forster has advised me I should consider an extended reading tour, perhaps to America. Everything I feared has come to pass. I've betrayed my public that had so much trust in me. I've betrayed all I believed in."

He was trembling.

In my heart, I knew what he said was true, but of course it pricked deeply, like a thousand hot pins sticking my throat and lungs. Now it was I who could hardly speak.

"Then, sir, it is truly I who must apologise."

We were both silent before he spoke again. This time his voice had a different quality to it, something I couldn't identify right away. "Alas," he said, "I've given up everything for you."

I did not turn to look at him, and he did not stir. Both of us waiting, I knew, for that critical moment of time when some blade would cleave or some bond would unite. And finally his words and the tone of his voice — the arrogance and conde-scension — swept over me, like a hot blush of anger: I had no reason to apologise to him. I was not responsible for his choices. I would not allow him to lay his anguish on my soul like a horsehair blanket. I would not allow him to free himself by passing on the guilt.

I chose the blade and sliced hard. "Sir, your words are un-acceptable to me. The terms of the relationship you've just of-fered me are rejected. Clearly, it would be best if I withdrew and left you to your sorrow. Any burden I bear is great enough for my thin shoulders. Do not think, sir, you can transfer yours to me as well."

And I left, shutting the front door behind me with firmness. The street was dark by then, except for a gas lamp almost directly in front of the doorstep. I crossed quickly into the night on the other side. Behind me, I heard the door open and Mr. Dickens' voice call out.

"Ellen. Wait. You misunderstood." I knew he was squinting into the blackness, trying to find me. "You misunderstood, Ellen. That's not what I meant. Please wait."

From the shadow in which I stood, I watched him come down a step or two, searching the street in both directions. "Ellen!" he cried.

But wait for what? Not even the most famous man in all of England, calling me in the blackest moment of hell, could have made me turn around. I would not be his angel in a broken house, nor his mistress in a palace. We had never been intimate, not once, and if he was no more man than the little boy he seemed to me then, I would have none of it. None of it.

"Ellen!" he cried.

At home, Mamma and Fanny informed me they'd told me so. They lifted their eyes and nodded their heads. I slammed my door and cried.

"Just as I thought," Mamma said to me from the corridor. "It should never have begun at all. You should never have allowed yourself to be so taken in. Consider yourself very, very fortunate you're not carrying that man's child."

"At least we hope she isn't," I heard Fanny say.

It was midnight, and Maria came in at that moment from her play at Covent Garden. She was wearing the cloak and bonnet Mr. Dickens had paid for.

"What's this?" she cried, hearing the tumult in the bedroom. She burst in. "Are you really with child? Are you such a fool? What can you have been thinking?"

"Tell us the truth," Fanny demanded, following close behind. "Is that what this is all about? There's no use trying to hide it from us. The whole world will know soon enough."

"Let her be," Mamma said. "Those of us with more rational minds will have to think this through."

I curled up in a small ball of pain on my bed, their voices coming at me from far away, underwater, and dull. For several hours I cried, listening to them in the sitting room bewail their misfortune. Toward dawn, Mamma came and held me. I curled into her warm bosom and sobbed again until there was nothing more in me. Mamma stroked my hair and kissed my forehead, whispering, "It will be all right, dear. You have the theatre, you have your family." I clung to her, knowing I suppose, that what she said was true, even though it seemed to have nothing to do with me at the moment. And yet, I was glad she cared enough to lie to me. Mamma believed that only when you accept the fiction of the role you've been given do you live it to the fullest.

None of us slept that night. At first light we fixed coffee and dry toast, talking all together about men. Marie remembered how the French actor Digasse had once exposed himself to her backstage, revealing his white and very limp member, as if he had just pulled out some kind of wilted arctic flower, grinning with full teeth, expecting her to faint or kneel down in worship. We'd heard the story before, but we laughed even harder this time.

Mamma told us for the first time how the Great Kibble had once proposed to her in Shropshire just before going onstage to play a sword-fighting scene. Kibble was considered all the handsome idol at the time. He had a bold broken nose, like a smashed pear on his face, and startling eyes emphasised with charcoal for his part as Eugenio. He had stabbed his sword into the boards, waiting for his cue, and suddenly turned to Mamma — who was only twenty at the time.

"My beautiful little duckling," Kibble whispered to her, wrapping his arm about her waist and pressing her hard against him, "as soon as this scene is ended, you and I will marry. You'll be my wife. The wife of the Great Kibble, eh? I'm going to play this scene for you, my love."

Kibble heard his cue and released Mamma. He whirled about to pull his sword form the boards, but the blade stayed in the board and Kibble rushed onstage with only the hilt raised in his hand.

"Beware, Condicio," he cried, "I've come at last with the full power of my manhood to avenge myself on you."

And then he thrust with his empty hilt at the actor playing Condicio, who collapsed in laughter on the stage.

Soon afterward, Kibble emigrated to Australia.

A week passed, and I received a note from Mr. Dickens, carried by Hubbard, who stood, bowler in hand, on our doorstep. For a moment I looked at the familiar handwriting on the envelope: "For My Princess." And I hesitated. It could have been the end or the beginning. I drew in my breath and returned the note to Hubbard's gloved hand.

"I am not receiving messages from Mr. Dickens," I said. "If he has anything to say to me, I would expect him to call in person." I closed the door politely on Hubbard's stricken look and slid to the floor, sobbing. I would have felt rather good about myself if I had not been so miserable.

Wilkie Collins

I STARED hard at Charles Dickens in disbelief. "What can you mean, sir? You haven't been intimate!"

We were drinking in the Olde Pelican in our private room on the first storey. Dickens looked sheepish and confused. Over the past few months his face had grown red and puffy from the strain of his separation. He turned away and stared at his own reflection in the black window, like a man peering from a jail cell at his own gallows.

"My God, man, a beautiful young woman waits for you to spread her thighs. And you only talk? You share companionship? You give her gifts? For this, you abandoned a wife and risked your reputation?"

Dickens slumped, as if too exhausted to explain. He studied his own dark prospect in the glass. "Wilkie, I'm afraid the state of my spirits little fits me for your society this evening. Over the past several days, I've had to consider whether a grave error in judgement has occurred. Have I freed myself or condemned myself? The ground seems to be shelving away in front of me, like a beach undercut by a secret current."

He sat silent again.

I tried to control my frustration. "Charles, you and I've

been friends for many years. What I'm about to say is inspired by deep gratitude for that friendship — and out of loyalty to your best interests."

Dickens seemed not to hear me. He appeared distracted and tired, but I went on anyway, out of desperation, I think. "Charles, there's an old saying: The only men condemned to hell are those who have turned down a willing woman. Now, let's face the truth, sir. Miss Ternan has shown herself to be a very willing woman."

Dickens spoke in a voice that made me lean across the board to hear him.

"Wilkie, sometimes I suspect every act of choice is self-deception. It makes almost no difference whether we act on rational fact or pure emotion, the game is always one of chance. And worst of all, the rules are perfectly clear — until the moment we choose. Then, the rules change." His mind seemed to be wandering over the ashes of his childhood, his marriage, his relation to Miss Ternan.

"Yes sir," I said. "That's why I write mystery novels."

He leaned back to relight his cigar. "I don't follow your thought, sir."

"I think you do, Charles. I read one of our great literary critics in *The Times* last week. He pointed out, with triumphant smugness, that the greatest peril in a novel occurs when virtue comes under threat."

Dickens nodded and puffed and seemed comforted. "Very true, very true."

"No sir. Not at all true. It is virtue itself creates the threat."

"Wilkie, you are talking literature," Dickens said. "I'm talking about choices in real life. How they turn back on you like sly foxes."

"So am I, sir. In your misguided attempt at preserving those virginal values you think Queen and country stand for, all this noble sense of virtue in you has led to nothing but misery, confusion, and disaster for everyone. There's the peril, don't you see?"

"No, no. The confusion and disaster comes from something else altogether."

He drew heavily on his cigar, collecting his thoughts.

"Here's the problem. I've always wanted to be a good man, an honourable man. But I was only good in my own eyes — like Oedipus. I set out to do a good thing, and it turned out bad. Yet in Catherine's eyes, I was an evil person from the beginning. She told her parents I had deceived her from the start of our marriage — that I had innumerable affairs. She claimed she'd always known the truth, but denied it to herself. Good and bad became so knotted neither of us could tell the difference."

He stopped, tangled in a web of confusion. "Wilkie, there's no honour anywhere in what I've done."

"My God, sir. All this stuff about 'goodness' and 'honour' — such noble values, so highly praised today, they're nothing but threads in an antique fabric. Try to follow the thread — as you've seen for yourself — and the thread disappears, or ties itself in a knot, or frays beyond repair. And then, we chose another thread, blindly or out of desperation."

"Enough metaphor, Wilkie. This leads nowhere."

"Sir, you must think of Ellen Ternan as a tapestry of luxury and eager sensuality. In your fear of passion, you're about to lose her. Stop worrying the threads, wondering where each one will lead, whether you've chosen the right one, the moral one, the evil one. Love the bloody tapestry. Celebrate it."

I held my voice in check, seeing the Great Charles Dickens in pain, wavering a little in his chair. The very beard on his

chin seemed splayed in all direction, unkempt, and shabby —
something Dickens' vanity would never have allowed in the
past. Only then did I realise several grease spots dotted his
waistcoat, his cuffs were frayed, his cravat roughly tied. When
he attempted to check his pocket watch, he stared at it blindly,
moving it in and out of range to find the time, which never
seemed to be the right time. He had always been proud of his
pocket watch. He snapped it shut with a bite.

Later, in the rain, we took a hack to Wellington Street. He
remained silent until we arrived, stopping under a flickering
gas lamp. Instead of jumping out with his usual vigour, he hesitated and, for a long moment, seemed unaware the cab had
stopped. I could hear the horse snorting and stamping impatiently.

"Wilkie," he said quietly, "I am especially worried about my
children."

"Yes sir."

"About Katie, you see."

"The enduring Georgina has things well in hand, I suspect."

"She does, Wilkie. It's Katie concerns me. She's more
aware than the other children, more sober and reflective, even
withdrawn now. Trying to play the role of mother, but desperate to escape, I believe."

"Katie is a fine, strong young woman."

"Living in sorrow and perhaps under more strain than I realised." He drew in his breath and held it, then released it with
an audible sigh. "You can't imagine how much love a father
feels for his daughter."

I left him there and went on in the rain to a sad and lovely
night with Caroline Graves. She, too, had grown somewhat
distant in recent months. We'd been experimenting with

opium — for her nerves — and although the drug worked to calm her wonderfully, it also seemed to separate us somewhat. She was often distracted now, somewhat distant, even when we consummated our desires — and that, too, seemed less frequent than it once had been. On my own, I was experimenting — just a little, you understand — with laudanum, which the doctor prescribed for aches and pains that racked my body. The laudanum made me groggy, dreamy, but in my dreams, which were wide awake, I found my story unfolding for me. I was writing better than ever before, drafting a new novel, one that made use of my first meeting with Caroline as she appeared so suddenly before me, a woman wearing only white, fleeing evil in the moonlight. I hadn't yet worked out the thousands of details, but I was furiously taking notes, drawing diagrams of relationships. It was to be a story of confused identity, of doubles and disguises. At times, I wasn't even certain from what evil my heroine was fleeing, but it had something to do with a Count who had befriended her. Money was probably involved. Sometimes, the story took on a life of its own, surprising me with twists and turns. The laudanum gave my imagination a heightened intensity. I could see everything so much more clearly. Plots interacting with plots. Mistakes intentionally made.

Then, it came to me in the hack — a possible way I could help Dickens. A diversionary plot altogether. I would introduce my brother Charlie to Katie. My younger brother, as usual, was in rather desperate shape, with no income and no likely chance of ever becoming the painter he envisioned. He had returned recently from France and begged Mother for an increase in his allowance. She wrote to me that he seemed at loose ends, uncertain of himself as usual, but she refused to increase his stipend. For Katie, he might be a perfect match. Katie was exactly the young woman who could give him backbone — or become the backbone he'd never had. And there was nothing more likely to help a young woman escape a depressing situation than a bright new lover, one who needed her strength to lean on. The opportunity was perfect. The timing surprisingly right for both of them.

I settled back in the cab as the horse clopped through the rainy streets, feeling rather clever. It was the laudanum, of course. The credit really had to be given to how perfectly laudanum intensified the mind. I was beginning to look forward to it each evening.

I'm certain you've already sensed the way it was then: the best of summers, the worst of summers. Dickens' struggle with Ellen Ternan was topsy-turvy. Rumour had it the young woman was edging toward reconciliation. The struggle with Catherine was topsy-turvy but crashing toward bitter finality. Charles Dickens took charge of his life again. In London, he worked like a madman, turning out novels, stories, managing his magazine, rewriting his will, buying and selling houses. He suddenly moved back to Gad's Hill, ordered repairs, turned a sitting room into a billiard room, adding lead-lined drawers to a cupboard where he could store several bottles of sherry and keep them cool.

On a Sunday afternoon when I knew Dickens would be there spending time with his children, I escorted Charlie to Gad's Hill for a social call. My brother was sickly as usual, coughing and sniffing, so nervous he could not speak in complete sentences for half an hour. I had dressed him in a short frock coat, and rehearsed him with some of my most charming approaches to women. Katie pretended to be reserved at first, as a woman should. By teatime, they had walked the yard together, looked out over the wheat fields behind the house, and circled about to Dickens' rose garden, where we couldn't see them for ever so long.

I don't think Dickens gave Charlie's presence any thought at all. He'd met my brother several times in early years, a failed painter, a would-be writer, still receiving a monthly allowance from our mother. Charlie was the kind of ineffectual man Dickens found distasteful. It was his very disinterest that freed Katie to take a long look, that allowed her to explore her own feelings. Charlie was perturbedly thin, self-deprecating, with a handsome face made more attractive to women because of melancholy eyes peering out from under a strong brow. His unruly hair was forever disheveled and tangled. He gave the impression of a handsome little boy who needed a woman to dress him. Katie was perfect for the role. The devoted daughter who had often served as surrogate mother, even as mistress of the house for numerous receptions and parties, making decisions and acting as hostess when Catherine was unable or unwilling to abandon her feather bed. Katie had reached that age when a young woman is deliciously plump and high-spirited in an innocent way. On that late spring day, she quickly realised Charlie's awkward shyness was genuine. Her own reserve began to fade. She showed him about the grounds, she introduced the dogs, she began to laugh and tease. Charlie did not know what to do with his hands, stuffing them one minute in his pockets, then sensing the ridiculousness of it, pulling them out, and clasping them behind his back, breathing deeply to maintain what little control he had. Katie began to glow confidently, as if saying, I'm a woman now and this young man is stumbling over his own feet because I'm pretty, because I smell like lilac, because my eyes look intently into his when he tries to talk.

Nothing I plotted could have worked more successfully than our first visit. At the end, without consulting her father, Katie became so bold she quietly invited Charlie to call again, and Charlie, seeing no impropriety at all in her invitation, immediately agreed and bumped into the open door on leaving.

In London, Dickens abruptly closed down his old weekly magazine, easier than casting off an old wife. Two hours later, he began a new magazine with boisterous enthusiasm, rehiring all the former staff on the same day he fired them. We heard Ellen had consented to see him again. Within days he purchased passage for Fanny and her mother to Italy, explaining repeatedly how Ellen's sister was such a brilliant student of opera, how she needed only the world's greatest teacher to launch her on a dazzling career. He was so impressed with Fanny, he told us. A true diva of the art, he argued. Essential that she study in Italy. And before Mrs. Ternan had even departed the country, he rushed out and rented new lodgings for Ellen and Maria on Berners Street. No sooner had they settled in than he moved them out, leasing a grand house on Ampthill Square. It was all quite dizzying. Forster drew up a secret deed, filed quite legally in the name of two "spinsters," Fanny and Maria Ternan. Ellen's name was not even mentioned, you see. Dickens felt he'd fooled everyone and he was immensely pleased with himself, although it was unclear who he thought might be spying on him.

He wrote yet another will, casting off and taking on according to his whim of the moment. At night, he hurried Ellen about London in dark cabs to secret taverns or outdoor concerts or hotel restaurants. There was a constant coming and going. All by darkness. Everyone he knew conspired to keep his secret — which must have been most of the better class of London. Dickens convinced himself, however, that he had successfully hidden his life from the public he cared about, his readers, the housemaids and schoolmasters and widows.

His new novel flowed from his pen as none before, a novel of revolution and sacrifice. It would tell an heroic story of compassion and Christian forgiveness during the French Revolution. He saw himself as the hero, only slightly transformed. And he ran the first installment of the story in his new magazine, publicly committing himself to a chapter a week, driving himself to work with ever more frenzy.

While Dickens worked, Charlie began visiting Katie on a regular basis. Calling often at Gad's Hill, bringing small presents. Katie received him, offered proper tea, went for quiet walks along the marshy paths that led down to the Thames, or through back lanes and hedgerows to Cobham. At one point, urged on by me, Charlie spoke formally to Dickens, who he found in his study at Gad's Hill. Charlie, of course, stuttered about honourable intentions, about the privilege of joining his name to such a distinguished family, needing only permission, and so on. Dickens must have half-listened, his mind on a thousand other things. He seems to have passed off Charlie with a convivial pat on the back, thinking only that Katie seemed happier of late and enjoyed the friendship of this ne'er-do-well. He tolerated Charlie's visit to his study as one would a small child or a pet dog that dropped by for a momentary distraction. Perhaps he saw my brother as a valuable tool at the moment, someone to distract Katie from her sorrow. But Charlie had indeed approached him, had formally asked for her hand, and Dickens, unintentionally or jokingly, had given boisterous approval — all the while distracted by his own romance with Ellen, his novel, his accounts, his admirers who lined the streets and doffed their hats as he sprang from his carriage and stomped into the magazine office. In some way, he failed to recognise the truth of Katie's sentiment.

Suddenly, Dickens burst in. I heard his boots pounding across the boards, and my door flew open. "What is the meaning of this?" he shouted.

"Sir?"

"You know bloody well what I mean. You have sicced your brother on my daughter, and he's caught her unaware in the briars, duped her in a moment of sorrow, taken advantage of her loss, and deceived the bitch into marrying him!"

Charles Dickens hovered over me, red-faced, and breathing heavily.

"Sir, I'm sure this must be a misunderstanding."

"Not at all, Mr. Collins. You're behind this. I see your hand in it now. They're to be married, and you're responsible for the disaster."

"Perhaps we can discuss this when you . . ."

"Don't interrupt me, Collins. I've no choice now but to allow Katie entry into what will prove a disastrous relationship, no doubt about it, but I do have a choice about you, Mr. Collins, and you will know that you've greatly strained the bounds of our friendship. You've taken advantage of me and my family at a time of our weakness. Don't throw up your hands in protest. I know your art. I've seen this kind of trickery and duplicity in your stories. Great fun to read about, I assure you. But damn you, Mr. Collins, not at all fun to find you've done it to my life."

He spun about, stomping back across the floor and out the door, while I sat in trembling silence.

*

Early one morning in July, Charlie and Katie were married at St. Mary's Church. As usual, the Great Man found it necessary to make his Grand Gesture. He hired a private train to haul over sixty guests from London to the station at Highham, near Rochester. The ladies wore flowered bonnets, and some of the younger women sported new-style hoop skirts, as big around as aerial balloons. They swayed and toppled and caused no end of laughter and embarrassment. The absurdity offended me. The gigantic hoops disguised a woman's actual proportions. It was impossible to judge the true span of her waist or the shape of her buttocks. Everything about the way a female now dressed had become deceptive. Hoop skirts were the ultimate disguise, a violent offence against nature.

But all was lost in the shout of the crowd. Villagers from Highham had turned out with rather handsome floral arches and great "Huzzahs!" When Katie and Charlie emerged on the church steps, hundreds of Dickens' working-class followers rushed forward, tossing their caps, shooting off guns, and proving a general nuisance. The invited guests shoved through to hired carriages and carts. Drivers snapped their whips and shouted at the crowd to move away. Eventually, the procession turned slowly onto Gravesend Road, rumbling and bouncing on the ruts up the long rise. As we passed the Falstaff, Dickens' local drinking companions stood on the outdoor tables and sang salacious songs at us. All in all, the whole thing had been a rather unpleasant experience. It made me even more determined never to marry.

For the wedding breakfast, Dickens invited a garland of famous writers and artists. We drank champagne with strawberries in the glass, and ate scones layered in clotted cream hauled all the way from Devon. The feast was held in the newly enlarged drawing room, where Dickens had installed a great bow window at one end and added a gallery of huge mirrors along the walls. The effect of all the mirrors was to double and triple the crowd in its celebration. Summer light danced off the mirrors and over our faces. Every woman took on a painterly glow. After half a dozen glasses of champagne, I began to feel quite civilised again. The whole experience did not seem as bad as I'd feared. A faint breeze blew through open windows. Curtains lifted and fell.

I became aware that all around me, everyone was whispering about Catherine's absence. Dickens, in a fit of pique, had apparently refused the mother of the bride the right to attend. But then, he hadn't invited his own mother either. Georgina served as hostess, taking on her role with pompous servility. I found the scandal rather petty. We had all the mothers we needed in my own ancient dame, who seemed to be there with a vengeance, wearing a bright pink frock and old-fashioned bonnet. At the age of many an ancient relic, my mother flirted unconscionably with all the men, even the bishop of Rochester Cathedral, who had just arrived in a fine barouche. It was quite shameful and quite funny.

Earlier that morning, I'd dressed dear brother Charlie in a dove grey morning coat with long tails. He looked surprisingly respectable, even if he wavered a little from nerves. Dickens called him forward, and he stood in silent panic at the head of the room with the Bishop, both haloed by sunlight from the bow window behind them. The Bishop gave a short speech on the joy and sanctity of the occasion, then raised his glass and set off the usual series of toasts, cheers, and goodwill. Charlie was required to say something. He muttered and stumbled about, finally ending with an acknowledgement that he supposed he was, in light of everything, probably married after all.

Everyone laughed and thought him a rather jolly good sport about it.

Katie reappeared down the stairs for her departure in a black frock with a large black bonnet that hid her face in shadow.

I heard an intake of breath from Mother, who gripped my hand like a hawk's claws clutching a field mouse. "This is atrocious!"

"It's for travel, Mother."

"Nonsense! The creature has put on a mourning gown."

Dickens took Katie to his shoulder, and both cried. The litter of other Dickens children gathered around and cried. The women in the room held handkerchiefs to their eyes as one person, and all cried. Was it a wedding or a funeral?

"God bless you," Dickens said to Katie.

It was picked up by all the male guests hovering about trying to figure out their role in all this. "God bless you!"

"God bless!"

"Three cheers!"

Everyone suddenly felt the obligation to shout out, "God bless," at the top of their nervous lungs. Georgina took her turn hugging Katie, and it began all over again. Dickens hugged Katie, and both cried. Everyone shouted, "God bless!" I was afraid it might go on all afternoon. Charlie looked as green and lumpy as pea soup, having no idea in the world what he should do. I pushed him forward to claim his bride in black, and guided them both out the door to a carriage festooned in garlands and flowers.

There was more obligatory shouting.

"Three cheers!"

"God bless!"

The carriage pulled away with all the women waving white

handkerchiefs as if some sort of ship were sinking. Some of the local men threw old shoes. Dickens followed the carriage to the road and stood longingly at the gate, watching it disappear toward Dover, where Charlie and Katie would sail to France for a honeymoon.

Everyone drifted back to the house for more champagne and more whispers about Katie's black frock. Mother refused to participate further in the festivities. She gripped my arm furiously. "That young woman has shamed our family, and I will never forgive her." Upon which she removed herself to a back parlour and sat stubbornly in an old oak rocking chair until her carriage arrived.

Mr. Dickens abandoned the party and locked himself in his study. No one saw him the rest of the afternoon.

Georgina played saint and martyr, hostess to a wedding party that tottered on disaster. Eventually, carriages and carts began the slow process of hauling everyone back to the train station. There were tired farewells and final strained attempts at good fellowship among the men. Georgina went about gathering up children who had fallen asleep on the lawn. I was the last to leave when Dickens finally appeared, smelling heavily of his own best brandy. He looked like Marley's Ghost, holding himself up in his doorway and staring at me with hollow eyes, his face grey as ashes.

"It's all my fault, Wilkie. My God! It's all my fault."

It wasn't, of course. It was the fault of the institution itself — of marriage as a devious excuse for legalising the periodic seduction of a female. I was always quite convinced the concept of marriage was a personal and social disaster. Marriage bears no possible relationship to the real needs and desires of men or women. It leads only to cross-purpose and conflict. In truth, marriage seems a grossly idealised form of slavery. The woman — who assumes total control of the courtship, the engagement, and the wedding — enslaves the male and whips him into a condition of simpering obedience. The male allows himself to be put through a ceremony of shameful artificiality, forced to act as if he were deliriously happy, all the while repressing his misery and guilt. Yet when the final act of the ceremony ends — for reasons equally obscure and absurd — the man suddenly abrogates superiority to himself, humbling and humiliating the bride into meek subservience, rudely violating her hitherto celebrated virginity and damning her to live thereafter according to his own arrogant will. All of which the female dutifully accepts as the natural state of human relations.

I thought long and hard about how to say all this to Dickens, steeling myself to speak what had to be.

"Ah, Mr. Dickens," I said, in my most sincere voice. "I know that deep in your soul, you feel only joy for them. You can scarcely blame yourself for anything but wanting the best for Katie. They are young lovers, delightfully happy."

"No, no, no. She's married to escape the horrible thing I've done to the family. Don't you see, Katie's done this to flee the scene of the crime."

"Nonsense. I've never seen a happier bride. Radiant! If I might say so."

Dickens took a deep breath and tried to listen to me, tried to subdue the anguish churning inside his chest.

"Katie married Charlie because she fell in love," I said. "That's what young people do, my dear friend. They fall in love."

Dickens looked relieved. "Do you really think so, Wilkie?"

"Of course. Didn't you see their faces?"

He chewed on his moustache and breathed deeply again,

holding it in this time. Finally, he placed one giant paw on my shoulder. "You always know my heart better than I do myself."

Gravesend Road looked deserted as far as one could see. The last of the carriages was long out of sight. "Quite right, Wilkie. I shan't blame myself, although I can't yet rid my soul of a sense of dread."

"Merely the natural feeling of a father for his daughter."

Dickens nodded. "The feeling of a father for his daughter," he repeated. "I can't bear to think about it. I'm sure you're right."

"Yes sir. A joyful occasion for everyone."

Dickens nodded. "Absolutely. A joyful occasion. Everything did go rather well, didn't it? An almost perfect wedding, I should say."

"Absolutely. A wedding to remember."

Dickens looked long and hard down Gravesend Road one last time. Several old shoes lay about in the dust, like castoffs from some odd army that marched by a century ago. Dickens' face turned dark and he closed his eyes.

"You're a great storyteller, Wilkie, but you're a damned awful liar."

In the autumn, after Katie and my brother Charlie returned from France, Dickens held a bonfire in the field behind Gad's Hill. Charlie told me about it. How Katie helped Dickens cart out several baskets of private letters from the great and famous. The younger boys staggered out with even more from Dickens' office, laughing and cheering as they dumped them on the bonfire. Mamie alone seemed upset by it all. Mamie had always been so much more reserved and quiet, and much too plump, like her mother in so many ways with her shy virginal eyes. She cried and begged Dickens not to do it, while Katie seemed oddly committed to the project. Katie was a married woman now, and something about the violence of it attracted her. She stirred the fire with a hoe, ensuring that every page burned. Some of the letters were personal, from friends and family, from Dickens' father, in crude charcoal. From his mother, in a tiny scroll with ink spots and misspelled words pleading for money. From his brothers and sisters. Baskets of letters were dumped on the fire as it blazed up, a swirling stream of grey smoke rising into the clear autumn sky above the fields and distant hedgerows.

Some of the letters were about business, from Forster and Wills. Some from publishers, like poor Bradbury and Evans, who sided with Catherine in their separation. There were letters from long dead friends, like Washington Irving, and letters from friends who were now dead to Dickens, like Miss Coutts. There were letters from his most bitter critics, including Ralph Waldo Emerson, who once complained that "truth was never an object for Dickens."

Dickens took the hoe from Katie and personally stirred Emerson into the flames. Servants watched from back windows of the house, nervous and thrilled. The flames built up and up into the sky. His boys brought out more bundles of letters, twenty years' worth it was said. From Leigh Hunt and Tennyson and Carlyle. From Mrs. Gaskell and Thackeray. Mamie drifted off to her room, where she locked herself in to cry. Katie stayed until the end. As the fire turned to ashes that evening, she and the boys roasted onions on the coals.

There were no letters from Ellen Ternan. They had an agreement never to write to each other. No correspondence between them would ever be found. They lived only in the presence of each other, in the here and now. Their lives were closed to the rest of us, and nothing — Dickens told me — nothing, nothing would ever be put into writing. Future generations must never know. There was his reputation, wasn't there. His duty to England.

Later that evening, a heavy bank of storm clouds swept the channel from France, and the sky began to rain. The bonfire steamed and hissed. Dickens told me he felt purged forever of his past.

"I burned your letters, too," he said. "Including the one in which you urged me to burn all my letters. I burned them as if I were burning correspondence of the devil himself."

We were drinking in the smoke and haze of the Olde Pelican when he told me about it.

"And no letters from Ellen survive," I asked.

"There have never been letters from Ellen," he repeated.

"Best to burn everything. Close the world to your private life, or they'll take it away from you."

"I even burned the letters Katie sent me this summer." His voice had a distant quality to it. "She wrote to me from France." Dickens put down his pint and looked me in the eye. I could tell he was waiting for some response. Waiting to see if I knew something he seemed to know.

"She wrote about it. I suppose you've heard."

"I've heard nothing at all."

"The poverty. Living like paupers." Dickens stared hard at me. It was his daughter, his favourite daughter.

"Nothing," I said. "Mother conveyed nothing at all to me, and I received only the slightest of messages from Charlie."

I could see Dickens was distressed. He turned his head away and told me the story.

"It seems they rented a secondhand gig and traveled about

looking for cheap taverns to live over. Wandering through France and Switzerland. They didn't even have a servant. Katie was forced to peel potatoes and fry bacon for their single daily meal. Charlie did the laundry when he wasn't daydreaming about his failure as a painter. Or visiting churches, where he seemed to have intense fainting spells. At night, they huddled under a thin blanket without a fire."

Dickens stared hard at me, waiting for an explanation, a justification. But I had none. I'd heard nothing like this.

"It's your brother, Wilkie. You knew he was a failure, and you foisted him off on my daughter."

"You have ever right to be angry, sir. I had no idea he was in this much trouble."

Dickens took a slow deep breath. "There's one more thing."

"Yes?"

He hesitated, sipped twice at his pint, and turned his head from me as he spoke. "The marriage has not been consummated."

I felt staggered. "At Katie's request?" I asked, hopefully.

"Because of Charlie's failure."

"Ah, my God!"

"In one sense, I suppose I'm actually relieved. I proposed to Katie we seek an annulment, but she refuses. She says she likes Charlie. She plans to stay with him. But this failure to consummate may wear thin for her. A woman will not tolerate a man long who fails to be a man."

"True," I said. "I can only beg your forgiveness, Charles. This is far worse than anything I could have dreamed of."

My apology seemed to affect him. Dickens visibly relaxed and slumped back in his chair. He called for the waiter to lay a fire, and after it was prepared, he moved us to large armchairs in front of the burning coals. We took our drinks and sat in the amber glow, absorbing the heat, feeling closer perhaps than we had in several years. We needed only something to roast in the smouldering ashes. Dickens seemed comfortable again. He began to talk of Ellen, began to smile, even laughed. Ellen had become so important to him, he said. He was working her into one of his female characters in the novel. Could I guess who? She was there, but in disguise.

He seemed well-pleased with his little deception. No one would ever know. His life was moving inescapably toward a dark secret world of private mystery. For a gentleman of our era, it could be only in such a world that the illicit fullness of living could take place, where the heart could pound, the heat of the blood be felt in the supple passing of air through the lungs. For the first time, I felt my plan had been successful. The former anger, the bitterness, the loneliness of his marriage with Catherine had burned out of him. He checked the gold pocket watch on his chain. He ordered more drinks. I felt as I had with him ten years earlier, as if he accepted me as an equal, as if I could tease him and laugh together with him.

"Sir," I said, lifting my glass in toast, "here's to love, to passion, and to pleasure. I have to confess my dreams have finally come true. I'm pleased and relieved to see you and Ellen have become lovers. You'll not regret it. You'll never go back to the horrid institution of marriage." I drank off my ale in celebration.

Dickens did not respond. He stared into the fire.

"I may have misled you, Wilkie. Ellen and I are still not lovers. There has never been an intimacy between us, you see."

"What can you mean, sir? What can you possibly mean?"

"She's not a fallen woman, Mr. Collins. She has a pure heart and a fine mind. I'm proud to say ours is a pure relationship, as pure and delicate as one between father and daughter."

"My God, man, she's an actress!"

"And I'm sure you'll agree, there is no profession more honourable."

"Sir, let me put it bluntly. Actresses are paid to flaunt their parts on the stage. They are talented, even charming, often enticing, but they're not women of purity. And thank God for it! We have enough of those in England to fill a vanilla cake. Let us celebrate the woman who knows she's a sexual being. Let us take joy diving into the muff of life, dark and wet and mysterious as it is."

Dickens had to think this through for a while. In the haze of the Olde Pelican, I could hear a party of men's voices laughing somewhere. Over our head, the sound of a waiter crossed back and forth, stepping in time. For reasons I can't explain, I felt a dark fury building inside me, as if in some way Dickens had betrayed me.

"She's a woman of pure heart," he said. "Of pure mind. I wouldn't dream of approaching her for purposes of lust."

"Great God! Charles. Where's the difference between lust — which everyone condemns — and love — which everyone praises? Call this love if you wish, whisper in her ear, bury your face in her throat, in her bosom — and whisper of love. Are you mad? Don't you know that she feels it too?"

Dickens raised an eyebrow at me. "Science has long since proven a pure woman does not feel the animal passions, Wilkie."

"Science is a hog! No different than our novels, sir. Mere stories we tell each other. A striving of fancy to give shape to what we don't understand."

I leaned forward in my chair and placed my face closer to

the Great Man's broomlike beard. He stared intensely at the fire, deliberately avoiding my eyes. "Sir, you must listen to me. I've known hundreds of women intimately, and all of them — including a nun I met on a train to Marseille — all of them have hot, wet thighs."

"I don't want to hear this, Wilkie. French nuns are papists."

"You don't want to hear the truth, sir. Ellen Ternan is waiting for you. Waiting, I tell you. Like all well-bred women, she's been faithfully trained not to initiate the deed with two backs, but sir, she must by this point feel in her heart confusion and doubt about your very manhood. She must question her own role in your life. Why did you seek her out? What can you want from her?

"She's like a daughter to me. And a friend."

"Daughter be damned! You have a kettle full of daughters already, sir. And the whole nation is your admiring friend. Ellen Ternan is not your daughter, she's your lover — if you will use her so — and if not, you will lose her."

"Enough, Wilkie. Our relationship is special." He rose from his chair grandly. His eyes avoiding me. "I'll hear no more of this. It is impossible for a sensualist like yourself to understand the sanctity of a higher relationship."

"My God, sir . . ."

"I will listen no further." And with great dignity, one booming step at a time, chest out, head high, he left our private room.

"My God, sir," I shouted after him. "Fuck her, Mr. Dickens, fuck her!"

Ellen Ternan

SUMMER faded into August. Maria found a starring role at the Strand, a comedy called *The Maid and the Magpie*. Reviewers praised her. They said she was beautiful, charming, full of high spirits. At the last moment, I picked up a small part in *The Soldier's Daughter*, a light farce at the Haymarket. I ran onstage in a risqué costume, pretending to be a child but making sure the audience knew I was a naughty woman playing a child. After a silly line or two, I fell down, revealing my legs, and ran off. Always to laughter, but never applause. The reviewers never mentioned me. Each of my roles seemed to grow smaller. The company used me to fill in a crowd or play the part of a pretty maid. I loved dressing up, I loved opening nights, the audiences, the clean smell of starched costumes, the thrill of anticipation. One night, after coming home late, I dreamt I ran onstage at the sound of my cue. The theater was empty, but in some strange dark way a looking glass occupied every seat, reflecting my own figure back at me. I pranced onto the blackened stage, said my silly lines, and tumbled upon the boards, waiting for someone somewhere to laugh, to applaud. In my dream, there was only silence. I kicked and struggled to raise my skirt so my legs would show — my pretty legs that once brought men leaping to the stage. I showed my legs in a very pretty way, cried out my funny lines. A hundred silent mirrors betrayed me, and all about, a steady slide of darkness fell, like a curtain going down.

I made no reply to the notes Mr. Dickens sent, waiting for him to call upon me. Mamma and Fanny paced the floors, worrying about their trip to Florence. Should they pack or abandon hope? Fanny practised her scales every day, hour after hour, as if nothing were wrong. She was terribly upset. She began wearing her green spectacles even to dinner. We would sit about the table in tense silence, listening to the muffled racket of dishes and silverware shuffled on the basement floor below us. On summer evenings, Mamma seldom lit the lamp until very late. Mr. Dickens had purchased velvet drapery for our windows. Only a hint of fading daylight slipped through cracks. We felt trapped in a stuffy tomb of lost possibilities.

Mamma rang for Molly to take away the dishes. We had gone through several housemaids by that point. Molly was the oddest. Mr. Dickens recommended her, and we were afraid to offend him by letting her go. She had been called to his attention by one of his many solicitors, a gentleman retiring to a farm in Cornwall who wanted to find Molly a new position. Still, she was cold and distant, a strong-looking woman with nervous hands. She wore long sleeves always and, from time to time, tugged at them, as if to hide her wrists. Her face seemed drained of colour, like someone who'd spent a number of years in prison. We had to admit she was efficient, but when she entered the room, her sullen presence made us all feel uncomfortable.

Mamma was about to ring again when we realised Molly

had answered a knock at our door. We sat in stiff silence, avoiding each other's eyes as if attending a wake. We could hear a man's voice and then the door closing. Molly was coming through the hall.

"A package for you, ma'am."

"Was it Mr. Dickens at the door, Molly?"

"No, ma'am, it was Hubbard, bringing a package."

Molly brought scissors, and we sat like children in church, watching Mamma cut the string. The package contained half a dozen letters from Mr. Dickens. The first was addressed in Mr. Dickens' own hand to "Pietro Romani, Singing Master, Firenze," followed by others to several of Mr. Dickens' closest friends in Italy. We were especially excited about a letter addressed to Frances Trollope, an elderly gentlewoman who we heard was quite as much the novelist as her son Anthony. Yet another letter was addressed to Tom Trollope, her younger son — or older son — we weren't sure. All of us recognised his name as one we had seen on numerous stories and articles in Mr. Dickens' magazine. We had no idea that Florence was such a cultured city. Indeed, we weren't really certain just where in Italy Florence might be found.

"I hear it's definitely near Venice," Maria said.

Fanny shook her head. "They tell me it's close to Naples."

Everyone looked thrilled by the possibilities.

The package also contained a personal note in a small cream-coloured envelope addressed to Mamma.

My Dear Mrs. Ternan,

I hope these letters of introduction prove satisfactory. Please be informed I have taken the liberty of making all arrangements for you and Fanny to depart from Dover on the last day of September. Because the ferry sails at dawn, you may wish to go down the previous day. I have arranged for you to stay at the boardinghouse of Mrs. Halbot, a hearty woman who serves a hearty breakfast of tomatoes and black pudding for those who must catch the early sailing.

If there is any other way I might be of service, please let me know. I have such high hopes and confidence in Fanny on this adventure. Both of you have my best wishes and cheers for success.

Y'rs,
C. Dickens

Mamma read the letter aloud twice. Fanny said nothing, holding her hands tightly in her lap. After we looked over the whole package one more time, Fanny rose rather grandly, seeing us now as a distant part of her past. She excused herself, kissed Mamma on the cheek, and walked straight to the spinet, where she practised singing her scales well past midnight.

There was no note for me.

Mamma hurried about each day in a flurry of packing. Fanny sang obsessively. She studied Italian. Maria and I went to the theatre late each afternoon. At the Haymarket, I helped others with their costumes and makeup. My character did not even appear until the second act, so I had little to do. The play was a success and promised to run until Christmas. Everyone was excited. No one really noticed me. I kept busy, and when there was nothing else, I read Carlyle by gaslight in the dressing room, waiting until the last moment to slip into my tights and my little girl's white frock with the tight pink sash. I wore my hair in gold ringlets under a narrow-brimmed straw boater. For a few minutes, a life of sorts would flood over me. I rushed onstage, feeling the hot presence of the audience out there in the dark, knowing gentlemen were admiring me as I tripped about pretending to be a child, flouncing my skirt. The other actors got all the best lines and the best laughs. I pretended to slip and fall — just so — showing my legs in their tights all the way to my knees, and on a few occasions even farther. The gentlemen gasped, then roared with laughter. Within a moment, I was offstage, in the dark where old furniture was stacked. I could hear the actors going on, raising their voices, pausing while the audience laughed again, and yet again.

I could have left the theatre at that point. My part was over. But I always found something to do in the dressing room. I studied my face in the old mirrors. Hung up a frock. Sewed a hem. Read a little more Carlyle. Later, when all the women burst in after the play, talking and laughing, removing hats, tossing petticoats, I busied myself and joined in. I was one of them. We wiped off our makeup, gossiped about who might be having an affair with the leading man, laughing at the possibility. At some point, Mr. Adersley, the company manager, always appeared and made a few announcements or pointed to some error that had occurred. We teased him and flounced about bare-armed in our shifts or corsets until he gave up and withdrew. Sometimes I waited until midnight, when I could meet Maria coming back from the Strand. We would take a hackney cab to Gloucester Crescent. Maria would tell me all the gossip and chat on about how she had played her part and who was seen in the audience and about productions she heard might be auditioning in the spring. The theatre life was a full life. Mamma was right. Theatre *was* my life.

I dawdled about until almost midnight before leaving. Everyone else had departed and the building was empty. Finally, I wandered to the side door on an alley near Charles II Street.

Maria had not yet arrived. I open the door and peeked out for her. It had rained earlier, and the darkness smelled wet and heavy, as night air so often does smell in summer.

A few yards down the alley, a closed brougham waited with curtains partly drawn. A driver with a lantern sat on the box. Two horses stamped and rippled their skin in the damp. I knew the carriage. When the driver saw me, he tied the reins to the post and jumped down, tipping his hat and opening the carriage door. In the dark it was impossible to see who, if anyone, was inside. My lungs felt as if they'd collapsed. I tried desperately to breathe. I had worn my oldest frock, a grey one Fanny insisted made me look as poor and pathetic as Jane Eyre. My hair still hung in golden locks, like a schoolgirl on her way to lessons. And my gloves! They were tattered and stained, a pair I should have thrown away long ago — but no one of consequence ever saw me. I realised how slovenly I'd become of late and suddenly felt ashamed and humiliated and about to cry.

The driver held the door for me. The horses snorted. In the street around the corner I heard a couple laughing. Whoever was in the carriage sat hidden in a dark corner, waiting, as silent as God hoping to catch a sinner.

I stepped in and could make him out, a shadow of power and strength, with a white silk cravat and white gloves. I sat on the bench across from him and spread my skirt. The door closed with a snap, and the carriage tipped momentarily as the driver climbed aboard the box. We began to move, rocking steadily over the cobbles, listening to the horses' hooves and our own heavy breathing.

"I've missed you, Ellen."

"And I have missed you, Mr. Dickens."

I felt the damp of the night driving into my soul. I wanted him to touch me. At such a moment, what could be more than a touch to me?

"You did not answer my letters."

"I did not read them."

"Had you read them, you would've known how sorry I was for the unforgivable attitude I took with you. And for the unacceptable things I said."

We rounded a corner. The carriage tipped slightly, and for a moment Mr. Dickens' waistcoat with his gold watch chain was illuminated by the passing light of a gas lamp. I could smell faintly his evening brandy and cigar. The odour made my throat tight with desire and fear. I hated myself for being so vulnerable.

"Perhaps you would consent to accompanying me to a small café I know. I'm told it's become quite fashionable with the after-theatre crowd. We could have Turkish coffee — or an aperitif, if you like."

"I'm afraid I'm not dressed for a public appearance. And Mamma is expecting me home."

"Ah, Mamma. Of course, and rightly so. She would be concerned."

For a moment we rode in silence.

"My family is deeply grateful for all you've done for them. Fanny is so very excited about studying in Italy. You've been a kind and generous man. We have no way to repay you."

"No, no. Never think such thoughts."

The leather harnesses creaked, and the driver's voice called out. The carriage rumbled over cobblestones in the dark, passing through the glow of another streetlamp, where two lovers strolled. Lamps and lovers, the soggy clop of the horses, the squeaking carriage springs. My brain felt unsettled. What is less or more than a touch? If only he would touch me.

"Ellen, I consider your family as close to me as my very own. I'm not being generous at all. It's a pleasure to serve, to have an opportunity to share. I grew up so poor — so destitute — if truth be known. No, no, I don't provide for others in order to stimulate gratitude or indebtedness. I provide because it gives me great pleasure. Pure selfish pleasure. Because I have the good fortune to be able to."

He paused for a moment, and spoke softly. "I fear I've revealed an intimacy that must make you think badly of me."

"Not at all."

"The world says it's improper to confess our charity is for our own gratification."

"So the world says. But I'm sure if I ever had such an opportunity, I would feel the same."

"We understand each other fairly well, don't we, Ellen."

"Yes, Mr. Dickens."

"Perhaps you would consent to forgive me for being a fool in the past. I hesitate to recall it. In my distress, I lost manliness. I sought to lash out, to blame others, anyone but myself."

In the dark dampness I felt the heart in my chest, felt we had reached a place where the essence of hope for each other must be fulfilled or abandoned. I knew that what must have been so with every set of lovers in the past must now be so with us. Lamplight and rain and the odour of cigar were the whole of it to me. If only he would touch me.

I stretched forth my shabby gloved hand in the dark as he stretched forth his, gloved in finest calfskin, with a pearl button that glimmered.

*

"English weather is far too moody," Fanny complained in a whisper.

She whispered all the time now to save her voice. She wore a wool scarf about her throat, twist after twist, carrying herself with a stiff back, her chin raised high by the scarf. She wore green spectacles.

"This house is so very small and damp." Her head tilted with melancholy, and she lifted one arm in a grand gesture. "To sing well" — she sighed — "one does so need grand vistas."

Maria complained about suffering a diva in the family, but Mamma shushed her. Talent had to be encouraged. Mr. Dickens opened an account for Mamma and Fanny at Moses & Son in New Oxford Street. Elias Moses was a friend of his, he reported, and as such, he had been ordered to provide a complete travelling wardrobe for both Mamma and Fanny. All of us went together and found the shop selling ready-made, but of the finest cuts. Moses must have been at least seventy years old and almost bent double as he opened the door for us.

"Truly an honour," he observed, looking up at us from his bent position. "A true honour to be of service for which I am most honoured, indeed, yes, I must repeat it, most honoured, indeed, indeed."

The sentence reached an end of sorts, and Moses made a point of clicking his yellow false teeth, as if to punctuate his gratitude for the great favour we had done him.

"So proud to have been called upon for service." He bowed even lower, as if to say the entire shop belonged to us. "Mr. Dickens informed me I should expect you." Again he clicked his teeth for punctuation.

Maria and I gave each other a look and smiled, but Mamma

saw the situation more clearly. She pulled herself up and accepted the role assigned to her.

"Yes, yes, fetch me the very best." She sounded quite impatient.

"Jacob and Joseph!" Moses shouted. "This instant, you hear! Bring our best Italian Travelling Outfit this instant."

The old gentleman spun about like a top, returning in midspin to Mamma. He bowed and clicked. "So very sorry to keep you waiting, madam. My sons are still new to the business, and I must acknowledge their incompetence of sorts, indeed, yes, ladies, a pity of sorts, indeed, yes."

Once again, the sentence seemed to reach a vague ending.

"We don't have time to waste, my dear sir."

"Of course not. A distinguished lady like yourself and her very beautiful daughters, whom I have the honor of meeting now for the first time."

He grinned and nodded curiously at Fanny, who was still cocooned in a wool scarf. Then he bowed to Maria and me, tipping so low he seemed in danger of tumbling over until he caught himself with one hand on the corner of the table.

"I caution you, sir," Mamma said. "We're not spendthrifts. But we want the best."

Mamma was enjoying herself.

"Jacob and Joseph!" Moses shouted. "A lady's Italian Outfit, this instant!"

The sons of Mr. Moses came running, grey-haired men in their fifties, carrying bundles of clothing and boxes. Each was clearly terrified of his father.

"What villains!" he shouted at them. "You've kept these fine ladies waiting, I should say, although I won't say it. Take note that I won't say it this time."

The two sons seemed remarkably grateful their father was not going to say it this time.

"Ladies!" Moses cried. And he spun about like a top, bent double. "Here, you will find only the finest quality. You have my personal guarantee."

This seemed to be some kind of signal. The two grey-haired sons began spreading out dry goods on top of a nearby table, piles and piles of goods.

"I shall die with confusion," Mamma said sincerely.

"Fetch the lady a chair!"

On the instant, one of the sons produced a chair for our long-suffering mamma to collapse into.

"Now here, madam," Mr. Moses proposed, "here we have the complete travelling wardrobe for Italy. Nothing is left out, absolutely nothing. I shall now demonstrate it, upon my personal honour, indeed, I shall."

He spun about and clawed with ancient fingers at the closest fabric.

"First, I recommend thirty long cotton chemises," Mr. Moses said. "The standard number. Plus eighteen long night-dresses and the same number of cambric slips, and on those colder days of winter four Welsh flannel petticoats."

"Of course," Mamma said. "Just as we expected. However, I should think sixteen nightdresses would be plenty."

"Sixteen, madam?"

Mamma leaned over from her chair and whispered in Mr. Moses' ear, which because of his bent position was exactly at Mamma's level. "We're not planning to emigrate," she confided.

"Ahhhh," Moses said. "I understand perfectly. Sixteen it is then." He clicked his teeth to punctuate the excellent finality of the decision.

"Next!"

One of the grey-headed sons spread out nightcaps, hand-kerchiefs, and linen.

"Here I recommend twenty-one long cotton drawers and three flannel drawers."

This time it was his turn to speak confidentially in Mamma's ear. "We no longer feel mosquito drawers are necessary for Italy."

Mamma nodded, as if it were something she'd been wondering about. "I am glad to hear it."

"And, of course, thirty-six cambric pocket handkerchiefs, with an additional thirty-six linen pocket handkerchiefs."

Mamma nodded again.

"Next!" Moses shouted. Another box of goods was cast out on the increasing pile of clothing.

"Here we have dressing gowns. Two would seem enough, but some women do prefer four."

Mamma did not hesitate.

"Four."

"Quite the better choice." Moses snapped his teeth, like the sound of a door latch closing. "Plus no doubt, you'll want at least one white satin striped dressing gown."

"Naturally."

"I also recommend thirty-six pair of white cotton stockings, twelve pair of merino stockings, and six pair of our finest silk stocking, imported from China."

"Absolutely necessary."

After that came three cloaks, six mantles, and nineteen frocks of various assorted fabrics and colours, plus one seaside hat, which Mr. Moses admitted was rather risqué for some women, but for ladies of character and beauty, it was all the rage.

Mamma selected three: one black, one yellow, and one white.

"Pack it up!" Moses shouted.

The sons rushed into a flurry of sorting and folding. Then Moses began all over again for Fanny, who, it turned out, was far more selective and insisted on touching and sniffing each garment.

Moses spun, clicked, and bowed, ordering his sons about until sometime after midday, when all of us felt exhausted. Fanny also realised, of a sudden, that she absolutely needed a new sailing trunk with leather straps.

"These voyages do so wear out sailing trunks," she said to Moses.

"So very true."

Mamma agreed she might as well select a new trunk as well, the old one being somewhat scuffed on the corners.

"Pack it up!" Moses shouted to his sons. "No more dawdling. Take note, I won't say it this time."

Both sons seemed eminently relieved.

Moses bowed us out the door, bent nearly double. "It has been my pleasure I assure you, ladies, quite the full pleasure, a great honour, indeed, the honour, indeed."

He snapped the door shut with the finality of a steel trap.

We hired a hack to take us home, but we were too worn out to talk. It was so exciting, so frightening. Our lives seemed out of control. We were like puppets with some grey-bearded Prospero moving us here and there about the stage.

Fanny and Mamma left for Dover on the last day of September. Maria and I saw them off from Victoria Station, a grand cathedral with high iron beams and rafters that always reminded me of flying buttresses. A throng of other families waved and cheered their departing friends. We pushed through the crowd, standing below the carriage window until the pierce of the conductor's whistle startled us, and we shouted *bon voyage* for the hundredth time. The engine blew steam and smoke, the bell began to ring, the wheels turned, the carriages jerked and rattled forward. My last glimpse of Fanny sitting back on the leather seat made me think she looked rather pale and frightened after all. We waved and watched as the train grew smaller and smaller down the tracks.

Maria and I glanced at each other. We were alone — without Mamma — for the first time in our lives. It felt so very odd. We smiled nervously, guilty at our thoughts.

"We'll miss them," Maria said.

"Terribly. We'll miss them terribly."

Two young women alone in London without a chaperon. We grinned wickedly, laughed aloud, and hid our faces from each other in embarrassment. The crowds parted, the bright sunlight outside gave the city an air of ripeness and anticipation. We strolled arm in arm through crowded streets, chatting over the top of each other, watching our figures float by in mirrored shop windows. We lifted our faces to the glorious autumn, wanting ever-so-much to stop by this tavern or that, bemoaning the lot of women, and setting each other off with laughter. We walked all the way to Gloucester Crescent, where Molly fixed cucumber sandwiches and cider for tea. And we celebrated.

Mr. Dickens took everything in hand. He hadn't realised how far Gloucester Crescent was from the theatre district, and, of course, the house was rather large for two young women who were hardly ever there. He rented new lodgings for us on Berners Street, only a short walk through Soho to Covent

Garden, which was far more convenient, he explained to us. It was also a rather dark and private street, where a carriage might pick up or drop off without attracting attention. And he bought a small library from the estate of a wealthy widower who had recently died in Exmouth. We were suddenly rich in leather-bound volumes by Ruskin and William Godwin and Mrs. Gaskell — to which we added Mamma's collection of plays, ragged and well-marked. Most of the plays lacked bindings of any kind, but we displayed them proudly. They were like a private genealogy of our family.

One foggy October morning, Mr. Dickens appeared at the door before we had finished breakfast, both of us in our wrappers and giggling with embarrassment for being so slovenly. He stood on the stoop, grinning under that delightful moustache, holding out to us in his arms a shiny-nosed puppy, a female spaniel. Maria and I squealed like schoolgirls and stroked and petted her, while Mr. Dickens beamed. The puppy wiggled and wagged her tail and pushed her wet nose into our faces, making us giggle the more. I felt so happy, so full of riches, and so loved, that right there in front of Maria, I lifted up on my toes and quickly kissed a shocked Mr. Dickens on the lips, feeling for the first time the scratchy delight of that lion's moustache, feeling for the first time the warmth and fullness of his lips, feeling my breasts under the wrap push against his chest without a corset to protect me, and seeing him blush bright as a schoolboy. I wanted to kiss him again, but stepped back, letting my fingers linger a moment on his shoulder, then slide down his sleeve and across the warm surface of his hand.

I named the puppy Miranda.

Mr. Dickens moved his own bachelor quarters from Wellington to York Street, where he had a small balcony with double doors. He hired a housekeeper to assist Hubbard and announced he had settled both of us at last. A few days later, he began talking about finding some secluded cottage outside of London where we might take the air and walk about through some orchard or back country lane.

"I have hardly unpacked, Mr. Dickens."

"Of course, of course. Just something to be thinking about."

Maria and I slept late, breakfasting long after decent folks had finished their midday meal. We spent afternoons reading or strolling in the park, and later we dressed for our walk to the theatre. Molly adjusted easily to our new schedule, serving tea late. At night, she waited up for our return — except on those evenings when Mr. Dickens picked me up from the theatre in his carriage. Molly always seemed to anticipate Mr. Dickens' schedule. When Maria returned home alone, Molly would be long asleep. I began to suspect she felt she was working for Mr. Dickens, rather than for Maria and me. She did, after all, receive a small wage from him each month, delivered by Hubbard. And on occasion, I found Hubbard and Molly talking in hushed voices in the kitchen. But I can't say she had any particular gossip to spread, since our routine was so clearly established by the Great Man himself.

We might have gone on forever like that, except for Maria's tendency to flirt with every male she happened to meet. Every evening on our walk to the theatre, we met two young bobbies in dark helmets, one quite handsome and sporting a military moustache. They would each lift a finger to their helmets in salute to us, and Maria would imitate them, raising her own finger to her bonnet. Sometimes, we stopped for a minute and laughed together or chatted about the weather. Decent young men, it seemed. Rather bored and fully pleased for two pretty girls to give them notice. We were glad for their presence. The

London streets at night were rather frightening. Rats scurried back and forth across the cobbles, child prostitutes — both girls and boys — hung about the iron railings, waiting for a customer or waiting to pick your pocket. More than once we had to step around sleeping drunks or a dead woman or man — their shoes stolen — or even their clothing ripped off their curled up bodies. Fresh horse dung and urine were everywhere. Sometimes, men followed us out of the theatre, or at least we imagined they did. The presence of the bobbies gave us some little assurance, and for the rest, we closed our eyes to it.

Long past midnight, in early December, I believe, only a month or so after moving to Berners Street, when the walk through Soho took Maria and me along deserted sidewalks, we passed under a gas lamp where the circle of light caught us momentarily like a bright moon. As we moved out of it into the darkness, we heard steps approaching from the other side of the street, and truly, we gave it no thought until an old tar wearing a sailor's jacket and a scrump hat staggered across the cobbles, hurrying to place himself in our way. We picked up our pace, but he was able to cut us off, forcing us to stop.

He leaned into my face with a parrot's beak of a red nose, his breath reeking of gin and stale tobacco. "Hellooo, me sweeties."

We tried to step around him, holding tightly to each other, but he pressed forward.

"How much for the twinning of me? Be brisk now, the price up front. It's the deed we want, doubled by your charming friend here."

"Leave us alone," I whispered.

"I'll pay the price," he bellowed. "I've a pocket full of more than either of ye've ever seen. My lucky night, I says, and here's the luck again, two of you for the price of one, eh?"

He matched each of our steps and dodges with his own, forbidding us passage.

"Come now, ladies, I'm good enough for you, ain't I? A little silver in my pocket can make for a right pleasant evening."

All of us together heard the footsteps behind him, running almost in unison, boot soles beating on the pavement, and then the stinging cry of the bobby's whistle in the dark.

In a moment, our old drunk had vanished, and the bobbies arrived.

"Oh, thank goodness," Maria said. "Thank you so much for helping us. He ran that way, I believe. You can still catch him."

The bobbies made no attempt to follow our attacker. Instead, the one with the dark moustache — standing erect and military as a guard at Buckingham Palace — said, "So, my two young friends, perhaps you'd let us know your interests, walking the streets this late at night."

"We've been keeping our eye on you two," the other bobby said.

They took us to the station house and held us in a room with three "other" ladies of the night, young women who were tipsy and scraggled and who sneered at our clean frocks and boots.

We were able to send a boy with a note to Mr. Dickens, who, an hour or so later, came roaring in with proper outrage. The police apologised, but we could hear the captain on duty explaining.

"We've had our eye on 'em for some time, sir. No decent woman walks through Soho at that time of night."

Mr. Dickens threw out his chest. "Innocent young women — pure women, mind you — accosted on a public street by the very police who are supposed to protect them." He bellowed loud enough to wake the Prime Minister.

"They had no male escort," the captain said. "None whatsoever."

Behind us, one of the prostitutes was singing.

> She was a pure young thing
> When she met him . . .

"Scotland Yard will hear of this," Mr. Dickens bellowed. "And if I get no satisfaction, I'll take it to the Queen herself." He turned red with a fury out of proportion to the crime.

> But the red of his coat
> And the flash of his sword
> Weakened her faint resooooolve.

The girls were laughing. The police were standing firm.

"Prostitutes!" he whispered. "You accuse these pure things of being prostitutes?"

> She looked in a mirror and spied herself
> Oh me, oh my, she cried
> I'm all of a thing to yooooou.

The women hooted. The police captain folded his arms.

"Sir," I said to Mr. Dickens, taking him by the arm. "Sir, I'm sure these gentlemen were only doing their duty. It was a mistake with no harm done."

I led him out of the station house. He was still trembling and bitter, but we found a hack, and he escorted us home.

Three days later, he signed an eighty-four-year lease on a new house — as a gift for me. The movers and carts appeared, and overnight, we were moved.

"Shipped out," Maria complained.

To Number 2 Houghton Place on Ampthill Square, not far from Mornington Crescent. It seems Mr. Dickens had been thinking for some time about purchasing some grand present for me. And then, it had come to him. We would be only a few blocks from his magazine office. He could check in regularly. Regent's Park was a short stroll. We could take delightful walks. Except to the theatre. For the theatre, we would take a hack.

In truth, the house was rather grand, if a little discomforting: four stories tall, with terraces and an iron gate and balconies. In back, Maria discovered a ragged garden that only needed tending, a place Miranda could run and bark without supervision. Mr. Dickens personally supervised the move, ordering workmen about, directing where furniture should be placed, rugs thrown, books shelved. The dining room seated twelve. He purchased three original oils for the parlour, two by Landseer and one by his friend Augustus Egg, along with a tapestry from Persia. Molly was ordered to stock the larder. Hubbard assisted with bedding and linens. Chimney sweepers cleaned nine chimneys. Windows were washed. Before we moved in, Mr. Dickens retained a cook — a woman as big and white-faced as a Hereford. Then he found a crippled young orphan girl to serve her as scullery maid. Finally, he announced he had located a woman whose mother was Scottish to be the upstairs maid.

"Scottish women make the best upstairs maids," he explained.

On Molly, he bestowed the new title of housekeeper, presenting her with a ring of keys which she wore, with no little amount of arrogance, on a belt around her waist.

Hubbard was named butler and given sole possession of the butler's pantry with a private bedroom attached.

Maria and I found ourselves in the way, tossed here and there, ordered about. We struggled to wear a positive face. The changes were coming too fast.

"I hardly know who I am anymore," Maria whispered.

More than anything, I'd begun to recognise who *I* was, and the role I was to play. Even a young girl knows the meaning of such a grand present. I was still pure, you see, still sitting on his lap and combing his hair, still teasing his moustache, and scampering in frightened delight when he chased me about a room. But when a man gives you a house, a great man, a married man who has decided he needs more than another daughter, you accept the gift with a different kind of knowledge, with a heaviness and a new sense of being a woman — of being about to become a woman.

"I have made arrangements for us to sail to France," he told me in private. "You'll want to visit the shop of Mrs. Merriweather for the latest in Parisian fashions. She's expecting you."

"What about Moses?" I asked.

Mr. Dickens looked up to see if I were joking. "Surely you wouldn't wear ready-made to Paris."

"Actually, Mamma always made our clothing by hand."

"Mrs. Merriweather will create a superb wardrobe for you. And to please your friend Moses, I'll ask him to send over several trunks to Mrs. Merriweather's for her to pack."

"Are you sure you want to go to Paris?"

"Yes, yes. In France, we can be free of all things British. I'll show you wonderful sights, museums, superior cafés, remarkable wines. There are several new plays and operas I've been wanting to attend. We could go to the Folies, if you're feeling risqué."

He took my hand. "We will have to hide from no one. The

world will be open to us — every door — day or night. There's no telling when we'll return. We're going to have a marvellous trip, just the two of us."

And so I provided notice to Mr. Adersley that a Wednesday evening, a fortnight hence, would be my last performance.

"To be sure," he said, offhand, as if he already knew.

Several players gave me a small party. After my final appearance onstage, I returned to the dressing room and changed into a delicious silk frock Mrs. Merriweather had just made for me. It was a lovely piece, robin's egg blue, with a full skirt shaped by gores and finished about the waist with a sash. Mrs. Merriweather had given it a new, rounder, and somewhat higher waistline to emphasize my small figure. The hoops underneath were slightly flattened in front, making my waist look smaller. I dressed my own hair, pulling it up as a woman should wear it, abandoning my girlish curls. With my hair lifted, my bare throat seemed more striking, even to me. I had always been pretty. But I had to admit that in those cracked and rusty dressing-room mirrors, I looked stunning.

It was a mistake. When the other women arrived backstage, they fell silent and avoided looking at me. I tried to joke with them as I always did, but they studied their faces in the mirrors and seemed quite taken with scrubbing away stage makeup. Several tossed on patched robes or faded frocks. A final few pretended to tease me about the identity of my mysterious "someone." They seemed to feel I'd never been serious about acting. I was only one of those many young women who pass through the theatre until they find a husband — or a *provider* — as one actress termed it.

"I've always dreamed of having a *provider*." She sighed.

"A rich one would be nice," said another.

"One with a closed carriage and two horses."

"Oh yes, someone very rich. Someone who could *provide* me with a frock of — say — robin's egg blue."

They broke up with giggles and laughter. A few male actors made brief appearances. They shook my hand delicately, as if I were someone else's property. I was no longer the silly young thing who showed her legs. One actress — Fanny'a age, perhaps — with the beginnings of lines about her eyes, excused herself early because of a splitting headache.

Maria joined me afterward, and we rode home together, silent and sitting apart. Our lives, once so focused on being a family of women, a family centred in our own tradition and our own independence — all that had vanished. We had been dispersed across Europe, our careers disrupted. I felt already as if I were a Great Man's mistress in France. And the woman riding across from me was not even my older sister — only some distant relative from childhood, being polite in hopes of further favours, somewhat afraid of me, now, inferior, lonely, and very far away.

At our grand new house, windows were illuminated with beeswax candles. The carriage driver handed me down and walked me to the door with the polished brass knocker. Hubbard opened up, bowing his head slightly. Molly escorted me to my room, where she helped me undress. On my bed lay a hand-stitched nightgown of Indian linen. The bodice was decorated with embroidered bouquets of posies. Mr. Dickens had purchased a new four-poster with a luxurious feather mattress and piles of down pillows. After Molly left me, I snuffed out the candle, eased myself between fine sheets and, for a long time, lay in the lonely dark feeling the weight of emptiness on my breast. I heard the faint click of Miranda's toenails on the floor as she scurried in. She leapt on the bed and snuggled next to me, pushing her wet warm nose into my breast. That was when I cried. After that, I never cried again, except once out of anger when Mr. Dickens refused to take me to America. And later, when they stole my baby. But that night, alone with Miranda, guarded by Hubbard and Molly, in a house with iron gates, I went over it all in my heart. I could find no place for myself. The stage was empty. The theatre dark. What had I done? And why? For what end? Hour after hour, I peered into the mirrored blackness, sensing only the quick sharp snake of dread, waiting for me in France.

We took the night ferry to Caen, and a steam train to the Gare du Nord, sleeping fitfully sitting up. The sight of Paris, with domes and cathedrals and wide streets lined with bare forked trees brought us to life. We bundled in furs, and Mr. Dickens held my hand. He was excited and pleased, in full power of his manhood, talking incessantly, pointing out the Opéra, the Louvre, the Ile de la Cité. Soon enough, we were in a country of rolling hills south of the city. Hubbard followed behind, in charge of three carts loaded with luggage. Peasants ploughed winter fields against the skyline. Poplar-lined drives led to manor houses half hidden by woods. Mr. Dickens had rented a château overlooking the Seine, where broken skiffs of ice floated slowly, like Nordic sailing vessels. The air smelled spectacularly clean after London. In England, one would never see a winter sun with such clarity. Geese babbled on the banks of a frozen pond. Inside the château, all was dreary and cold. In the Grand Hall, ancient battle flags with fleur-de-lis drooped heavily overhead in vaulted darkness. Thin arrows of sunlight entered here and there through narrow slits in the stone. At one end, a blackened fireplace was so grand I could have walked into it. Flames roared and logs crackled, but I could feel the fire only when standing close by. I had the impression the Grand Hall was generally impervious to light and heat.

An army of French servants unloaded our carts, carried trunks, uncovered furniture. Hubbard was appointed steward. Mr. Dickens set him up in a special command post in the pantry, and that created several arguments with the French butler. Mr. Dickens intervened, speaking the language rather well, it seemed to me, and resolving disputes gracefully but firmly. A dozen men and boys carried, loaded, unloaded, and served. We had a staff of six housemaids, two kitchen maids, a scullery maid, two cooks, and an ancient English widow dressed in black with a white cap, called Mrs. Smarthy, who lived now in France and who — I was told — would be my lady's maid during the stay. She was somewhat blind and hard of hearing. At times, she confused me with her granddaughter and called me Dorene.

"Mrs. Smarthy will take good care of you," Mr. Dickens explained. "When we've settled somewhere, I'll find you a permanent maid, if you wish, someone you might feel more comfortable with." He leaned over and whispered. "I couldn't bring Molly, you see, because of her past. She wouldn't be at all suitable for a lady. I'm sure you've heard more than enough about that."

He was quite happy providing for me. He never seemed happier than when he had given me a present or added another servant to the household. It made him stride about stomping his boots like a schoolboy carrying a secret frog in his pocket.

Our château belonged to an ancient Count who wintered in Portugal and who claimed Voltaire had once hidden in the château's wine cellar before fleeing to England. Mr. Dickens considered it all rather questionable. He was still writing his novel on the French Revolution, and seemed to feel he was an expert in all things French.

That first evening, sitting alone in the great cold dining room, we ate roast duck in some strangely wonderful orange sauce. Mr. Dickens suggested we have dessert in front of the fire in the Grand Hall. Dessert consisted of numerous kinds of cheese, which seemed odd to me but which Mr. Dickens explained was a French custom. We began with something called Camembert, accompanied by a chilled Sauterne. Mr. Dickens opened the wine himself. I drank more than I should, feeling flushed and sometimes faint. I tried to listen to Mr. Dickens. I kept going over advice Maria had given to me about what was going to happen later. She explained how it all worked — the mechanics of it — but in the heat of the wine and the fire, I wasn't at all convinced.

Mr. Dickens seemed equally uncomfortable about what was to come. He talked especially hard, telling old stories. He recalled hiking through the Italian Alps with Mr. Collins and Mr. Egg. He laughed about their moustache-growing contest, recounted some odd accident in Rome with his son. He described a garden party in Aix, suddenly remembered visiting Balmoral in Scotland. He hardly knew what he was saying. I laughed politely at his stories. Poured more wine. Straightened my frock. Tried to remember everything Maria said. In truth, the heat flowed through my whole body, and in some frightening way I realised I wanted him to possess me. I felt embarrassed, even humiliated at such a thought. I tried to push it away. My throat grew so hot and tight I could hardly swallow.

Mr. Dickens stopped talking in midsentence. We stared at the fire. The logs crackled and burst. All around us the house clicked softly. And finally, he found his courage, stood with rather slow, silent decisiveness, and selected a candle to light our way. On the grand stairs, I took his arm, and we climbed to the first marble landing, then the second marble landing, barely breathing. I wanted desperately for him to hold me for a long, long time. I felt ready to cry at my own fear and my own ignorance, knowing nothing about how I was to please him, a man so very much older and wiser, so much more experienced in the world than me. I let my fingers rest upon his sleeve, accompanying him silently, step by step. His trouser leg whispered against the fabric of my frock, like someone breathing heavily. In the top hallway, his candlelight danced in macabre shadows over oil paintings of the Count's long-dead ancestors, framed now in tarnished gold. A Baron stared down at me with insolence. A cruel-looking woman, burdened with jewels, watched me with condescension. Their eyes followed me, all of them dead, long dead in their tombs.

But we were not to be alone. Not yet. We retired to our own bedrooms, where housemaids laid fires and an army of water boys hauled up buckets of hot water for our baths. A great brass tub stood near the fire. Mrs. Smarthy directed traffic, eventually adding rose oil to the steaming water, then ordering everyone out so I could bathe in private. The truth was, in all the steaming heat from fire and water, I almost fell asleep from exhaustion. All about the room hung gilt-framed mirrors from the eighteenth century, some with naked cherubs and laughing seraphim. The water steamed, I soaked and drifted, breathing deeply and slowly, controlling my breath. I wanted to slide down deeply into that womb of water, but I couldn't let my hair get wet. Mrs. Smarthy brought towels, more than I would normally use in a month.

"Unless there's something else, Dorene, I'll leave you to

yourself. Mr. Dickens has ordered the nightgown on the bed for you as a surprise."

I had seen it when I came in. A creamy silk gown with long lace cuffs, a lace bodice, and a high neck, tied with a single magenta ribbon.

"Would you like me to dress your hair?"

"That will be all, Mrs. Smarthy. You might want to carry away some of these towels."

"Yes, ma'am. And if I may say so, you look quite lovely."

"Thank you."

She hesitated, as if wanting to say something else. "It will be all right, ma'am," she whispered kindly. "You'll see. God gets us past the difficult hour. You'll see."

"Thank you, Mrs. Smarthy."

In Mr. Dickens' room next door, I could hear the same commotion. Water pouring, feet moving back and forth, doors closing. And then, long silence.

I soaked as long as I could, until I heard the water in the next room splash, signalling that Mr. Dickens had probably stood up. And so I stood as well, water flowing off me. I rose from the water like Venus, standing in the light of half a dozen candles, and looking suddenly at myself — fully naked — defined in one of those Marie Antoinette mirrors. I had seen myself in a mirror many times. An actress lives around mirrors. I had not looked at my flesh in the same way. The warm candlelight flickered over the swelling curves of my thin little body, and I knew I was indeed lovely. My shoulders were white and wet, like a shoreline where the breath of the sea whispers at sunset. Slowly, deliberately, I watched myself cup the weight of my breasts, feeling their small heaviness in the palms of my hands. I was dripping wet and trembling. I had never so deliberately touched myself. A woman should not. It was impure, I

knew. Everything wrong had always been beyond consideration. Mamma made it so. But I was so very alone. Mamma and
Fanny were in Florence, Maria in London. I was alone and
naked in a château outside of Paris. I could hear nothing in
that great house, no voices, no horses clopping by outside, no
sounds of someone in the kitchen. My lungs thickened with
fear or lust. I did not know which. I was alone with my body
and soul. I realised I would be from now on. It made me suddenly want to be bad, very bad. I was beautiful.

Did I love him?

What can a woman know of love on her first night? Mr.
Dickens snuffed out the candles. I remember only the pain
and discomfort, the odd smell of a man's pomade, a pressure
and weight, like the full heaviness of some grunting beast im-
prisoning me. How can I help but remember the awkward
hands, so much more impatient than I imagined, or the hairy
leg forcing its way? Yet I felt my blood swelling, felt it in the
flesh of my bones, unable and unwilling to resist, pulsing and
quickening, my fists held tight at my sides. Did I learn wisdom
then? Was there some quickening of my soul when the Great
Man suddenly flung himself away, panting, and announcing it
was over? So soon. With so little accomplished. Somewhere
between Sodom and Bethlehem.

Did I love him?

I desired him. My green apple breasts burned to be
touched and suckled. After long silence, I reached out, finding
his damp chest in the dark, searching through unexpected
hair on his belly, wanting to grasp the odd source of such violence. But how shall I say this? Like some sweet power in me,
hot and driving, where the pulse quickens, rising unexpectedly to my dark energy, a whisper between his teeth told me I

had found my way. I forgot for a moment in France that I was unhappy to be there. I felt powers I'd never known as a girl in a pink sash with a straw hat and golden curls. I felt what other women must have known, at some time, some place, or always: a thin, invisible tug of female history pulled me along, as if I were not me or, rather, more than me. All about me, in that great bed of promise and betrayal, somewhere outside of Paris, hung dark mirrors in which I could see nothing at all, as if I had already disappeared. A new script had been handed me, as a woman. I took the part and made it mine. I became what I had to become.

Georgina Hogarth

CHARLES needed a woman to believe in him, trust him, stand beside him. He had no one to depend upon. The stress had taken such toll upon his person and his soul. He'd grown thinner, his face and eyes looked strained. His shoulders slumped. The pain of it all caused me to suffer as well — a degeneration of the heart, our physician said. My heart pounded so hard and fast I couldn't breathe. I took up fainting. Charles invited me to Dover for a holiday. We walked upon the windy cliffs, where a green sea beat and thrust below us.

He gripped my arm to keep me from being swept away. "My best and dearest friend," he said. "You must take better care."

"And who will take care of you, Charles?"

"I shall be fine. It's you I'm concerned about."

No one knew how devoted I was to him — or he to me. Our love was silent, unspoken, but no less tangible. The wind whipped my bonnet off, tearing out my pins and loosing my hair. The wind threw the bonnet over the cliffs to whirl and spin out to sea below. Charles made a desperate effort to catch it, but the bonnet was gone in an instant.

"I'm so sorry." He hurried back to me. My hair swirled

about me, loose and sensuous in the wind. For a moment, we could only cling to one another, like two lovers buffeted by the lashing the world gives those who care too deeply. I felt like the heroine in an old novel by Sir Walter Scott.

On our walk back, he mentioned I'd lost my cheery spirit of old. "I do so miss that former devotion." His eyes told me he was pretending to joke, but I knew he was serious.

"I feel much better already, I assure you."

I could feel my heart flagging, my strength weakening. I knew I could never be the woman I had been. He seemed well-pleased that I should pretend. He required it for peace of mind. How could I not help him? It was a spiritual debt I owed to Charles, as every woman owes it to a husband. I never again let him know the truth. He was not my husband then, of course. You'll find it in none of the official biographies. But the truth no longer needs to be guarded.

For appearances, Charles spent much of his time with Ellen Ternan, meeting her "secretly" in distant towns or pretending to hide her at the back of his theatre box. He worked carefully to establish a grand charade that would protect me from the gossiping eye of the public. He took her to France, where he kept her oh so many years. I suppose he paid her well for the deceit. Charles was clever. Those who knew about Catherine's departure were willingly deceived by gossip about a young actress. So many great men do keep a mistress, don't they? And Ellen Ternan played the role with ease: the kept woman hidden away in an immoral country. Everyone overlooked the fact that Charles spent most of his time in London, working hard as always on his magazine, writing plays and novels, giving readings to his devoted public, and living at Gad's Hill. On occasion, he even invited Ellen Ternan to

Gad's Hill for tea. When she heard about it, Katie thought it very improper, but I confess I found Miss Ternan mildly likeable. We never became friends, of course. We came from such different social standings. But we shared a grand secret that gave us an unusual tie. Both of us knew our roles, the ones Charles assigned to us, and we had no reason to feel competition or jealousy. We sat down to tea together, with Charles presiding, and chatted about oh so many things that had nothing whatsoever to do with our real thoughts.

Over the next several years, Ellen Ternan lived most of the time in France or visiting her family in Italy. The old rumours about Charles and me faded away — as he knew they would. Eventually, Mamma and Papa reconciled with me. We wrote to each other several times a year — a little formally and with great reserve. We avoided mentioning Catherine. All the terrible turmoil of recent times seemed something from a former life. Katie was married into the Collins family, although not well, it seemed. Charlie, Catherine's eldest son, continued to reside with his mother at my parents' home. He and his father never really spoke to each other again, although they did sometimes communicate by letter. One by one, Mr. Dickens sent his other sons off to begin their own lives. Each boy had great expectations that his father would provide some large trust to ensure a life at the level to which he was accustomed — something to invest or build upon. It was not to be, however. More and more, Charles came to believe that every young man should make his own way in the world — as he had done so many years earlier — rise or fall as one's talents dictated.

Walter and Frank were shipped off to India, Sydney to South Africa, Alfred to Australia. And after Alfred seemed to prosper there, Dickens insisted Plorn join him, even though Plorn was only sixteen at the time. He had always been a weak-eyed young man who seldom spoke. The forgotten boy in a large family. At the train station, I gave him a box of cigars as a farewell present, thinking he would accept it proudly — a symbol of his approaching manhood. Plorn grew teary-eyed in confusion.

Charles patted him on the back. "Don't fret, my boy. Life is little more than a series of partings. You'll grow accustomed to it."

In order to give Plorn courage, Charles pretended to be quite casual about the boy's departure, checking his gold watch, impatient that the train was late. In my heart, I knew Charles was deeply pained by the dwindling size of his family, the loss of all those darling children. He put on a brave front, as a father must, and each boy in turn took heart as best he could, setting out alone in the world, to achieve or fail as fortune would have it. We never saw Plorn again, or any of the sons, really. They ended up as lonely clerks in countinghouses throughout the Empire. Walter died in Calcutta, still writing desperate letters home, begging for some portion of an inheritance. Gad's Hill seemed empty, and Charles spent more and more time in France. I think he found retreat there from the sad dispersal of family, the failure of his sons. It was about this time Charles began to think of starting a new novel on such a subject — about a young man going forth in the world with false hopes — and how we do lose our way. What more could he have done for them? he must have asked himself. I remained the only person he confided in. I alone knew how he grieved.

Many years earlier, he'd told me about his travels through Europe with Collins and Egg: hiking in Switzerland, smoking cigars on loggias in Italy, eating oranges in Southern France. I liked Egg the best by far. He was Augustus Egg, the famous painter, and he had already been appointed to the Royal Academy, as he so richly deserved. Wilkie Collins' father was a painter also, and that was how he came to know Egg. But Collins was too much the sly snake for my taste, and too flamboyant. He was not the kind of man Charles — or Egg, for that matter — should have associated with. All England loved those great mystery novels Collins seemed to write so regularly, but his personal reputation was a disgrace. He openly kept a mistress. Rumour had it she was the cast-off lover of some Italian aristocrat by whom she'd had an illegitimate child. Then one day, Charles revealed Collins had taken a second mistress, setting her up in a home just around the corner from the first. Impossible to believe, it was so blatantly defiant of public taste.

"It's disgraceful," I said. "The man should be brought up on charges for immoral behaviour."

Charles only laughed.

"She's just a girl from the north country," he told me. "I met her yesterday. Martha Muddy, or Ruddy — something like that. Rather tall and awkward, with country manners. Slimly educated, I should think, and barely nineteen. That's the real crime of it. A middle-aged man like Wilkie taking advantage of a mere girl for his sport."

Charles never brought it up again because he and Collins were friends. One did hear rumours, however. Everyone in London whispered about it. How Collins would put on his Bohemian hat in one house and walk around the corner to the next, where he would hang up the hat and shamefully pretend all was right and moral in the world.

Augustus Egg was far the better companion to Charles: so much more a gentleman, and so much more discerning.

Collins was short and vulgar. Mr. Egg was tall and gentle. He had a delicacy one expects of the better classes. It was unfortunate he had such a large head. It seemed somehow mismatched for his body. When he got excited — usually when talking about art — his head would bob and wobble, as if it might fall off. The truth is he looked like a tall spike with a loose lantern on top. Yet I always felt he was a man of refinement and intellect. In public, he dressed all in black, with a top hat, as was the fashion, and he sometimes wore a goatee, but he seemed unaware that even when perfectly dressed, he always had various coloured paint under his fingernails. Some days, it would be green, other days, black. Charles admired him a great deal, but behind his back he made fun of him, especially because Egg had an odd tendency to wheeze all the time — even while you were talking to him. It was disconcerting really. Sometimes he would wheeze and whistle whole overtures, as if several players with wind instruments were warming up. You had to learn not to listen or you might lose your train of thought altogether.

He visited Gad's Hill rather frequently at one point, calling on Charles and sharing a small glass of port with him. He even spoke about doing a portrait of Charles, but it never came about. And then one day, in early spring, Mr. Egg asked me to accompany him to a new showing of his work at the Academy. I'd seen several of his shows, including the one which brought him so much recognition, the one that featured a painting titled *Queen Elizabeth Discovers She is No Longer Young*. I recall being quite overwhelmed with it. But on that occasion, I had accompanied the entire Dickens family. We traveled in two carriages with all the children. This time, Mr. Egg made it quite clear he was inviting me personally, and we would be going alone.

I felt flustered and shamed. To accompany him without a chaperon, I felt sure, constituted a betrayal to Charles. Something I absolutely could not do.

That evening, Charles came home with a special bounce in his step, boots pounding across the floor. "Ah! Georgina! I understand you may have something to tell me." He grinned like Mr. Carroll's Cheshire Cat.

"Sir?"

"Come, come now. Out with it. You've been invited somewhere by a secret admirer, if I'm not mistaken. No deception, now!"

"Sir, I hardly know what to say."

"Well, just say it! This is quite an invitation, rather remarkable, don't you think?"

"You're speaking of Mr. Egg, then."

"Of course, I'm speaking of Egg! Who else would we be talking about? Do you have other beaux who give you private invitations to the Royal Academy?"

"But I haven't accepted, sir."

"Of course you've accepted. I told Egg you'd be delighted. Nothing could be more thrilling, eh? And here I thought all these years old Egg was calling upon me. The old dog! What a deceiver he is. And you, too, Miss Hogarth! All these years, eh?"

"Oh, no sir, not at all."

"Come come come, I'm never mistaken about these things." He hurried off in great spirits, leaving me burning and faint. Was there really something more to this than I'd thought? I was certain there wasn't. Augustus Egg had long been a confirmed bachelor. He was married to his art, as he should be. Nonetheless I found myself dressing that afternoon with shaky hands and a dry tongue.

Egg and I took the train together from Rochester to London and then went by open hack to the Academy. I remember so very little. And yet I remember every detail. How the late spring sun beat down upon the cab. How I struggled to carry a conversation over the incessant wheezing of Egg, talking mostly about Dickens because he was the easiest subject for us both. I remember climbing the granite steps to the Academy, one at a time, my hand tucked into his arm. And the sudden cold darkness when we entered the marble lobby. Others were there, of course, women in hoop skirts and bonnets, like myself. Men dressed in black. Clusters of talkers gathered about each painting. From the high ceiling, an echo of voices came back at us as if all the angels of heaven were babbling in some distant temple at once.

Most of all, I remember a crowd gathered around three related paintings — a triptych. The crowd was remarkably silent, several women shivered with teary eyes, and men held their chins high, as if hearing the distant song of a great choir, moved by the angel of truth herself to recognise greatness. There, in front of that series of canvases, no one spoke. Only the faint shuffle of feet could be heard. One after another, couples moved closer, gripping each other unknowingly with firm hands. In the stunning stillness, standing there with Egg — the most startling, most painful collection of pictures I had ever encountered — I felt faint and overwhelmed. This was art that spoke to the soul alone.

"I call it *Past and Present*," he said, humbly. And during a moment of intense immersion, all Egg's strange tics and manners disappeared, as he too must have sensed the higher truth of what he'd accomplished. He and I entered the paintings themselves, felt the pain and beauty of them, the great tragedy the story revealed. There could be no question, ever, as to whether they would be chosen for permanent display in the Royal Gallery to bring a moral lesson to every decent man and woman.

The first of the three panels showed a parlour where presumably — moments before — a happy family must have gathered. Two small children must have been playing quietly. The father, whose top hat still lies upon the table, must have just returned home, and the mother — what would the mother have been doing? The painting does not focus on that moment. Instead, we are shown an event several minutes later. The father sits stunned at the parlour table, a letter crumpled in his hand, and the mother (with braided hair) seems to have thrown herself in despair upon the floor. One child looks up at the sudden shock.

Nothing explains this dramatic event.

In the second panel, a woman in black — a widow, perhaps — sits at a bedroom window, gazing in resigned sadness at a distant moon. Another woman, with braided hair, kneels before the widow with her head buried in the seated woman's lap, as if she has been crying or pleading. Again, nothing explains the anguish.

Only when the eye moves to the third panel does the purport of the crushed letter and the distraught mother's actions become clear. One can only assume the father has discovered a note from his wife's secret lover or perhaps received a letter from a friend warning him of his wife's betrayal, for in the third painting, the same mother with braided hair now stands in grief under a bridge, and in her arms she carries a small infant bundled in rags. Over the scene, a cold and distant moon shines down.

In the painting, Egg has revealed the blackest story — the consequence of adultery. A family destroyed, children in shock, and the betrayer rightly punished with eternal despair for such vile transgression. No series of images could have been more truthful, more burning, more morally effective. It was my own guess that the woman in the pictures must have been reading French novels. She'd clearly been seduced away from her solemn vows by the vileness of romance. Yet that was no excuse. The painting rightly revealed the destructive power of lust, whatever the cause. Once married, always married. Anything else was forbidden. Augustus Egg had painted the most important emblem of our time.

I gripped his arm tightly, feeling almost faint. Perhaps no statement about the truth of all our lives had ever been so profoundly made. This was Shakespeare in art. It would forever represent our highest values to future generations.

The next morning, I had hardly time to dress when Mrs. Potsherd in her white cap hurried into my room and announced that Egg was arrived downstairs and waiting. It seemed oddly inappropriate to call at such an early hour. My poor, weak heart hammered with anticipation. He stood when I entered the drawing room, still holding his black top hat in his hand.

"I do ask your forgiveness for this early call. Would you mind if we went for a walk — in the garden, perhaps?"

"I would be delighted." Although we had no garden — except for the tiny rose garden Mr. Dickens personally attended to — and it was not a place to walk. Instead, I led Mr. Egg to the grounds behind the house, outside the brick wall, where one could look out over wheat fields and woods. The morning sun had not yet burned off a low-lying mist. All about us birds sang and whistled as if we were strolling through an aviary. Mr. Egg whistled, too, under his breath, and for the longest, most awkward while, we seemed to stroll here and there with no other purpose but wheezing and whistling. I attempted efforts at conversation, but Egg resounded with little more than "Ah, yes" and "Hmmmm."

Finally, he halted, seeming to have reached a decision. He turned to me and gripped me by both arms.

"Miss Hogarth," he said bluntly. "I'm sure you've long known you have been my choice in life for so many years. It is my own fears and reservations have prevented me from speaking."

His hands trembled on my arms, and his head wobbled ever so slightly, but he looked me directly in the eye.

"I've known no woman with more grace and charm than you possess. I've known none with such wit, such devotion, such — hmmmm."

He seemed to run out of praise entirely. And while his eyes gazed into mine, he wheezed a moment through his nose. Then he recalled his place in the text.

"Miss Hogarth — Georgina — may I call you Georgina? You hold it in your powers to make me the happiest man in the world. I understand you may need time to think this over, but I've waited so many years, I can surely give you the time necessary to search your heart."

My weak heart exploded against the walls of my chest. Nothing like this could have been expected. He was such a tender, gentle man, so clearly sincere and generous in his praise. My cheeks and throat raged with heat. I could hardly breathe.

"Oh, sir," I finally whispered. "My feelings are too great and too confused at this moment to express. Nothing in my life will equal the great honour you've given me."

He nodded, almost bowed, as if he knew what I was about to say — as of course, he must have known.

"My dear Mr. Egg, I shall cherish your expression and the dear warmth of your feelings forever. But, sir, I'm already betrothed."

He stopped wheezing. For a moment, his dear large head bobbed about without focus. Slowly, deliberately, he withdrew his hands from my arms. I could see bluish paint under his fingernails.

"Do I understand correctly?"

"You do, sir. I'm ashamed you should not have known. I would have done anything to spare your feelings. And I'm ashamed to confess it's a secret betrothal, so very dishonourable in the public' eye should it be found out. But there it is, sir, nonetheless. I can never return your great gesture without receiving even more dishonour."

His large head quavered ever so slightly. And then, because he was a gentleman, he gathered up his feelings, looked me directly in the eye, and said, "Whoever the person is, he has won the grandest prize in England. I congratulate him. And I assure you, Miss Hogarth, your secret will remain sealed forever in my heart."

He bowed, offered me his arm, and walked me back to the house, where he declined my offer of breakfast coffee, mentioning a pressing engagement in London. I watched him drive away in his carriage, down Gravesend Road as far as I could see, the carriage growing smaller and smaller, like the sun moving behind a cloud. Had my emotions not already been engaged and the ceremony itself already arranged, I should have felt more pain. Mr. Egg was, without doubt, the second greatest man in England.

For the sake of the servants, Charles pretended to be upset with me. He spent several days barking and stomping. He did it all for others. Our own fate was already settled. I dressed in white, of course — a simple white gown with a delicate lace overlay. I'd chosen a modest older style without hoops, although I still wore several crinolines. And I selected a delicate, rather demure poke bonnet that seemed so much more proper for that time of evening, and so much more conservative. Of course, I wore a white silk mantle over my shoulders, and glad I was, because although Gad's Hill was twenty miles from the sea, the marsh country across Gravesend Road leading down to the river was full of raw mist and sudden pockets of chill. The sun had already set when Mr. Dickens took my arm and we crossed the road. In the slant of chill and fading light, we passed first through the alder trees and pollards, stepping on into the bleak marshes, where scattered cattle fed, crossing through gates and over dykes and mounds. The leaden line of the river beckoned to us. A mist rose up and hid the lowing cattle. I shivered once, and Charles pressed my arm closer to him. My dress caught frequently on the grasses, tugging at me, like nature trying to warn me, to hold me back from what we were about to do. Charles never hesitated, taking large, manly strides.

As the darkness drew closer, he told me about his childhood. How when he was only five or six — "Just a pip of a lad," he said — his father had more than once walked with him up Gravesend Road, and how his father, a ne'er-do-well, a failure, pointed one dirty finger at Gad's Hill and said, "There, boy. See that house? When you thrive, you'll be able to own such a house as that. Mark me well, boy."

I'd heard the story many times. Long before he purchased the house, Charles had used it as the model for Scrooge's former school in *A Christmas Carol*. But I knew how important all this was to him. He had succeeded on his own talents, he had become the greatest author in England, perhaps the world, all through his own effort. On this night, as the grey mist continued to flow in off the river, we marched through reeds and over mounds, toward some vague memory of a church once located there, with a half-sunken graveyard, it was said. In my pocket I held tight to the wedding ring I knew Charles would present to me. The time had come and the secret would be mine forever. I was not dreaming it, not this time. This time, Charles held me close, pushing ahead toward the past that would seal our future. Sometimes even now I'm not sure how it all was. The images are unstable now. But we were so mystically transported it must have been true. The mist became a swirling fog, wrapping about us both like the cold breath of the old river. Through the fog, I thought I could make out the ghostly outlines of a church surrounded by leaning monuments to the dead. The door seemed open, and in the approaching darkness, a faint candle must have burned inside, the only light for the ceremony we might have performed.

"It's strange," I said to Charles, "for although I've never walked here before, it reminds me, too, of my own childhood. A time when I got lost in a marsh near Swansea. My family was on holiday and I wandered away — I must have been very small, perhaps three or four — and I could hear my brothers calling out to me. 'Biddy!' — that was my childhood name — 'Biddy!' they called, but for reasons I couldn't explain, even knowing I was lost, I hid from them and ran farther into the marsh. I think I believed I was playing a game, but in my heart I also knew it was one of those few chances I would ever have to control my own destiny. I didn't do it without thinking. It was a choice, and I made it, knowing I might be lost forever."

Ellen Ternan

WHEN you think back on the great passions of your life, the temptations, the insanity, driven by your body, your anger, your desire, it seems so foreign. You know it happened. Memory tells you so. The event, the passion, the pulse of excitement in the flesh. But memory sees it darkly. As if it happened to someone else. You remember the feeling without the feeling. You remember you were in love without the love. You struggle to recall what it felt like, and in some way it seems only queer.

Do you want to know what I remember? How strange it is, the small sad things that never leave us. You recall the big things, of course. They seem perfunctory. Obligatory. As if they were official papers carried about in your pocketbook. What your heart remembers are other things, little moments no one else will ever know.

Mr. Dickens was obsessed with keeping himself clean. He liked me to cut his toenails, his ear hairs, his nose hairs. When he bathed, he might take an hour or more, sloshing and scrubbing and blowing. I would wash his back with a sponge. Mrs. Smarthy would bring new buckets of cold water every so often. He had a theory about cold water being better for you. I would wash his hair, his beard — or soap his chest or clean between his toes. Mrs. Smarthy would come in with another bucket and dump it over his head to wash out the soap, and Mr. Dickens would bellow and howl and moan. He loved being pampered, like all little boys.

I kept Mrs. Smarthy with me whenever I was on the Continent. She was like a grandmother to me. She chattered for hours as we rode a train to Marseille or Vienna. In Paris, she laid out silk frocks for the theatre, guarded my jewellery from prying maids, dressed my hair.

"You're not to be late, Dorene," she said. "You know you have a cold. It won't do to stay out late with a cold."

"I'll try to be home early, Mrs. Smarthy."

"And wear your mantle at all times."

"Yes, Mrs. Smarthy."

She hugged me, smelling like soap. She was one of those old women whose skin had grown tighter instead of wrinkling. It looked like polished marble. The whites of her eyes had yellowed. Behind the eyes, she was tender, and she guarded me well. She leaned close to my ear, as if she were about to impart the secret of life.

"When you get to be a very old lady like I am," she whispered, "you'll know."

I nodded, waiting for her to go on.

She studied my face carefully, considering whether I was mature enough to understand. Then she whispered, "The only wisdom is the heft of the resurrection," and she nodded several times as if to assure me she meant it.

"Thank you, Mrs. Smarthy."

"Think nothing of it."

*

Mr. Dickens began a new novel called *Great Expectations*. He had to write one or two chapters every week. The pressure was terrible. He rushed to France to visit me, taking the night train from London, crossing on the morning ferry, then hiring a carriage with a driver to rush him to me at a hidden villa in Condette. We spent a day together, a night together. He talked about Pip and Biddy and Joe Gargery, working out the plot while he talked. Sometimes, he jotted down quick notes, but he seemed to envision it all in his head. The characters spoke to him, he said. Sometimes they objected to something he wanted them to do or say. Sometimes, they told him the exact words to write down. It sounded all rather odd to me.

Plots evolved rapidly, changed, were abandoned. Sudden breakthroughs made him swing me about in his arms before disappearing to his writing table, where he scribbled outlines or reminders or whole chapters. Then he was gone, leaving in the rushed blackness before dawn the next morning. Back to London, writing on his lap on the boat, in the train, rushing pages to the printer.

When the pressure became too great, he would cable me to hurry immediately to London, and I would gather up Miranda and travel alone, leaving Mrs. Smarthy behind to care for the house. Mr. Dickens did not like me to travel without a chaperon. There was always a certain amount of grumbling and barking, but he would grow lonely or need my advice on a new chapter, and then he would give in and send another cable, *Come now*. In London, I stayed at Ampthill Square, but sometimes it would be a day or two before Mr. Dickens could find a moment to see me.

I remember most vividly the morning I heard the Great

Man pounding on the door for Hubbard to let him in this instant.

Mr. Dickens picked me up and swirled me around.

"We're going to America," he cried. "Yes, yes, America. It's all arranged. To America!"

"Mr. Dickens, what can you mean?"

"A reading tour. The Americans love me. Forster and Wills think it a good time to take advantage of it, while everyone is still clamouring over the first chapters of *Great Expectations*. New York! Boston! Philadelphia! Everywhere there is to go, just you and me."

"Me?"

"Yes, yes, that's the idea, don't you see. The two of us. And Hubbard, of course." Mr. Dickens nodded at Hubbard, who stood behind him holding Mr. Dickens' top hat. Hubbard smiled nervously and ran his free hand over his bald head, as if he were already concerned about making a good appearance in America.

Mr. Dickens swirled me about. "And Mrs. Smarthy, of course. And an American manager. And a publicist, I suppose. I don't know yet who that shall be. It's a wonderful opportunity for the two of us to be alone."

He swung me about again and hugged me to him. I was still wearing my morning gown, and he looked down into my face with the grin of an orphan who's just found tuppence in the street.

"It's all settled then?" I asked.

"No, no, not quite. A million details to work out." He slipped his gold watch from his pocket. "I've got to hurry back to the office. No more time."

I gave him a peck on the cheek as he stomped out the door. *America!* I thought. *I'm going to America!*

*

Sometimes, Mamma and Fanny would travel from Florence to Genoa, where I would meet them. We would luxuriate under a brilliant sky the colour of bluebells. Several times, Mamma came alone to visit me at Condette. She still wore scoop bonnets that were very out of fashion, insisting she was too old to change. There was nothing to do but try not to appear embarrassed by her lack of fashion. When Mr. Dickens was with us, it seemed not to matter. He spent so much time teasing her and laughing with her, I felt almost ignored. We would go to Paris together for the ballet. Or travel by train — to Aix or Zurich or Cherbourg. The three of us, Mr. Dickens, Mamma, and me, with Miranda on my lap, hidden under my mantle because the railroads had silly rules against carrying dogs in public carriages. Sometimes, we returned with Mr. Dickens to England, where we caught the Mail Train to York or Bristol or Coventry so that he could give another of his famous readings. Afterward—after the crowds had finished cheering him, even chasing his carriage through the streets—he would return to the inn where Mamma and I waited up.

We played all fours by the light of a coal-oil lamp. When he played cards, Mr. Dickens kept a bottle of claret beside him. Every so often he poured a little more into his glass, and sometimes he poured a tiny portion for Mamma.

"No, no." She pushed the glass away.

"Just this once, madam. A small drop for the digestive system."

"Perhaps just one tiny drop."

And then, with her cheeks flushed, Mamma played the trump.

"Ah!" cried Dickens. "My dear Mrs. Ternan! What's the

meaning of this!" He loved to win, but when he lost, he laughed graciously and congratulated everyone all around.

"A triumph." he said. "A real triumph!"

Later, after the lamps were snuffed and I climbed up into the four-poster in the damp English night, Mr. Dickens pouted. He changed in the dressing room, appearing in the moonlight in his wool nightshirt and nightcap. Georgina had embroidered the nightcap in fancy red stitching. The red stitching swirled about lovingly to form flowers and vines.

Mr. Dickens hemmed and hawed about the room, waiting for me to sink deep into the cold white feather bed. Finally, he climbed in on his side and pretended to sleep, adjusting and readjusting the nightcap firmly over his head.

"Is something the matter, Mr. Dickens?"

"Nothing at all, no, no. Of course not. A little tired, I believe."

He turned his back to me and pretended to settle down. I knew he was pouting because he had lost. I waited for a while, silently, until he began again to adjust his nightcap and punch his pillow.

Finally, I said, "You know, Mr. Dickens, you looked especially handsome tonight. You must have been a great success at the reading."

"Well, it did go well, I thought."

"So many young women seeking your autograph, I suspect."

"No, Princess. Are you jealous?"

He laughed then, softening. Rolling back to me and snuggling. We were almost never intimate in England. But he liked to cuddle, and by the next morning he would wake up feeling boisterous and loud and happy again. He was always a new man in the morning. As if in some way, just by awakening and still being Charles Dickens, he had proven his own triumph. Nothing could defeat him. Certainly not his own pettiness.

I took Mamma aside and told her it would be better to lose at all fours, and she would try for a while. Then she would get a certain look in her eye, especially after a drop of claret, and she would trump him again.

Mr. Dickens took a lease on a small farmhouse for me in the Loire Valley. The old white stone building was not very pretty, but it sat on a hill where one could look out over patches of woods and blue-green pastures of sheep and horses. The house was called La Sainte Vie, and the stone walls were two feet thick. Looking through the window was like looking through a deep picture frame. Inside, it was dark and cool, a little damp. Outside, the light was so bright it hurt your eyes, like a flash of sunlight in a mirror. Through a break in the hills, you could see a slow river, magnetic blue and quivering, with a sensuous curve, like the waist of a dancing girl. The air smelled ripe with vineyards, a warm perfume in the blood. I was leaning on the cool deep window ledge and wearing only a chemise. Mr. Dickens came quietly up behind me and, with both hands, lifted my hair. My hair was thick and golden, and when he lifted it the air cooled the back of my neck.

He could have pressed against me, but he held back, both of us silent, until finally he bent forward, his mouth brushing my neck, and blew gently on it, tenderly. I could smell that faint odour of cigar that never left his beard.

I turned into him, the chemise tangling about me, twisted over my breasts. In France, Mr. Dickens was always charged with sensual energy. I thought he would sweep me up and carry me back to the still-rumpled bed.

He said, "For a moment, from behind, I thought you were Catherine—when we were young, of course. Catherine is changed now, very changed. But for a moment . . ."

He walked to the mirror and adjusted his coat. "Isn't it odd," he said, "how the memory works. From behind, I could have sworn you were Catherine when she was young." He strolled out of the room. I did not know what had happened. Then, slowly, as if my soul had left my body, my hands began to shake. My teeth began to grind. I could hear him come out below through the French doors onto the terrace. He was talking to the gardener in French, his voice going on and on about something. He wanted "*les fleurs*" planted along a stone walkway. I was shaking so hard I had to grip the dresser. In the mirror, I could see my face all blotched, crying silently, then gasping to find my breath. It was the same mirror he had adjusted his lapels in. I hated him, despised him. I turned and ran to the window, leaning out all at once and shouting down, "You pig, you baboon, you arse's mother!"

The old gardener looked up at me in puzzled shock. Mr. Dickens had vanished, and the gardener was all alone with his flowers.

"Oh," I whispered.

The gardener tipped his hat and bowed with great dignity. "*Je crois, Mademoiselle, que vous plaisantez ce matin.*"

The time wasn't right. Forster and Wills talked it over. Legal problems. The American tour couldn't be arranged. A short delay. Several months. Perhaps next year. Forster and Wills decided this and that, wrote letters, huddled in secret, discussed options. Mr. Dickens was cheerful as always. More important now was the ending to *Great Expectations*. The public queued at newsstands to buy each issue of the magazine. No one talked of anything else. The ending had to be a triumph. But Forster and Wills didn't like it. Pip loses Estella forever. No, no, they cried. Too advanced for today's public. Too harsh. His readers would never accept it, they needed a wedding. But Dickens didn't want a happy ending. Instinct, he said. His artistic instinct told him the usual wedding was all wrong, simply all wrong.

Wilkie Collins proposed a new ending in which Estella dies of malaria in India, leaving the wealth of her first husband to Pip. And Pip, in his grief, having learned generosity and humility, would place all the money into a trust for Biddy's Little Joe, giving him — tra la — Great Expectations. It would be a wonderful irony, Collins argued. Dickens tried writing it, but after showing it about to several colleagues, he burned the only copy.

Finally, another friend, a man named Bulwer-Lytton, proposed a compromise. Mr. Dickens liked his suggestion and brought it to me for my opinion. I was with Mamma in Paris, where we were attending the opera. Mr. Dickens was waiting when we returned to the hotel. He was pacing in a circle about an Oriental carpet, reading and rereading five sheets of paper. What did I think? He would wait. My advice would decide the issue. Mamma withdrew, and I sat in a chair near the curtained balcony. Above me, a flickering gas lamp hissed, casting a yellow glow about the room. Mr. Dickens took up pacing again. His original ending covered two sheets of paper. The second ending, the new one, covered almost three.

"Everyone thinks Bulwer-Lytton is right," he said. "It goes against my original vision. But my fans. I have to think of my public. They expect the ending of a novel to give them what they've never had — a dream fulfilled. Maybe I was wrong. How could Estella look down at Pip from her carriage window and not see love on his face? How could she not realise the right thing to do?"

He paced in a circle, unknowingly tracing the pattern on the carpet as he stomped about. He turned to me in my chair. In the tarnished flicker of the gas lamp, his face seemed more aged than ever, doubting his friends, doubting the inner voice that always served him well.

He knelt in front of me.

"It's up to you, Princess. I trust you. You'll tell me the absolute truth. You'll not tell me what the public wants or what the effect on sales will be. You'll tell me the truth, I know you will."

He looked into my eyes.

In the first ending, Estella's heart has not changed, even though her husband has mistreated her, even though Pip still loves her. It's true, she has learned something, but her heart remains cold and white as a distant star. She rides away forever in her carriage, leaving Pip alone. The first ending was very sad and very real. I read it several times with great dread for the life I had chosen.

In the second ending — the one all his friends were now recommending — Estella's heart has changed. Or at least, because of her years of tragedy, she has the potential for changing, for seeing that Pip is the man she should have chosen. She is a woman. She has chosen wrong in the past. She must right the past. In the second ending, Pip thinks Estella's heart is softened. The second ending offered hope. A shadow of hope. Dickens' fans would be uplifted. But Pip is only a man. He doesn't understand how a woman plays many roles. He thinks it is for him Estella has softened.

I didn't know Bulwer-Lytton, but it was what a man *would* think. Mr. Dickens could easily believe it. Mr. Dickens thought he was Pip. He thought a beautiful woman couldn't help but see the error of her ways. Her heart would soften and she would realise it was always him she had loved. Men are like that. Men have only one truth and they cling to it. Like a mathematical problem. Estella has added up her life incorrectly and then she discovers her error and adds it up again with such logical results. The correct answer is Pip. But if Estella did change, it was only because she saw one of the other truths in her life. Men don't have a clue how it works. For a woman, truth is not the answer or the solution or the destination. It's only a shady stopping place along the road.

I looked at Mr. Dickens kneeling at my feet. I looked at him with as much sincerity as I could muster.

"You must go with the second ending," I said. "Your friends in London are right. The greatness of your art lies there, in hope and comfort and prayer."

He squeezed my hands. "I knew I could trust you."

I stood up and moved into the bedroom, where Mamma was laying out her nightgown. She'd overheard everything. "Don't worry, Ellen," she said. "It's often necessary to lie to a man — especially when it's the only kind of truth he can hear."

The trip to America was settled. Next year, certain. Then, it was cancelled. We must await a more propitious time. Something about the Lyceum Circuit. Travelling through Ohio in winter would be a disaster. Ohio, it seemed, was somewhere on the frontier where roads were nonexistent. We would be forced to travel on canal barges, but the canals froze over in winter. Next summer would be better. The financial arrangements were not at all satisfactory. Soon, very soon, we would be going to America. I must be patient.

*

Over the years, I fell into a pattern. I summered in France. Mamma would visit from Florence. Or Maria would travel from London and stay with me a month or two. The theatre season in London was slow each summer. In spite of Mr. Dickens' continued efforts to help her, Maria's career seemed to be fading. She picked up only small parts, here and there. There were always touring groups, but she no longer wanted to play in dirty little towns or sleep in faded hotels. The following winter, there was nothing for her at all in London. She wrote that she had agreed, out of desperation, to join a tour the next spring, and she would visit me later, or perhaps join Fanny in Florence. All of us seemed to know the tour would be her final appearance on the stage. Her letters sounded afraid and sad, confused, and not a little bitter. Her beauty was fading. No one dared tell her the truth, but she knew it anyway.

Then, in early January, I received a thick letter from Oxford. After a performance of *Cymbeline* — the previous November — she had met a prosperous young man with high connections. Now, he had proposed, and Maria accepted. The family was upset at the idea of their son marrying an actress. He belonged to a family of clergy, solicitors, and brewers. They were all very dull, respectable people. Maria was working hard to charm them. She told them she had gone onstage at the suggestion of the famous Charles Dickens, after personally appearing with the Great Man in one of his own plays. She left everyone with the idea she was really only an amateur doing it for a lark. The possibility of a connection to Charles Dickens — even a remote connection — brought about a decided change. The young man's mother invited Maria to tea, where they got along quite well indeed. Arrangements for the wedding were begun. She and Rowland were to be married in

London at St. Matthew's in June. Her letters were full of jokes, high spirits, and energy.

Later, in May, only two weeks before the wedding, just as I was talking with Mrs. Smarthy about which frocks to take with me, Mamma and Fanny arrived from Florence. It seemed that after an exchange of many upsetting letters, and much heartfelt discussion, everyone had decided — that is, Maria, Fanny, and Mamma had decided — under the circumstances, you see, that it might be best — for the time being, just this once — if I did not attend the wedding.

Maria felt very bad about it all, afraid to bring up the subject with me herself. But her young man's family did have to be considered. They were so very respectable in Oxford, which was a very respectable town, as everyone knew. A respectable family might well ask questions. They might even investigate if their suspicions were aroused. Respectability had a price, and for Maria, at the moment, as her wedding approached, the price she was paying was fear.

Mrs. Smarthy withdrew. Fanny stood by the window, looking out through two-foot-thick stone walls. The old wooden sashes were flung open, and a warm, sunshiny breeze lifted the curtains about her. She stood with her back to me.

"You have to understand," she said, quietly. "All of us know the truth. Without you, Ellen, we would probably be on Gin Row by this time. We owe you everything. This is not easy for us to say. But Maria needs you to do this one thing more for her."

Mamma cried quietly. Her hair had begun to streak with grey. Fanny stood at the window, reluctant to turn around. Mamma sat in the wing-back chair, her face buried in her handkerchief, afraid to look up.

My heart closed tight in my chest. But not tight with anger

or hatred or bitterness. They were my family, and I under-stood about family. Maria was playing the most important role of her life, and in *her* performance I was, after all, a mere extra. Extras cannot appear onstage and drop a tray or knock over a candle. Extras can do absolutely nothing to distract the audi-ence from its rightful attention on the main players. I knew how to perform either part and had done so many times. For a brief moment, I considered going to the wedding in disguise, but there was only one proper action to take.

I sent a cable to Maria and her fiancé — a Mr. Taylor of the respectable Taylor family of Oxford — expressing my deepest regrets. It seemed I was suddenly taken with ill health. I wished them a most happy and quiet married life together, promising a visit as soon as my health improved. In truth, Mamma — perhaps from the strain or from her age — did take to her bed with exhaustion. She remained behind with me, sit-ting each afternoon in the shade on the terrace and drinking tea with just a tiny drop of brandy to help her recover.

Fanny travelled on alone and reported it was a very grand marriage indeed. So many had expressed their regrets that Mamma and I had been unable to attend. Best of all, Fanny wrote, Maria glowed with happiness. In some unexplained way, through some confusion, her husband had misunder-stood her age and thought she was only twenty. A good time was had by all.

I was reading *Jane Eyre* on the lawn at La Sainte Vie when I came across a passage toward the end. Jane, now the mis-tress of a small country school, sits in the doorway fantasizing what it might have been like had she run off to France with Rochester.

What is better? *(she asks)* — To have surrendered to temptation; listened to passion; made no painful effort — no struggle — but to have sunk down in the silken snare; fallen asleep on the flowers covering it; wakened in a southern clime, amongst the luxuries of a pleasure villa; to have been now living in France, Mr. Rochester's mistress; delirious with his love half my time — for he would — oh, yes, he would have loved me well for a while. He *did* love me — no one will ever love me so again. . . . Whether it is better, I ask, to be a slave in a fool's paradise at Marseilles — fevered with delusive bliss one hour — suffocating with the bitterest tears of remorse and shame the next — or to be a village schoolmistress, free and honest, in a breezy mountain nook in the healthy heart of England?

I had never realised with such overwhelming force that those who write books have no idea what real life is like. The passage was so jejune I tossed the novel aside. I found it no more difficult to acknowledge I was now a mistress than to acknowledge I had once been an actress. All my life I had been an outlaw in society. Actress, mistress — both were damned in sermons on Sunday. We were railed at in Parliament by those who passed laws against us. Gentlemen dallied with us but hid us from the public, using us only in secret. The ordinary bloke leered or snickered, even while fantasising about our wicked ways, wishing just once, on some hot summer's night, his dull wife would smell so sweet or reach out and touch him with so bold a hand. All of them lusted for our persons, yet they would have felt shamed to walk openly on the street by our side.

Ladies pretended we did not exist. Homely wives of merchants bore their bitterness with bile and despised their husbands for dreaming silent fantasies. Women in every walk of life hated us because we lived in comfort and sensual luxury —

and with a power they could never find courage to even dream about, except as Jane Eyre dreamed, retreating always in the end to that breezy mountain nook of their commonness, justifying their cowardice, their fear, with words like "principle" and "duty" and "purity."

I scoffed at Jane Eyre. She makes the wrong choice. Then, through her tears, she tries to justify it. I was supposed to feel happy for her at the end of the novel because she marries a maimed and blinded Rochester, a man who has lost his ancestral manor and his fierce male pride. Mr. Rochester was a giant of dark passion, a true man who could have loved her with brute strength and tender desire. Instead, because she listens to *principle,* he's destroyed, and she marries a ghost. I suppose the common reader must have cheered. Rochester has been tamed. Jane claims she is "in her ascendancy." But the breezy mountain nook is nothing more than conventional dullness, lacking in spirit and denying madness and joy. An hour of madness in defiance of the world is worth our all, and lump the rest.

The American trip was finally settled. Mr. Dickens and I would sail for New York, where we would spend several weeks. Then we would travel variously by train and stagecoach to places like Boston and Chicago. I would need to limit myself to a single trunk. Mr. Dickens proposed I speak with Moses & Sons about the proper travelling outfits. Before I could make arrangements, the trip was cancelled, scheduled now for next fall, certain.

Mr. Dickens and I were staying in a chalet at Zell am See when I received a cable from Fanny. Could I come to Florence as soon as possible? Something important to confide, she said. I knew her career in opera was not going well, and now, I realised, she needed me to give support, to cheer her up. Mamma had been staying with Fanny throughout the spring, but it was clear Fanny needed a confidante her own age. Would Mr. Dickens be so kind as to spare me?

As always, Mr. Dickens was understanding. Helping my family had become an almost full-time emotional commitment. In any case, it was necessary for him to return to England in a few weeks, and this would relieve his mind at my being lonely. We travelled together by coach to Vienna, where he put me on a train alone to Italy. He waved his top hat in the station, and I leaned out the window, waving back, watching him grow smaller and smaller. Mrs. Smarthy travelled with me, carrying Miranda hidden in a picnic basket. We took only six trunks, and they were stored in the baggage car. The train rumbled and rattled and jerked, soot flew in the windows, and outside, the most spectacular white-capped mountains in the world passed slowly by. Three days later, we steamed our way through sun-dried hills of Tuscany. Fanny met me at the station, a soot-blackened building in a city of white stone and red tile. The heat was stunning. It seemed to envelop my body like a man's hands. I felt almost faint.

Thomas Trollope was there as well. Extraordinarily tall, he towered over everyone, bearish and full of laughter. "So very glad," he shouted. "So very glad." He helped me into the carriage, a brougham with lacy spoked wheels painted the colour of raspberries — so very Italian, I thought.

"Don't worry about your trunks," he bellowed. "The servants will take care of everything." And then he disappeared in the crowd to personally oversee the loading of my trunks, as if the servants indeed could not be trusted.

Fanny did not seem at all distraught. I expected to find her disconsolate, but she was wearing her green spectacles and a Zouave jacket with a Garibaldi chemisette, and on her left wrist, a heavy pearl bracelet that certainly had not been among her effects when she last left England. She seemed Bohemian in a delightfully free way.

"Tom," she said — carelessly waving the hand with the bracelet — "Tom does take care of everything. You'll find his mother just as eager, I assure you."

"I'm glad to hear it," I said.

"Absolutely charming. And so very intelligent. Did I mention she writes novels, too? Oh yes, the whole family writes novels."

The carriage started with a jerk and lumbered slowly through hot crowded streets.

"Now for the surprise." Fanny leaned forward, her face glowing. "I am writing a novel, as well."

"A novel?"

"Absolutely."

She settled back and waited for the huzzahs she seemed to think would float down from wisps of high white clouds overhead.

"I've been in touch with your very own Charles Dickens, who speaks well of it and believes he might find a place for it in his magazine."

She might as well have told me Mr. Dickens had joined a monastery in Macedonia.

"You're not serious, of course. Mr. Dickens has said nothing about this to me."

"Oh yes, very serious. Of course, he hasn't *promised* to publish me, but he has indeed sent encouragement."

"Encouragement?"

"Yes, is that so shocking to you? Did you think I have no talents?"

"Many talents, Fanny. What happened to opera?"

She raised one arm and pointed. "The Uffizi is down that street. You can almost see it. We'll go there soon. Wonderful paintings, I must say. You'll be very impressed."

"Fanny, what happened to opera?"

She leaned forward again, reaching out to take one of my hands in hers. The carriage bounced and edged its way slowly through narrow streets.

"I have become a governess," she whispered.

"What!"

"Tom has hired me as governess for his daughter, Bice. His wife died, you know."

"Several years ago, I understand."

"But Bice needed a woman's guidance. I give her singing lessons. We draw together."

"Fanny, slow down. Tell me what's going on here."

"You'll love the Villa Ricorboli. It was a disaster when I arrived, books everywhere, carpenters building shelves, painters painting. Someone had to take charge, don't you see? And Tom was so grateful."

"This is leading somewhere, isn't it?"

"He writes all the time. Standing up! Can you imagine? He was so grateful for my efforts, organising his library, taking command of the servants, giving much needed affection to Bice."

"Tell me the truth, Fanny."

The carriage bumped over the last of the cobbles, and we travelled away from Florence, with all its domes and churches, following a winding path through an olive orchard, climbing steadily.

Fanny sat back, smiling and fanning herself. "Ellen, we're to be married."

"What?"

"It's a very distinguished family, you know. I haven't met Anthony Trollope yet. But he's almost as famous as your Mr. Dickens. And Tom publishes novels in Mr. Dickens' magazine. His mother is a delightful writer, too, and she plays any number of instruments with such grace. Everyone is distinguished, you see. We've all become quite proper, haven't we?"

I looked at her face, deviously happy in the bouncing carriage, the mottled shade of olive trees passing overhead, and everything came to me then, like a burst of hot Italian sunshine. Fanny wanted to become distinguished.

Count Bertoni dined with us on several occasions. Tom Trollope ordered a table set in the afternoon shade behind the house. The air had that warm sensuous smell of ripening grapes and wine and fine cheese. Mamma wore her black scoop bonnet, but even she seemed to have relaxed more as she aged. She laughed and teased and openly drank several glasses of bright red Chianti. Huge round loaves of bread were passed about. The way to eat the bread was to break off a chunk and dip it — bite by bite — into a bowl of fragrant oil and spices. We ate various kinds of pasta with white sauces and tangy olives. Seldom in my life had I ever allowed myself to take more than a sip or two of any wine, but there, in the laughter and heat and the burring murmur of insects in the orchard — with Tom Trollope laughing and Count Bertoni leaning over and teasing Bice in her pink dress — there, where Mrs. Trollope wore her white cap and presided over the table with grace and good humour, insisting I take one more glass, there I found nothing so much in all the world but a desire to lean back in my chair — something I had always been taught a lady never does — and to breathe in the sharp aroma of a wine that must have been pressed from bitter cherries.

"Chianti Classico," Tom Trollope called it. "Made from our own vineyards." He poured me another glass despite my weak protests. "They say these vineyards date from the Renaissance. Think of it! You could be drinking wine from the same vine Dante drank from."

Fanny made a toast. "To *Il Paradiso,* where the light of love is forever."

"No, no." Bertoni lifted his glass. "To *Il Purgatorio,* where the darkest passion burns brightest."

Tom shook his head. "No again! Let us raise our glasses to the *Commedia* of life itself!"

"Hear! Hear!"

We spent long afternoons chatting. We went for walks with umbrellas to protect us from the ripe sun. I grew lazy like a cat. It was so easy to cease being British and luxuriate in becoming Italian.

Bertoni had lovely dark eyes, almost black, with a dark Mediterranean skin, having come from a family in Sicily. He was not really a Count, he confessed to me as we walked behind the others through a field of blood red poppies. His family owned sulphur mines and had grown rich and greedy. They married a daughter off to a Baron from an old aristocratic family in Rome, and without any legal right whatsoever, his parents adopted the crest as their own. The family name wasn't even Bertoni, and although he had studied poetry briefly at Palermo and, later, the University of Rome, it was all halfhearted.

"I'm not a gentleman," he said. "I'm a fraud, really. Not

what I seem. And in a few years, I must return and take over the business." He sighed. For a moment, we walked in silence.

"Sulphur mines," he said. "Can you imagine? *Il diavolo incarnato.* And there will be an arranged marriage, no doubt, with some horribly plump but very wealthy girl from a family that sells salt."

He laughed, throwing back his head and at the same time placing one hand in the small of my back.

"Can't you see me married with five or six little black bambinos?"

"Sir, I cannot at all see you like that."

The others had pulled ahead of us and were waiting about vaguely on top of a hill.

"No, no, neither can I. No doubt I will take a lover. Don't you agree, no matter what the world does to you, you still have a right — in the heat of a dark night — to find at least one private moment of passion? Shouldn't everyone have at least one moment in a lifetime? Do you think badly of me for having such thoughts?"

He did not remove his hand. And then he did, and we went on up the hill to join the others where everyone was chatting about the weather.

Several months after I returned to England, Fanny married Mr. Trollope. Her letters were excited and happy. It had been a very Italian wedding with a hundred English guests. A string quartet played Vivaldi. Pietro Romano, Fanny's former opera master, sang an aria that brought tears to everyone's eyes. And toasts to their happiness had gone on into early morning hours. Before Fanny and Tom retired to their rooms, Bice hugged Fanny and called her Mother. They hugged and cried.

After a short honeymoon in Trieste, which, Fanny explained, was a small village on the Adriatic, they would settle in the Villa Ricorboli, which was a very distinguished place to live.

Mamma wrote to me that she was so pleased and her life seemed so fulfilled now that Maria and Fanny were successfully married.

Mr. Dickens decided to rent out my house in Ampthill Square. It would provide me with a small annual income, he explained, and he leased a new home for me at Peckham Rye, a small village south of London, nicely located on the rail link to both Waterloo Station, near his offices — and to Gad's Hill, twenty miles or so farther south. Windsor Lodge was set on a gentle rise near a field of grain that sloped to a crooked stream. The stream held back a line of tangled wood. A short distance up the road lay the old Nunhead Cemetery, as beautifully landscaped as if it were a park. The house itself had been recently constructed, and seemed quite modern and imposing. Molly complained greatly because we brought only nine servants with us from Ampthill Square. Her authority had been tampered with. Mr. Dickens noticed nothing, but to me, she was cold and impudent, as if I were responsible for her diminishment.

We had just moved in, and I was directing placement of various pieces of furniture when Mr. Dickens arrived on foot, puffing and proud of himself. He had walked, it seemed, all the way from Gad's Hill.

"I have come to ask you for tea," he said.

"I'll ring for Molly."

"No, no. I've come to ask you to Gad's Hill for tea." He took both my hands and grinned. "I very much want you to see it. And Georgina quite approves. If you change now, the ride by carriage will not take long. We'll be there by five o'clock, certain."

Because I had so long been an actress, I was always prepared for the unexpected: a good actress adjusts, ad-libs a line or two, finds a way to incorporate the surprise into her part. But for this, I was not prepared. I felt myself flush. The heat rushed into my throat, as if I'd swallowed scalding milk. For a moment, I actually wanted to turn and dash out of the room with my apron over my head. Only I didn't have an apron. And Mr. Dickens was obviously so pleased with himself.

I knew in my soul I could not decline his request, although every voice in my heart said no. Gad's Hill had always been the centre of his life away from me. At Gad's Hill, he had been intimate with his wife, or if that ceased long before my time (something he confessed to me late one night), the house was still considered the family home: a place where he raised nine rowdy, adoring children, celebrated birthdays, married off daughters, bid farewell to sons. He had landscaped, planted roses, remodelled rooms, and was even now thinking about adding a magnificent, grand conservatory, one he expected to be among England's finest. Gad's Hill *was* Charles Dickens. Not my Charles Dickens, not the one whose beard smelled of cigars, who wore a nightcap to bed, who sometimes rushed me back to France just so we could love each other with the sashes thrown open in the hot French night at La Sainte Vie. Not *that* Charles Dickens, but the other one, England's Charles Dickens: admired father, playwright, novelist — the one who had risen from a childhood in the blacking factory to a gentleman who accepted commands for tea with Queen Victoria. The one who hosted over a hundred guests at Gad's Hill for Christmas and played a ferocious game of billiards with the Lord Mayor of London.

"Come, come," he said, impatiently. "I've promised Georgina, five o'clock sharp."

Mrs. Smarthy was growing old and more and more declined to travel. I'd left her behind in France, so I changed my frock and dressed my own hair hurriedly. It was still golden, but not so much so. It seemed to have dulled over time, and recently, although I was not yet thirty, I had discovered a grey hair. In the looking glass I could tell I was both angry and frightened. I swept the hair up in a bun and stabbed a comb into it.

On the way to Gad's Hill, every jolt of the gig drove a nail of dread into me. For an hour, I practised my breathing and rehearsed my part. Mr. Dickens talked the whole way. I was about to meet Georgina. She had been such a delightful helpmate to him. "She practically raised my children by hand." He flicked the whip lightly at the horse. "One couldn't find better help anywhere."

He told me how Georgina had turned down a proposal of marriage from Mr. Egg, how she felt the children — his children — needed her too much. "I feel sorry for her," Mr. Dickens confided. "A woman needs to be married, you know. It's part of woman's nature. Children, a home, servants. That's what any woman needs and has a right to expect." We were trotting past a meadow of miniature donkeys. I smoothed the skirt of my frock, a lovely violet satin with a tight bodice, something Mr. Dickens had purchased for me in Paris. I wore a gold brooch he had given me, and a white ribbon around my ankle he had put on me that morning.

"Really," Mr. Dickens said. "I do feel sorry for her sometimes. It's got to be hard on a woman of her delicate nature. So absolutely pure and devoted to the children, you see. With them mostly gone, she's at a loss. A woman needs those things. The truth is, a woman is never a complete woman without children, husband, and hearth. It's biological, isn't it?"

We were both silent, listening to the clop of the horse's hooves. We rode past the donkeys and came upon a field of sheep.

"I'm sure you'll like her," Mr. Dickens finally said. "She needs your support. She's given up everything a woman has a right to expect in life."

We rose up over a hill and started down the other side. "Here we are!" Mr. Dickens pointed. "My little Kentish freehold!"

He stopped the horses directly in front. His face glowed with pride. He was looking at the house through my eyes, and it looked grand to him.

"Five o'clock sharp."

Gad's Hill was a hefty Georgian house of red brick. A cupola perched on the roof, with a weather cock, which even at the moment was gently turning. I did not think the house at all grand. Rather, it seemed a portly English family home with a round porch in front, and great bow windows on each side. The front door opened, and a smallish woman appeared in a grey frock. She was rather thick in the waist and wearing an old-fashioned cap, but with a kindly face, her eyes watery, and breathing deeply, as if she were expecting a friend from long ago.

Mr. Dickens waved, turned the carriage around in the yard of the Falstaff Inn, and drove us back past the house again so I could see it "in the light."

When we finally brought the horses into the drive, Georgina waited for us, her face revealing how much she mirrored Mr. Dickens' pride.

"So pleased to have you call upon us. We've waited a long time for this moment, haven't we?"

She hugged me as I stepped down, smelling faintly of talcum. She was much older than me. I had not considered that Georgina might be old.

"Let me show you around," Mr. Dickens said. "The grand tour!"

He took my arm, and with Georgina following, we went into an entrance hall, where a winding staircase rose up to the first floor. "We're very proud of this." He waved his hand at the stairway. "I removed every other balustrade and inserted panels, you see. Then, Katie painted each panel by hand. Truly artistic, don't you think?"

"Very much so."

"And here's my library." He shuffled me into a room where he pointed out ceiling-high glass bookcases. A red-and-blue carpet covered the floor, and a monstrous desk stood at the bow window, piled high with papers and notes. "This is where I write," he said, with a reverent hush. To one side, a giant wicker wastebasket overflowed with crumpled notes and papers. "No one is allowed to empty this except me." He poked at it with his boot. "Sometimes, I'll realise I've tossed away a line or an image that will take me an hour to search for, but as long as the basket is full, I know nothing is lost."

He spun me about. "And see here."

A glass bookcase had been built onto the back of the door.

"Look closely." He grinned as if there were some kind of secret to be discovered.

For a moment, I could see only row after row of leather bindings, and then the titles began to clear: *Cats Lives, A History of the Middling Ages*. A three-volume set titled *Five Minutes in China*.

Mr. Dickens roared. "Fake titles," he cried. "Fake books. It's my little joke, don't you see?"

He wanted me to laugh, so I did, and I reached up and kissed him on the cheek. He needed so much admiring.

When he threw open the door, Georgina was standing on the other side, smiling like a dotty old aunt waiting for her nephew to appear. The three of us paraded room to room: drawing room, dining room, billiard room, bedrooms. Mr. Dickens pointed to the silk fabric on the sofa. Georgina pointed to the bevelled mirrors. Mr. Dickens pointed out how one could almost see the Castle in Rochester. He seemed quite proud of that. Georgina explained how the dumbwaiter in the hall worked with a pull rope to the kitchen below. And tour the kitchen we did — down another curved staircase — to see the walk-in fireplace and the flagstone floor and inspect the nine pantries.

Tea was served on the back lawn under a tree. For a moment, Mr. Dickens was called away to meet someone who had just arrived. Georgina was a gracious hostess. We chatted about the weather. Finally, as we grew more silent, awaiting Mr. Dickens' return, she turned to me.

"I do want to thank you."

"Thank me?"

"For the great sacrifice you've made." She reached out with one dry little hand and placed it on top of mine. Her eyes looked at me with great sincerity, even admiration. "Perhaps someday, when they write the biographies," she said, "perhaps, they'll give you the credit you deserve."

"What is it I've done?"

She smiled and nodded, as if it were our private little secret. "I knew you would be modest about it," she said. "We're like sisters, aren't we? Only I'm afraid you've paid a far greater price for so noble a deed."

I looked into the swelling tears in her eyes, feeling puzzled, uncomfortable at her sudden gesture of intimacy.

She leaned across and whispered. "I owe everything to you. Charles and I could never have united if you hadn't agreed to be his public diversion." She nodded, as if she knew all about my suffering. "His life and mine, you see." She held out her left hand to show me a simple gold band. "The symbol of our union," she said softly, admiring it, although admitting she usually wore it only when Mr. Dickens was away, as he often was, so very busy at his writing. "He's a novelist, you know. Perhaps you've read some of his works."

"I've had the opportunity," I said.

For a moment I wanted to laugh. But in her face I saw that idle intensity, that hint of fear and confusion that tightens pale skin like vellum. I had seen it before, in the eyes or in the face and hands of so many women, so many governesses, spinsters, maiden aunts — so very many women who had no real place in the world, and found themselves dependent on the charity of others. I could not be rude to her.

"Yes," I said. "I've had the pleasure of reading several of his novels."

"He and I have so little time together." She leaned across the table and whispered confidentially, "Without your help, even the little pleasures we share mightn't have been possible."

In the nearby wood, a lark began to sing, and both of us listened in admiration, silenced by natural beauty. It was then I began to sense that, over the coming years, there would be more visits to Gad's Hill. I could anticipate having coffee alone with Georgina in the new conservatory among the imported flowers and exotic plants. We would be like two strange birds held captive in Mr. Dickens' hothouse, each with our very different plumage, but nonetheless agreeing for the moment to share the same tree in an odd forest.

Mr. Dickens returned back across the lawn with a young woman on his arm. She wore a pale lavender frock with a short-waisted bodice and plain sleeves ending in turned-back cuffs. I had seen her before. She approached me with a quiet confidence.

"Ellen," Mr. Dickens cried out. "Ellen, I should like you to meet my daughter Katie."

Katie held out her gloved hand, a subtle smile on her face. "We met several years ago."

I lifted mine to hers while our eyes held each other. She stepped forward and kissed me lightly on each cheek.

"We're glad you could come. I've hoped for so long we could be friends."

Georgina smiled boldly. "That's already been taken care of."

The American trip was finally set.

"Get ready to leave immediately," Mr. Dickens cried.

Mr. Moses helped me select a travelling wardrobe that could be limited to a single trunk. "You needn't worry about America," he explained. "They have no sense of fashion, I assure you, none at all, indeed, I can assure you." He bowed almost double and clicked me out the door. "A great honour," I heard him say.

Forster and Wills made all the arrangements, although Forster was increasingly concerned about Mr. Dickens' health. Travelling in America was said to be exhausting. But the Great Man scoffed. The timing was right. His admirers needed him. We were to depart from Liverpool in November with a return the next April or May. Six months or more travelling together. I cabled Mrs. Smarthy to join me in London in late October, a few days before sailing. The house at Peckham was in a constant flurry of packing, changing our minds, repacking.

I was going to America! The thrill of it was not to be accounted for, although Mamma and Papa had done it once, long before I was born, acting on tour. Mamma had described America as a muddy wilderness, nothing more really than one great dark forest with a few ragged villages clinging to the Atlantic shore. But the word itself — America — had so much romance to it, I could not help feeling thrilled. Each evening, Mr. Dickens brought home a new report of where we would go: Boston, New York, Philadelphia, Washington. He warned me to be prepared for a land of barbarism and violence.

"America is populated with scoundrels, vagabonds, and hog buyers," he said. "I'll do light readings. Few Americans have a serious education, and they won't be able to appreciate a higher vision."

He planned to read from *The Old Curiosity Shop* and *A Christmas Carol*. Simple stories with sentimental characters.

"But why go?" I asked. "If you really don't like the place, you have fans enough in Britain."

He seemed flustered at the question. "The right opportunity," he said. And then something about finances. "I can't afford to turn it down." He looked tired, more so of late. His beard was almost white in places. He lit his cigar, puffed several times, and stomped from the room as if the issue were settled.

More arrangements were made. Baltimore and Chicago, although Chicago was doubtful, the distance was so great. His health might be affected. More certain, now, were Albany, Syracuse, and Buffalo.

"We'll visit Niagara Falls," he announced.

For a short time, he proposed taking Collins with us, but Mr. Collins' health was also bad. He was in the middle of a new novel called *The Moonstone*. The opportunity did not seem right.

I was greatly relieved.

As the season for departure drew closer, Mr. Dickens became more and more vague. I felt he was overworked. He travelled everywhere for readings, sometimes gone every night for a week, then home again by train, doing editorial work on his magazine on Saturday and Sunday. On those occasions when he passed a rare evening at Windsor Lodge, he would fall asleep sitting up in his old chair by the fire. He complained about his foot hurting him. He denied he had gout, but he could not pull his boot on without severe pain. If I pressed him to see a physician, he scoffed.

"When I come down to dinner, take my pulse, and if I'm still alive, I'll go ahead and eat."

Then, he mentioned doubts about my health. "Winter in America is like winter in the Arctic," he said. "Forster and Wills are concerned about you."

But the trip was on. I packed. Mrs. Smarthy cabled the date she would arrive. I wrote farewell letters to Fanny and Mamma in Florence.

"Perhaps you shouldn't go," Mr. Dickens said. "Such a rough crossing in November. And all the terrible trains and roads, the bad food."

"I'm very strong." I laughed, thinking he was only acting out the role a man is supposed to play.

"Forster and Wills have their doubts."

We were within a fortnight of final departure. The sun was setting much earlier, and I had already lit the lamp.

"You see," Mr. Dickens explained, "America is even more prudish than England. And our American contacts have grave concerns about my appearing with — as it were — a beautiful young woman on my arm."

"Are you ashamed of me?"

"Of course not. But my public, you see. We don't want to provoke scandal again, do we? We've been through all that once before. I can't suffer it again."

"Are you saying I shan't go, Mr. Dickens?"

"No, no. That isn't it. We would require separate cabins on the ship, and then we'd need separate hotel rooms everywhere. I could say you were my secretary, but everyone would know that to be false. The real question is, how to explain you?"

"How to explain me, Mr. Dickens? I didn't know I needed an explanation."

"Not explain. No, no, not explain. But Forster and Wills point out the press in America is rabid. Reporters are trained to sniff out blood. No sense of decorum. No sense of morality as you and I know it. The American press lacks the dignity of the British press. There would be no way to appeal to their sense of discretion, because they have no discretion."

The American trip would take place, but it seemed I was not to be included. I stayed in my room for several days, filled with such bitterness and anger I spoke to no one. I refused Mr. Dickens' appeals to come out. Molly brought my meals, but she did so with a sneer, as if what had happened was something I deserved.

Mr. Dickens used the trick of following her into the room one evening and then immediately sending her out.

"Do we have anything to say?" I asked him, holding back tears.

He grinned broadly at me. "We've come up with a new

plan, and believe me, I've worked hard for this, just to please you."

"I'm sure you have, Mr. Dickens."

"So here it is. I'll leave as scheduled in November — alone — and after I arrive in Boston, I'll scout the situation, like an American Indian." He was all grins, as if his simile alone ought to charm me into good humour.

"If the press is friendly, you see, and I can win some confidants, I'll send a cable that says for you to follow. But if the territory is fraught with scandal and danger, I'll send a cable that says you're to stay. We've decided on a coded message, one that only you will be in possession of. A secret code, eh?"

He rocked on his boots, checked his watch, and seemed all in all pleased with himself. "Actually," he admitted, "I consulted Collins about this. He's such a genius at mystery, you know, at tangling and untangling everything, I felt he could come up with a plan, and it's top notch, don't you think? A secret code. Quite the clever thing."

"Mr. Dickens, either I accompany you as planned, or I sail immediately for Italy. I have no intentions of spending a cold lonely winter in England while you romp about America and see Niagara Falls."

"But it's all arranged."

"Send the cable to me in Florence," I said. "If you order me to sail for America, I'll do so from there, but do not think this 'plan' is worthy of you."

"For God's sake, woman, Collins and I have spent an entire week on it."

"And you may spend another week before you sail, thinking of a way for me to forgive you."

In truth, as angry as I was, I so wanted to be with him, and he so wanted to be with me, the anger was no longer meaning-ful. I felt my breast overflowing with misery for the very reason I knew in my heart this was the world I had chosen, a world in which I lived in shadows. My very existence was denied by everyone who knew Mr. Dickens. More and more it was de-nied by my own family. Katie might want to be my friend. Mrs. Smarthy might want to be my grandmother. But they were strangers. Only my little dog, Miranda, seemed to love me for who I was, in spite of what I was. And in thinking so, I knew I had grown maudlin and felt ashamed.

My trunk had been taken down by Hubbard. I would sail for Italy instead of America. Mr. Dickens found me crying at the window of my bedroom. He entered softly, waited for me to acknowledge him, then turned and locked my bedroom door from the inside, something he'd never done before. He pulled the drapery over the window, and in the half dark, for our last time ever in England, he led me to my bed, and we were intimate. Mr. Dickens was tender, but as always, awkward and a little hurried. I knew in my soul such an act was almost impossible for him. In his heart, he still considered any inti-macy between us in England to constitute a betrayal of his le-gal wife, of his multitude of followers, of the Queen and Realm. It would never occur again. Nor would we ever men-tion it.

Two weeks later, I landed at Genoa and took a train to Flo-rence, with Miranda curled on my lap. I know what happened there; my memory tells me it did. The event, the loneliness, the empty driving pulse in the flesh. But memory sees so darkly. I remember the feeling without the feeling. Even now, as the train slows, pulling into the soot-blackened station in Florence, I see Count Bertoni waiting in the cold sunlight. A devilish cold wind blows hats and bits of paper into the air.

Fanny, it seems, is indisposed. Mamma has gone to Lauzon for the waters. Tom Trollope is writing and cannot be interrupted. The cold wind swirls about us and blows dry leaves and old newspapers. So much dust batters my eyes I cover my face with a scarf. The wind roars and swirls.

Bertoni must shout to be heard above the wind. "Do you mind if I serve as your escort today?"

He takes my gloved hand and lifts me into his carriage. "Will it be so very improper? Just the two of us?"

"Sir," I cry through the inferno, "there's no one I trust so well."

Ellen Ternan

FANNY and I huddled near a fire in the drawing room. Outside the Villa Ricorboli, an Italian winter swirled and roared. Branches beat against the window, and gusts of rain shook the frame. I had not been out of the house since I arrived. Each day, I awaited a cable from Mr. Dickens. Each day, Count Bertoni drove up in a closed carriage and dashed into the house, slapping a soaked hat against his trousers. When he laughed, his eyes brightened.

"As soon as the weather clears, I will personally show to you the beautiful sights of Florence." He scowled at lowering clouds outside the window, as if by showing his personal displeasure he could surely change the weather. "Perhaps today for sure, I think. You must know Italy as only an Italian can know it."

Fanny grew desperate and pulled me aside. "I've married into a distinguished family," she whispered. "I can't let you run about alone with a man of Bertoni's reputation."

I didn't tell her it was weather, not respectability, that kept me indoors.

"Perhaps," I said, "you should be more concerned that Count Bertoni not be seen with a woman of *my* reputation."

She sniffed, and no more was spoken. Later, I learned that thirteen-year-old Bice had been appointed chaperon and permanent guardian of my virtue — should the rain ever cease.

Two weeks passed.

Everyone said it was the worst weather — the coldest and darkest in anyone's memory. The rain did not stop, and a cable from Mr. Dickens did not arrive. Our fires became smaller and more smokey. The logs were soaked. In the parlour, tile floors were almost slippery from dampness that seemed to have settled permanently over everything. We all worked hard to be cheerful. Bertoni would talk with Tom Trollope for an hour about some new novel they'd both read. He looked through handwritten drafts of Fanny's writing, offering candid responses, often comparing some image or line to this or that poet he had studied at university. He was always encouraging. When Mrs. Trollope was not indisposed, or working on one of her own novels, Bertoni sat in front of the fire with us while Fanny in her silk gown, and Mrs. Trollope in her white cap, worked on their needlepoint. Fanny, of course, had never done needlepoint in her life, but she bent over it intently, if awkwardly, complaining the cold weather made her hands so very, very stiff. Didn't Mrs. Trollope feel the same way?

Bertoni and I eventually wandered to the far end of the room, where we studied wind and rain through the window. He stood with folded arms, looking out, pretending to be deeply interested in the weather.

"I have not yet seen *your* needlepoint," he whispered.

"And you never will." I looked up at him. "I confess I detest it. Sitting about with needle and thread is so very boring."

"But isn't it proper occupation for all English ladies?"

"For ladies, yes."

We laughed. Fanny and Mrs. Trollope glanced up from their chairs by the fire and eyed each other.

Bertoni and I tried to look innocent, but that only made us laugh the more. The real object of Bertoni's visits lay in the few minutes each day we managed to be alone. It had become an unspoken game with us to find those moments together.

"I believe," he said, "I have never pointed out a special painting in the music room. Tom has collected some fine works by our greatest artists. This one will interest you, I'm sure."

We wandered casually back through the parlor. Fanny did not look up, but she stabbed her needle faster and faster through the fabric.

No fire had been laid in the music room, and no lamp lighted. Double doors led onto a terrace puddled with rainwater. The room was dim and chilled. Heavy shadows darkened the corners.

Bertoni pressed something into my hand. "I hope you won't think it forward of me to offer you a small token. I saw this last week in one of those quaint shops on the Ponte Vecchio. It struck me at once you might like it. If you'll accept it as an offering of friendship, I shall be greatly honoured."

In my palm lay a brass box with a latch. The brass lid was delightfully wrought with intricate vines and flowers. On the lid there seemed to be a scene, difficult to make out in the dimness. I felt sure it portrayed a flowered garden, a miniature Garden of Eden. In the darkness I could not see whether a snake lurked among the ripened fruit.

"How charming. It's really quite lovely. I'm embarrassed I have nothing I can offer you." I looked up at him. "Perhaps I must take up needlepoint after all."

"No, no." He laughed. "Here, open it. The present isn't the

box. The present is inside. One must enter the Garden to experience the pleasure." He laughed at his own joke. One of the qualities that made Count Bertoni attractive was that he never quite took himself seriously.

I unlocked the tiny latch and lifted the lid, where I found a delicate gold ring with a single pearl setting, the kind a young girl might receive for her fifteenth birthday. I felt flattered and embarrassed at the same time.

"It's so very — innocent. Truly lovely. But I'm not sure I should accept such a gift, sir. Is this appropriate in Italy?"

"For friendship only, I assure you."

We were standing close to the double doors, and cold rain pelted the puddles outside. Grey Tuscan hills beyond rose up faintly into heavy clouds.

"I shall be very proud to keep this." I looked up at his dark face, and yet it did not seem dark to me then, but full of light and good humour. His eyes were bright with mirth. I suddenly realised his eyes were the warmest thing in all of Italy.

He took the ring from the box and lifted my hand to him, slipping the ring on my finger. It would not quite fit my ring finger, and so he laughed and slipped it onto my smallest finger. I could feel the warmth of his hand holding mine for those few moments. It was firm, but gentle, the touch of his flesh brushing softly against my palm.

"Friendship only," I said.

"Of course. In Italy, we believe friendship between a man and a woman is very important."

"In England, we might question whether a man and a woman can truly be friends. Other things do so often get in the way, don't they?"

"Really?" Bertoni seemed genuinely surprised. "In Italy, nothing gets in the way of a man and woman who wish to share companionship." He did not let go my hand, or perhaps I did not withdraw it.

Mamma arrived with Maria after a long stormy trip from England. Mamma was ill. She looked old and weak. We put her to bed immediately, but she complained about the cold.

"I've come all this way for warm Italian weather. What a pity. A hardship for an old woman like myself. What a pity."

Mamma was too weak to travel alone, and Maria had used her illness as an excuse to flee the dull respectability of Oxford.

"Marriage is so respectable," Maria whispered. "I had to escape. There are only so many teas you can attend, so many 'delightful conversations,' so many explanations from your husband on how beer is brewed — and then you want to scream."

Fanny could not understand. "Tom and I have so much to talk about. Every day has been an absolute delight." Fanny looked admiringly at Tom, who stood across the parlour talking to Count Bertoni.

Maria waited until Fanny returned to her needlepoint, then rolled her eyes at me. We laughed again, and Fanny took offence, especially since the two of us were younger and had not yet acquired her wisdom.

Our family had been apart for so long I forgot almost everything else. Mornings and afternoons were spent huddled together, telling stories, remembering, forgetting, holding hands, arguing. It was a wonderful time, and Tom Trollope was a gracious host, setting ever grander tables, serving his best wine and cheese.

The rain ceased finally, as all rain must, and the clouds were blown away like old rags. The sun came out faintly and hovered in a foreign sky. I was surrounded by my family, and I should have been happy. Still, I felt chilled and alone. Mr. Dickens seemed to have abandoned me.

With Bice as chaperon, Bertoni was gracious enough to transport me to the cable office in Florence. I sent cables to Forster and Wilkie Collins. *Have you heard from our Friend? Did he arrive safely? Am I to know anything soon?*

Afterward, bundled in coats and scarves — to hold our bonnets upon our heads — Bice and I turned remarkably cheerful, exuberant on realising we had escaped the house. Bertoni drove us up and down cobbled streets, pointing out the sights. We trotted through puddles in the almost empty Piazza del Duomo and then to the Cathedral, where Bertoni took pains to describe how the dome had been designed by Brunelleschi. "The dome," he said proudly, "is the largest since the Pantheon in Rome." He brought the carriage to a halt so we could admire it. "Truly elegant."

He wanted to say more, shaping his thoughts. "It's both Classical and Renaissance, you see. Brunelleschi was looking back to . . . what? . . . a celebration of sacred imaginations, let us say. Maybe as far back as pagan imaginations."

Bertoni turned to us in the carriage, looking directly into my eyes, as if he felt something he wanted to share with me. Neither Bice nor I had any idea what we should say.

He laughed at our perplexed faces. "Especially the pagan, don't you think?"

I could only laugh with him. "I'm sure you must be right, sir."

We drove on, and Bertoni continued to talk about Brunelleschi, as if he were a distant cousin. Later, I realised all Italians feel the great Renaissance artists are part of their families: cousins, nephews, distant uncles, grandfathers. Bertoni was born in Sicily, but Florence was his hometown, as were

Padua and Naples and Rome. Wherever he was in Italy, Bertoni was at home. They were all family.

We visited the Pazzi Chapel at Santa Croce, and the Santa Maria Novella, made of green and grey marble. Bertoni pointed to details, laughed, joked. Bice and I sat back and rode through a chilled and fading sunlight, our arms about each other, our cheeks red. But very alive, it seemed to me then. I felt amazed Bertoni could derive such pleasure from taking a whole afternoon to show silly girls about.

The sun grew warmer as the afternoon shortened. Bice huddled against me, enjoying our ride. Bertoni drove up and down through narrow streets, pointing this way and that.

"There, there!" he cried. "On that bridge Dante spoke to Beatrice."

"I thought he only admired her from afar."

"No, no. But yes, of course, from afar. They never spoke. On this bridge, he tipped his hat and signalled his love for her."

"How does one do that, Count Bertoni? How does a man signal his love?"

"Ah, you ask the most important question." He looked back at us and seemed almost to laugh. "Even Bice knows the answer to that."

Bice blushed and buried her face against my shoulder.

"It is a miracle, isn't it," Bertoni said. "That a man and a woman know — with the eyes, the voice, or even a mere presence of the body, in the same room, on a bridge — in a carriage."

The carriage made a sudden turn down an even narrower street. "Here," he said, pointing to a long arcade on the upper floor. "Here is a fine old loggia designed by a student of Alberti, and — if I may say so — my present home."

The house with the loggia seemed more like something a Londoner would associate with a heavy government building.

Black soot disguised granite walls. Fortresslike wooden doors barely revealed old carvings that were now unidentifiable. Yet the upper floors were enlightened by arcades of windows, and the roof of the loggia was supported by surprisingly white marble columns.

"Naturally, it would be improper to invite you in, and in any case, Piccolo is probably still wandering about in his bathrobe. Piccolo is my manservant. A decrepit, dottering old man, but he's been with me since I was a boy. He's absolutely indispensable."

Bertoni pointed to one far corner of the loggia above our heads. "If you stand there, at that corner, and twist your neck, you can see the Uffizi." He assured us the Uffizi contained a hundred different excitements for eye and soul.

When he finally brought us back to the Villa Ricorboli, he helped Bice down from the carriage first, and then, taking a little longer to help me down, he deliberately held me back, waiting for Bice to go into the house.

"Soon we must visit the Uffizi. Just the two of us."

"Quite daring of you, sir, but I don't think we can escape without Bice."

"Oh, of course we would include Bice. I would not dream of taking you anywhere without chaperon." He scanned my face with dark, mischievous eyes.

Cables arrived from England. Forster said I must be patient.

> Storm on Atlantic. Ship delayed. Our friend settling in. Message soon no doubt.

Wilkie Collins was more condescending.

> Mr. Pickwick abroad. Thought you knew. Very busy. All in good time.

*

Plans for visiting the Uffizi were made and remade. We were to go on Saturday, but Tom's birthday was Saturday, and our plans were cancelled. Then we were to go on Wednesday, but the galleys for Fanny's novel arrived, and we all worked to seek out misspelled words, stray commas, and lost passages.

The sun came out like a Roman god, warm, generous, confident, and something of a tyrant. We shed our heavy garments and opened doors for mild breezes to blow through the house. Servants cleaned fireplaces. Mamma found a chair in the sun on the verandah. She wore her black scoop bonnet and sipped small drops of a fine old sherry called Amontillado. Although it was still winter, we felt as if it were spring. The air seemed brightly polished. We laughed too much and talked about taking a holiday to Trieste or Venice. Italy had become Italy again.

A cable from Forster arrived. It said, *Our friend safe and well.* Nothing more.

I carried it to my bedroom and, from my trunk, retrieved the instructions Mr. Dickens had prepared for me — "the code," as he called it. He had sealed his letter in a cold white envelope and told me to open it only when the cable arrived. Inside was a short note in his own hand.

Dear Princess,
    If my telegram says: "All means well," it will signal you to come. It means I have made all secure arrangements. You should probably sail from Genoa. Be sure to send me a cable by return and let me know the name of the ship and date of departure. I'll be waiting for you. Do not use your own name. Sign the cable "Nelly," and I will understand.

If my telegram says: "Safe and well," it will signal you to stay. I still look forward to working out the details and believe all will turn out satisfactorily.

I will contact you only through Forster and Wilkie. They will make sure you receive my messages by sending cables to you at Villa Trollope. Should you decide to travel or visit elsewhere, leave word on how their cables should be forwarded.

Do not try to contact me directly. Remember, if an emergency arises and you absolutely must cable me, do not sign your name. Use the code, "Nelly."

I read Forster's cable again. And then again. *Our friend safe and well.* But was Forster responding to my earlier concern? I had asked him whether Dickens arrived safely. I reread Mr. Dickens' letter, then Forster's cable. *Our friend safe and well. Our friend safe and well.* Should I be happy or distressed? My heart beat like a kettledrum, and I began to cry. To Mr. Dickens, I *was* an old drum. He played me like a circus entertainer pounding out rough melodies for trained dogs to prance to. I was the drum. No, I was the dancing dog. It didn't matter. Nothing mattered. Was Mr. Dickens safe and well? Or was I commanded to stay behind?

Maria knocked.

"Another telegram," she called to me. "Just arrived from Mr. Collins."

I flung open the door and tore the message from her hand.

Word from America. Safe and Well. Hope you are enjoying Italy.

As ever, Wilkie

I was about to faint. Hot tears ran down my face, and I threw myself sobbing into Maria's arms. A sister can be a wonderful thing. She held me, rocked me, and never once asked me what the problem could be. For a while, I grew worse. Perhaps I was hysterical. Mamma and Fanny and Mrs. Trollope hurried to my aid. My stays were loosened. Cold compresses were placed on my forehead. I was told to sip hot tea. Then brandy. Maria never stopped holding me, rocking me like a baby. I could hear everyone discussing the telegrams, puzzling over why I should be upset if Mr. Dickens was safe and well. A plaster was prepared for my chest. Servants hurried in and out. In the hallway, I heard Tom Trollope being told he was forbidden to enter the room. It was a female matter, a voice explained.

That night, Maria slept beside me while I lay awake, staring at the blackness all about, blackness in my heart, in my blood. Early in the morning hours, still in darkness, I rose softly and crossed to the window, opened the window shutter, and peered out, hoping for a moment to look as far away as possible — at the furthermost star or a cold and lonely moon. But there were no stars. No moon. Only more darkness. My heart continued to pound, slowly now, with heavy strokes beating on a drum that must have cracked. There was no music, only bitterness. My chest throbbed in bitterness.

I gripped the window and hung on. I waited, letting the cold morning air dry the dampness from my skin. I waited. I refused to submit to all that bitter darkness. Eventually, I knew, a bloody sun must rise. And I would not submit. Some kind of bird, vaguely like a nightingale, began to sing. Others joined in. There was promise in it, even though the sky was dark. I could see a dividing line between distant hills and sky. The light grew slowly, as if filtered through my own being. But it did come. "I will find my own America," I whispered. The light was gradual but steadying and revealing. I knew I would not submit.

On a bright afternoon, only a few days later, when the light seemed clear as crystal, Count Bertoni again invited me to visit the Uffizi. Maria helped me dress, convincing me to abandon my crinolines even though the new flowing look was still risqué. She insisted it had become all the rage in London and Bath. For dramatic effect, she attached a short train, which she said was now appropriate for an indoor frock. In the looking glass, I appeared quite bold and startling. Maria also loaned me a hat, a lamballe plateau with a small feather on top, something her husband had purchased for her on a business trip to Paris.

Bice wore pale pink satin with a white ribbon in her hair, and she carried a pink umbrella. The weather was delightful. We rode in Count Bertoni's carriage with the top down and within twenty minutes entered the dark old palace itself.

Just inside, on a temporary easel, a hand-lettered sign had been posted: "Professor Cantori will lecture this Evening on Leonardo's questions on the Eternal analytics."

"My," I said to the Count, "I didn't know Italians were so well-read."

"Professor Cantori is quite famous. He lectures on books that do not exist, and we applaud him for making Italians seem as intelligent as the English."

"Oh sir, it is quite out of fashion in England to seem intelligent."

"Then, you are Italians, after all."

I laughed, but Bice thought perhaps the English had been insulted, and for a while, she clung to my arm. For more than an hour, we strolled through room after room of pictures. A few other gentlemen carried top hats, and a few women, mostly sombre matrons in old-fashioned bird-caged crinolines, wandered about peering at obscure drawings. Some rooms were dimly lit from dirty windows high above. Several interior rooms offered gas lights that hissed and flickered. Almost no one spoke. We could hear the shuffling of feet in other galleries. We climbed staircases, wound about through webs of hallways, crossed through rooms we had already visited and circled back to others, a labyrinth of dark portraits, scenes of sinking ships, mythological warriors, and religious piety. In almost every room, we saw another Madonna, another bleeding Christ. We walked past countless Medici ancestors, looking grim and arrogant. We admired the ethereal calmness of Filippo Lippi angels. In the Flemish room, the eyes of sober Puritans followed us with disapproval. Bice and I grimaced at the *Martyrdom of St. Justina*, where a slave thrusts a dagger into the bosom of the kneeling saint.

Finally, we paused in front of Leonardo's *Annunciation*. The Virgin was unbelievably beautiful and serene, hardly more than a girl of Bice's age, with golden brown hair curled in Renaissance fashion. She might have been thirteen or fourteen, at most. She might have been Bice, and I knew Bice was thinking the same. Such innocence, confronted by such awesome knowledge.

Bice dropped onto the bench in front of the painting and sighed. She looked exhausted. Bertoni hovered over her with concern. "Would you like to rest awhile? Why not sit here while Ellen and I visit a few last galleries?"

Bice nodded, fully agreeable to anything that did not require her to walk through another endless maze of rooms.

"Wait for us here, and when we return, we'll stop by my

lodgings. I have a surprise for you. The most delicious chocolates you've ever tasted. Piccolo has gone out for them."

Bertoni turned to me and whispered, "And perhaps he'll
find a small bottle of champagne for you and me to celebrate
our excursion today."

Throughout the museum, I had rested my hand lightly on
Count Bertoni's arm. Now he took my arm firmly and guided
me away.

"Some paintings," he whispered, "are perhaps not appropriate for Bice's innocence."

"Are you implying, sir, that I'm not innocent?"

"No, no, no." He laughed. "I know very well you are innocent as a lamb."

"You mock me, I'm afraid. The people of England — if
they knew about me — would not call me innocent."

"That, my dear, is because the English are confused about
the relation between innocence, purity, and knowledge. They
do not understand all these concepts are merely different
forms of the same thing."

Before I could consider what his meaning might be, we
stopped in front of two side-by-side paintings titled *Adam* and
Eve. I have never heard of the artist, one Cranach the Elder
from the sixteenth century. In each painting, a fully nude figure stood silhouetted against a dark background. Their life-
sized forms were casual and slender. Eve was portrayed as a
young woman — barely more than a girl — yet mature and
shameless, with both breasts exposed and both nipples
brightly pink. In one hand, Eve held out to Adam the apple
from which she had already taken a bite. Over her head, the
evil snake curled down from a bough of bright red apples. But
it was Eve's eyes that seemed most striking. Perhaps because
she had already tasted knowledge. Her eyes were seductive, al-

most hard, their gaze challenging Adam, taunting him, tempting him. Her hair flowed down behind her, curled again in the Renaissance style, suggesting thin snakes writhing in darkness. In her other hand, she held a slender branch with a few small leaves covering — barely covering — her most private flesh.

By contrast, Adam projected boyish innocence. His eyes seemed puzzled if intrigued. They looked outside the frame and directly into Eve's on the next canvas. One hand was raised to scratch his head, as if he were perplexed by her offer of the apple. Clearly, he bore no responsibility for what was happening. Eve had lost her innocence, if only in her imagination, and Adam was caught in her gaze, just as Eve was caught in the gaze of the snake above her head. Adam, too, covered himself with a single branch, but the leaves were larger and elongated, hiding his surprised power.

I was far more intrigued by Eve and *her* power. I did not know if Bertoni felt the same way. Inside my breast, I felt confused, not only as to why he had chosen this picture for us to pause before, but by my own emotions.

Bertoni squeezed my arm, and we moved on to an adjacent room, where we found Botticelli's *Birth of Venus*. It was a huge canvas with a nude Venus having just risen on a shell out of the ocean. She covered one breast with her hand. The other breast was fully exposed. I studied the canvas in silence, telling myself that I should appreciate the painting for its mythological quality, but I could not take my eyes from the life-sized woman's body in front of me. She was surely pure, and surely innocent — even shyly hesitant, exposed as she was to wind and sea — but she was nonetheless a beautiful young woman, fully and nobly naked. It was her innocence that made her so sexual, her innocence that seemed to give her magic.

I could hear Bertoni's breathing. He took my arm, and we moved again to another gallery, not talking, but intensely aware of each other. He stopped me in front of Titian's *Venus and Cupid*. This time the painting was larger than life size. A luxurious Venus, the Greek Aphrodite, golden-fleshed, fully mature — and totally naked — reclined on a couch, facing us without modesty, her full rounded breasts exposed, a dark patch of hair between her legs. She looked back at an angelic winged cherub I assumed to be Cupid. One of Cupid's hands, in turn, reached over her shoulder and rested lightly on her breast. Behind Venus and to both sides, red velvet curtains were draped across a window. Her body reclined on a dark satin coverlet. A string of pearls warmed her throat. A pearl drop earring hung motionless at one ear. On both wrists, she wore wide-banded gold and jewelled bracelets. She was marvellously beautiful, serene, exposed and waiting. The cherub looked concerned, his eyes by contrast were intent, almost pleading, as if he had offered the Goddess of Love one more conquest and she had hesitated, gazing off canvas for a moment, recalling her past or future.

No, it was definitely her future. She had known too many lovers to be concerned with her past. One could read it in her face, the momentary glaze of her eyes, knowing the naked little cherub had announced yet another lover for her to take and that she would take him, but for a moment, there was only the blurred memory of so very many lovers, sweating and heaving on her body.

I breathed deeply, trying to think of anything I could say. "You see, my Count, even Venus must pause and consider — even when she is naked and fully ready for love."

I could feel his fingers on the inside of my arm, feel the heat of his hand through my sleeve. "I admit the question is clearly whether she will say yes. That's why Cupid looks so concerned. All women — including Venus herself — may say no if they choose. Yet we are in Italy, Ellen, and here — like Venus — we need not pretend to English purity. Quite the contrary, we find love is always waiting for us."

"No doubt that's her point," I boldly said. "It is hesitation itself that heightens desire."

Bertoni laughed and turned me about.

"One final picture, if you're ready for it?"

We crossed the gallery to another large painting, *Venus of Urbino* by Titian, and this time, I found myself taking a deep breath. Not that I was shocked by nakedness, as Bertoni had perhaps hoped I would be. I grew up in the theatre. In dressing rooms, there is no time for modesty. Women's bodies were all about me, rushing to step out of one costume into another, sometimes wearing only a shift or nothing at all. I had seen women's bosoms, seen their thighs, seen their pubic hair and rounded flanks. I had seen my own, standing in front of mirrors, side by side with other women, all of us hurrying our makeup, dressing our hair, powdering bosoms.

And on tour, where there were no dressing rooms, only a crowded space behind a wagon or a sheet hung over a rope, men and women dressed and undressed together without thought. It was only business. I had seen men naked, and they had seen me or my sisters or other women. We knew each other. We were not sheltered as the great masses of the English public were. But nonetheless, the Venus of Urbino was different.

This Venus was not a girl, not even a girl who was almost a woman. She was a fully experienced woman. Still young of course, but a woman who had lost all innocence willingly and eagerly a long time ago. Nor was this Venus an immortal goddess listening to winged cherubs. She was not a mythological Aphrodite, not serene, not richly and warmly seductive even while remaining distant and aloof.

The Venus of Urbino was truly a woman. A seductress of men. A luxurious mistress of the royal bordello. She looked the viewer directly in the eye, gazed at the viewer with all the temptation of Eve, all the expectation and teasing challenge of Salome, all the confidence of a woman who can pick any man she chooses, and does so. A woman who has never been rejected. A woman who hesitates only because she wants a man to fill himself with the fantasy of her, to burst into flame, to take her with ecstasy, with primal passion, like Europa filled with the seed of Zeus' immortality.

This Venus, too, lay reclined on her couch, this time on white silk, that only heightened the sensual tones of her golden body. Again, she leaned back on several pillows covered also in white silk. Her hair flowed over her shoulder. A single pearl droplet shimmered at one ear. Like the others, she was fully naked. This time, however, one hand lay casually at the "v" of her thighs. I could say that her hand partly hid her pubic hair, but that was not true. In reality, the presence of her hand made you feel she was partly *exposing* her pubic hair, making it suddenly part of the temptation. Her breasts were flattened somewhat because she lay back on her pillows, but her bright nipples were ripely erect, and the colour of the nipples saturated the area around them with more pink ripeness.

Behind her, in a far room, two maids busily searched through trunks for dresses, but it was too late. The look on her face showed clearly her lover had already arrived. She gazed directly at him. The lover was the viewer. We were there to seduce her. She was there to be seduced.

I could feel my lungs tighten. Never before had a painting

excited me. Never before had a woman excited me. Never before had I felt such heat spreading through my body. In one sense, the heat seemed to flow downward from my lips and throat into my breasts and stomach. In another sense, it seemed to pulsate from Bertoni's hand gripping my arm, as if the blood pounding through me was not my blood but his.

Taking my cue from the painting, I looked up at Count Bertoni and said, "I believe you mentioned something about champagne, sir. At your lodgings."

Bertoni's dark eyes were full of sudden admiration for me, as well as the humour of his successful little plan.

When we arrived at Count Bertoni's, Piccolo opened the door instantly, as if he had been waiting on the other side. He was a frazzled-looking man with a white goatee, rather small and old. Dark like a Sicilian, with a comforting smile and many nods of his head, yet dignified in his quiet way. One got the impression Piccolo might have been the true Count the family had stolen its name from.

"I did not expect you so soon. No, no, not this soon. There has been no time, you see. I've had much to do. No time at all. Perhaps a little cheese and wine would substitute. I'm sure I can find cheese and wine."

Bertoni looked awkwardly surprised. "And the chocolates?"

"No time at all." Piccolo bowed slightly. "This, that, and the other, as the English say. No time at all."

Bertoni's eyes darkened. "I have promised these ladies chocolates, Piccolo, and chocolates they shall have. Get your coat immediately. You may take my carriage, but I want all due speed, do you understand?"

Piccolo seemed flustered, perhaps even a bit frightened. "Of course, sir. Yes, sir. I'll get my coat."

In the moment that he was gone, Bertoni turned quickly to Bice. "I do so beg your pardon, my dear child."

"It's nothing, sir."

"No, no, it's a promise, and this fool has wasted the morning dawdling, thinking I would not want to make a scene and he could get out of going."

Bertoni took Bice's arm and spoke softly, as if in strictest confidence. "I'm not even sure he knows where to find these chocolates. He doesn't get about much here in Florence. Would it be a great burden on you if I begged you to accompany him, just to make sure the fool doesn't wander off and get lost?"

"It would be no problem at all, Count Bertoni."

"Wonderful, wonderful. Now, I've given Piccolo directions, but I'm going to repeat them to you. The chocolates I want are an incredible delicacy, made of genuine Brazilian chocolate with a dark creamy centre — and you can find them only at one place in all the world: a special shop called the Grand Duke's Pleasure, where Signora Buontalenti makes each chocolate confection by hand."

Bertoni gave very explicit directions, and Bice listened attentively. When Piccolo returned, Bertoni again berated him, asking him to repeat the directions. But when Piccolo and Bice started out the door, Bertoni stopped them, as if something had just occurred to him.

"If Signora Buontalenti's shop is closed," he said, "you must try the Sala Chocolate on the Via de Tornabuoni. It's on the other side of the city. Piccolo knows it well."

Bice and Piccolo had started down the dark staircase when

Bertoni suddenly remembered something else and ran to the landing.

"Piccolo, don't forget the champagne. Go to Leopoldo's near the *stazione*. Do you understand? I want everything done right this time."

I heard Piccolo's frightened voice from below. "Of course, sir. I won't fail you, sir."

And they were gone. Count Bertoni and I were alone in his rooms. The only light seeped in through double doors opening onto the loggia, a filtered light through sheer curtains. From another room I could hear a clock ticking. In the street below, the carriage started up and rattled away over the cobbles.

Bertoni stepped up to me. "May I remove your hat?" Without waiting for an answer, he reached over and slipped the pin from my hair, carefully lifting the hat away, and setting it on a table.

"You have such golden hair," he said softly. "That is the correct term, isn't it?"

I had no time to think of a response before he deftly removed both combs from my hair and let it tumble about my shoulders. I felt in the fall of my hair I had already committed adultery. I could hardly breathe.

"You are no gentleman, sir."

"Of course not."

We both laughed, and I hid my face.

"Now, what do you think," he suddenly cried. "I have just recalled a place where I'm sure some of Signora Buontalenti's chocolates must be hidden away for us."

He opened a cabinet and came forth with a package wrapped in brown paper. He untied the string and opened it on the table next to my hat. The hat seemed oddly out of place. For a moment, I couldn't imagine how it had left my head, where it belonged. But I *could* imagine, and the repeated image of removing my hat and loosening my hair made my throat flushed and tight.

"Ah!" Bertoni cried. "What a fool I am. I completely forgot I ordered champagne yesterday and it was chilled all night for us in the cellar. Why, I brought it up myself this very morning."

He drew open another drawer in the cabinet and brought forth a bottle.

"Poor Piccolo. I've so unjustly sent him on an errand for nothing." He looked at me with the most devious, delightful, evil eyes.

I forced myself to find my voice. "You recall, sir, a woman always has the choice of saying no."

"Of course." He popped the cork and poured us each a glass. "I also recall that hesitation builds passion, makes the blood hot, the heart pound."

We sipped our champagne, and Bertoni moved close, looking down into me in such a way his eyes silenced and enclosed me. "Hesitation," he said softly, "is not the same as innocence; knowledge is not the same as guilt."

We finished the champagne and chocolates in his bedroom on a giant four-poster bed. Watching us, from another wall, were three painted figures in an elaborate gold frame. The first and largest figure was of some dark god, naked and struggling to hold down a golden-skinned woman with tangled hair. His eyes were devilish and laughing with anger, while hers were filled with false fright and lust. She writhed and fought, not to escape, but to fulfill. Behind them and above, watching from a swirl of clouds, a Pan-like figure laughed and ogled, admiring their heavy-thighed beauty, their passion.

I no longer thought about breathing. I thought of nothing. I felt only the heat of Bertoni's face as it bent toward me, moving slowly down my throat, pressed against the warm flesh of my breasts, while his hands lifted and turned me. His slow weight seemed to break my bones softly. The breath went out of me, until I felt one with him, as if some immortal god pressed down upon me, with the fullness of his mouth over my mouth, taking my soul into himself, so forcefully I felt my body arch against him. My breath came like a deep series of heavy moans, like the heaving swell of ocean washing over me. And then Bertoni settled heavily, his body hot and wet. It was not enough. I grabbed his hair and pulled with both hands, rubbing my nose and face back and forth across his throat and shoulder, smelling his male sweat, which was sweet and awful at the same time. I had the urge to lick him, but held back until I realised that to hold back was to hold back from living, and living was so short, a two-act play on the road. I licked his throat in one long swipe of my tongue, and then his shoulder, and stretched until I could lick his ear. I rose up in new strength and pushed him off and over, following with my own body, and licking his lips and his hardened nipples and the wet hair of his belly and his groin. I licked and sucked the soul out of him, and his manhood rose up again, hard against me as I moved down him, and took hold of it and opened my eyes to it, seeing a man's risen cock for the first time ever, shocked by its bruised — almost absurd — ferociousness. I held on to him and sucked gently the hot salty man balls, instinctively using my teeth lightly to pull and stretch the skin. I licked his inner thighs and the insides of his ankles, like a mother wolf cleaning its cub.

It was not enough.

I rolled him over and licked the backs of his knees, and nipped the backs of his heavy thighs, surprised to find even there the soft curly hair. I pressed my face against his buttocks and his back, brushing my lips and tongue along the skin, starting at the small of his spine and moving slowly, wetly, tenderly up to between his shoulders. I found my teeth biting into the flesh of his shoulders and neck, tasting the salt on his wet skin, tasting in his sweat the basil and the wine and the heat of all Italian lovers who would never be mine, but were mine now. Biting tenderly at first, unable to control myself. No, that wasn't it. I didn't want to control myself. Biting hard, until I drew blood, and Bertoni bellowed and threw me away, knocking me almost off the goose-feather mattress. For a moment I felt terrified. He pinned my wrists and hovered above me, his face angry and hot. His black eyes were no longer bright with humour. They frightened me. He lowered himself slowly and covered my mouth with his mouth, until I felt myself open for him, until I threw my head back and forth, and there were no words left, and no breath even, only deep animal sounds from someone somewhere in the room. Surely I would die. But it was death to be desired. I realised with such disbelieving surprise how innocent I had always been.

It was not enough. I want more, I thought. I want it all, I thought. I want. I want. I want.

Wilkie Collins

THE TELEGRAM arrived about two A.M. with a banging on the door.

Emergency cable from Florence. Nelly pregnant. Wants return to England. Must absolutely avoid scandal. Depending on you to develop cover. Much gratitude.

The cable wasn't signed, of course. It was just like Dickens to expect someone else to clean up his problem. We were still best of friends, but over the years our relationship had reversed. More and more, I became *his* mentor. More and more, the older man turned to the younger for guidance. Not that he ever needed help with his writing. Dickens was always in complete command of his writing. But his personal life, that was another matter.

My first response to the cable was anger, or rather disgust. After all these years, he still possessed no common sense about women, least of all manipulative women — the kind Ellen turned out to be. He treated her as if she were a street waif in one of his novels. I could just hear her saying, "Please, sir, I want some more porridge."

He gave her everything, coddling her, like an innocent child, assuming all she told him must be innocent truth. Dickens had no sense of her deceit, and you see how he was betrayed. The cable from Ellen was nothing more than a ruse, a fiction designed to draw Dickens home from his successful American tour. It was Ellen trying to push herself back into the story of his life, and Dickens, as always, playing the part of victim.

Let me begin again. I speak here from far greater experience with women. Not only had I successfully lived with a much wilder woman than Ellen Ternan, I trained my own Caroline to obey my every wish. Not that she had any real desire to go her own way. None whatsoever. She put herself in my hands, and I guided her destiny. I commanded, she obeyed. We found that mutually satisfying.

A few years ago, during a walking holiday in Norfolk, I met a delightful young maiden — Martha Rudd was her name — and I brought her back to London with me. Caroline raised no concern whatsoever. Or at least nothing serious. Caroline's only objection was to my proposal that Martha move in with us — a *ménage à trois,* as it were. (I was feeling very French on the occasion.)

But no, Caroline felt uncomfortable with such arrangements, and I respected her opinion. After submitting to her refusal to allow Martha to move in with us, she could hardly deny me the right to establish Martha in a separate house, which from my point of view was only slightly less desirable, and in some ways better because it settled the issue of jealousy that women are prone to.

This was about the time a twisted little man began following Caroline about. At first, we thought it humorous. As best we could determine, he was younger than Caroline by a decade or more and oddly deformed. One shoulder was hitched up higher than the other. He didn't walk so much as lope, rather like a rabbit might hop with one paralysed leg. Caroline believed she first saw him in the open market one afternoon, loping along behind the stalls, keeping her in his eye. She had no reason to pay attention until he sprung at her, bearing broken stalks of several rusted daffodils he found discarded behind a flower stand.

Caroline, in her surprise, accepted the gift, and the young man loped off with one shoulder twisting and falling, as if it refused to obey his body's instructions.

We discovered his name was Joseph Clow, or perhaps Klowgh. Through some private enquiry, we found he considered himself a petty merchant. He owned a wine and spirits shop on Fitzroy Square, although it was so dark and dust-filled — so piled with old clothing and empty bottles — it seemed more like a shop for hulking mudlarks. No one ever recalled seeing a customer enter the establishment through the front door, but he did sell gin through the back. Rumour had it that he kept several stray dogs on the premises. When I hired a man to investigate him, he was quickly driven out of the shop by the scurry of guinea pigs rushing about in blind panic under his feet.

Whoever he was, Mr. Clow seemed to have fallen madly in love with Caroline. He would appear in the strangest places. Peeking over the fence behind our back garden. Huddled in the rain near a bakery where Caroline sometimes bought a loaf. On one occasion, we believe he came to our door in the night and slid a message under it. The paper it was written on was greasy and ancient, as if it had been found on a shelf under an old ham bone. The writing trembled with odd spellings and random letters. Yet it seemed passionate enough.

Yes! Cryed the lonely Soule,
a Sea of life ensiled,
with echoing strayts between Us thrown,
Dotting the Shoreless Waters
We mortal millions Live Alune!

Neither of us could make any sense of it. My brother Charlie thought he recognised an echo of something from Matthew Arnold. But what was it supposed to mean?

I teased Caroline about having a secret lover. She was in her late thirties then, and modestly flattered that a younger man — even one so odd — should be attracted to her. She took no offence, and he was no real bother to anyone. Indeed, I suddenly found his presence useful, pointing out to Caroline that Martha Rudd had followed me about in just the same way, attaching herself as it were, and because I felt sorry for her, I'd made certain promises. Caroline didn't like the comparison one bit, but since I showed no jealousy over Joseph Clow, her twisted little gnome, how could she suggest any objection to my giving assistance — charity as it were — to a poor soul like Martha Rudd?

And so Martha, barely more than nineteen years old, became mistress of a charming little house on Bolsover Street, a shady side lane in London, conveniently around the corner from where I lived with Caroline. We all lived in tandem, well-rewarded by each other's charity.

Martha's story was neither as odd nor as long in the telling as Caroline's. Martha's life was merely dreary. She escaped from a family of eight children, running away at sixteen to make her way in the world. When I met her, she was a maid at a certain tavern in Great Yarmouth. I was struck with her immediately, even though she was hardly older than Caroline's own daugh-

ter, Harriet, who still lived with us and whom Caroline continued to introduce as her niece. Martha was tall and slender,
with strong eyes and a firm mouth. It was her eyes attracted
me. Her eyes, and a rather ripe bosom that seemed to sway
and flow under her bodice (I've always preferred women with
a fullness of growth). Martha was dark-complected and wore
dark hair parted severely in the middle, raked back into a large
bun with several sharp pins stuck into it. I was afraid she
might turn out to be stern or cold, but those dark eyes looked
into mine as she served me at the table, and I felt sure she was
not so much stern as intense. I sensed a spirited girl who knew
what she wanted. The first night at the tavern, she refused my
bed. The second night, she laughed at my proposal and
tweaked my nose, which I considered encouraging. On the
third night, catching her alone in a hallway, I grabbed at her
roughly, pushing her against the wall and taking a number of
liberties with her person. I feared she might cry out until
sensed her hand sliding its way between my thighs, and I
knew we would soon be tumbling upon my bed.

Instead, she grabbed me hard and paralysed me with fright.
One slight twist of her fist, and I might find myself crippled for
days. And that twist was clearly threatened in those hard eyes.
Of course, I tried to unhand her, tried to back away, tried — as
it were — to disengage my affections. Even that did not convince her to let go of my most sacred parts. Instead, she
laughed through her nose, then out loud. Her eyes never
stopped looking into mine, as if she were a mentalist.

"I been keeping watch on you since you arrived in the
coach," she said. "But I want you to know I'm a good girl, I
am, so I don't take lightly being treated like one of y'r ordinary
whores."

"Never once thought of it," said I. "Your breeding was apparent to me from the moment I first saw you bending over my table with a plate of oysters."

"Yes, sir," she said, still holding tight and still grinning. "I leaned over so's you'd notice me, and now you have, haven't you."

"You have my full attention."

"Got y'r attention, have I?" She laughed. "Just you remember who's got y'r attention in her fist, and if I catch you treating me badly, I'll have your holy hanging flesh for breakfast, I will."

She kissed me hard, then leaned back and popped me over the ear with a cupped hand before pushing away.

"My work ain't done yet. You call down about midnight for a fresh candle, and I'll deliver it. We'll see then if you've got any fire to light it."

When the time finally came to introduce her to Caroline, I prepared the way, retelling how she was a poor waif forced from home due to poverty.

I sensed they didn't particularly like each other, but they both knew a good thing when they had one, and so long as I didn't talk about one in front of the other, they lived comfortably in their separate houses, without a further hint of conflict. It was a good lesson on how all of us can learn to live with more love and compassion for our fellows.

After I received the cable from Dickens, my first thought was to ignore it, but our friendship had lasted twenty years, so I let myself lie awake, studying how to solve his newest problem. Indeed, I lay awake most nights anyway, especially when I failed to take my laudanum. I had grown old, it seemed, and various pains seared my body. Sometimes, my mind felt as if a hot poker had pierced my temples, day and night. I found more and more need to husband my energies. The physician said it all began with a rheumatic gout in my right foot. He prescribed sea air. The swelling and fiery pain spread to my left foot, and he prescribed colchicum, advising sternly that at all cost I should avoid sea air. My legs felt as if I were roasting them in a bonfire. Caroline's remedies did far more good than the physician's. She prepared a poultice out of cabbage leaves wrapped in silk about each leg. Then she heated a small jug of oil and poured it evenly over the poultice. It gave just enough relief to allow me to sleep a few hours each night. The laudanum worked even better.

Caroline herself suffered now from a nervous disorder, sometimes collapsing on a sofa with nervous palpitations. I would bring her a mixture of quinine and hot tea — which many of the great ladies swore by. Most days it would help, except when she suffered a complete hysterical attack. There was no remedy, then, except the laudanum.

My writing suffered. I passed whole days in pain and accomplished nothing. We took tiring journeys across Europe in search of relief. Caroline organised expeditions to the baths at Wildbad and Rome, where we submerged ourselves in sulphur waters. When Caroline heard the baths at Aix-la-Chapelle contained an electric influence, she made immediate arrangements. But again, the journey was exhausting. I wrote little. After a while, the trips became more painful than staying home. The food was always wretched. Only the laudanum saved us.

When I took laudanum, my brain was energised. Ideas and images broke through like golden chicks hatching from eggs. And later, the body would be energised as well. The pain was numbed. I sometimes felt good enough to service Caroline, dress myself, snap on my floppy Wide-Awake, walk around the corner, and stir up Martha, who at her age was always ready for a hard romp. The laudanum had also helped immensely throughout writing *The Moonstone,* and I felt creatively renewed. My mind seemed unstoppable. The mastery of plot and design and mystery had returned to me with remarkable power. Dickens was fortunate that his cable arrived at a moment of such brilliance. The novel was almost complete, the ending secured in my mind. And lying in bed, awake, I could give full powers to saving the Great Man's life once again.

If Ellen were indeed with child, she must have conceived in late October, before she and Dickens went their separate ways. Hence, she would be due July or August, about three months after Dickens staggered off the boat from New York. The first thing to do was prevent her from returning to England with a swollen belly. She must be made to understand there was no secure way for her to bear an illegitimate heir in England without the word spreading. No, she must stay on the Continent, drop her litter into the discreet arms of a French midwife, and either dispose of it there — if she would accept that plan — or put it out for fostering in England, by some country maid far away from London, where she could, if she must, visit the little puker from time to time.

The problem was, the plan was horribly dull. A good mystery must have diversion, false clues, odd twists. As I lay there in the dark, *The Moonstone* still swimming in my mind, I realised Dickens was entrusting me to do more than arrive at commonsense arrangements. Where was the fun of it, after all? A mystery should have unexpected surprises, something to keep the reader interested. Something delightfully deceptive, something with terrifying possibilities where someone is rescued or saved only at the last minute.

That's when I thought of Joseph Clow, and I laughed out loud in the dark. My God! It was perfect. The whole of it came to me in a single flash of laudanum lightning. Pure pleasure, pure delight, pure deception. It would be the talk of the town, and not one soul would ever know the scandal they were talking about was only a shadow of the real scandal they would never fathom. It was brilliant! Absolutely brilliant!

Here's how I laid it out for Caroline the next afternoon. Our parlour curtains were drawn as always. We sat in the yellow shadows of a single gas light that hissed subtly as a snake. I poured out a few drops — a teaspoon or so — of laudanum. One teaspoon for each of us, and almost immediately, we began to feel our health improving.

"Here is the plot, my lovely one, and you will be the central star. The entire city of London will be focused on you, or at least all the better classes, which is all we care about in a case like this."

She stretched back on the sofa and waited, her eyes growing dull.

"First, it will be publicly announced that you'll be leaving one Wilkie Collins — novelist *par excellence* — to marry one Joseph Clow, Official Gin Dealer to the Destitute."

Caroline did little more than raise an eyebrow, but I knew she could not stop listening now — which was exactly the point. All of London had gossiped so often about my various arrangements, titillated most recently by my installation of a second mistress around the corner from the first, that every living member of the social set would be stunned. Absolutely stunned.

"Second, my dear, you will not only make a public display of leaving me, you will indeed make a very public wedding —

to which everyone will be invited — including the Great Charles Dickens himself. We'll do it openly without a hint of shame, respectable, don't you see. My God," I cried, "we'll even do it legally!"

I was already laughing. The plot was delicious.

"A church wedding! Great God, Caroline, we'll publicly reveal your aristocratic blood — I'm a genius, I tell you. And we'll invent an equally absurd bloodline for young Joseph Clow, for I haven't a doubt in the world he's the illegitimate son of some Grand Duke."

Caroline rose up momentarily, looking newly interested. "Do you think so? Well, then, it's settled." She lay back and withdrew into herself.

And settled it was. The first thing we had to do was convince Ellen Ternan to abandon plans for a return to England. She must seclude herself at La Sainte Vie, where she would have the best attention from French doctors, midwives, servants — anything her heart desired. In the meantime, in London, we would mount a distraction, the like of which the social world had never seen before.

Word has it that Wilkie Collins' mistress — the crazy one — is leaving him. That's what we hear. Going to publicly marry a cripple ten years younger than she. Everyone says it's true.

And — suddenly it came to me — I would personally attend the wedding! Perhaps I would even give away the bride. Everyone would be stunned! My brain was alive with brilliance!

Not one grand dame in all of London would miss such an opportunity. Caroline and I would be the centre of attention for weeks. And then, there was Joseph Clow. We could easily make him think all this was serious. Caroline would lead him to believe she was swept off her feet by his charm, his wit, his brilliant poetry. We might even pay *The Times* to print a little of it. Surely, we could convince the idiot his attractiveness to women was overwhelming, especially with an aristocratic blood-line I would suddenly discover in hitherto sealed documents.

"Here's the plan, my darling. The two of you will marry in a garish, bizarre ceremony, attracting all of London, and after an appropriate honeymoon to, say, Romantic Manchester, you'll return to settle at Joseph Clow's town house above his mealy shop, and you will take out an advertisement in *The Times,* announcing you are *At Home* on Tuesdays. Who knows, perhaps some grand ladies with a sense of the absurd will find it irresistible to call on you."

Caroline had fallen asleep. It didn't matter. I had come up with a brilliant diversion. Not a soul in Great Britain would pay heed to Charles Dickens. His life would be more private and obscure than any time since his youth. We would drag all this out until after Ellen's own nine-months' dwarf was delivered and disposed of, in whatever means might best suit her. And then, she would return from an "extended visit" to her family on the Continent, to settle in quietly and unnoticed at Peckham.

I could not help but enjoy myself.

We set the plot in motion by sending a cable to Ellen in Florence.

> Under no circumstances return to England. D. forbids. Suggest immediate departure for La Sainte Vie. Will meet you there in fortnight. Tell no one.
>
> Wilkie

Meanwhile, Caroline composed a simple note to Joseph Clow, posted to his shop on Fitzroy Square.

I cannot tell you how much your poetry has moved me. Although I would greatly desire to meet you, I realise you must be a famous poet already overburdened with adoring women. Someone as simple as I would have no chance at touching your heart. But write to you I must, regardless of the consequences.

                                        An Admirer

Overnight a return note was slipped under our door. Again it seemed to have been scrawled in desperate haste on paper stained with oil drippings. We decided the odd letters and spellings might not be accidental. They were probably Clow's way of giving his poem as antique mystery. I sent for my brother Charlie, and we sorted through a dozen books on my shelf, searching for the source. Finally, we decided it might be an odd paraphrasing of a poem by Robert Browning.

> Hist! But a word, my Faire and soft Caroline —
> You see, I knowe your Name, and it is love.
> Make the word Prick uyp its Ear!
> Truyth's Golden o'er us although we Refuge it
> Nature, through Cobwebs we string her
> Well, I Forgat the rest.

We needed no laudanum to laugh ourselves silly. But Charlie raised a point I hadn't thought about.

"Are you sure you can trust the man? Do you feel safe turning Catherine over to him, even for a few months?"

"Safe! Of course. The man's an idiot, not a murderer."

"Yet, he might be dangerous."

I was still basking in the glee of my plot. "No, no," I insisted. "No, Joseph Clow merely has the mind of a child. He'll do for an easy tool, and when the time's up, he'll have no idea at all what's happened to him."

*

I took Caroline with me to visit Ellen in France, where she was being waited on by an old lady — a Mrs. Smathers — who seemed to have no hearing and no sense. It spoke well of Ellen that she surrounded herself with fools. But Ellen was sickly, her face looked puffy, her hands appeared painfully swollen. The jewellery she always draped about her person was gone. Her golden curls seemed flat and dull. When we explained our plan to her — Caroline and I laughing out loud at the delight of it — Ellen listened with only faint interest. She spoke little, as if her old spirit had been gravely wounded. We retired early and fled quickly the next morning. I felt inspired by how successfully everything was going. If anything, I was disappointed that everyone I knew was so easy to manipulate. My fictional characters gave me more trouble than Ellen Ternan and Joseph Clow.

Dickens and I were drinking in the Olde Pelican. The usual crowd had gathered about in the street, waiting to see the Great Man after his return from America. For the past week, the London papers had trumpeted his success. When he stepped off the train in Rochester, church bells rang. Banners and garlands of flowers dangled from lampposts. Newspapers reported several thousand farmers lined Gravesend Road all the way to Gad's Hill, throwing hats in the air and cheering. He was like a general returned triumphant from some foreign victory.

"They loved me in Boston," he said, lighting his cigar on the candle. "I tell you, a crowd stood in the street all night before reading. The line stretched half a mile in the dark. Tickets were being hawked at six times face value. I made five hundred pounds a night."

He grinned, leaning back in the chair. "The newspaper called it the most important social event since the Boston Tea Party. Every American writer of the age was there."

Dickens' hand trembled continuously. Several times, he reached for his ale and, several times, drew back, letting it set on the board untouched. He told me he was still suffering from a bad cold. He looked much worse. His eyes had an odd blankness to them, like the eyes of a doll that had been painted on, once bright and green, now faded and empty. The skin on his face sagged from exhaustion.

"The best of them are dead, now." He blew a thin line of cigar smoke toward the ceiling. "Cornelious Felton is dead, and Nathaniel Hawthorne is dead." He drew out his gold watch and opened the cover. The tremble in his hand was unmistakable. He snapped the cover closed without ever looking at the time.

"But let me tell you, Wilkie, I had the pleasure of meeting Emerson again — the old rhinoceros — and to my surprise he up and apologised for his early words, blaming it on youth and jealousy. I heard later from Longfellow that Emerson told him — confidentially, of course — that Dickens had too much talent for his genius. Not that he could have said it to my face. Emerson still spreads it about that he's the only genius in the Western world."

I laughed and ordered another round. Dickens seemed unstoppable, but he repeatedly lost his train of thought. His hair stood up oddly, as if he slept with his head under his pillow. His beard had turned almost white and even more untidy.

"Sir," I said, "I hope you'll allow me to say how pleased I am for you. I must also say you seem worn down by the strain of it all."

"Did I tell you about my dinner with Charles Sumner and

Edwin Stanton? It seems the two of them were in a cabinet meeting with Lincoln only hours before the assassination. And the President, they said — this is what they told me — the President was more serious than normal, sitting up very formal and dignified instead of his usual lolling about on his chair, and finally the President said, 'I've had a dream about a great broad rolling river, and I was drifting about — just drifting about.'"

Dickens' eyes grew even more distant. His hand ceased to tremble. "Lincoln claimed the dream had come to him three times."

Dickens seemed transfixed. He lifted his chin and gazed off toward some imaginary horizon on the western prairie. He had become Abraham Lincoln. "I've had a dream about a great broad rolling river," he said, imitating a sort of broad American twang. He was onstage again, the old actor in him taking over. "I've dreamed about a wide rolling river. And I drift — I drift."

The waiter came by with more ale. Dickens drew back into himself and relit his dead cigar on the candle.

"It's your health I'm concerned about, sir."

"Oh, it's true, in New York I had to take to my bed for a while. Frightful cold, you know. In Philadelphia, it got worse. They brought in some doctor so young he could have been one of my own children. He poked and prodded for a while and said it was a serious catarrh that had spread to the nervous system. Thought he detected some low action of the heart. But he was a mere boy, and I had a schedule to keep."

His cigar went out again. He tossed it away in disgust. "My God, it was exhausting. Albany, Utica, Syracuse, Rochester, Buffalo. Night after night, I read from *The Old Curiosity Shop* until I could recite it backwards. I was so weary. And the weather so bloody cold my whiskers froze on my face. It's a god-awful country, ruined by war, fouled by slavery. There was nothing to love there. I missed everything I love."

"I'm very proud of your success, sir. You deserve a long rest from such a triumph."

"No time at all. I've asked Wills to set up a whole new series of readings here in England. I've got to strike quickly while the newspapers are full of my American reception. We're going to draw the greatest crowds in history by calling it the Farewell Tour." He grinned with delight at his own cleverness.

"But sir," I complained, "your health must be attended to. And there's the matter of Ellen Ternan."

He flinched, as if I had slapped him.

"Yes," he said softly, like a child who has been caught and must confess. He lowered his eyes. "How is she, Wilkie?"

"Very much into her condition."

"Yes, yes, but how is she?"

"Full of sorrow, I should think. She feels she's betrayed you."

"It was my fault."

"The fault of human nature, sir."

"No. I have to accept it as entirely my responsibility. Not one word of blame can be attributed to her. Everyone frightened me about the consequences of taking her to America. I became obsessed with my reputation, and I abandoned her. It was disgraceful. She should have been with me."

"It can't be helped now," I pointed out. "And besides, I've come up with a wonderful diversion, a simply delightful plot-line that will distract all of London and most of Paris."

I laid out the plan for him, describing Joseph Clow in great detail — perhaps exaggerating a bit for the humour. He nodded at all the right points, but like Ellen, there seemed no laughter left in him. It was very disappointing to have striven so hard to accommodate his hour of need and find him so disinterested.

"I have several commitments this week," he said. "Then, I'll go immediately to France."

"There is one thing, sir. Ellen seems determined to bring the snivelling little infant back to England. Perhaps you could use your influence with her. It would complicate everything, and I fear the ruse would quickly be discovered by the press."

Dickens nodded.

"Do you think I should send a wire to Ellen? Let her know I'm home safe? I'll be there in a fortnight."

"I was speaking about our plans, sir. About the diversion."

"Yes, yes, I understand. A cable would be appropriate, necessary even. I've always trusted your advice, Wilkie."

I knew an out-of-work actor named Barlow Cheltenham. For a small sum, he agreed to call upon Joseph Clow and present himself as a solicitor for the Duke of Marlborough, who had recently died, leaving a secret letter (which I wrote myself). The letter explained how Clow was, in fact, the natural son of the Duke, twice removed, and therefore entitled to call himself the Baron of Barchester Towers. The solicitor explained to Clow that no land or fortune was attached to the title, but the Duke, in his generous love for the boy, had privately left him a token of esteem, some ten pounds, on condition he marry before the age of thirty.

"It's always good news to hear you've come into your fortune!" the solicitor exclaimed.

Clow nodded, accepting the shock soberly. He sighed. "With this here title comes the burden those of you amongst the lower classes can't never understand."

The next morning, we found on our doorstep a new love poem, accompanied by a package wrapped in greasy papers. Inside the paper was a dead guinea pig.

> This Gyft is left In her body's lieu.
> For Grand the Pleasure known in thee
> But my poor Faiths poor first-fruits be
> What! quintessential, Ethereal blyss
> For death's sweet chrism retained
> Quicke, tender, Virginal, and Unprofaned!

Charlie identified the verse as something butchered from Coventry Patmore, a poet long admired by many in the lower stations of life. Still, the symbolism of the dead guinea pig escaped us. I ordered our maid to throw it away, but Caroline had a better idea. Why not roast it up in a fine dish and return it to Mr. Clow, with her own poem of deepest gratitude?

We all laughed ourselves silly and then followed suit, dressing out the guinea pig with truffles and pastry. Cook objected greatly, but did as she was told, and we returned the dead beastie that very night, with a note from Caroline.

> This offering seems the least I can do for such gallantry.
> If you love me, you will eat its heart, as mine is eaten up
> with love for you.

Within a week, Caroline made a great and public display of moving out of our house. Trunks were stacked on the walk, with much delay and shouting and confusion. Several roughs were hired to load them on carts. Charlie mentioned it to a few friends, and by the following week, London was buzzing.

Caroline Graves has walked out on Wilkie Collins — with intent to marry another man — a prosperous merchant no one has heard of.

Collins is said to be under sedation.

Quite the contrary, Collins tossed her out. The gentleman in question is the third son of a well-known member of the House of Lords. He has a large plantation in Jamaica.

No, no, the man is a cripple, with an estate in the south. Caroline and Collins fought publicly on the sidewalk. It was disgraceful. Seems she wanted him to marry her, and when Collins refused, Caroline swore to find someone who would.

He's a dwarf! A gin dealer, with a secret past. Caroline's trunks were seen being carried into his shop.

It turns out they're cousins on Caroline's mother's side, who was once mistress of a lascivious Bulgarian count.

No, no, Clow is the natural son of Lord Carlton by a blind chambermaid with one arm.

They say he's a poet — like Lord Byron — crippled but wealthy beyond belief, an unknown mystery to the best society. Collins is said to have attempted suicide.

It's just been found out! Clow gives abortions in the alley behind his shop.

The newspapers continued to write about Dickens, but he was relegated to inside pages. Wilkie Collins and his former mistress became the new sensation of London. I delighted in it, as if everyone were whispering about a new mystery novel I'd just created. And in a sense, they were, don't you see? I was the author of real life. No one understood the plot, but everyone tried to guess the outcome. It was my grandest work, with motives so obtuse even future generations would never figure it out. If I reveal it now, it's because events turned out far differently than I planned. Like everything in Dickens' world, the plot took on a momentum of its own. The mystery became bizarrely heightened, fearfully so, in ways I could never have anticipated.

Dickens, in disguise, took the night crossing to France once every fortnight, returning within a few days, pale and exhausted. His eyes were sunken, his cheeks deeply lined. The relationship was strained, and the Great Man blamed himself. I couldn't seem to talk with him, not intimately, as we had in the past. He was too busy to talk. Portraits of him were offered for sale in almost every shop window. In the portraits, his eyes looked haunted, his hair too thin. He had become the Ancient Mariner, compelled to tell us the darkest truth about his soul. No one was listening. His public wanted him only as their beloved Mr. England. It took all my contrivance to keep him silent.

Engraved invitations were delivered by hand to everyone in the best society. The wedding would be conducted by the Rector of St. Marylebone (for a bribe somewhat higher than I anticipated). No expense was spared. Garlands of roses and iris draped the aisles, bouquets of peonies blanketed the altar. A choir was hired. An open white carriage with four horses would whisk the happy couple away. We rounded up fifteen street urchins to run behind the carriage throwing old shoes. The only problem came from Caroline herself. Her notes to me began to complain forcefully about living under vile conditions — with a creature who sometimes frightened her.

At her insistence, I finally paid a formal visit, entering Mr. Clow's shop through the front door on Fitzroy Square. A bell rang with iron dullness. No one appeared. The shop was dank, almost black. The horrific odour of pig turds slapped my nostrils. My boots squished and slid about in the stuff, which seemed generously spread about a dirt floor. I felt for a moment I might choke or panic. Here and there, small unidentified creatures scurried behind boxes and old barrels. I held my will steady and waited in the dark. The shop windows had long ceased to let in light. At best, a dim mortuary haze filtered through the smudge of twenty years.

On slanted board shelves, I could make out stacks of old newspaper, boxes that had lost their shape years ago, rusted tools, and here and there, any number of mildewed books.

"Hello!" I called out. My voice sounded tentative in the darkness. I did not make the mistake of calling again since it required me to take a deep breath.

A hollow clunking began overhead, then moved arhythmically down some hidden staircase. It seemed the only answer I would receive, for no sound of greeting rang out. I realised the clunking was more a series of odd swishes, followed by a skip and a thump. It seemed to beat out some horrifically strange rhythm: *puddle-dee-thump, sloshsssssss, ki-shooo, ssssszz, thump-de-swish,* like an industrial machine gone berserk in a deserted factory. Mr. Joseph Clow himself did not appear so much as manifest himself out of the darkness, like a pagan gnome crawling out from some Celtic forest, one shoulder higher than the other. Greasy hair drooped in tangles down his back. His eyes glowed with pricks of yellow light. He swivelled his leg about, loping oddly, and twisting as he approached.

"Mr. Collins," he snarled in a voice full of unease and discomfort, as if he must live continuously in bodily pain.

"Yes. I assume I have the pleasure of Mr. Joseph Clow."

He corrected me. "Sir Baron, the Duke of Barchester Towers." A heavy sigh signalled how deeply the burden of his new title weighed upon him.

"Are you quite sure?" I asked.

"Absolutely." He lifted his head and looked past me, as if I had greatly insulted him.

"Well then, congratulations are in order."

For a brief moment, Clow's head lolled about.

"None intended," he finally said.

"No, I should think not."

I had no idea of his meaning. The conversation did not seem to be starting well, and worse, several unidentified creatures — guinea pigs, I assumed — continued to scatter about under our feet with frightening squeaks.

"They keep mice away," Clow explained. "Few recognize their fat can be boiled down for candle wax."

"I confess I didn't know."

He nodded gravely. "Their bladder, when rubbed across a wart, will completely remove it in three days."

"Amazing."

"Few people know."

"You should write an essay for the papers."

"They've all been turned down."

"Shameful. Absolutely shameful."

I heard Caroline's voice above. "Please come up." She sounded strained, a little desperate.

The newly titled Sir Baron led the way up a shaky stairwell so low I had to bend over. In the living quarters the foul smell from below was somewhat fainter — but only somewhat. Caroline looked as pale as an inmate in a Turkish prison.

She looked hard into my eyes. "Delighted you could call."

The apartment seemed all one room, with an old cot to one side, separated from the main area by a stained sheet hanging on a rope. Everywhere stacks of yellowed newspapers toppled over. Candle wax dripped like ancient stalactites from bookshelves and windowsills. Piles of ragged books — mostly poetry, it seemed — littered the shelves randomly, looking as if they too would topple at any moment. Other books were heaped on the floor. A leg of books supported a table in the centre of the room. In spite of the benefit of guinea-pig-wax candles, the Baron seemed to have squandered a part of his inheritance on a shiny new oil lamp that occupied the middle of the table. The lamp smoked badly, but no one offered to trim the wick.

Caroline pointed me toward a seat on an oilcloth sofa with stuffing hanging out. I sank into it almost to the floor, my knees nearly touching my chin. I flailed about, trying not to topple in completely.

Caroline laughed, but there was no humor in it. Clow said nothing at all, merely loped about with one shoulder rising and falling in an odd rhythm, like a wolf with an old wound.

"Well, then," I finally said. "I've come to offer my services at your wedding. Anything at all that I might do to make the occasion bright and festive."

Neither Clow nor Caroline spoke.

"And, of course, to wish you hearty congratulations."

"You've come to claim your female," Clow barked. "But you can't have her. She's mine now, and she's in love with me. You can't get her back."

"I understand, sir. Truly I do. No hard feelings at all."

Clow kicked wildly with his bad leg — a looping blow at a slop pot, nearly toppling it. The vile liquid inside sloshed about, some of it splashing out on the greasy board floor. Clow almost toppled as well, catching himself with one hand on a shelf, which instantly cracked and tilted forward. About twenty books and several mouldy-green sausages crashed to the floor.

"You can't have her," he snarled.

Caroline didn't flinch. She turned to me with lidded eyes. I knew there would be some debt accrued here between the two of us, and I would be expected to pay rather handsomely when the time came.

"Now, now, sir," I said. "She's entirely yours, as you see. I accept that the better man has won."

Clow glared at me, breathing heavily, suspicious, and ready if necessary to declare a duel between gentlemen.

"It was your poetry, Sir Baron. She was won over by it. And, I must confess, so was I. So much so I've used what little influence I have in the literary world to arrange publication of one or two small pieces in *The Times*."

Clow did not trust me, or perhaps the words did not sink in.

"This is my study," he suddenly said, pointing to the shelves of books. It seemed only then that he realised a pile of them had fallen to the floor. "I've always been a scholar, you see."

"And a poet," I reminded him.

For the first time, he seemed affected by words. He turned himself about slowly, and with difficulty. Every movement of his body caused him to flinch. He turned until he came face-to-face with Caroline. He pointed at the vile green liquid on the board floor. "Clean up the slop."

Caroline glanced at me and walked to the far side of the room, lost in the darkness.

Clow hobbled over to where I still sat on the sofa, knees to my chin. "I keep the slop pot to drown the guinea pigs." He nodded, as if it were something only gentlemen like ourselves could understand.

"Naturally," I said.

He continued to stare down at me. "*The Times,* you said."

"Absolutely. If you wish to, of course. I sense you're not one of those who seeks fame and glory, and you may not like crowds of adoring readers gathering at your shop door."

He waved me away. "I'm accustomed to all that."

"Naturally."

"You're sure it's *The Times*."

"Quite certain."

"Well then, I'll have to accept that burden, too." He suddenly spun about, almost toppling over but catching himself on the table and knocking the lamp backward, until it tilted and fell, breaking the chimney and spilling oil across the floor. I sat in terror the whole place would catch fire, but the wick snuffed out quickly.

Clow stood shaking for a moment, then shouted at Caroline, "Wipe up the slop!"

My darling Caroline emerged slowly from the darkness with a dirty rag. She dropped it deliberately to the floor and, using the toe of her shoe, rubbed the rag back and forth a bit across the spilled slop. Then, with a delicate thumb and forefinger, she picked it up and carried it back into the dark, but not before she gave me another glance, this one of tears and desperation.

The Baron did not turn around to look at me. "You're excused, Mr. Collins. I'll have a runner deliver my poems to *The Times*."

"Well, then, I've enjoyed my visit."

There was no response, and I let myself out, feeling my way down the black stairs and hurrying through the pig dung, and stepping over the whispered scurry of frightened guineas racing blindly about my feet.

*

Charles Dickens was finally persuaded to attend the wedding. He sat toward the rear, forcing a tentative smile amidst a large crowd of celebrities and London socialites. It was a bright mid-summer day with elegant sunlight wafting through stained-glass windows in the transept. The men wore dove grey morning coats. The women wore gowns and bustles and straw bonnets trimmed in roses and lilies. I waited until the church was almost full, then walked boldly the length of the centre aisle to a front-row seat, hearing the hushed whispering flow like a wave through the congregation. A choir sang "For Lo, the Winter's Past." The rector entered in white vestments. Then, Sir Baron, the Duke of Barchester Towers — born Joe Clow — clumped in from a side door wearing an ill-fitting coat, one I had selected for him myself, one that happened to be several sizes too large with tails that dragged behind him on the floor. He looked like a small boy dressed in his father's clothing. Our bride wore white satin with a white veil and a ten-foot white lace train — to symbolise her purity. For the fun of it, she carried a bouquet of straw, with one blood red rose in the centre.

The rector said all the appropriate words. The new Duke placed a tin ring on the bride's finger, lifted her veil, and tugged her face down to his. Caroline showed no emotion. She pulled back deliberately, and in front of everyone wiped the kiss from her lips. The choir burst into song: "My Beloved Spake." And the happy couple hurried down the centre aisle with sober faces, setting off for their honeymoon in a hired carriage before most of us could even exit the pews.

As a sign the gods looked favourably on all this, we later heard that Ellen Ternan, far away in France, had spread her legs and heaved out a bloody boy at almost exactly the same time as the wedding ceremony. I took it as a clear sign the gods have a sense of humour and, no doubt, as confirmation my little scheme was being propelled from powers on high.

Unfortunately, that's when Dickens also revealed Ellen remained determined to bring the baby back to England. She would remain in confinement a few weeks more at La Sainte Vie, then return with Mrs. Smathers to Windsor Lodge at Peckham. Nor would she agree to placing the infant out with a wet nurse in the countryside. The baby must be close by, she insisted. Purely for spite, I assume, she wanted to visit it frequently. It was a mean twist I hadn't prepared for, a meanness on the part of Ellen that revealed her lack of compassion for Dickens.

I worked out a new plot, with less than a fortnight to set it in motion. Joseph Clow and Caroline would return on July 9, the same day Ellen planned to leave France. Two problems had to be solved immediately. Ellen couldn't be seen getting off a train at London Bridge Station with a swaddling child in her arms. And she couldn't keep the stinky little creature at Peckham. It remained a fact that common folks still did not know about Ellen and her relationship to the Great Man. But that kind of secret can't be kept from everyone. Over the years, Dickens had gradually revealed the illicit relationship to most of his male companions. Early on he invited twenty of us for a boating excursion on the Thames, in the summer of what — 1861, perhaps. I recall the air was clear and sunlight danced on the water. We were all eating cold roast beef and drinking cider. And Ellen was there — it may have been to celebrate Ellen's birthday. She was the only woman onboard. Forster was in attendance, of course, and Wills and Townsend and Thackeray. If I remember correctly, Browne and Cruikshank were there, and Evans, Dickens' publisher. I'm sure Bulwer-Lytton was there, with Macready and Edmund Yeats. All of Dickens' intimate friends. But no wives, no other women at all.

Ellen Ternan was just twenty-one or twenty-two that day, and smelling of lavender. I remember how those famous golden locks flowed out from under a most fashionable bonnet of rich silk, the colour of pearl. She always looked much younger than she was, and in those days she had a kind of innocent sexuality that drove Dickens wild. She would tilt her head at the Great Man, and she would smile, ever so subtly, as if she understood him, as if she saw through him to a vastly earlier time or as if there were some great secret between them. Dickens would suddenly remember where he had come from: the shoe blacking factory, the humiliation of a father imprisoned for debt, a servant they couldn't afford to pay, a dog named Maggot, a little boy lost who wanted love. For a while, he would become little Charlie again. For a few minutes, talking to Ellen at the back of the boat or allowing her to feed him morsels of cold roast beef under the awning. Standing by her, smoking a cigar, the two of them leaning lightly against the railing and studying the water, as if they were surveying lives yet to come, his hand on the rail, his little finger almost touching her hand on the rail, like Russian ballet dancers who meet at midstage and pause as the music hovers about them, holding the note, their bodies almost touching but not quite — infinitely long, until you think the pressure unbearable, until suddenly they drew away at the same time, choreographed, Dickens talking loudly and laughing with Forster, and Ellen sweeping out from the shade of the awning into the sunlight, her face flushed with sweet cunning. No one onboard could have doubted their relationship, although, being gentlemen all, none of us said a word, even to each other.

If Ellen Ternan stepped off a train in London Bridge Station, looking pale and swollen, carrying in her arms a crying baby barely two weeks old, someone of importance was bound to see her. One could not pass through London Bridge without meeting any number of charming acquaintances coming and going. Everyone could overlook the affair. No one could overlook the delightful scandal of an illegitimate son.

I poured myself a drop of laudanum and settled in for a night of plotting. I long believed no conflict in plot is ever unreconcilable. All the mysterious twists and turns, all the unscheduled events, all the recalcitrant characters can be handled with imagination and clever skill.

Indeed, everything progressed even better than planned. Dickens returned from a hurried trip to France with good news. Ellen agreed, reluctantly, that someone else could carry the baby into London, and I immediately arranged that the "someone" would be none other than Martha Rudd, exactly the right age and demeanor for a single mother travelling alone with her infant.

Then, Caroline and Joseph Clow returned from their honeymoon two days early. And who better to play nurse to Ellen's baby than Caroline herself. It was only necessary for Martha to deliver the baby on arrival in London to Caroline, who would immediately present it to Sir Baron of Barchester Towers as their own child, sired in the course of their honeymoon. The Baron would never understand what had happened. The image of Joseph Clow being told that his new wife had already been delivered of an heir was one I treasured with absolute delight.

Martha Rudd left a day early to ensure she would be waiting at the customs area in Caen. Her cable arrived at midnight.

*

All well. Departure tomorrow morning. Arrive London
Bridge 10:39 P.M.

The next day, when it was all over, Martha told me everything that happened. She had worn a frayed grey dress with no
hoops or bustle. Her black hair had been wrapped in a scarf
and tied with an ordinary knot. To most people, she would
have been unnoticeable, a servant or factory girl travelling
alone. She had never seen Ellen Ternan before, but she spot-
ted her immediately. A brightly attractive woman, still somewhat heavy from her condition, in a richly tailored travelling
outfit with lace collar and cuffs, and carrying a small spaniel in
her arms. Ellen was accompanied by an older companion,
who carried an infant wrapped in rich blue cotton. Four male
servants unloaded two carts of baggage and trunks. Another
servant, probably a butler, was sent to take care of tickets and
customs. Clearly, she was a woman of stature. She would not
be kept waiting in line for a customs inspection but would be
escorted aboard immediately on first call.

Martha held back until the luggage had been taken away.
Then she approached Mrs. Smarthy, who nodded, as if they
had some distant acquaintance. Ellen Ternan did not look
around. She stood with chin raised, gazing toward the first-
class doors, as if nothing of any importance could possibly be
going on around her in such a location.

"I do appreciate y'r taking care of the baby for me," Martha
said. "My affairs are in order now, and I'll take 'im back, if you
please."

It was the code we had worked out in advance.

At that point, Ellen could not resist. She turned briefly and
stared hard at Martha, as if memorising her face, then turned

her back and paid no more attention, as if it were nothing more than a bothersome affair between servants.

"You promise to take good care of him now," Mrs. Smarthy said, reluctant at first to hand over the bundle.

"Oh, yes'm. I wouldn't let no harm come to me own son, now, would I?"

Mrs. Smarthy still hesitated. "And you've arranged now for a wet nurse, haven't you? It will be a long journey."

Martha looked at Mrs. Smarthy intensely. She'd been a servant too recently herself to have forgotten the feeling of humiliation at being treated like an idiot.

"I swear I have. It was kind of you to hold 'im for me, but all the arrangements' taken care of, I swear they are, ma'am."

Ellen again took a quick, desperate look — this time at the sleeping child in the bundle — then walked away, trying not to show emotion. Mrs. Smarthy held the bundle out for Martha, and the transfer was made. In a busy terminal, no one noticed. Within moments, Ellen Ternan and Mrs. Smarthy had been escorted onto the boat. Martha got her first look at the baby then. He was some three or four weeks old, rather small for a boy, with a frizzle of hair and tiny fingers that opened and closed of their own volition. He had been sleeping to that point, but he opened his eyes and gazed blankly about. The colour of the eyes was always in question. On the one hand, they were dark. Very dark. On the other hand, they might have been blue, or black with hints of blue. Several hours passed before second-class passengers were allowed to board the ferry, climbing a steep gangplank before being pushed below deck. In the hold of the ship, Martha clearly remembered the baby looking at her with a long steady gaze, lifting its little pink hand, and opening and closing its fingers.

"Something happened to me," she confessed. "I never once

in my life thought of having a baby. Coming from a family of nine, all squalling and fighting and hungry, I never once even considered it. But that little thing looked up at me, and I felt some strange tightening in that place where a woman feels it, and it grew all hot, and my bosom grew hot, and I wanted then what I'd never wanted before."

Earlier that evening, Caroline appeared at my door. The humour of her situation with Joe Clow had long since worn off. I held her in my arms for the longest time while she cried and swore she could not return. Nor would I have asked her, except for the foolishness of Ellan Ternan. Caroline would have to be at Clow's shop to accept the transfer of the baby. But that was hours away, and we settled down with a small teaspoon of laudanum. In some ways, our separation had been good for us. We felt strongly about being alone together again. We were tentative with each other, yet laughing and relaxed. She was home at last, and I dreaded losing her again, even for a short while.

Caroline kept saying, "Oh God, please don't make me go back."

We laughed about Sir Baron and mocked him, and after a while, we celebrated surviving him with another dose of laudanum. This time I used the needle and injected us both. The effect is so much more swift in that manner. Within moments, we were both swimming in a blue haze, settling down in each other's arms, and drifting through the pleasures of old memories and warm feelings.

In fact, I had not forgotten to arrange for a wet nurse. She boarded the ferry separately at Caen and, several times during the crossing, suckled Ellen's little beastie in the rolling hold.

The sailing was late, as it always is, and the boat missed the first two trains to London, catching the last possible one at 9:10 P.M. Martha rode in a smoke-filled second-class car with wooden bench seats. The train rocked and swayed and rumbled for an incredible number of hours to London Bridge Station, being held up at every small station and crossing. When they arrived, it was long after midnight. The crowds were heavy getting off, all of them frustrated and tired. Martha never again saw Ellen Ternan, who travelled first class. Presumably, she departed immediately for Peckham.

The wet nurse demanded to be paid extra and held the child captive until Martha had slipped her two pounds more than agreed upon.

"We was late," the wet nurse said. "I've missed my train to Slough, and I'll need to stay the night, won't I?"

The rain from earlier in the day had let up, but the streets were still wet, and a hack could not be found. By the time Martha reached Fitzroy Square on foot, it was almost dawn. After that she found an available cab and returned to Gloucester Place. Caroline and I had passed out in a drugged sleep on the sofa. Martha's knocking did not wake us. The downstairs maid was finally roused by the pounding. She and Martha quarrelled on the doorstep, but Martha pushed her way in and woke us both by shaking us. We ordered tea, and that caused more rumpus. The fire was not lit. Cook was not awake. For a while, the house was bedlam. We finally settled down with a pot of hot tea and some yesterday's scones. The morning sun was just up.

That's when Martha told us about it. We made her start from the beginning, listening to every delicious twist and turn I had thought up, and how it unfolded so excellently.

We laughed. Sipping the last of the tea.

Caroline still had a mouthful of scone. "But where's the baby?"

"You wasn't there," Martha said.

"Wasn't where?" Caroline asked.

"At Joe Clow's shop. Wilkie told me to give you the baby at Joe Clow's shop. When I finally roused him, he said you wasn't there and didn't know where you'd gone out."

In the fog of the waning laudanum, I listened with puzzled good humour.

Martha turned to me. "So I told him what Caroline was supposed to tell him."

"And what was that?" I spread strawberry preserves over my stale scone.

"Why, that it was Caroline's baby. And you should'a seen his face. He looked mighty funny, like he was trying to take it all in. He kept saying, 'Whose baby?' and I kept saying, 'Your baby. This here's your baby, and Caroline will be home soon to help you take care of it.'"

"Like hell I will," Caroline said, and we all burst into laughter.

Caroline poured more tea. We talked for a while about other things.

I finally asked, "So where did you leave the baby?"

"I told you, I left it with Joe Clow."

For another long moment, we sat chewing and sipping, and then the fog of my mind began to grow red hot.

"My great God! You didn't!"

"Caroline wasn't there."

I shouted for the downstairs maid, and Caroline was on her feet at the same time. Everyone in the house began to run and shout.

"A cab! Flag down a cab! We need a hack now!"

I grabbed my old Wide-Awake, and Caroline snagged the very shawl off Martha's shoulders as the two of us ran for the front door.

Outside, the streets still showed a faint glistening from the rain. Here and there, a carriage moved through thin morning fog. We could hear the clopping of horses' feet. The sun was rising gradually above heavy clouds in the east. Not a hack could be seen anywhere. The two of us ran as fast as we could to York Street.

"There's one. There's one."

"Cab! Here!"

"Fitzroy Square," I shouted, "as fast as you can fly."

"Where is it, mate?"

"To Marylebone, then right, fast as you can." I flung the young driver a sovereign. "Now!"

The carriage leapt into motion, and we bounced and flew across the cobbles, the driver's whip snapping and his voice crying out to pedestrians ahead, "Make way! Make way! Emergency here!"

Caroline and I said not another word, clinging to each other and the bouncing hack. In our hearts, we heard each other cry again and again, "My God, my God."

At Marylebone, we slipped into the flow of morning traffic, stalled behind lorries and ale wagons. I leaned out.

"Faster! Faster!" Ahead I could see the Royal Academy of Music on the left. "It's the first right past Cleveland," I shouted. "Just after you enter Euston."

The driver whipped his animal, and we swung wildly about, barely missing a slow-moving hansom cab carrying an old lady, who peered out at us with sudden fright.

Joseph Clow's shop looked dark and shut up, as it always

did. I threw the driver another sovereign for a tip. He looked as if he would faint. The horse heaved with gasping and snorting. Caroline ran to the front door. It was locked, but she had a key. Still, it took a frantic moment or two for her to find it in her cloth purse. We burst in together, hearing the clang of the iron bell in the rooms above. Even in our rush, the overwhelming odour of pig dung slapped me in the face like a wet towel that has gone horribly sour. Guinea pigs scurried hysterically across the slippery floor.

I led the way up, two steps at a time, our feet echoing in the narrow staircase like twenty drummers.

"Clow!" I shouted.

"Joseph! Joseph!" Caroline called.

At the top, I flung open the door. The room was silent as a black mausoleum.

"Joseph!"

"It's Collins," I said. "Where are you, Clow? We're not here to hurt you. Don't be afraid."

We stopped dead, our heavy breathing the loudest sound in the embalmed dark.

"The lamp," Caroline whispered. But we had nothing to light it with.

I ran to a window and ripped away the rag curtain. Only a faint lick of light seeped through the glass. The sash wouldn't budge. In the stumbling dark my hands found a book, and I threw it through the glass. I found another book and, pane by blackened pane, I broke out every barrier to the morning sun.

I was still struggling to let in the light when I heard Caroline moan behind me.

"What?"

She pointed.

The slop pot overflowed. A greenish slush of garbage and human turds lay on the floor. Above the rim of the pot, two infant feet bobbed and floated oddly.

At the inquest a week later, Joseph Clow was indicted for murder, but Clow was never found. Some heard on the street he was hiding in Liverpool. Many believed he slipped away to Australia — as others of his kind have. Others said he sailed to America and joined the masses of migrating poor heading west in long wagon trains. On one occasion, I received an odd letter from a solicitor in Warsaw, demanding payment of one hundred pounds for causing the estrangement of a wife from her husband, a gentleman, described as a man of some repute who continued to suffer grievously from my actions. I hired a detective to trace the origin of the letter, but he was unable to locate the supposed solicitor. The last rumour that came to me suggested one Joe Clowsky, a midget, had been shot in a gun fight near Rock Springs, Wyoming. By then, it no longer mattered.

Mr. Dickens and I saw little of each other after that. Ellen Ternan blamed me for everything. I heard through friends she thought I'd planned it all, a murder for hire, paying off Clow and even helping him escape. All the rest — Clow's inheritance from a supposed aristocrat, Caroline's wedding and her honeymoon — all of it was nothing more than a distraction from the real evil I'd intended all along.

Caroline Graves returned to Gloucester Place, of course, and that seemed to give substance to Ellen's argument. There was no way to correct it all. No way to explain. For days, Caroline and I slipped silently into each other's arms and held on tight. But it was not enough. Caroline was never able to be intimate with me again. I can't explain it. Our friendship remained strong, but she could not recover. I turned to playwriting with modest success, but my fiction dried up. All those devious plots and suspenseful twists that entertained me so much through the years now seemed to avoid me. Nothing came from my pen. My gout worsened. My body ached and burned. I began to spend more and more of my life with Martha in our quiet little house on Bolsover Street. We consoled each other, as it were. It was Martha gave me the calm and forgiveness I needed, the sense of family I never knew I wanted. We both recognised in our heart a heavy burden for a terrible tragedy. I knew it more deeply than I could express to others. I never blamed Martha or Caroline. I alone was responsible. It was my own hubris. The Greeks revealed it first so very long ago. We are blind to our failings as well as our fate. I could not see to see. And then I saw, and my already racked body became twisted with pain and unforgiving regret.

Over the years, the laudanum helped briefly, but did not stop ghosts from appearing in my bedroom. My father appeared often, angry and silent. On one occasion, a woman with green teeth accosted me on the stairs, causing me to fall violently. Worst of all, late one night, as I struggled to write, alone in my bedroom, crumpling page after miserable page, I looked up in horror to see myself sitting across from me. The other — the other Wilkie Collins, my double — reached out and grabbed at my writing tablet, attempting to twist it away from me. I held on, and he clawed for the very pen in my hand. I fought him, clawing back. We wrestled violently over the table, spilling ink across my gown and across the white Persian rug under me. The splash looked like blood dripping off the table, and I thought for a moment I could see the face of Ellen Ternan in it, looking back at me. Others heard my scream, heard me fall, and rushed to help me into bed.

I seldom leave here now. From time to time, I receive a note from Charles Dickens. Usually something formal concerning old business contracts. He signs the note with his initials. Never with a salutation. I would see him if I could, explain to him if he would allow me the privilege. Instead, I write a formal missive in reply, but I sign it, "Yours, Wilkie," or sometimes "In Friendship, Wilkie." I expect no response and there is none. I watch shadows of failing sunlight slip across the wall of my bedroom. Carriages rumble by in the cobbled street below. Am I worse than Dickens? Did I not serve at his calling? If the plot went wrong, was it not because the plot of Dickens' life itself seemed always to fail him? To what end does a man do everything for others, for reputation, for wealth? Hadn't Charles Dickens created the man he wanted to become? He had always been magnificent at inventing characters. But had he lived a full life? Had he found the plot that gives support and substance to the character? No. His life was rich in art but empty of more simple human experiences. The plot of his life always disappointed him. In that sense, he failed us all. We idolised him and made him more than he was, until he couldn't become what we needed him to be. What he wanted to be; not a writer loved, but a man loved — intimately. That's where he failed. He couldn't control the players, couldn't shape the dialogue, couldn't untangle the mystery. And mystery is what it's all about, isn't it? That's where I tried to help. I can't blame Charles Dickens. Only myself. In the end, the plot failed me as well. Or I failed the plot. Could I have foreseen the consequences? And does it matter? If I had known all in advance, wouldn't I have constructed it differently? And yet. Oedipus knew in advance, and the plot he wrote to avoid what he knew destroyed all he loved. It's the mystery we want, not knowledge of the ending, which can never be satisfactory. Knowing in advance, after all, is nothing more than knowing our sorrow in advance. The mystery alone gives life to it. The mystery we live into every day and wish for and love and fear. Nothing else matters.

Georgina Hogarth

A T GAD'S HILL, we cowered in silence. Charles moved slowly from room to room, like an old grey elephant searching vaguely for something lost. Sometimes he locked himself in his library, where he called for a fire but let no one in.

Hubbard ran one hand across his bald head, straightening invisible hairs. "I tell you, it's some great loss of funds. A man never acts like this except when he's lost money."

And it was true, the eldest son, Charlie, had gone bankrupt. But he and his father had never been close since Catherine's departure. Charlie's situation couldn't have driven the Great Man to such brooding darkness.

Hubbard argued his point. "Consider what it must be like to raise a family of failures," he said. "Consider how it must feel to be known as the greatest gentleman in England and to have failed with all those you care most about."

Hubbard pointed to Plorn, who had only just cabled another plea from Australia to let him come home.

And there was Sydney in South Africa, asking his father to cover gambling bills.

And Frederick, a brother who died recently, leaving his family destitute.

Then there was Katie's husband, a handsome man, so charmingly ineffectual he couldn't support Katie, even on an inheritance from his mother.

And tax collectors. That was another matter altogether. The government fought with him almost daily for ever higher taxes on the fortune he brought from America.

And, of course, Ellen Ternan, with all her houses and jewels.

"I can't deny the weight of the problem," I said. "But my heart tells me this grief is about something preying on his soul. I know him better than anyone. I feel it wrapped about him like winter fog. He has closed his heart and won't open it again, I fear."

Only months earlier, Charles returned from America in triumph, full of new plans and ideas. He ordered a conservatory built on the back of Gad's Hill. "Glass and tile," he instructed the architect. "I want to compete with the Crystal Palace."

He turned to me and whispered, "It will be my last great renovation, and I'm determined to enjoy it in the time I have left."

He and the architect hiked about the lawn in great bold strides, measuring imaginary walls of glass. Dickens pointed out where doorways would open into the dining room on one side and into the drawing room at the back. From the conservatory, the lawn would slope gradually downward toward a brick wall at the rear. The view would look across fields of wheat and distant woods toward Cobham. Charles was never happier than when he was making plans. And although his face showed ever-deepening lines of stress and pain, he assured me he was happy.

"I'm looking toward the future," he whispered. "A time when I might even decide to retire. Can you imagine me retired? No, no, I can't either. But somehow, it begins to close in on me. Even Shakespeare retired. I begin to know the future is no longer open-ended, you see. It's like some dark wall approaching, sometimes slowly, sometimes with disturbing speed." He pointed to the conservatory construction. "I think that's why I'm building out of glass now. I want to be surrounded by glass."

His plans for the Farewell Tour were as inspired as his plans for the conservatory. "I want this last tour to be the boldest ever undertaken," he said. "I want everyone talking about it into the next century."

Arrangements were made in Manchester and Liverpool, at St James' Hall, and at Cheltenham, York and Canterbury, Leeds, and Bury St. Edmunds. Readings were scheduled at Chester and Saltergill and Edinburgh. Dozens of halls were rented. Dublin and Galway were added to the list. Bills printed. Advertisements arranged in the papers. Hotel rooms reserved. Forster and Wills worked full-time on the project every day for months. Throughout the summer, advance ticket sales were recorded on the front pages of the newspapers.

And then, something happened. Ellen Ternan returned from France, and something had gone wrong. I found Charles alone in his library, having walked all night from Peckham, twenty miles in heavy fog. He had often walked that far before, but never had it tired him so seriously. His white hair lay wet and straggled about his head. His beard hung limp on his chest. I wrapped him in a cotton blanket and brought towels to dry him. He would not touch hot tea carried in on a tray by Cook. And when the usual bag of mail arrived later that morning, he ignored it — something unheard of in thirty years.

I thought he spoke, but I wasn't sure.

"Sir?"

He said it again, softly.

"I'm sorry, Charles, I didn't catch what you said."

He stared vaguely out the window at the rose garden, planted so many years ago, when the house tumbled over with children and dogs. For a long moment more, he continued his silence. I waited, unsure whether to stay or go.

I heard him whisper. "I dreamed I was floating on a broad river."

What he said made no sense, but I climbed straightaway to my bedroom and cried for half an hour.

In the sitting room, they were arguing. Charles paced up and down in front of the mirrors. Mr. Wills and Mr. Forster were there taking notes, arguing about a change in the Farewell Tour Charles had suddenly proposed. I carried in a tray of glasses and a decanter of brandy from the billiard room, where Charles kept his private stock.

"My God, sir, you can't be serious." Wills stared at him.

"I've been thinking about it for some weeks. It will be absolutely unexpected. Perhaps unsettling to some, but I have no comedy left in me, none at all."

He stopped in front of a mirror and studied his haggard face. The mirrors were something he'd insisted on years ago, when he first moved into Gad's Hill. At that time the sitting room had been fairly small, with a single window facing Gravesend Road. Almost immediately Charles ordered an addition, doubling the length of the room, opening up new windows. But the interior wall was still long and blank until Charles thought of adding a row of mirrors. The mirrors reflected the opposite windows, bringing sudden light and brilliance. After that, he had gone through the house calling for more mirrors in almost every room.

When I came into the sitting room, Forster was trying to explain something to Charles. "All it will take," he said, "is for one woman at the back of the hall to cry out, 'Murther!' and faint dead away. The crowd will panic in hysteria."

"Or, at the least, be revolted," Wills added. "Word will get about. Ticket sales will plummet."

"Quite possibly." His tone clearly said he didn't care. "All my instincts tell me I must."

Wills acknowledged my arrival for the first time. "Let's ask this worthy woman." He pointed at me as if I were some stranger walked in off the street. I'm quite sure I blushed.

Charles spun about to confront me, as if I had challenged him directly. "So!" he cried. "Your feelings at once, madam! Don't think it over, just give us your true response."

I could hardly breathe I was so astonished.

"I was bringing brandy, sir, and I've not the privilege of overhearing your discussion."

"You see!" Charles shouted at Forster and Wills. "You've upset this fine lady for no reason."

He turned back to me with gentleness. "Sit down here, won't you?" He led me to a bench seat in one of the bow windows. Bright summer light fell across him like a spotlight on the stage. The mirrors behind reflected more light, illuminating him, so that he was no longer my Charles but some dramatic figure, enlarged and immortalised in front of my eyes.

"Madam," he said, "I propose to do something different for my Farewell Tour, and these two learned gentlemen have expressed their reservation." He bowed slightly at Forster and Wills, who sat in shrunken silence.

Charles began again. "Georgina, instead of reading from

Pickwick or *A Christmas Carol* — instead of providing a comical evening — I've decided to reveal the bloody truth, which will out anyway someday, as Shakespeare himself so often said."

He stood over me, like Edmund Kean onstage, playing Hamlet's father and dragging a heavy chain, his face as stricken and white as his wild beard.

"Madam, I have determined to read from *Oliver Twist!*"

He said it in such a way he clearly thought I would be shocked, but when I wasn't shocked and, no doubt, looked only puzzled, he spun about to Forster and Wills. "You see, gentlemen! She doesn't flinch."

Wills leaned forward in his chair. "Miss Hogarth," he said gently, as if explaining something complicated to a young child. "Charles is proposing to read the scene in *Oliver Twist* where Bill Sikes murders Nancy."

For a moment, no one spoke. The three gentlemen stared at me for reaction. I could hear them breathing. They waited. Yet I knew of no response. My brain burned with old images: the flash of Sikes' pistol, a young girl blinded with blood, the violent bludgeoning with a heavy club while the most innocent Nancy staggers and falls to her knees, breathing one last prayer of mercy to heaven.

"It would be quite stunning," I finally whispered. "The nation has waited, too patiently I fear, all these many decades."

I turned and looked directly into Charles's eyes, eyes that had always seemed so dear to me and that now appeared hollow and foreign. Burning in an odd way. They pierced my weakened heart and made me want to shiver. Something in him, I thought. Something, indeed, must out.

I turned to Forster and Wills, their heads not quite reaching as high as the mirrors, so that above them there was no reflection of their existence at all, only the image of Charles Dickens, illuminated and shimmering with light, as if it were the ghost of Dickens, and not the man himself, hovering there in the sitting room where he had held so many happy parties and happy readings, sometimes with a hundred guests or more. As he turned and walked the length of the room, his image passed through each mirror, until he stopped at the bow window with his back to us, a black silhouette enveloped in light.

I explained it all to the two mortal men sitting across from me, their knees together in puzzled humility.

"My husband," I began — and caught myself. The gentlemen glanced at each other out of the corners of their eyes. I dared not look at Charles.

Slowly, I refolded my hands and tried to focus my mind.

"Charles," I said under my breath. "Charles is proposing a tragic act of atonement for the nation. It will be his greatest triumph, the *Macbeth* of our time, where murder and the haunting memory of blood will serve as our redemption."

I heard my own voice speaking, but truthfully, I couldn't recall where I'd ever got such a notion, and then I thought I might have heard Bulwer-Lytton saying something similar once, about another author, but for the life of me I couldn't remember who or where.

Forster and Wills stared at me. Even Charles turned and looked from across the room, although in the brightness I could not see his shadowed face. I tried very hard to focus my mind. A woman like myself is supposed to defer to a gentleman, especially three such learned gentlemen — a writer, an editor, and a lawyer. No one knew me as anything more than a silent caretaker of Charles' children, a nanny of sorts, a befuddled governess at best. I realised my hands were folded tightly in my lap, cold as splintered ice in summer, and I dared not let go for fear of trembling.

"There!" Charles shouted at his companions. "That's exactly what I've been trying to tell you."

He stomped up to me in his boots. His face softened. Eyes that recently had become so hardened and distant warmed to my own.

He looked down at me and shook his head gently. "Once again, you've known my heart better than me. I only knew I had to do this and not why it drove me so."

He held out his hand, and I took it, rising and straightening my skirts.

"Gentlemen." I nodded to all three.

Their silence followed me out. I went straight upstairs to my bedroom over the sitting room. Muffled voices below kept on for several minutes, then I heard all go out the front door. From my front window, I could see them politely inspecting Charles' rose garden, pretending nothing of significance had happened. I sat in my chair by the empty fireplace and cried, long and hard. When the time came to stop crying, the house was silent, and Charles again locked himself in his library.

Charles thought best to revise his will. Lawyers came and went for days, scriveners, copyists, advisors. He joined me in the newly finished conservatory. We arranged a small table, and he asked me to bring two glasses and a bottle from the billiard room. It seemed a special moment to him, and although I never much cared for the taste of brandy, I did as he asked. He toasted our life together, and we sat quietly for a long time, watching a farmer ploughing misty fields near the woods of Cobham. The ploughman was too far away for us to hear him.

He crossed slowly back and forth behind two horses, his plough unearthing dark, wet soil. A spiral of crows dived and swooped behind him, making a raucous cawing.

"In my will," Charles said, "I've named Ellen Ternan first."

For a moment, my weakened heart slipped away. "Yes sir," I finally agreed.

"One thousand pounds." He poured himself another glass of port.

We sat in long silence, watching the plough furrow the black earth.

"For Catherine, I've set up a large trust. She can't be worried with the monies directly. Henry will take charge of the funds and provide her with living expenses. After she dies, the capital will be divided among the living children."

"Yes sir."

"For Charlie, I've also left my library."

"Very appropriate and generous."

"For Forster, I've bequeathed my favourite watch." He drew the gold piece from his pocket and checked the time, snapping it shut again.

"Yes sir."

"And all my manuscripts."

"I understand."

In the far distance, angry crows whirled about, fighting and squabbling over spoils. The ploughman ignored them, treading steadily behind his horse. For him, there was only the horse and the soil.

"And for you, Georgina, I've left my single largest bequest."

I closed my eyes, not wanting to hear, my breath already dead in my chest, as if my heart had seized my lungs and squeezed them shut.

"For you, eight thousand pounds directly. And instructions

to all my children to remember how much they owe you. I don't think they'll need instruction, but I want to ensure you'll never be wanting in affection."

"Thank you, Charles."

"There's one other thing." He reached across the table and held out his hand for me. I placed my small hand in his, dry and trembling.

"Georgina, I've assigned you to be my executor. Along with Forster, of course."

"I understand."

"It's a great burden, but I can't leave the responsibility to Catherine. She has no sense in these matters, no strength of conviction without someone else to tell her what to do."

I nodded, feeling his fingers close around mine. We sat in long silence. All about us rose exotic plants Charles had ordered, with blooms as bright as South American parrots. Early spring sun burned through the glass over our heads, and the wet heat inside the conservatory began to fill my lungs, as if I had been crying, although I hadn't.

"There's one last thing. I've directed this to Catherine, but I want you to ensure it happens exactly."

"I would never fail you."

"I've directed an inexpensive and unostentatious funeral. I want it completely private, you see. No announcements in the newspapers. No posters on church walls. This is vital to me, Georgina. I've lived such a public life, I want this one last moment of privacy."

"A burial," I said, "should belong to the family."

"Exactly. I want to be buried at home, in Rochester, in the Cathedral churchyard. Don't let them do anything else to me, Georgina. None of that hideous pomp the mob uses to advertise their grief in public. No black ribbons, no black bows or hatbands. No one hired to walk behind a coach with handkerchiefs to their noses."

"I understand, Charles. After all these years, I know your heart."

We were silent a moment. He nodded, his face wasted and grim. "I feel exhausted. You stay here and enjoy the spring sunshine."

I heard him move slowly, limping on painful legs through the dining room to his study, where he locked the door. The house was so quiet I could hear the hall clock ticking. Far away, the ploughman cut through the earth for one more season. Crows dived and cawed about his head. He took off his cap and flailed at them, beating them away.

I ordered two of the servants bring an old rocking chair from the attic of the carriage house. It was a chair we used whenever there were new babies tumbling about. I had rocked almost all of them in it, so long ago. We cleaned and oiled the ancient chair. One arm was almost broken off, and we called in a furniture maker from Rochester to repair it. Then I placed it in the conservatory, on the tile floor among the ferns and hothouse blooms of angel's-trumpets and hibiscus. The blue spangles Charles insisted on for the upper windows glittered in the sun, like blue eyes watching down from heaven. Mrs. Potsherd — almost ninety — doddled about in her white cap with a cup of tea, and I set myself in the old chair, facing out over the fields behind Gad's Hill toward a distant hedgerow, with woods farther on.

I began rocking, slowly, almost unnoticeably, waiting, knowing all the memories would flood back over me if I waited long enough. And they did. Memories of Catherine when she and I were young girls in white dresses. Memories of Catherine

meeting a young writer of no means at all, handsome and boyish, yet somewhat frightening in his determination and confidence. I rocked and remembered the time when Catherine
and our sister Mary attended one of Charles' early plays, a
comedy, and how they all went home together after the play,
and Mary, only seventeen years old, took ill of a sudden after
midnight and died the very next day. Mother and Charles and
Catherine held her and cried hysterically, and none more than
Charles, who called her his very own sister — more his sister
than Catherine's — and to me privately, in the upper attic of
the house he had rented for his new family, to me in a whisper,
saying Mary should have been his wife. It was Mary he loved.
That was when I knew I loved *him*, and even though Catherine was already large with their first child, I would replace
Mary in his heart, because he had already pushed Catherine
out of it. He knelt down in sobs before me. "Mary was so
slight, so excellent, so mild," he cried. "The earth has seen no
element of her anywhere before." Even though I was barely
more than a child myself, I wrapped my arms about his dear
head and pressed his face to my chest, letting him sob against
my heart. From that moment on, he was my husband, my
dearest friend, my lover on winter nights when I burrowed
under coverlets alone, hearing him arguing with Catherine
somewhere else in the house — so many houses over the
years. I knew if I became everything to him, he would wear out
with Catherine, and we would have the only true marriage.
They say the future is only a dream, but a dream is really who
we are now.

I rocked there in the conservatory, sipping tea, and reliving
our life together. Perhaps it was a life others would have dis-
paraged. I was not the weak-minded sister so many thought. I
knew that for both of us, it had been a life joined only by hid-

den hearts and shared imaginations. What else could it have been, seeing the times in which we lived?

In Chelsea, where I grew up, I looked out from the nursery window over unending orchards, as if the world were one great Garden of Eden. Like so many large families, we daughters were a burden to our parents. Raised properly to serve father and brothers, we were destined to marry early, and if that did not happen, our options were slim indeed. I didn't want to be a grey-frocked governess or a spinster aunt. Perhaps I could have written novels like Walter Scott, who was a friend of my father's. I might have organised grand music festivals as my grandfather had in Edinburgh. I knew in my heart I had more imagination, more dreams, more talent then Catherine. Dull, plump Catherine. But she was nineteen and wanting to be plucked when Charles Dickens came boot-stomping into our home, a young reporter trying to write fiction before dawn or after midnight. He hardly noticed me, the youngest girl. What was there to notice? My figure had not even started to develop. It was Mary who had all the talent, Mary whose imagination bubbled over with ideas and jokes and dreams. But Catherine, dull Catherine, was the oldest, the ripest — and there's a time in man's life when ripeness is all. Catherine held out promise of being supporting and docile, something I knew even then Charles wanted in a wife. I also knew he would become quickly bored with a mind as empty as a sheep's. With a woman without spark or soul. Even before they were married, I saw him turning to Mary, and with Mary dead, I knew like a steel trap that he was mine for the rest of our lives. And that was my dream forever.

Yet there might have been other things for me if the world had been different. If the world had allowed it. I fancied I might have studied law or become a music critic like my fa-

ther — or an architect like my brother. But the world didn't allow it and is no different now. In the beginning, I thought I
might faint from all the pressure building inside me. Like
other women I knew, I might spend a tiring life, stretched out
on a fainting couch with a wet cloth on my forehead. I was a
girl, and then I was a woman, and the man I loved married my
sister. The world offered me no choices. Only fantasy. As I
rocked in the wet heat of the conservatory, I felt the old twist in
my womb, that contraction of love and fear and heat. I knew
by the age of twelve I would be a ghost all my life. But I would
be Charles Dickens' ghost — the ghostly lover who would
haunt his bed and roll out the wife or mistress, pressing my
small presence against him in the dark. I would be his companion, invisible to everyone else, a mere whisper coming and
going to his study, where no one else was allowed. I would wait
and hide, appearing only when I was wanted or needed, before he even knew I was wanted or needed, like a shadow of
his will. I would be a spectre, a shade, but I would be his wife.
The world would never know, but I knew. And Charles knew.
And I made the right decision, for there were no other women
in the house now, only me, and there had been no others for
more than a decade. In a short while, my husband would be
coming down to join me, in his old age, to sit near me while we
talked softly of the past and of our life to come. We would rock
in our glass house, where no one could see us. He would reach
out and hold my hand, and he would say, "You have always
known my heart better than I." I reached into the pocket of my
apron and found the slim gold ring, sliding it onto my finger,
rocking and rocking in the ancient chair with the broken arm.

Death is never what we think it ought to be. Charles Dickens
should have died peacefully in bed, wearing a nightcap and

surrounded by his children, like a painting by Augustus Egg. In the background, there should have been all those close friends from a lifetime of labour and shared values. We should have held handkerchiefs to our noses, weeping quietly, while the fading breath passed slowly from that great bearded face. I would have combed his thinning hair, combed the beard. Someone would have folded his hands in a prayerful position on his chest. We would have felt the presence of his soul and known the calm spirit of all those years of generosity was lifting toward heaven. Even Catherine should have been there — in the background, perhaps — bitter, no doubt, but sobbing at the loss of one who had fathered her children. And Henry, the quiet son, the only son who possessed his father's dignity and grace, Henry would have led us in prayer.

Charles Dickens deserved that. We all did. But he died crunched between the wall and several chairs in the dining room. Hubbard and I were too old to lift him. I remember I was sobbing and shouting for help. Hubbard was crying, too, attempting to push back the mahogany table that seated twelve. One chair had fallen over and become tangled with another so that Charles lay partly on his back and partly on his side, with his legs twisted in the tangle of chairs. Mrs. Potsherd, who had been carrying a tray of soup and biscuits, threw up her hands in fright. The bowls broke against each other and the soup splashed across the wall in a wet arch, like a black rainbow on the wallpaper. Spoons and napkins lay scattered as if we'd had a wild party. Cook came huffing and running with hot bricks from the oven downstairs. We wrapped them in towels and held them against Charles' feet, but he did not respond.

By then, the liveryman came running, too, and all of us together put our backs against the table and heaved until it moved just enough to allow Charles to slide fully down to the floor. Hubbard climbed to the attic and returned with a cot. The five of us were able to drag and lift Charles onto it — he seemed so much heavier than any of us could have imagined. Then, we ordered the liveryman to ride horseback to Rochester as fast as he might to fetch the doctor. He had only just dropped over the top of the hill when we realised we had forgotten to tell him to send wires to London. Hubbard and I hitched a partly lame horse to the fly, and Hubbard set off following the liveryman as fast as an old horse could limp. It was long after dark when Katie arrived from London with Mamie and Frank Beard. Later, an angry Charlie came bursting in, followed shortly by Henry with his new family. Sometime after midnight, Wills appeared, staying a short while, then returning hurriedly to London to prepare all the legal documents. The house was full of people moving aimlessly about, speaking in whispers, or not speaking at all. Mrs. Potsherd broke down and was put to bed in hysterics. Millais arrived in a hansom cab to make the death cast. We had not yet wired Catherine, and I thought it best to send Katie to tell her mother. Although I cared nothing for Catherine's feelings, a wire seemed too impersonal. Only then did I realise that dawn had broken hours ago. Morning sun reflected off empty mirrors in every room, into every corner with a splash of shimmering brightness pure as honey. The light seemed almost blinding, and we had been blind to it for so long I had to close my eyes.

In the afternoon, Katie returned with Ellen Ternan. After notifying Catherine, she had gone straight to Ellen's cottage. Ellen wore a black frock with a black veil covering her face. She seemed to be trembling. Katie steadied her arm, escorting her inside. They moved silently, with only a faint hiss of skirts, up the stairs to the bed where Charles had finally been carried. I waited downstairs, alone in the growing crowd of confused mourners until Ellen came down. She had raised the veil over her hat. We stood in the hallway a moment together under an old horseshoe Charles had nailed above the entrance when he first took possession of the house so many years ago. He'd hung the horseshoe upside down. Many a guest pointed out to him that it was bad luck. But his answer had always been jolly and booming.

"No! No!" he cried, placing a bear paw about their shoulders. "I've lived a lifetime of such wonderfully good luck that I've hung the horseshoe upside down in hopes a little of that grace will tumble out upon my guests."

Standing there awkwardly under the horseshoe, Ellen held out her hand to me. Momentarily, we looked each other in the eye. I could tell she knew her role had ended now. The secret between Charles and me no longer had to be protected. Her presence in our life was no longer needed. I felt sorry for her.

"If only you could have known him as I did," I said. "He would have wished you well, I'm sure."

She searched my face, a friend at last, having performed her duty to the end with — I admit — sacrifice and dignity. For the first time, I felt admiration for her. A little. But it was time for her to go. Charles Dickens belonged now to those of us who loved him. Ellen Ternan lowered her veil and passed silently out of our lives.

Her carriage shuttled onto Gravesend Road just as Catherine's arrived.

Catherine had cloaked herself in layers of new and expensive black crepe and bombasine, lustreless and dreary. Her darkness muted the sunlight that had filled the house. She blocked the front door like a bulbous general, pulling off black gloves with a snap.

"I've arranged for burial at Westminster Abbey. I'll brook no exceptions to my will." She stared coldly, daring me to disagree. "It's my house. My husband. No one will challenge me, do you think?"

"Of course, Catherine, but . . ."

"Settled, then!"

She passed me like a black steam engine, huffing up the stairs to command her husband to stay dead. At the top of the steps she looked back. "I'm not the same woman, Georgina. Don't try to interfere."

She draped the outside of Gad's Hill with black bunting. A black wreath was mounted on the front door. Two boys in black were hired to stand on either side, and at the approach of a visitor, they snapped out black handkerchiefs and began to sob. Black-bordered announcements appeared in all the papers, posters were hung on walls throughout London. Catherine abruptly cancelled funeral plans at the Rochester Cathedral

"He will be buried at Westminster Abbey," she announced. "I'll have nothing less."

The grave, already dug in Rochester, was ordered filled in.

For three hours, Forster and Wills huddled with Catherine in Charles' study. Everyone in the house could hear her screaming. They reached a bitter compromise. Charles would be buried at Westminster Abbey, but the ceremony would be private. Catherine would not send an invitation to the Queen, as she had planned.

That night, Charles' body was moved by slow train to Charing Cross. Hubbard accompanied the casket in the baggage car, refusing to sleep. It rained most of the way. Next morning, the sun rose with that kind of clear brilliance seen only after light showers. As our procession reached the Dean's Yard, the bell of St. Stephen's was ringing nine o'clock. We arrived in three black coaches, passing under the archway to the echo of horses' hooves and carriage wheels rumbling over cobbles. As we stopped, horses shaking and snorting, the great cathedral bell began to toll. In my dark corner, I trembled inside the swelling sound, as if every slow gong of the bell tolled my own soul's departure. The dream, outlived, settled finally about my heart like a lead casket.

A still bitter Catherine refused to climb out of her carriage. She yanked her curtains closed in Katie's face. We left her there, sealed alone in a tomb of her own bitterness. The rest of us — Charlie and Mary and Kate and Henry — and, of course, Forster — and, at the last minute, a dazed Wilkie Collins — the rest of us followed the casket through the western cloister and along the nave to the south transept, where a grave had been dug in Poets' Corner. I remember most a nameless burly man with a beaked nose, huddled in a long overcoat and a tattered scarf about his neck. He was one of the gravediggers, I believe, and he stood to one side, twisting his hat while the Dean of Westminster conducted a quiet service. At the end, when the organ sounded a Dead March, the burly man began to sob. It was the only other sound in the cathedral. Forster and Katie reached out to hold the old man, but he was too heavy. He collapsed on his knees in the shadows at the side of the black grave.

By the time we came out of Westminster, hundreds — and then thousands — of common mourners had begun to crush through the gates. Catherine's carriage had departed. We climbed awkwardly onto each other's laps in the two black carriages that remained behind. A moaning crowd folded about us, faces dark with loss. Knowing, I suppose, the mob could not be forbidden, the Dean ordered the great bell to continue tolling. A polished sky, bright as a mirror, was darkened by starlings and pigeons, swirling about in ceremonious confusion. They say the bell rang all day.

In the weeks that followed, I moved through empty rooms in Gad's Hill. Again and again, I found myself drawn to the conservatory, where I rocked incessantly, alone, refusing the aid of servants, refusing to answer callers at our door. I sat in the old rocking chair, staring out across ripening wheat to the hedgerows of Cobham. I rocked and listened for a sign in my heart, trying not to remember, and doing nothing but remembering.

I remembered our summer trips to France. It was the ferry crossing I saw most in my memory. The whole family, Catherine in her billowing white frock looked like a hot-air balloon. Six or seven or eight children ran up and down the deck, with Katie in pink, leading them. Charles would lean on a railing, smoking a cigar and looking over the grey waters of the channel. He would always have a friend with him. Augustus Egg or Wilkie Collins or Bulwer-Lytton, and if they weren't available, he would order Wills or Forster to take a holiday with him. Nannies and maids seemed everywhere. Liverymen stayed below with the luggage and a small trunk full of Charles' writing materials. The ship lifted and dropped with a gentle sway. Even as a young man, Hubbard wrapped himself in a woollen coat with a woollen scarf, afraid of the wind, even when the cold sun was bright and encouraging.

We were all one family, it seemed to me then. Before Charles began to imagine himself with a mistress. I think he felt he couldn't really consider himself a writer of stature without a mistress. And his unhappiness with Catherine must have made him feel as if he'd fallen overboard into a cold northern ocean. Drowning would be such relief. The fantasy of sinking slowly into icy darkness must have been tempting.

He invented another dream, of an innocent little girl, one who would free him from the burden of a happy family. Perhaps he saw her as a seventeen-year-old, like Mary, with laughter and wit and the barest hint of sweet-smelling womanhood, a girl sitting on his lap and combing his hair. He must have known how pathetic it was, yet he dreamed it with all the intensity he could. And Ellen happened along at the moment, like a succubus, waiting for a time of weakness. I don't blame her. She must have had her own fantasy, dancing half-naked on the stage and hoping somewhere in the rowdy audience there might be some wealthy man who would ravish her with gifts: the bulbous-nosed owner of a boiler factory or the foppish son of a weak-minded baron. A dull vision, lacking romance, but vaguely more interesting than the life she led.

I know now, at my age, that only our dreams matter, not the quality of them. How else could we sustain the lack in our lives? How else face the tedious rising from bed each morning onto a cold floor? Are we any different from those who compose great symphonies? Or those who struggle with profound tomes of philosophy? Or great plays? Didn't Shakespeare fill the blank of his soul with a hundred lives more interesting than his? Dreaming and acting, he said. It was all the same. Charles Dickens knew about dreaming and acting. He was the great businessman of silken fantasies. Those of us whose minds are dull and timid have his visions to borrow. For a price, he would sell you one, and let you live it awhile. That's all we have, and we must be satisfied, especially when old age begins to show. Old themes play themselves out in every generation, I'm sure. Vanity alone makes us believe our dream is special, redeeming us from a life of straw and sawdust. I know now the dream alone, no matter how sad and pathetic, resolves the heart's mystery. Dreams are the rags and refuse that buoy the boat on an ebbing tide.

Ellen Ternan

ONCE he touched the small of my back, fingers and thumb spread apart, guiding me across the stage like a dancer. I could smell cigar smoke in his beard over my shoulder. "Here, Princess," he said. "This is where you belong." I could feel his breath in my hair.

It would have sufficed a lifetime.

At eighteen, I expected nothing from the world. I did not dream of houses and jewels and servants. I lived from one song to the next, from one stage to the next. I wore tights and golden curls. My legs were pretty.

I was part of a family. Mother, sisters, grandmothers. I memorised lines, sang in tune, stood where the director told me. Yet when I met Mr. Dickens, I must have made choices, decisions. My body made the decision. My heart. My blood. I chose to let others make decisions, something for which I bear full weight.

I was innocent and weightless. I dreamt a lot, like other girls.

After the American trip, Mr. Dickens was never really the same. For a while, he pounded about in his boots with crazed energy, planning his conservatory, planning a Farewell Tour that went on night after night in badly lit halls with bad food and no rest. When the readings first began, I took a separate train — to Liverpool, Wolverhampton, or Hull. He gave readings to packed houses that cheered and cheered. His heart was fed by it. All of them adored him. I dressed modestly in a grey cotton frock and sat far toward the rear so I could listen. I could not bear to hear the murder scene from *Oliver Twist*. Mr. Dickens read the passage with obsessed intensity. The first night, like others around me, I broke into strangled sobs and left the hall early. Each time, I waited in our hotel for Mr. Dickens to return, but it was always so late I fell asleep in tangled dreams. Mr. Dickens tiptoed in long after midnight. He paced the room on sore legs with a sore heart, unable to sleep. Like a very old lion in a cage, he rubbed his mane against the bars of his own anguish. Sometime before dawn, he dropped heavily into bed beside me, trying not to disturb me. The next morning, in half-light through the windows, he would hold me while I tried to cry.

Mr. Dickens did not cry. I felt age gnawing on his heart for the first time. Everyone wanted to take his picture now. None of the portraits pleased him. "That's not me," he whispered bitterly, "not that grim, wasted mariner you see looking out at you. That's not me." But he knew it was, and it frightened him. The world had narrowed. Sometimes, I felt more like one of his children or a close acquaintance from the past. He had become the ancient king passing through the antechamber of his subjects. He saw us through an imperial gaze, delighted by our pleasure in him. He carried all within himself now. I felt he loved me, perhaps even more deeply. He was leaving me. We were seldom intimate. And our intimacy, when it did occur, grew further and further apart. On rare occasions, his desire arose, but without passion,

To me, confidentially, softly, he said, "I drift alone on a wide river."

He seemed unable to explain. More and more, he turned to Georgina, who pampered him, brought hot milk, sang nursery songs for him, or so he told me.

"She sacrificed everything," he explained again and again. "Augustus Egg would have made her a grand husband. They might have had a family of their own, you see. Children of her own. She was in love with me, I'm afraid."

We settled again into Windsor Lodge in Peckham. Molly was still with us — or, to be accurate, she was with Mr. Dickens. She never liked me, it seemed, although I never knew how I offended her. Molly, too, had aged. Her right shoulder had begun to hump over. No one else was allowed to serve Mr. Dickens, except Hubbard from time to time. Hubbard often used a cane now and could not always carry a tray. Mr. Dickens lived in a forest of toppling trees. In some ways, I felt more alone than ever.

Once, I'd thought a woman plays many roles in her lifetime while a man plays only one. I began to see that Mr. Dickens, too, lived so many parts. He had been all the characters he created, a gallery of all Britain, the "Chaucer of his Age," one pandering critic called him. He had been an actor on the stage, playing the role of actor. And director and producer. In spite of everything, he played the model husband. The truth of the matter was of no concern to his followers. A gentleman of wealth, he played the role of philanthropist and reformer. He was the romantic lover whose passion was denied in Queen Victoria's England, a culture of rusted chastity belts. And still, all in all, perhaps the brittle centre of a man never changes, where a woman's centre if fluid, flowing, evolving. For Mr. Dickens, I realised, each role was adopted as he needed it or wanted it, like Hubbard choosing him a coat from his wardrobe.

For a woman, each role is inherited. Evolutionary, I believe, is the modern term. A woman plays all her various parts as one, even when they contradict each other, so that she is always whole, always herself, even when she is many selves. And never more so than when called upon to please a man. I grew more and more alone. The script handed me had few words on it now. I cuddled, stroked, whispered in his ear. He held me once more as he had in the beginning, on his lap, like a little girl. He seemed distracted, listening to some faint pulse of the distant stars.

I know all about the rumours, but there was no child.

No child at all, really, from our union. A baby boy would have weighed five pounds at birth, too small by far. And he would have had large blue-black eyes that looked up at mine in trust. He would have suckled my breast. He never existed. No one took that child from my arms. I would never have allowed it. Not after going through my confinement, swollen and afraid, the veins in my legs throbbing. Not after giving birth in an old farmhouse in France with walls two feet thick. Do you really think I would have handed over a baby less than four weeks old to someone else, after all the sickness, after sweating and squatting on the floor, giving birth before the midwife could get there, gripping the bedpost and Mamma catching it in a towel, crying, It's a boy! A beautiful beautiful boy! A child bathed in mucus and blood.

Do you think I haven't heard all the rumours about abandoning a baby, giving him up for adoption, losing him on a train, or even murdering him? What do you think all those whispers have done to me? Has my heart grown like a black tumour in my chest, until I can barely breathe? Have my eyes sunk into dead, hollow cavities? What do you think such rumours would have done to the feelings between Mr. Dickens and myself? Nothing like that could have happened without destroying us. We could never have looked each other in the eye again. How could we bear to be alone with each other? Or if something that terrible happened, what would we have said to each other? Could we ever accept? If my bodice was wet from flowing milk, my breasts aching, a knife thrust into my womb, could Mr. Dickens and I endure looking at each other? After he abandoned me to flee to America alone? After he left me exiled in France with only Mrs. Smarthy to comfort me with her pictures of the resurrection? Would I have thrown plates at the wall? Would I have cursed him and stabbed my fork into the table where I sat eating alone night after night? Would the child in my body have thrashed in fright and doubt? Whose baby? Whose baby, I say? Who was the betrayer and who the betrayed. My God, I could have clawed the very depth of desire and evil and love from my chest and stomped on it. Though, now, I have closed myself like a fist, ready to strike only my own temple of shame.

It must have been some horrible slanderer who began such talk, spread the gossip, arranged for nights of hell to descend upon us. Out of what? Jealousy? For a prank? For his own enjoyment? What devil could have devised such schemes, and for what end? And if it were Wilkie Collins, how could he go on living in comfort and ease, with his mistresses and his children, a family man of dubious parts and diabolic heart? Am I tissue to be ripped apart, does the blood not flow so fast that the midwife, arriving late, at the last minute, with Mamma and Mrs. Smarthy in hysterics, brushed aside for the pressing of herbs and plants, ancient remedies, and compresses, anything to slow down the flow, the rushing heart that would stop forever anyway when the baby that never happened would be lifted from that mother's arms, carrying a mother's soul wrapped in silk and cotton swaddling, dumped into hell with no more thought than a prank played for those who have never known the imprint of a tiny hand reaching out blindly, pressing the breast for nothing more than love? Only love. There was no child. Trust me. I'm not a mystery novelist relishing complicated plots. I'm not driven by a lifetime of delusion, unable to separate truth from fantasy.

I began my life dancing and singing, almost before I could walk. The rough crowd of men and whores cheered me on. It was not a good life, perhaps, for a little girl, but I felt proud, special. It would have sufficed. And was it better to leave all that public exhibition, so damned by the better sort, for more than a decade of hiding and disguise? Travelling at night with a cloak over my face. Staying in foreign hotels. Wearing jewellery and embroidered frocks and ordering servants about, but dining only in sad restaurants where no one might recognise me. Was my life more exposed, or less exposed? Was I in love? Was I a whore? Was I a whore in love? Was I only trapped in some mystery I didn't understand, a luxury of emotion I wanted and hated at the same time?

I received a note from Count Bertoni. His father was ill. The Count wrote that he'd been called home by his family to take over the sulphur mines. The family had arranged for him to marry the daughter of a local salt merchant. It seemed the merchant was quite important in Sicily and the wedding would be lavish. The Archbishop himself would preside over the ceremony. Bertoni did not want to return, but he had no choice. "Family is destiny," he said. He wrote that he recalled me with fondness. He hoped I would live a happy life.

Mr. Dickens grew old, and I cared for him. I held his cup when his age-spotted hand trembled too much and splashed tea across the linen. I combed his thinning beard. When I was with him, I almost never thought about myself, about my life or why or what I'd become. Or why or what I had gained. Or lost. Mr. Dickens could not help but brighten any room he entered. There is something about a Great Man, I suppose. And for reasons I can't explain, my own anguish was always swept away by his.

His feelings were as deep as mine. He did not have to tell me, but he did, finally, on one of those last days at Windsor Lodge.

Speaking barely above a whisper: "I've done so much wrong."

"Nothing wrong, sir."

"Everything, everything."

We were holding hands, sitting together on a sofa. Molly had left a tray of cakes and sandwiches on the side table. It was almost dark, past teatime. We had not touched our meal. Mr. Dickens held my hand tightly and would not let go. His skin felt cold, brittle. I could feel the bones in his hand and the slow faint throb of his pulse.

"We've had good times, I suppose?"

It was a question, and I nodded, yes.

"Yet I've hurt so many people, left so many things undone."

"No man in England is more loved than you."

"Yes, yes, I've heard that. It only makes regret worse, you see."

Hubbard moved quietly through the room, lighting oil lamps. We could speak openly in front of Hubbard. He could hear now only when you shouted at him.

Mr. Dickens waited for me to ask.

"Why is that, sir?"

"Because no one is large enough."

I waited for him to go on, and when he didn't, I said softly, "I understand."

"There's no way to know the empty weight of it all. How easy it was to abandon Catherine, to abandon Katie and all my children, to hurt them beyond their imagination. And the greatest guilt was I didn't feel any guilt at all."

"You were racked with guilt, sir."

"No, no. I felt only joy at being freed."

For a long moment, while the light outside faded and the lamplight rose about us with a yellow shade, we both tried to recall our feelings, but they were tangled and obscure, and memory, like storytelling, is never to be trusted.

"You were there," Mr. Dickens finally said, "and you received my attentions. I abandoned a woman I'd been married to for twenty years, and I did it hating her for not staying young, for growing fat, selfish, and darkly crazy."

I could tell he was about to say that if it hadn't been me, it would have been some other actress, some other young woman with firm bosom and slim hips. But he did not say so, and I was glad.

Hubbard blithely lighted more lamps, hearing nothing, happy inside his dreamy world of silence.

"Ellen." Mr. Dickens enclosed my hand with both his scraggy old hands. "You saved my life. You saved me from shrivelling up into a mean, empty old man. I would have retained my imagination, I suppose, but there would have been a failure of passion." He squeezed firmly. "It was my life you saved."

"And you saved mine."

He didn't hear me.

"You've always known my heart better than I do," he whispered under his breath.

He looked at me with eyes far away. For a moment, he seemed unsure who I was, a strange woman sitting beside him holding his cold hands in a house he didn't recognise.

Don't you see now, our life is more than mystery, more than fantasy or even love. Although all that, too. We have to face the hard stuff now. At the end, it isn't about spring showers, as it is when you're young and you open like petals — petal by petal — to the warm rain, to his slightest glance, his touch, the smell of cigar in his beard, or for no reason more than because he's a man, when the texture of his touch is like a flower imagining the rain. All of that matters. It matters so very much. Then, it no longer matters. Only the rain, everywhere descending about you like autumn coming back with gusts of cold. Mr. Dickens' hands enfolded my hands, and his head nodded. I knew there was no question of death because death was there, quietly waiting, listening as I was to the deep snoring that sometimes faltered, with long silent pauses when death and I held our breath before Mr. Dickens returned, a faint stir of wind in the night, his head snapping back, before he settled down again and slept so dearly we did not want to move him, and so we waited, death and I, falling asleep as well, with our head on Mr. Dicken's knees.

Mr. Dickens gave his farewell reading in Rochester. I remember because it was mid-March, 1870, and he asked me to accompany him openly, arm in arm. But I might have been his nurse for all the attention I received. The crush of followers in his hometown swept the Great Man away from me, carried him bodily to the stage in a roar of good cheer. I found myself pushed aside and standing against a wall for lack of a chair. The applause was thunderous. The silence, when he began to speak was reverently hushed. To everyone's surprise, perhaps even to Mr. Dickens', he did not read the murder scene from *Oliver Twist.* For several long, uncomfortable moments, he stood at the podium fumbling vaguely through his papers. The audience waited in silent embarrassment. Then he found what he wanted and began to read — from *A Christmas Carol* — his voice loud and clear, full of good cheer and love for his own words, for his admirers, for life itself, it seemed.

"God bless us, every one!" he cried, and the audience leapt to its feet, shouting it out with him, all together, "God bless us, every one!"

The hall exploded with cheers and huzzahs! They stamped, they cried, they hollered! They were his people: farmers, clerks, blacksmiths, downstairs maids, the Mayor and the Bishop. The applause went on and on. Waves of adoration surged like a tide that could not be stilled or held back. He was Charles Dickens. Their Charles Dickens. He was little Charlie Dickens, who some of them — wearing shawls and carrying canes — still remembered. I was pummelled in the crush, pushed back by mindless arms and legs and elbows.

Finally, he raised both hands and calmed the roaring sea. The crowd hushed while Mr. Dickens slowly let his arms fall to his sides. He spoke without notes, looking out over the heads of his audience at someone or something only he could see in the back of the hall.

"This episode of my life is over now." His voice sounded

strong and firm, as it had been that first time I acted onstage with him so many long years ago in Manchester. "For innumerable years, in this hall — and many kindred places — I've had the honour of presenting my own cherished ideas before you for your recognition." He searched the faces of his friends, one by one, as if he knew each of them personally, every ancient coalman, every shopgirl, every red-faced carpenter. And perhaps he did know them all. His breathing seemed to deepen, and his eyes penetrated their souls.

"From these garish lights I vanish now forevermore. With a heartfelt, grateful, respectful, and affectionate farewell." He bowed deeply, holding it as if in mourning, and then raised his face to everyone for the last time, avoiding our tears, so that he would not begin to cry. He walked heavily from the platform into the wings.

The audience sobbed softly. Then, as if all had taken a deep collective breath, they cheered, they stomped their feet. Hats flew in the air, women waved handkerchiefs. Shout after shout, *Encore! Encore!* did not bring him back, but neither did they stop applauding.

After ten minutes, Mr. Dickens entered slowly again from the wings, so very tired he could hardly carry himself without shaking. Impossible as it seemed, the cheering grew even louder. Everyone in the audience seemed to be crying. Those around me stood on chairs and waved their coats, shouting as if Christ himself had reappeared one last time to bid his farewell. Through the waving hats and arms, I saw Mr. Dickens kiss his hand to the audience, holding out his palm, slowly raising and lowering it in benediction.

On a late morning in June, Mr. Dickens and I sat in the garden under a sumac. For a while, he read to me from his new manuscript. It hadn't been going well, and he wanted to test a scene on me. He had rewritten it several times. There seemed more ink on the page than white space. His voice was slow but even, articulating each word carefully. One hand trembled slightly. He seemed not to notice. Near the house, Hubbard, balancing on a cane with one hand, waved a towel in the air with the other, attempting to drive away a flock of starlings racketing on the roof. Finally, Mr. Dickens stopped in midsentence and shook his head. "No. It isn't right."

I was about to assure him it sounded so much better than he believed. When I looked over at him he was drooling.

"The ship sand lag," he said. His eyes seemed vacant, almost white. "Parting," he said. "My tooth aches."

Like an ancient tree in a hushed forest, falling silently, Mr. Dickens toppled onto the grass. Pages of manuscript fluttered like ink-stained leaves floating down softly after him.

"Hubbard!" I screamed. Together we helped Mr. Dickens to the house. His legs did not seem to work. We half-dragged him to a sofa in the parlour before he collapsed, an old doll without any stuffing.

Hubbard tried to set him up, chastising him. "Now, now. No time for this behaviour, sir."

"On the ground," Mr. Dickens whispered.

"What? What?"

"Let me lie on the ground." His eyes closed, but his chest heaved. He sucked in air, sucked in air, sucked in air. Hubbard felt compelled to hold him up straight. Mr. Dickens was a much bigger man, heavy now, and he slid further and further into collapse.

"Molly!" I called. "Bring something, bring something!"

I realised I was crying and had not even known it. My heart jammed up, but my head was horribly clear: Mr. Dickens would not want to be found here. His reputation was too important. I could not let him down. Not now. Not now when he needed me most.

Molly threw her apron over her head and began sobbing in fright.

"Listen to me, Molly."

She kept sobbing, and I was sobbing, too, but I had to do the right thing. Never more in my life did I have to do the right thing. I had to do what Mr. Dickens would have wanted, and he wanted dignity, not shame. He wanted honour, not disgrace. He deserved that, he deserved that.

"Damn you, Molly, listen to me." I shook her hard. "Listen now to every word."

She looked at me with hatred in her eyes, but it was no matter at all.

"Run now, as hard as your legs can run. To the jobmaster on the Rye, near the post office. You know where I mean."

Molly nodded she did. She took a deep breath and held on to her emotions.

"Run now. Tell him we need a closed carriage with two horses. Tell him to drop the curtains and come now. I'll pay double. Triple. He's to come this minute, or I'll pay him nothing at all."

"Yes, ma'am." She was standing straight now, an old soldier who knew her duty. "I'll do it, ma'am. For him."

"Of course for him, you nit!"

She fled to the front door. "Wait." I suddenly remembered. "After you arrange for the carriage, run to the post office and send a wire to Georgina at Gad's Hill."

Molly seemed unable to handle two tasks at once. "I'm to order up the carriage, ma'am."

"Yes. The carriage first, then run to the post office. Wire

Georgina that a mutual friend has taken ill at Windsor Lodge. Tell her we're hurrying in a closed cab. No one is to know. She'll understand."

Molly sagged momentarily against the doorframe, overwhelmed with all the responsibility.

"Molly! Listen to me! Order up the carriage, then wire Georgina we're coming. No one is to know. Put that in the telegram twice, Molly. No one is to know."

Molly spun about and raced out the door and off the porch. I could see her running, an hysterical old lady with long skirts tripping her up. I knew her eyes could not see where she was going, but her feet would lead her. She would not fail Mr. Dickens, no matter what she thought of me.

Hubbard and I brought blankets and wrapped the Great Man. He trembled and drooled. His head lobbed about.

"It's apoplexy," Hubbard said. "No doubt about it." Hubbard was crying, too, now. My throat grew tighter as the noose of my future pulled about it. I had one duty only, to save a reputation for a man who had lived his life for it. I steeled myself, drew upon the core of my heritage, saw my mother's face, and straightened my back. And suddenly, for reasons I can't explain, I saw my mother whole in my mind and realised how badly I'd treated her, how I'd been so often ashamed of her, in her out-of-fashion black bonnet, and how I'd treated her with such condescension and disdain. The terrible pain of shame and humiliation washed over me.

The coach arrived within half an hour or less. I'd never met the jobmaster before, a man in his thirties, with a cap pulled firmly over a crab apple face. Molly had ridden back in the coach. The four of us struggled with the very limp and heavy Mr. Dickens, unable to carry him. Hubbard, without his cane, was of little use.

Finally, the jobmaster said, "Wrap him in the carpet, ma'am. That'll give him a bit of stiffness."

And so we rolled the Great Man up in a carpet, and with one of us straining at each corner, we staggered our way out of the house to the carriage, sliding him across the floorboard. Molly ran around to the other side and placed a round cushion from the sofa under his head.

The coachman leered down at me. "These old gents can't take their drink, can they?"

I climbed into the carriage over Mr. Dickens' body and tried to find some way not to place my feet on top of him. Hubbard crowded in on the opposite bench. Molly shut the door, and the coachman snapped his whip. I never saw Molly again. By the time I returned, later that night, she had packed her trunk and vanished. I still owed her a month's salary. She never wrote to claim it.

"As fast as you can," I called to the driver. He snapped his reins, and the horses began to canter through Hatcham and onto the Roman Road. I knew the sun was already dropping low over Kentish fields and woods. The carriage bounced and rocked. More than once I desperately wanted to open the curtains to let in fresh air. I could only remind myself this might be the final gift I could ever give Mr. Dickens. It had to be done as right as I could make it. From time to time, Mr. Dickens moaned lightly. Sometimes, he seemed to speak, but with the sound of the wheels and the horses' pounding, we could make out nothing. Hubbard and I said not a word. We did not even look at each other. Every so often, the old servant reached down and straightened Mr. Dickens' coat or ran a hand through his white hair to make it right. We jolted along, down the same road Pip had taken at the end of *Great Expectations,* toward Gad's Hill, where little Charlie Dickens, holding his father's hand, heard his father's voice say to him, "Work hard, lad, and someday a place like this will be yours."

Georgina met us at the door. She had been able to give all the servants tasks that took them elsewhere. The house seemed momentarily deserted. Again, four of us struggled to drag Mr. Dickens out of the carriage. He was a remarkably heavy man. How could we have known? I had thought we would whisk him upstairs to his bedroom, but by the time we passed through the door and into the hall, we had to drop him roughly on the floor. All of us were huffing and panting. Hubbard sagged against the wall.

Georgina took charge.

"We'll take him to the dining room and lay him on the table."

The idea was bizarre, but at the moment it seemed remarkably sensible.

"Unwrap him first," she said. The four of us gently turned him over and over, taking off the carpet, and then lifted, heaved, and gasped our way down the hall with the sagging body. We staggered past his library, past the hall clock, past the stairway to the kitchen, and into the dining room on the left. In trying to heft him up onto the table, it was the ancient Hubbard, almost fainting, who first began to sag. I could not hold on. In a crash of tablecloth and chairs, we dropped Charles Dickens, the body twisted and wedged in the wreckage. We knew the sound of the crash would bring servants running. Georgina grasped my hand.

"Go," she whispered. "Hurry. You've done as much as you can."

"It's what he would have wanted," I tried to explain.

She pushed me out. I ran down the hall alone, back to the hot carriage with the curtains already drawn. Within moments, I felt the driver climb on the box and heard the front door to Gad's Hill close solidly upon my life.

Then there was only a wooden loneliness, the empty bouncing ride back in the dark, much slower this time, back to Windsor Lodge in Peckham. The front door was still wide open, the house dark and empty. Molly gone. Hubbard, of course, at Gad's Hill with his master. I walked about ghostly rooms, followed by Miranda clicking her toenails. She whined softly to be picked up. I realised this was not my home at all. Nothing here belonged to me except memories, and they were not many, a few years' worth at best. I climbed stairs, opened doors, and looked into hollow spaces. Slight voices of wind called in the eaves from time to time. I felt my heart drumming slowly, soundly in my chest. I swallowed. I remembered to breathe. My hands felt unusually cold. Fully dressed, long after midnight, I collapsed on a bed somewhere, shivering, unable to sleep. Unable to stay awake. I burned with chills and dread, like a battered soul spun about in the hot wind of purgatory. Finally, before dawn when the first bird began to sing to the great broad world outside, I fell into a deepness that did not end until I realised that for some time, a pounding had been rocking the front door of the house.

A young postal boy, perhaps twelve or so, handed me a wire from Georgina.

Death came quietly early this morning.

In the afternoon, Katie called upon me. I was still wearing a nightgown. She was immensely kind, helping me wash my face in a porcelain basin. She found a black frock and veil for me to wear and, steadying my arm, guided me out of the vacant house, vacant of memories and life, steadying my efforts to climb into her carriage, and on the long ride — this time a journey that took forever — escorted me to Gad's Hill, where for a moment, in the confusion of mourners and whispering voices, I saw my dear friend in his bed, hands folded coldly over his chest, white hair and beard combed and brushed, but all so very very dead, the spirit of the man gone, his laughter, his bellowing, his stomping boots, all gone. And not even one last word for me to carry the rest of my life.

At the bottom of the stairs, I met Georgina.

"Services will be held at the Cathedral in Rochester," she whispered.

"Do you think I might attend?"

"Of course. You'll be veiled, and it will bring no shame to the rest of us."

On the morning of the funeral, alone in Windsor Lodge, I dressed myself. My footsteps echoed about my empty bedroom. The adjoining door led to Mr. Dickens' room, but I couldn't open it. Out the window, I could see an ancient chestnut tree in the garden, and for a while I stared at the tree, hoping I might find some revelation in it. A dove flew from the lower branches, making a great ruckus, but it seemed a random, inexplicable act. I latched the door behind me and walked to the station, where I waited alone on the platform, as if I were asleep and dreaming of an empty train station. In the carriage, I sat by a window, where my veiled face looked back, ghostly as it flew across fields and rivers.

Be quiet, I said to my soul. Wait now for whatever is to come. As if nothing had happened. But nothing seemed to fill the empty hollow of my heart beating, and I felt myself stiffening like a scarecrow in a field passing by my window. I felt as if it were me standing in those fields, straw arms spread wide to welcome or frighten whatever should come flying to me, per-

haps a dove in the morning light. Mr. Dickens had disappeared like a dove flying out of a chestnut tree, like someone
who says, I'll be back directly, but who does not come back, a
sudden lift of wings, a flutter of white in the dawn, I saw him
everywhere in my life. I stood with my straw arms spread apart
waiting for something that would never happen, waiting for
bright wings to flutter back to me.

Did I love him? My life was woven into his with so much
more than the word "love" can express, tied to him, bound to
him, until I became him. My blood had woven a tapestry with
his blood, his booming laughter, his fear, a Bayeux Tapestry of
love and war, of parades and cheering and dark train rides to
hidden assignations. A tapestry of crowds waving hats and old
women crying, of children left behind, and lost moments woven together.

At Rochester the guard did not collect my ticket. After I
stepped off, I kept studying the ticket in my gloved hand, as if
I could not quite understand why it was there, or what it
meant. Rochester station was also empty. I crossed the square
and started up the narrow curve of High Street toward the
Cathedral. The ancient mediaeval street was deserted. Tudor
storefronts on both sides were sealed tight. For a few moments, I thought it appropriate and right the village should be
closed down. Yet it seemed there might have been a few strag-
glers like myself making their way in mourning toward the
Cathedral. I passed the Guildhall and Watts Charity House.
Not a soul anywhere. The whole village seemed emptied out
that sunny morning. I began to walk faster, thinking I must be
late. I hurried past the Bull Hotel and the Corn Exchange,
with its ornate frontage. All about me, there was only the hush
of light wind on a June morning, with the Cathedral ahead of

me now on my left. The doors there, too, were sealed shut. I could hear no sound at all except the faint and distant pop of a flag on the castle tower across the way, a sound like snapping shut the cover of a book.

It seemed such an odd and vacant ending. I wandered about the grounds and found in the graveyard a recently filled-in grave with no marker. If it had been the grave of Mr. Dickens, there would have been flowers. I knew there would. And the ground about would have been trampled by some kind of crowd. Mourners would be gathered, even if I'd misunderstood the day and time. Still, I had no choice, and standing there alone in the empty wind, with no one to bury, I held a silent funeral.

Dear love, my dear Mr. Dickens, I would have broken this dream, this mystery, for no one less than thee.

And nothing more. My heart was empty by then. I did not understand why those words came to me or what they might mean. I took another breath and tried to assemble a more appropriate eulogy. Wisps of clouds passed overhead, like wings of angels. Yet in my mind, I found nothing so uplifting — only half-formed, aching images, dancing in a jumble. Something to piece together later. A story made up of fragments, it seemed: small findings in an old rag and bone shop, here and there a truth, overwrought, like love between a man and woman always is. Some bright nothing that pieces the soul together with disparity.

Out of the belfry, a flock of dirty pigeons swooped and circled before settling down again. An English sun grew warm, and because there was no reason not to I lifted the black veil over my bonnet and gazed about clearly. I was alone in the world, everywhere I looked. I wandered back from the Cathedral, down the cobbled High Street, meeting no one. At the train station, I found a ticket agent smoking a pipe and reading *The Times*.

"Why is the town deserted?" I asked.

He did not look up. "All gone to London for the funeral. Westminster Abbey, they say." He shook out the paper and turned to me, looking sceptically at my black mourning dress and veil. "You've come the wrong way, haven't you, miss."

I nodded and breathed deeply of the foul train smells in the station.

"It might seem like that," I said. My heart felt like straw.

"Would you be wanting a ticket to London, then?"

I gazed up the iron tracks. The rails beckoned and merged in the distance, curving silently into a shadowy wood. I breathed deeply and tried to say my good-byes. It was, you might say, an ending of sorts, empty and puzzling as endings always are, full of fear and anger, wordless, scattered love. What more could I have expected?

"A ticket to London, then?"

"I don't think so," I said. "I'll rest here for a while."

Acknowledgements

I feel deeply grateful to P. B. Parris, Eric Walburg, Levi Gardner, and Brian McGrady for their dedicated support, encouragement, and detailed critiquing of the manuscript. I am equally in debt to David Bowen at the University of Manchester, who provided critical editorial insights. A special expression of gratitude must go to Ann Everitt, Headmistress of the Gad's Hill School for Girls in Rochester, England, who gave so generously of her time and who offered so many wonderful stories and anecdotes about Charles Dickens. I must also acknowledge the assistance of Sean and Maureen Guyan-Lallor, who allowed me to use their home on the coast of Devon as a retreat for writing. The University of North Carolina, Asheville, provided me with a research grant for travel, which proved of great benefit. Finally, I must acknowledge the authors of numerous scholarly works that proved invaluable for background and historical details: Catherine Peters, *The King of Inventors: A Life of Wilkie Collins* (Princeton University Press, 1993); Alison Gernsheim, *Victorian and Edwardian Fashion* (Dover, 1981); Walter E. Houghton, *The Victorian Frame of Mind, 1830–1870* (Yale University Press, 1957); Patricia Ingham, *Dickens, Women, and Language* (Harvester Wheatsheaf,

1992); Fred Kaplan, *Dickens: A Biography* (Sceptre, 1988); Emmett Murphy, *Great Bordellos of the World* (Quartet Books, 1984); Daniel Pool, *What Jane Austen Ate and Charles Dickens Knew* (Simon & Schuster, 1993); John R. Reed, *Victorian Conventions* (Ohio University Press, 1975); William M. Clarke, *The Secret Life of Wilkie Collins* (Allison & Busby, 1989); and most important of all, Claire Tomalin's brilliantly researched and sympathetic biography of Ellen Ternan, *The Invisible Woman* (Knopf, 1991).